TYRANNOSAURUS RALPH

NATE EVANS *AND* **VINCE EVANS**

Andrews McMeel
PUBLISHING®

For three people who made a difference:
Caryn Wiseman, Wesley Asbell, and Paul Hindman.

—N.E.

For Laurie, tougher than a T. rex.

—V.E.

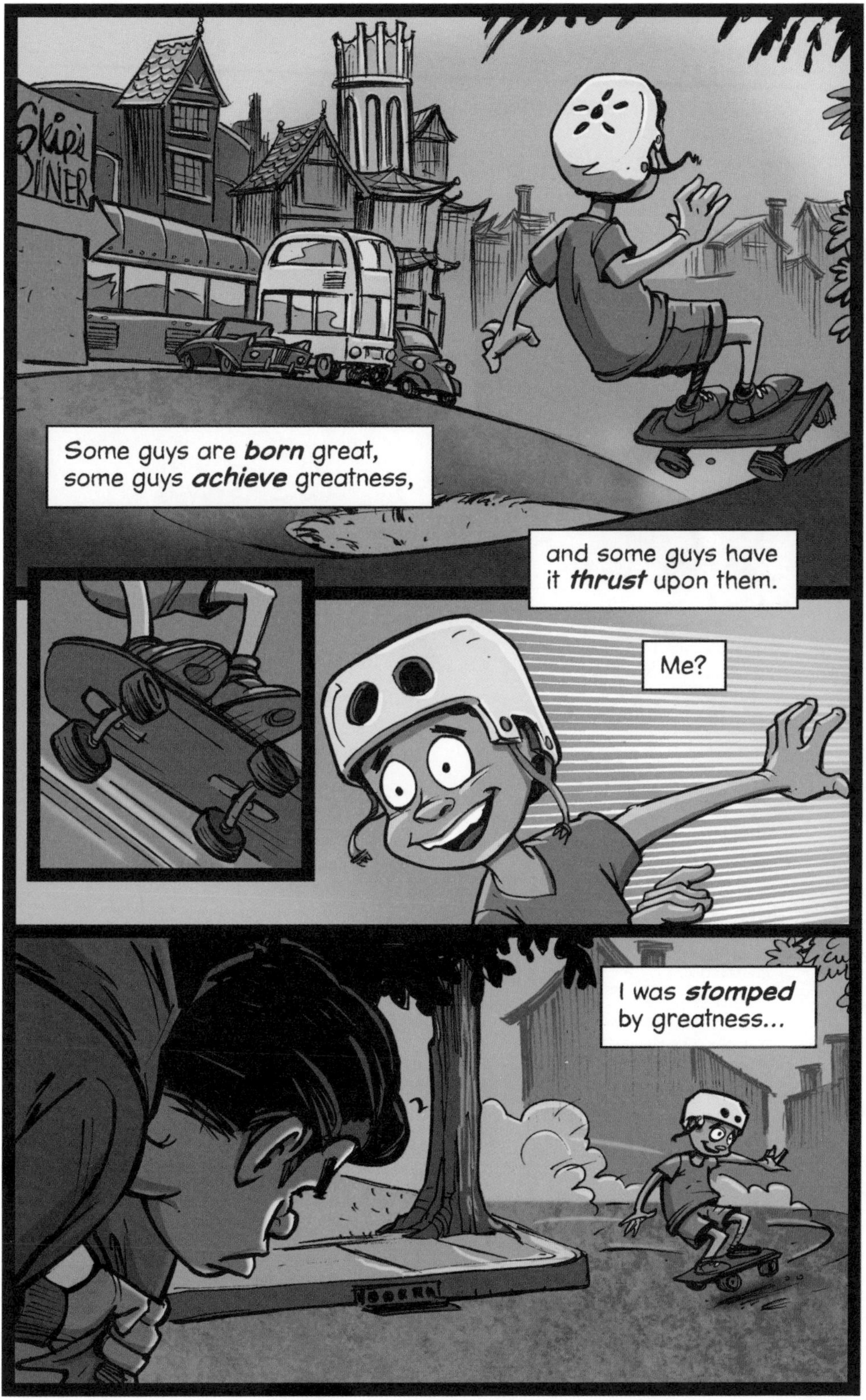
Skip's DINER
Some guys are **born** great, some guys **achieve** greatness,
and some guys have it **thrust** upon them.
Me?
I was **stomped** by greatness...

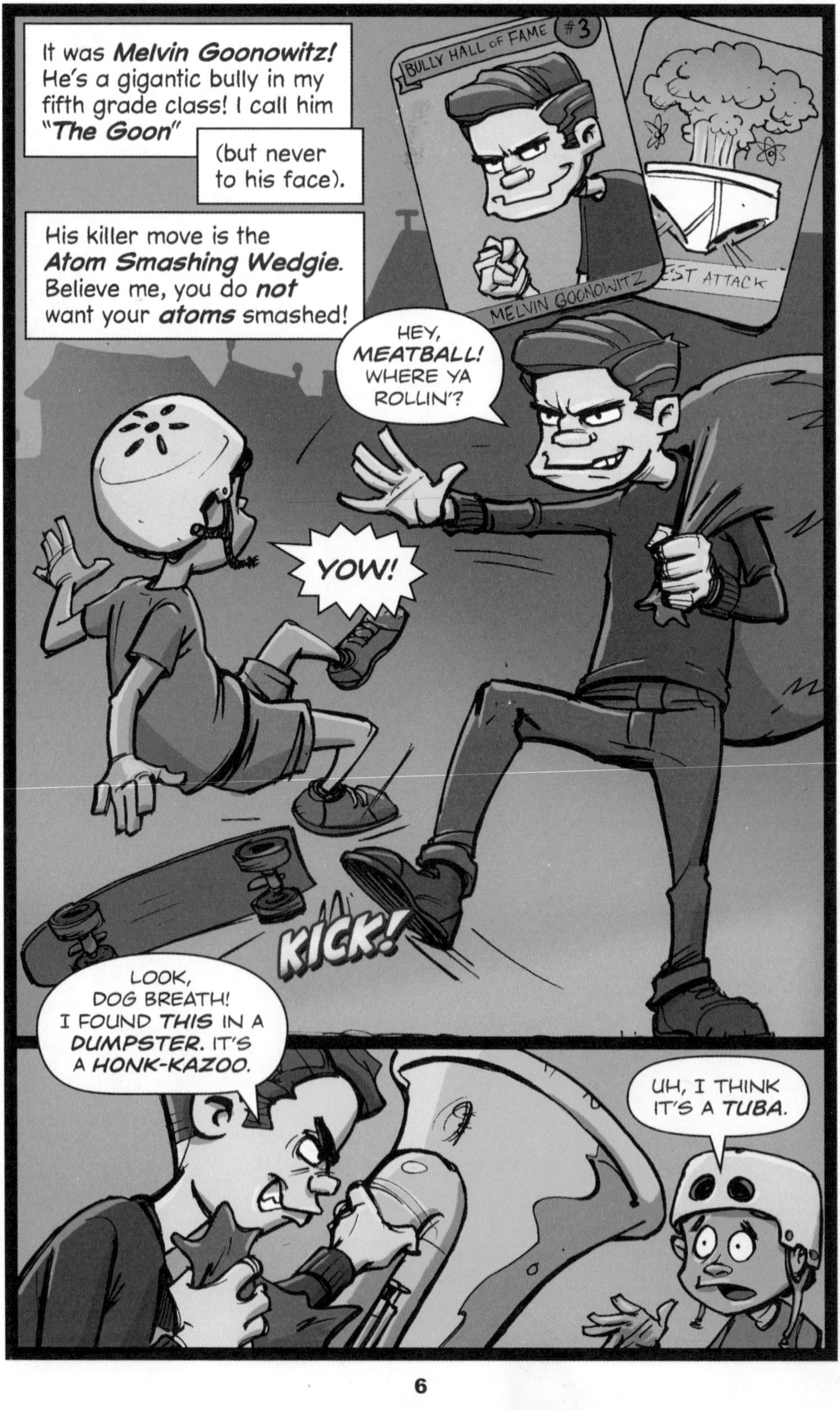
It was **Melvin Goonowitz!** He's a gigantic bully in my fifth grade class! I call him "**The Goon**"
(but never to his face).
BULLY HALL of FAME
#3
MELVIN GOONOWITZ
EST ATTACK
His killer move is the **Atom Smashing Wedgie**. Believe me, you do **not** want your **atoms** smashed!
HEY, **MEATBALL!** WHERE YA ROLLIN'?
YOW!
KICK!
LOOK, DOG BREATH! I FOUND **THIS** IN A **DUMPSTER**. IT'S A **HONK-KAZOO**.
UH, I THINK IT'S A **TUBA**.

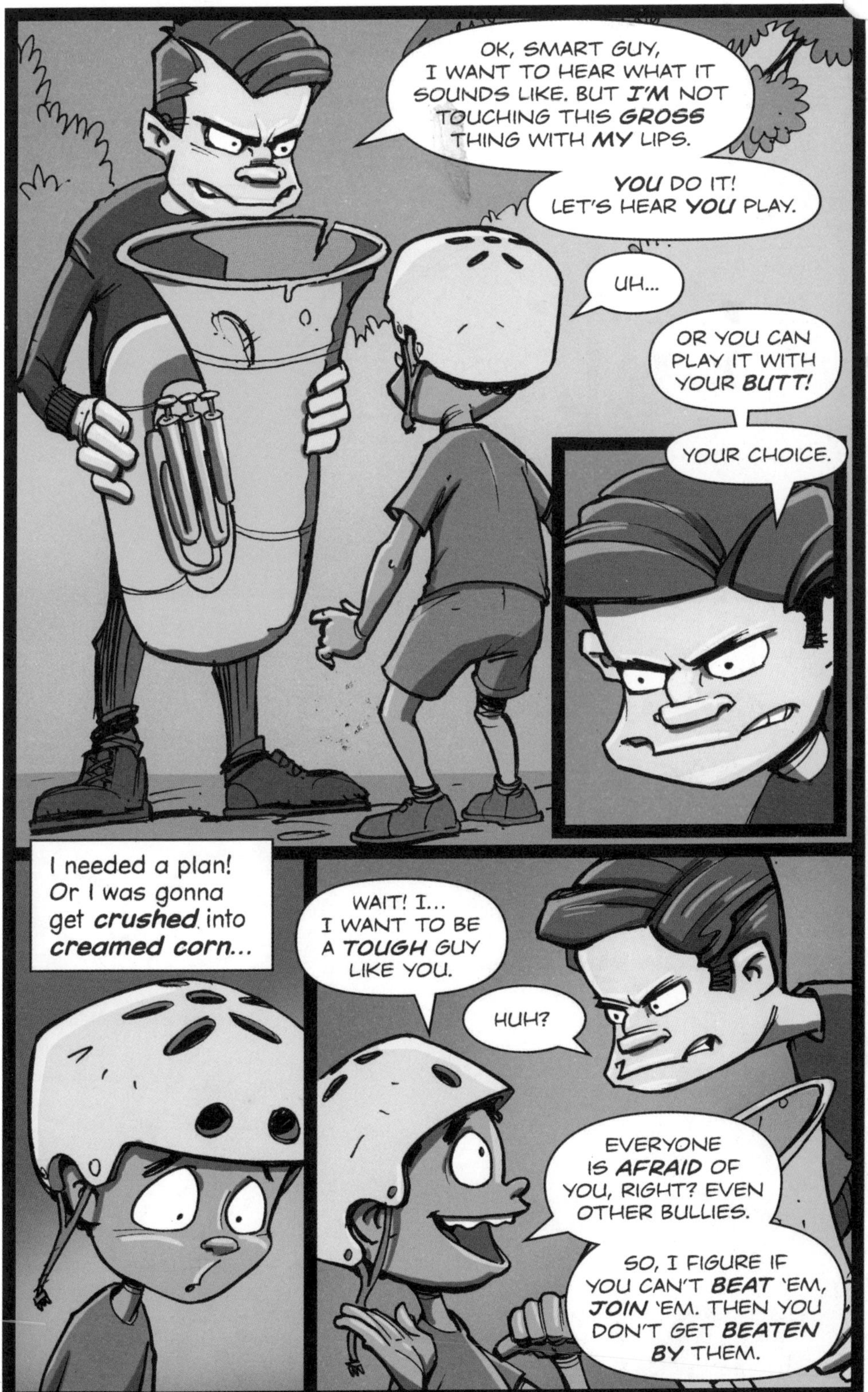
OK, SMART GUY, I WANT TO HEAR WHAT IT SOUNDS LIKE. BUT I'M NOT TOUCHING THIS GROSS THING WITH MY LIPS.
YOU DO IT! LET'S HEAR YOU PLAY.
UH...
OR YOU CAN PLAY IT WITH YOUR BUTT!
YOUR CHOICE.
I needed a plan! Or I was gonna get crushed into creamed corn...
WAIT! I... I WANT TO BE A TOUGH GUY LIKE YOU.
HUH?
EVERYONE IS AFRAID OF YOU, RIGHT? EVEN OTHER BULLIES.
SO, I FIGURE IF YOU CAN'T BEAT 'EM, JOIN 'EM. THEN YOU DON'T GET BEATEN BY THEM.

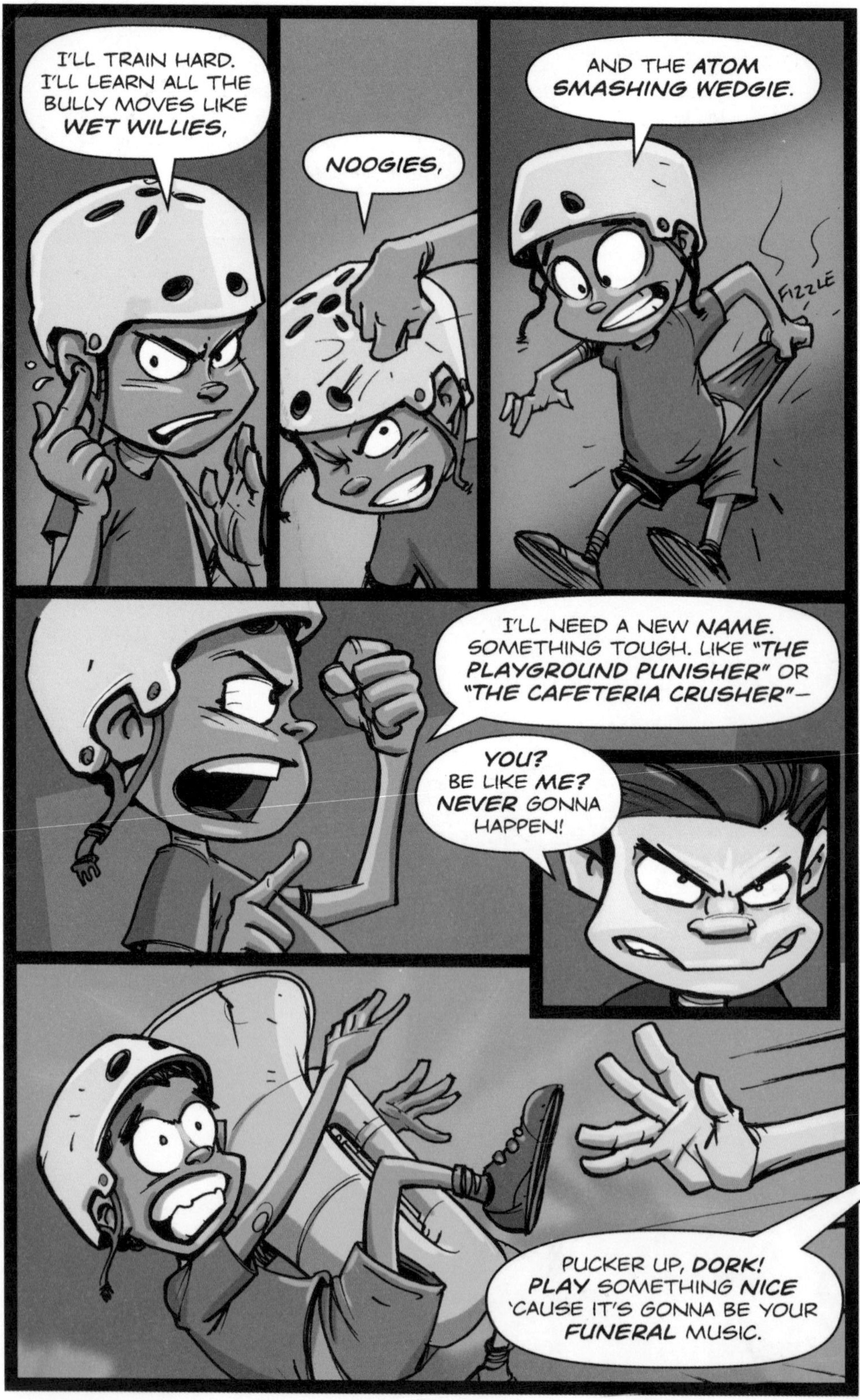
I'LL TRAIN HARD. I'LL LEARN ALL THE BULLY MOVES LIKE WET WILLIES,
NOOGIES,
AND THE ATOM SMASHING WEDGIE.
FIZZLE
I'LL NEED A NEW NAME. SOMETHING TOUGH. LIKE "THE PLAYGROUND PUNISHER" OR "THE CAFETERIA CRUSHER"—
YOU? BE LIKE ME? NEVER GONNA HAPPEN!
PUCKER UP, DORK! PLAY SOMETHING NICE 'CAUSE IT'S GONNA BE YOUR FUNERAL MUSIC.

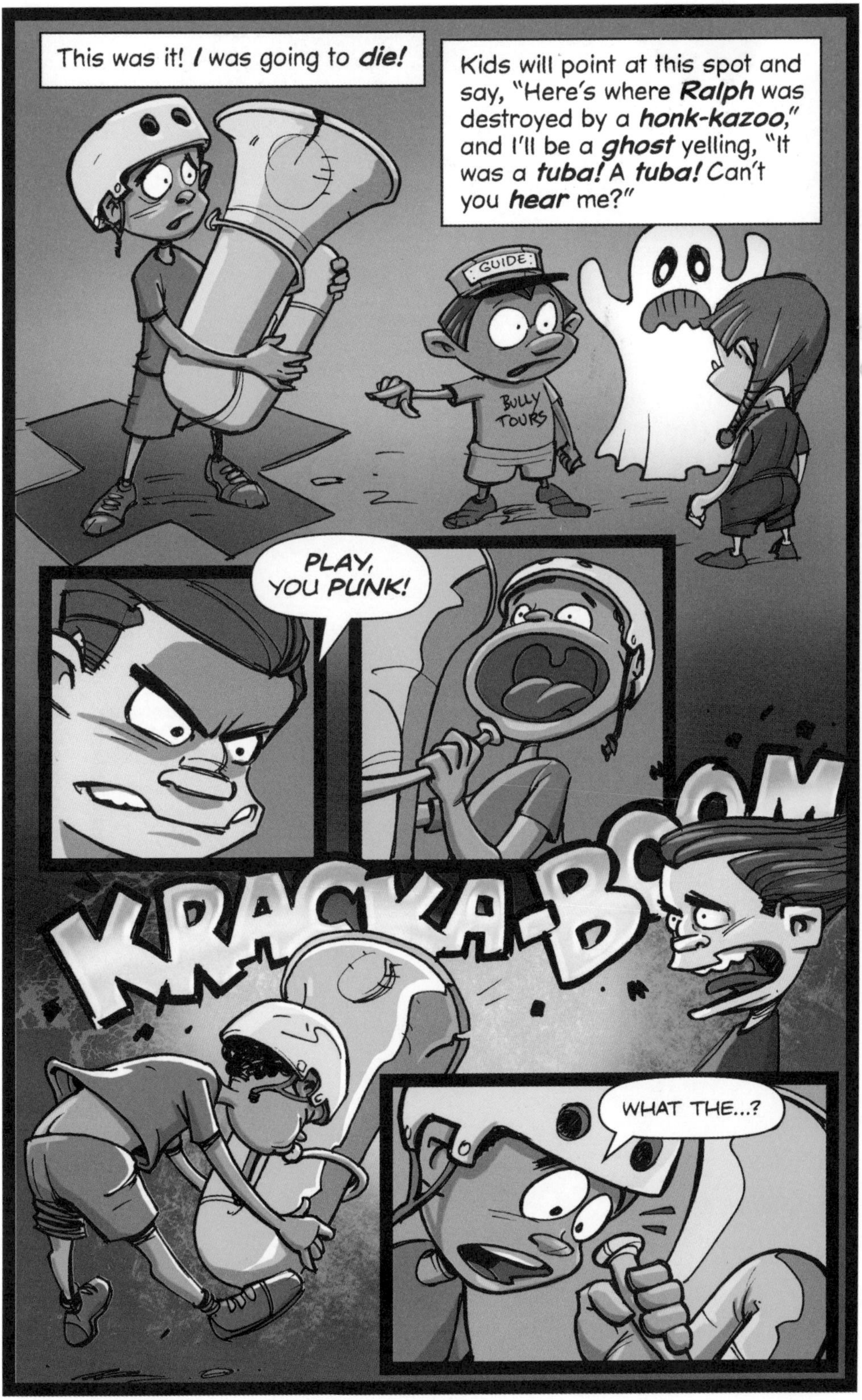

This was it! *I* was going to *die!*
Kids will point at this spot and say, "Here's where ***Ralph*** was destroyed by a ***honk-kazoo,***" and I'll be a ***ghost*** yelling, "It was a ***tuba!*** A ***tuba!*** Can't you ***hear*** me?"
GUIDE
BULLY TOURS
PLAY, YOU ***PUNK!***
KRACKA-BOOM
WHAT THE...?

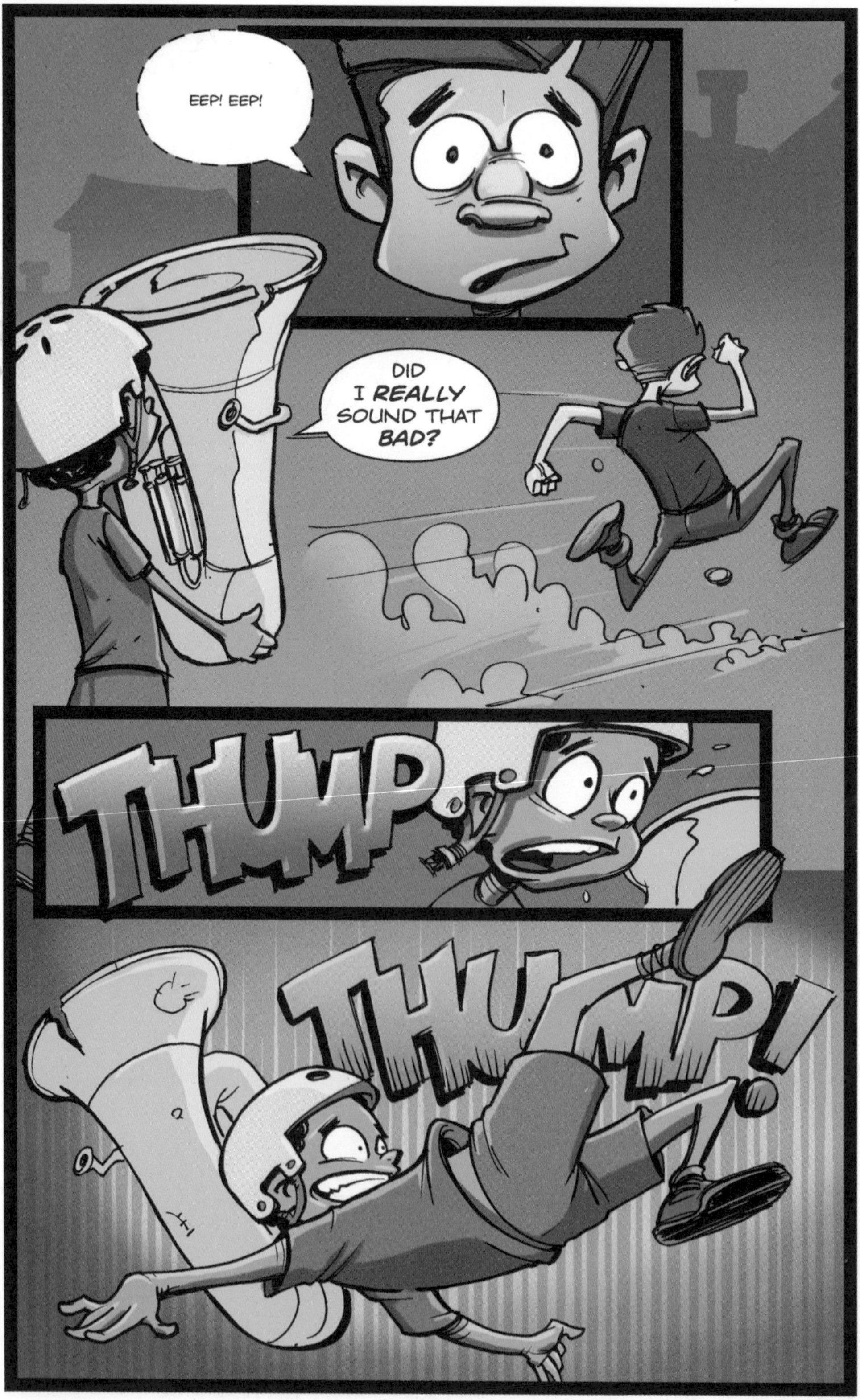
EEP! EEP!
DID I *REALLY* SOUND THAT *BAD?*
THUMP
THUMP!

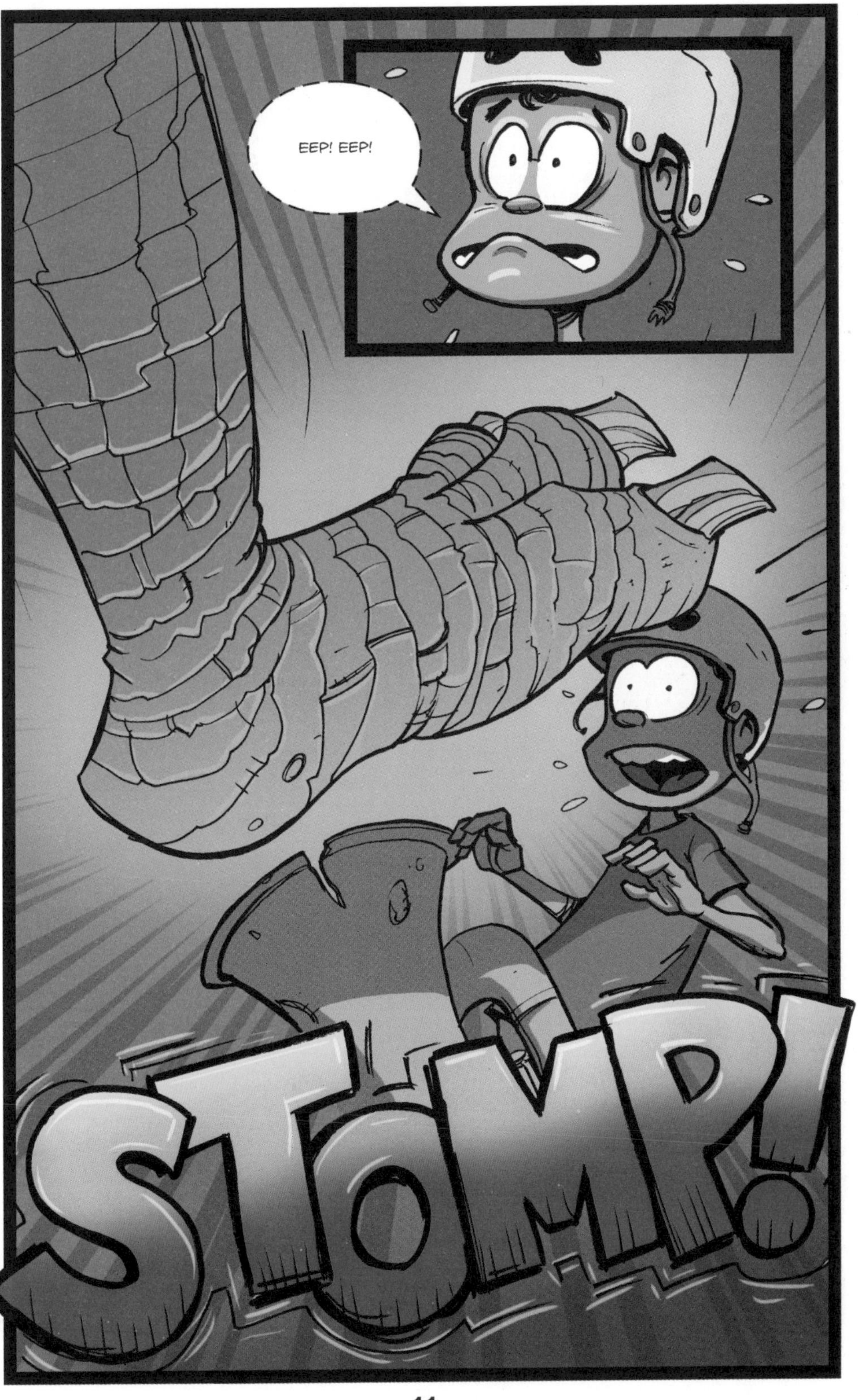
EEP! EEP!
STOMP!

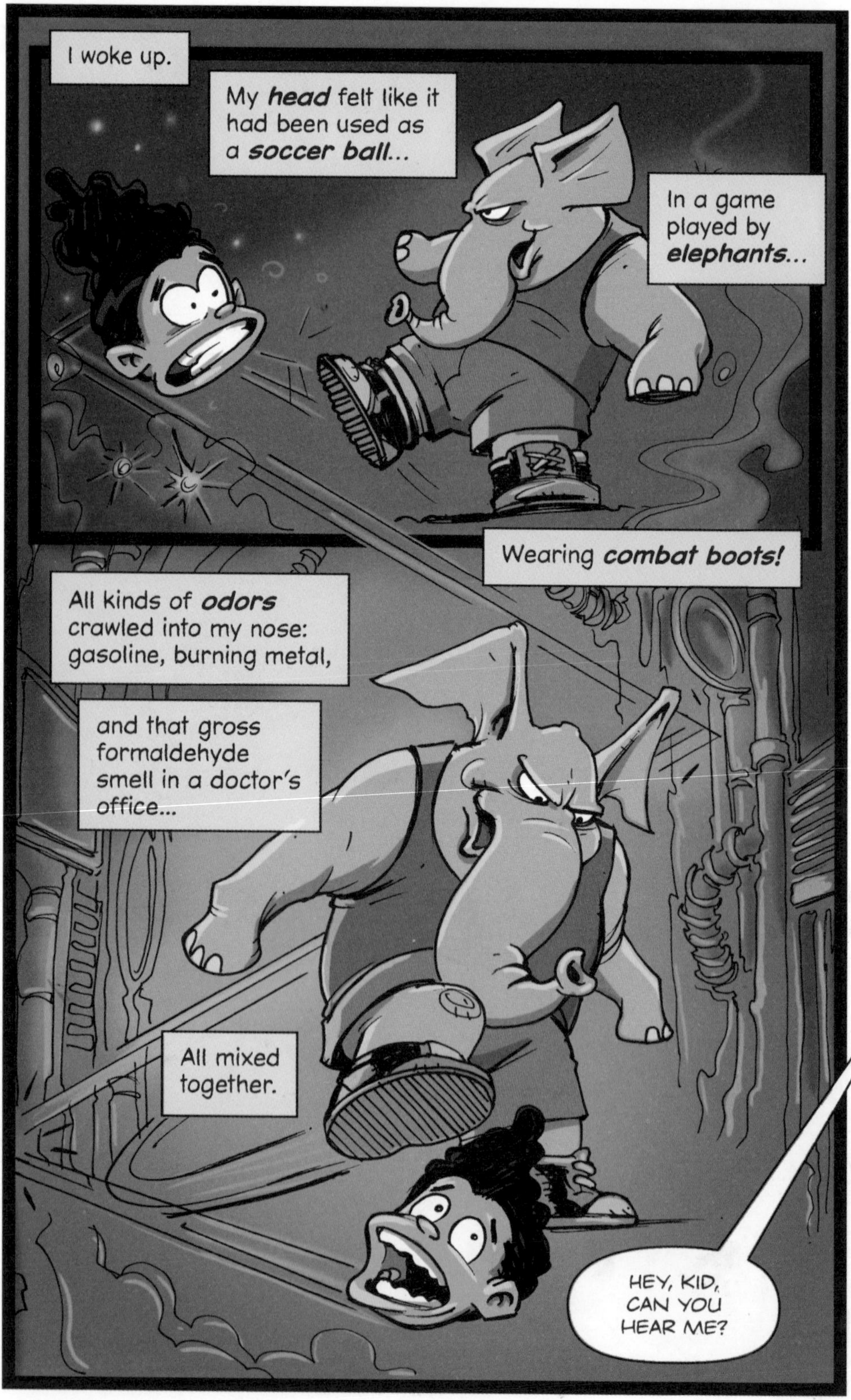
I woke up.
My head felt like it had been used as a soccer ball...
In a game played by elephants...
Wearing combat boots!
All kinds of odors crawled into my nose: gasoline, burning metal,
and that gross formaldehyde smell in a doctor's office...
All mixed together.
HEY, KID, CAN YOU HEAR ME?

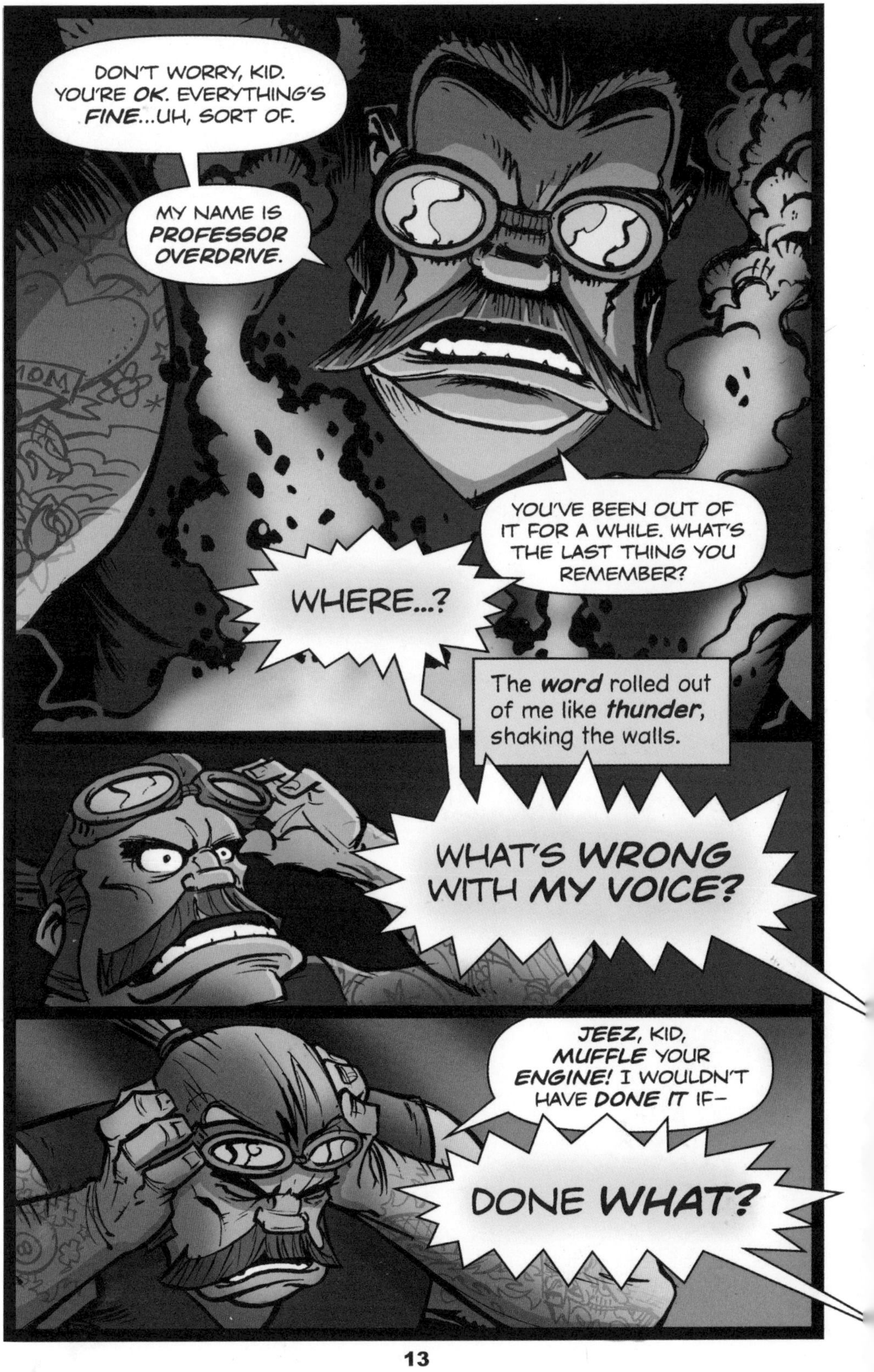

DON'T WORRY, KID. YOU'RE *OK*. EVERYTHING'S *FINE*...UH, SORT OF.
MY NAME IS *PROFESSOR OVERDRIVE*.
YOU'VE BEEN OUT OF IT FOR A WHILE. WHAT'S THE LAST THING YOU REMEMBER?
WHERE...?
The *word* rolled out of me like *thunder*, shaking the walls.
WHAT'S **WRONG** WITH **MY VOICE?**
JEEZ, KID, *MUFFLE* YOUR *ENGINE!* I WOULDN'T HAVE *DONE IT* IF–
DONE **WHAT?**

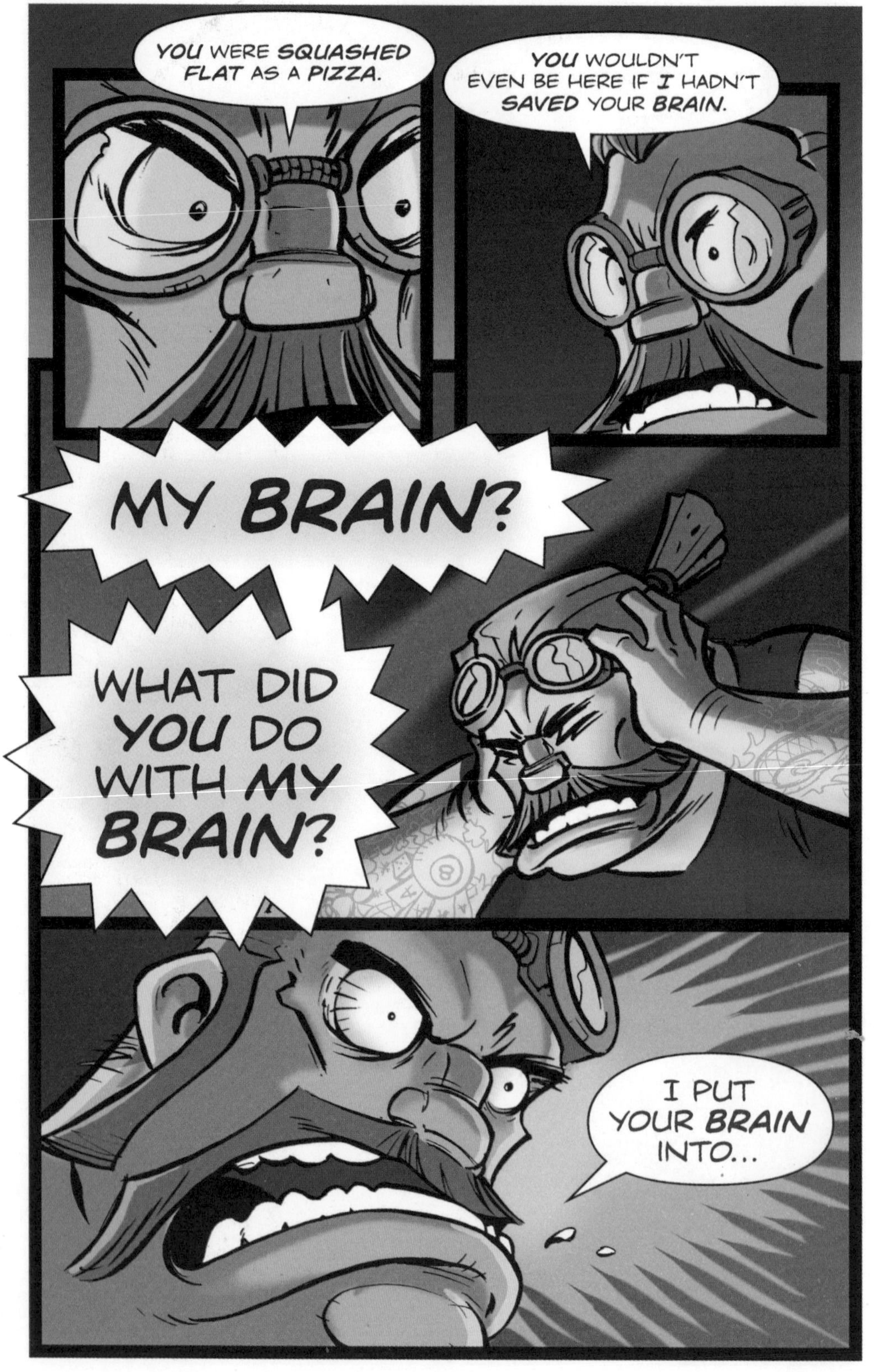
YOU WERE SQUASHED FLAT AS A PIZZA.
YOU WOULDN'T EVEN BE HERE IF I HADN'T SAVED YOUR BRAIN.
MY BRAIN?
WHAT DID YOU DO WITH MY BRAIN?
I PUT YOUR BRAIN INTO...

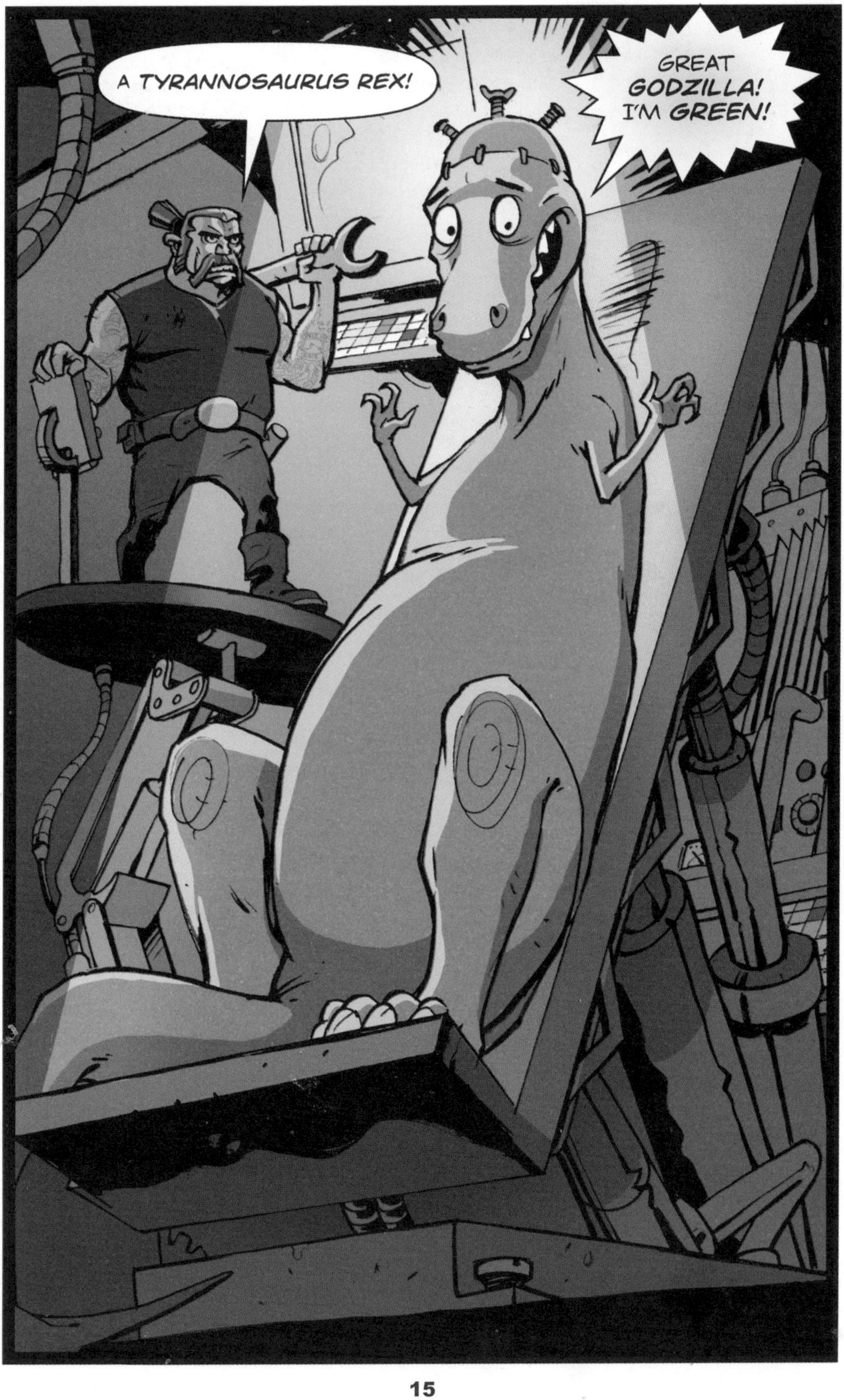
A TYRANNOSAURUS REX!
GREAT GODZILLA! I'M GREEN!

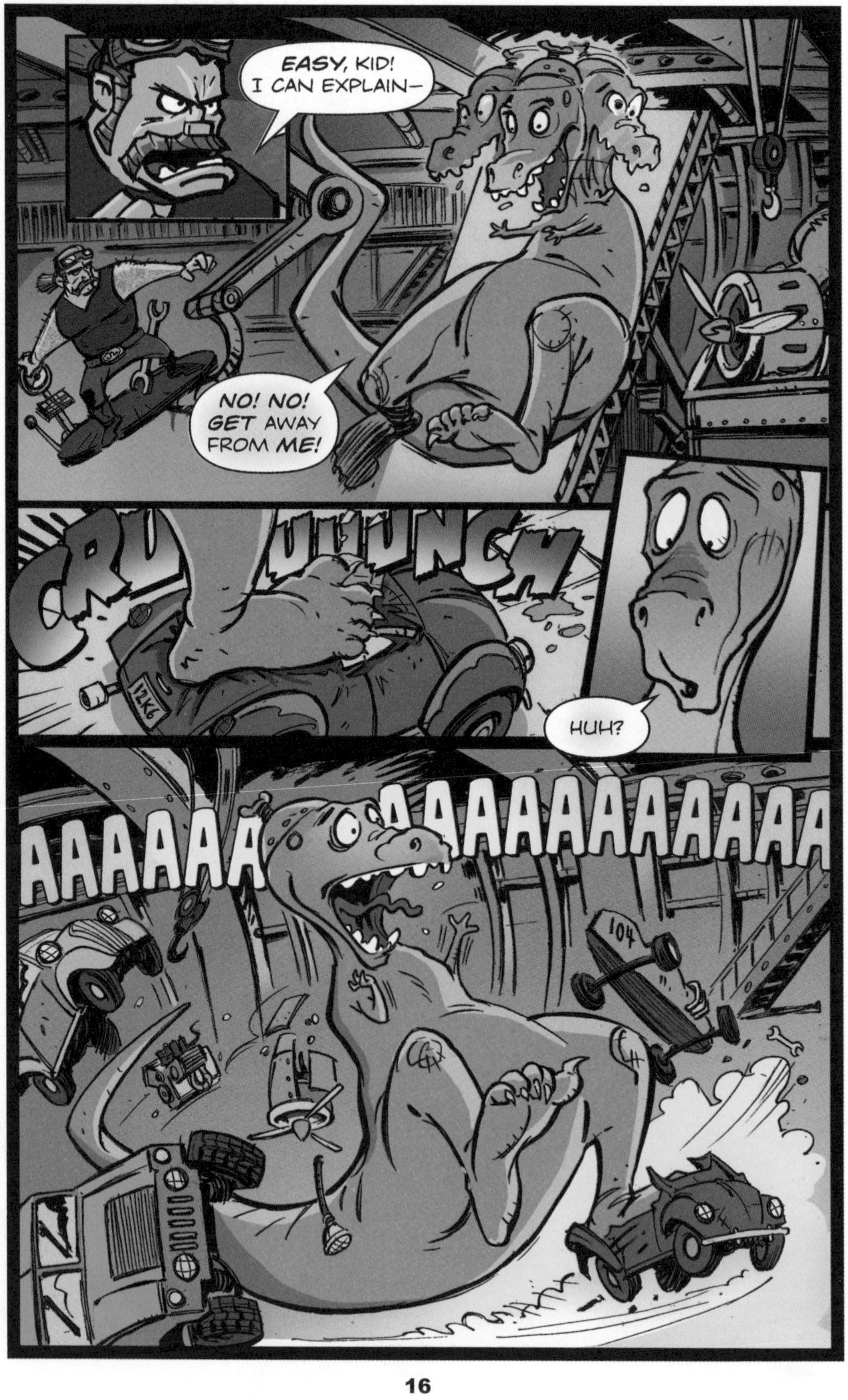
EASY, KID! I CAN EXPLAIN—
NO! NO! GET AWAY FROM ME!
CRUUUUNCH
HUH?
12K6
AAAAAAAAAAAAAAAAAA
104

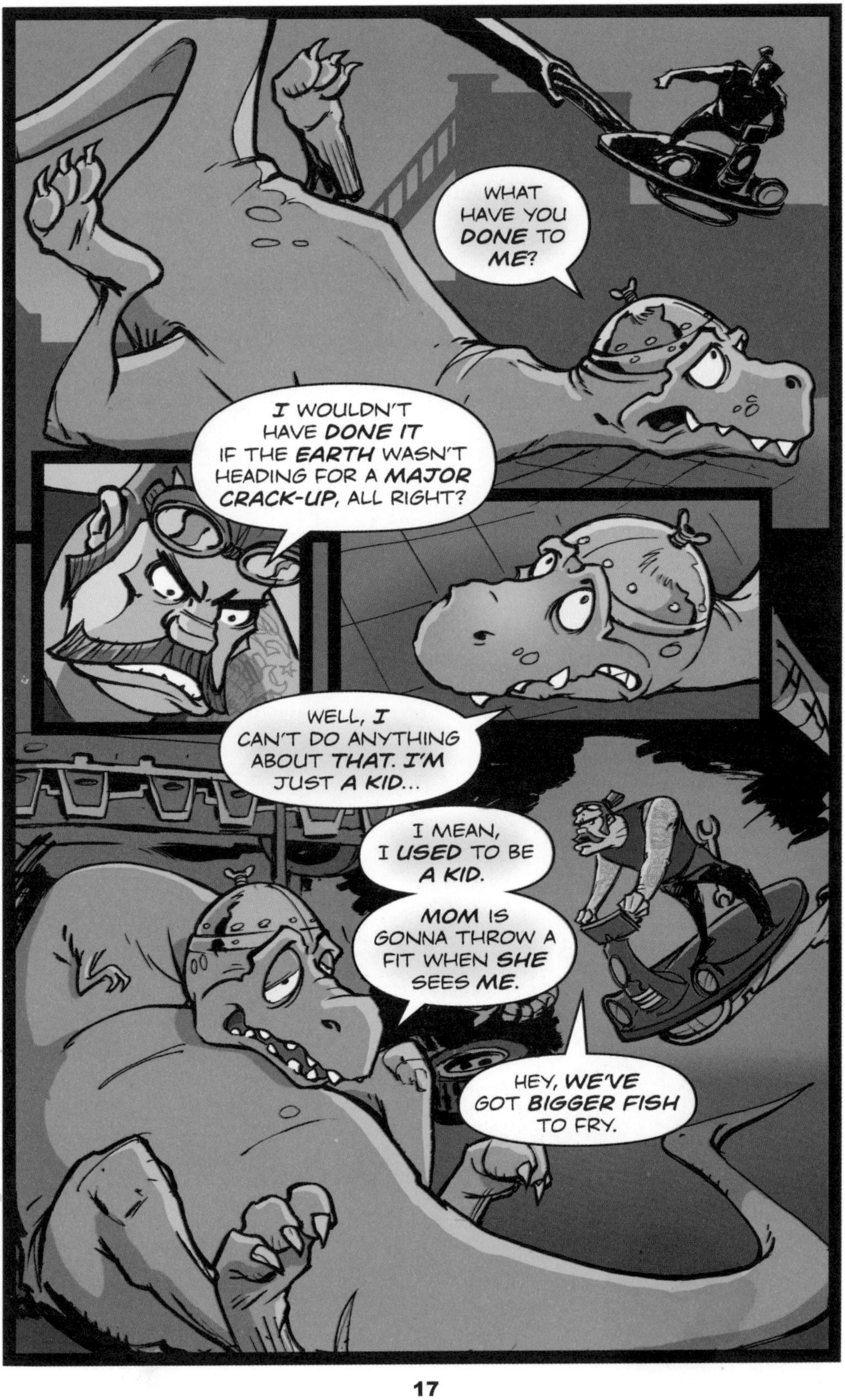
WHAT HAVE YOU DONE TO ME?
I WOULDN'T HAVE DONE IT IF THE EARTH WASN'T HEADING FOR A MAJOR CRACK-UP, ALL RIGHT?
WELL, I CAN'T DO ANYTHING ABOUT THAT. I'M JUST A KID...
I MEAN, I USED TO BE A KID.
MOM IS GONNA THROW A FIT WHEN SHE SEES ME.
HEY, WE'VE GOT BIGGER FISH TO FRY.

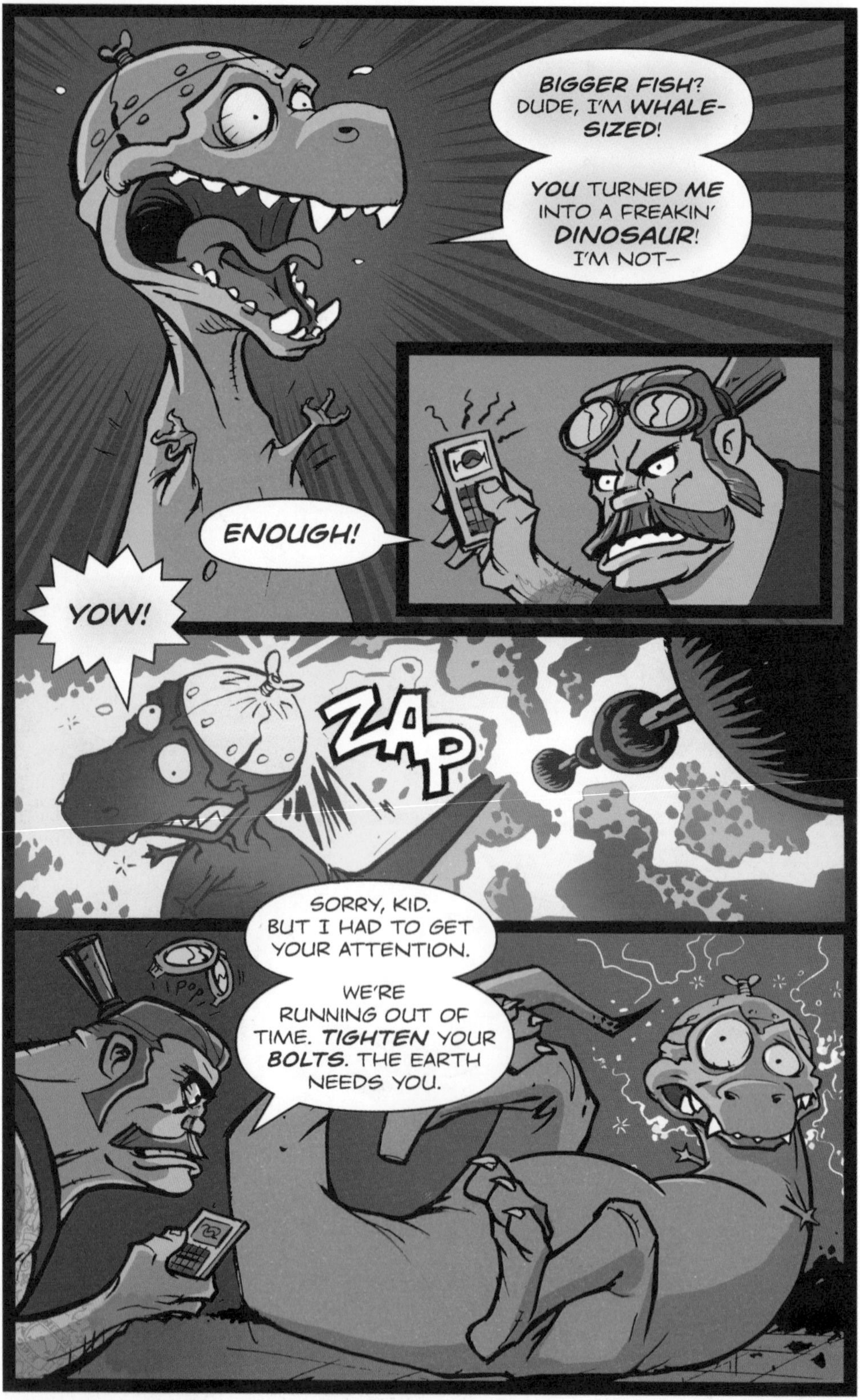
BIGGER FISH? DUDE, I'M WHALE-SIZED!
YOU TURNED ME INTO A FREAKIN' DINOSAUR! I'M NOT–
ENOUGH!
YOW!
ZAP
SORRY, KID. BUT I HAD TO GET YOUR ATTENTION.
WE'RE RUNNING OUT OF TIME. TIGHTEN YOUR BOLTS. THE EARTH NEEDS YOU.

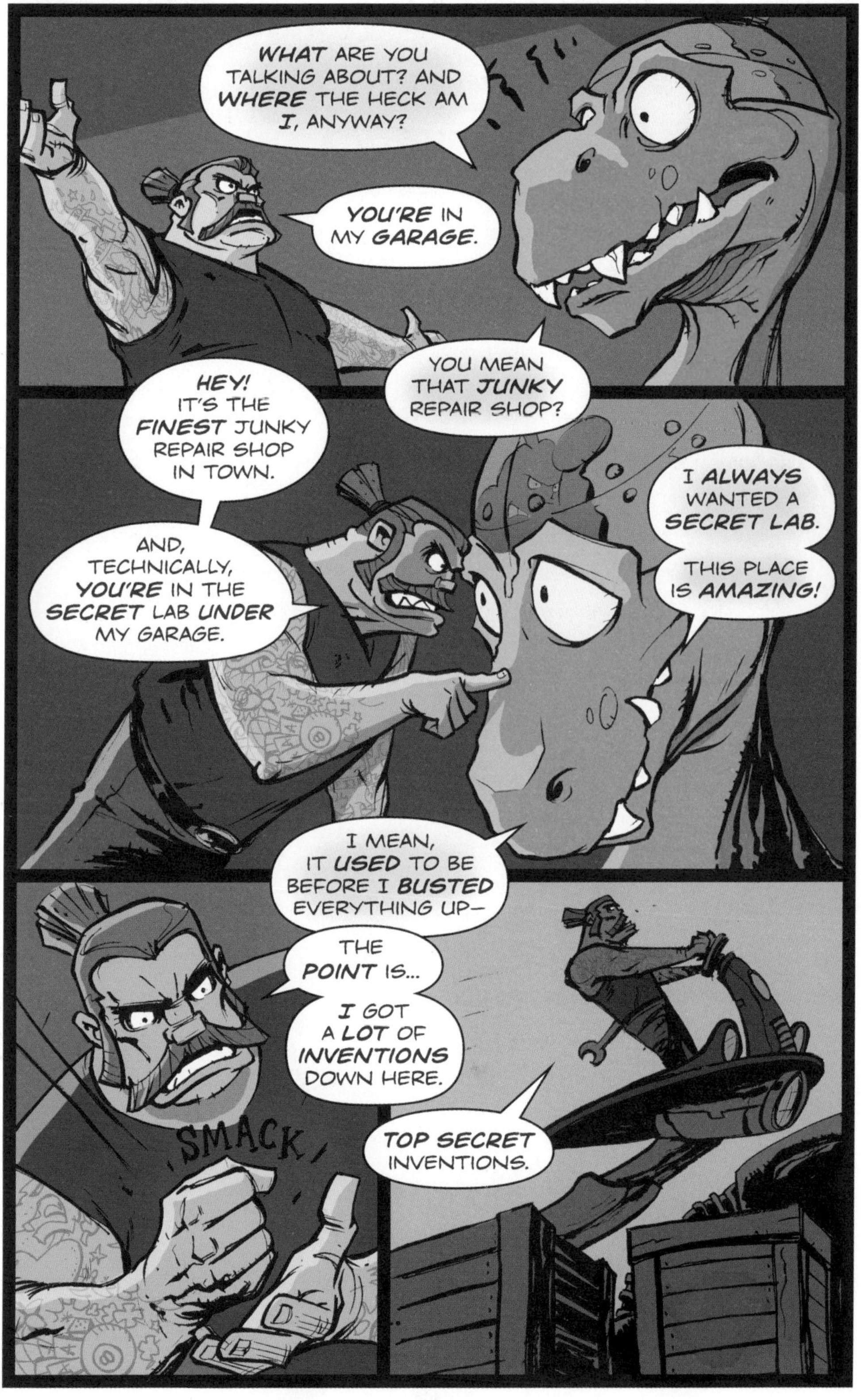

WHAT ARE YOU TALKING ABOUT? AND WHERE THE HECK AM I, ANYWAY?
YOU'RE IN MY GARAGE.
YOU MEAN THAT JUNKY REPAIR SHOP?
HEY! IT'S THE FINEST JUNKY REPAIR SHOP IN TOWN.
AND, TECHNICALLY, YOU'RE IN THE SECRET LAB UNDER MY GARAGE.
I ALWAYS WANTED A SECRET LAB.
THIS PLACE IS AMAZING!
I MEAN, IT USED TO BE BEFORE I BUSTED EVERYTHING UP—
THE POINT IS...
I GOT A LOT OF INVENTIONS DOWN HERE.
SMACK
TOP SECRET INVENTIONS.

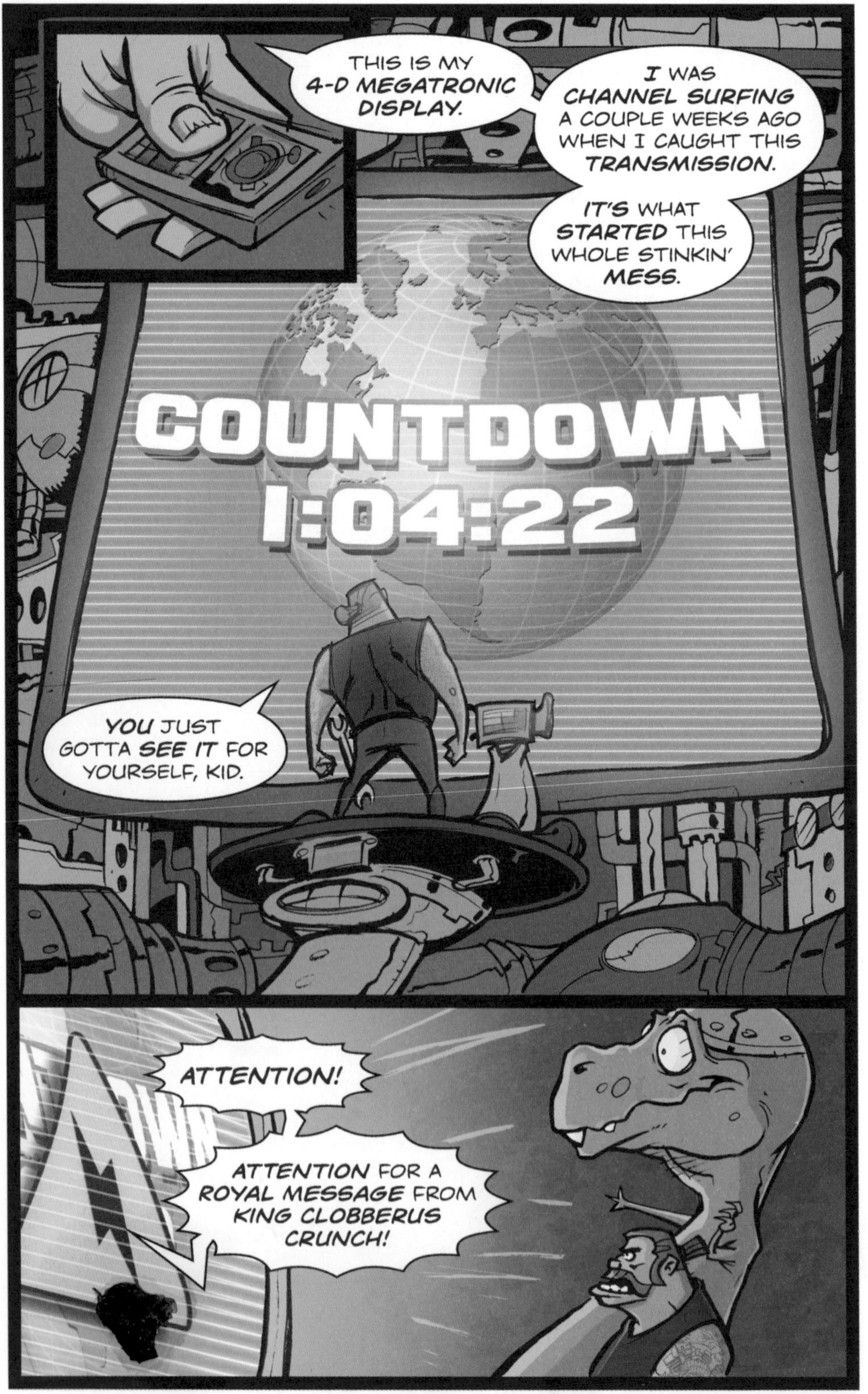
THIS IS MY 4-D MEGATRONIC DISPLAY.
I WAS CHANNEL SURFING A COUPLE WEEKS AGO WHEN I CAUGHT THIS TRANSMISSION.
IT'S WHAT STARTED THIS WHOLE STINKIN' MESS.
COUNTDOWN 1:04:22
YOU JUST GOTTA SEE IT FOR YOURSELF, KID.
ATTENTION!
ATTENTION FOR A ROYAL MESSAGE FROM KING CLOBBERUS CRUNCH!

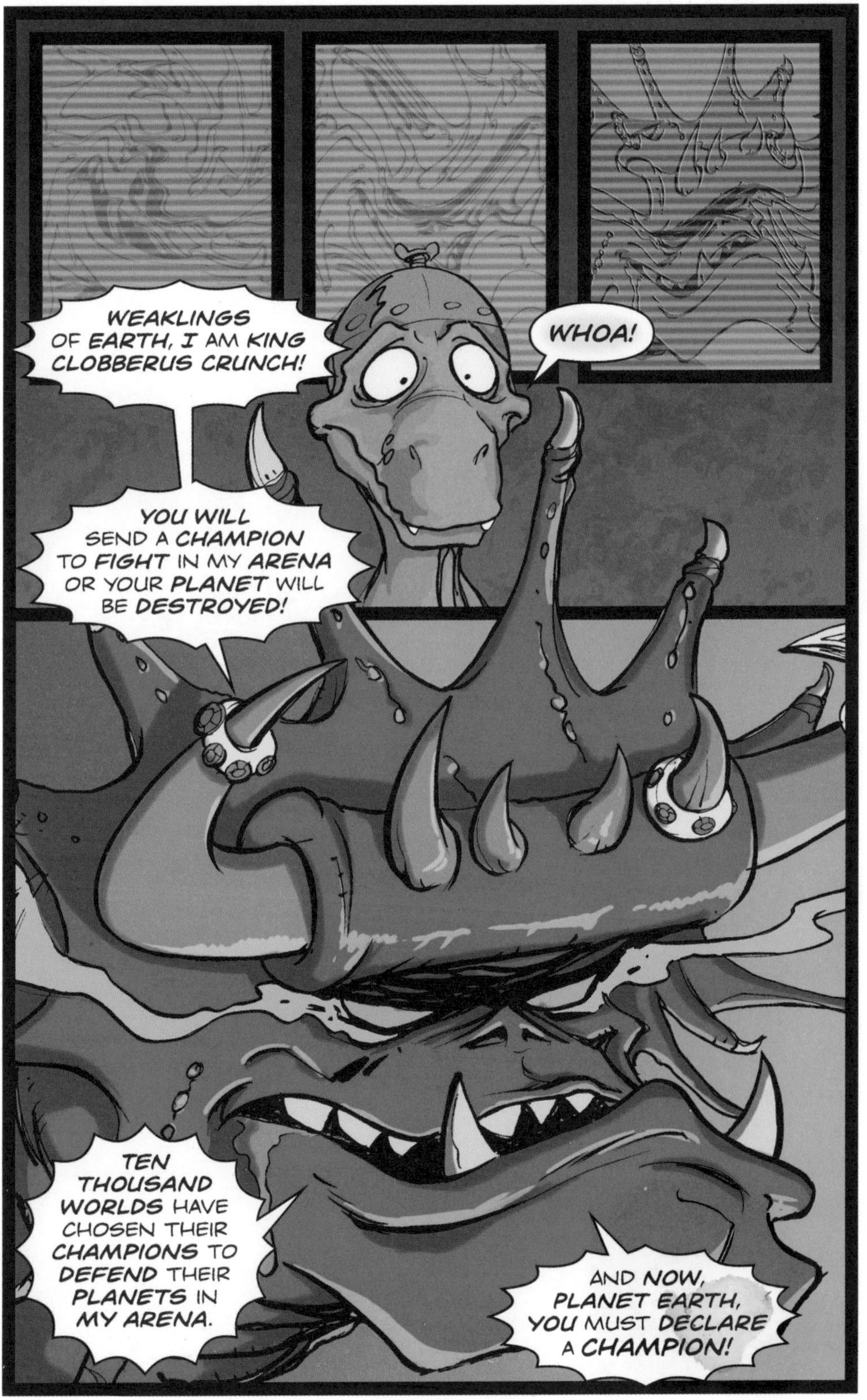
WEAKLINGS OF EARTH, I AM KING CLOBBERUS CRUNCH!
WHOA!
YOU WILL SEND A CHAMPION TO FIGHT IN MY ARENA OR YOUR PLANET WILL BE DESTROYED!
TEN THOUSAND WORLDS HAVE CHOSEN THEIR CHAMPIONS TO DEFEND THEIR PLANETS IN MY ARENA.
AND NOW, PLANET EARTH, YOU MUST DECLARE A CHAMPION!

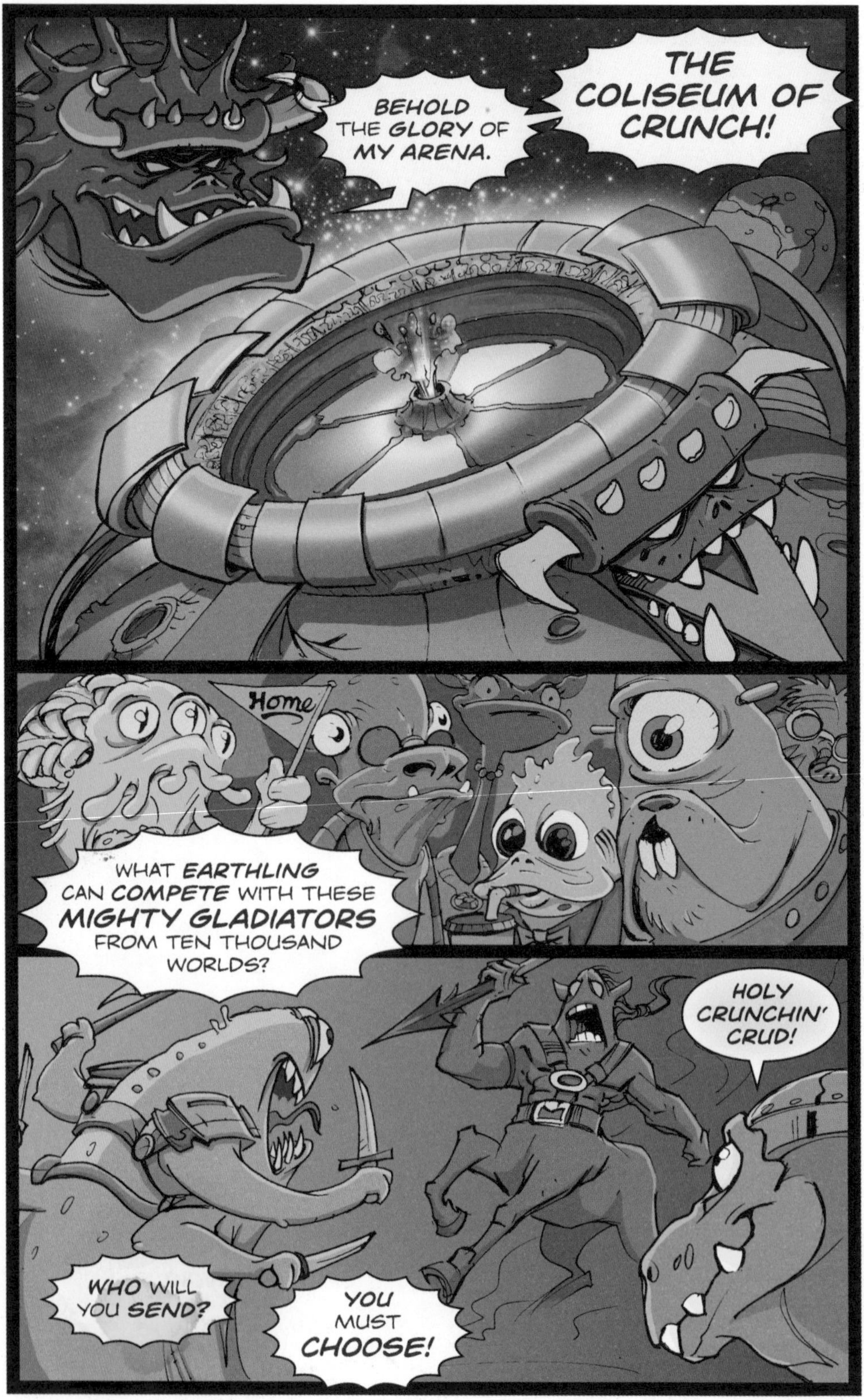
BEHOLD THE GLORY OF MY ARENA.
THE COLISEUM OF CRUNCH!
Home
WHAT EARTHLING CAN COMPETE WITH THESE MIGHTY GLADIATORS FROM TEN THOUSAND WORLDS?
HOLY CRUNCHIN' CRUD!
WHO WILL YOU SEND?
YOU MUST CHOOSE!

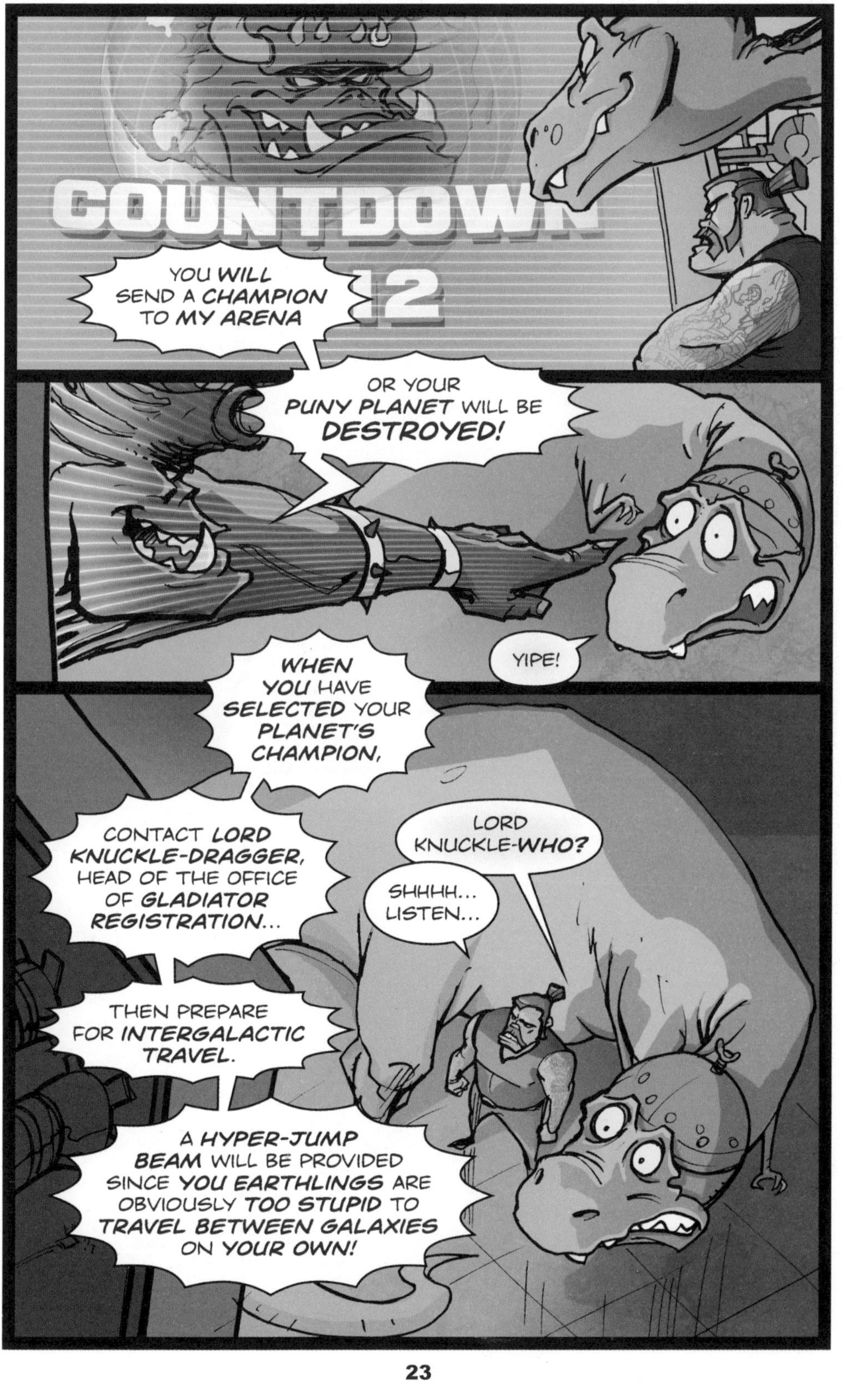
COUNTDOWN
12
YOU WILL SEND A CHAMPION TO MY ARENA
OR YOUR PUNY PLANET WILL BE DESTROYED!
YIPE!
WHEN YOU HAVE SELECTED YOUR PLANET'S CHAMPION,
CONTACT LORD KNUCKLE-DRAGGER, HEAD OF THE OFFICE OF GLADIATOR REGISTRATION...
LORD KNUCKLE-WHO?
SHHHH... LISTEN...
THEN PREPARE FOR INTERGALACTIC TRAVEL.
A HYPER-JUMP BEAM WILL BE PROVIDED SINCE YOU EARTHLINGS ARE OBVIOUSLY TOO STUPID TO TRAVEL BETWEEN GALAXIES ON YOUR OWN!

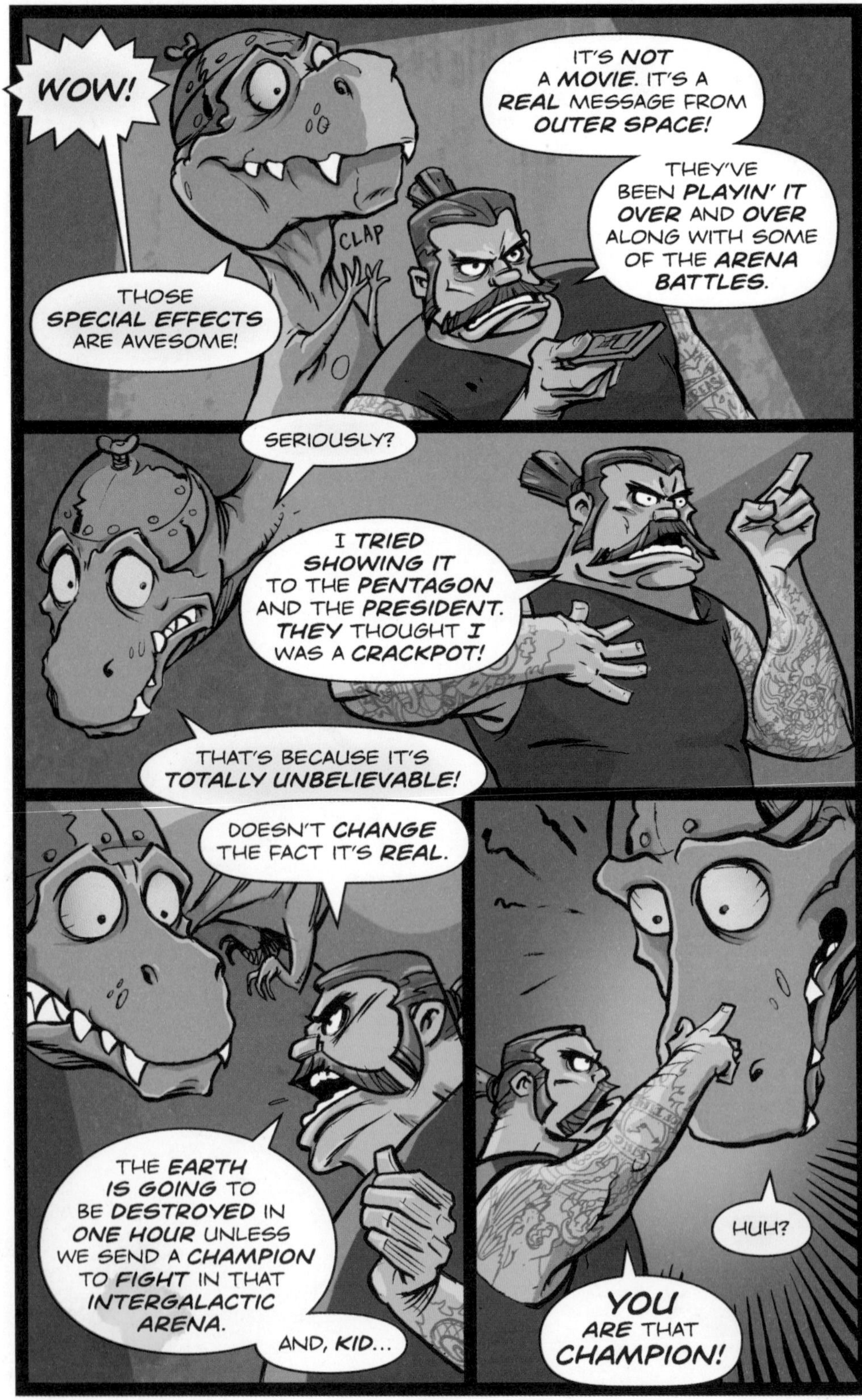
WOW!
IT'S NOT A MOVIE. IT'S A REAL MESSAGE FROM OUTER SPACE!
THEY'VE BEEN PLAYIN' IT OVER AND OVER ALONG WITH SOME OF THE ARENA BATTLES.
THOSE SPECIAL EFFECTS ARE AWESOME!
CLAP
SERIOUSLY?
I TRIED SHOWING IT TO THE PENTAGON AND THE PRESIDENT. THEY THOUGHT I WAS A CRACKPOT!
THAT'S BECAUSE IT'S TOTALLY UNBELIEVABLE!
DOESN'T CHANGE THE FACT IT'S REAL.
THE EARTH IS GOING TO BE DESTROYED IN ONE HOUR UNLESS WE SEND A CHAMPION TO FIGHT IN THAT INTERGALACTIC ARENA.
AND, KID...
YOU ARE THAT CHAMPION!
HUH?

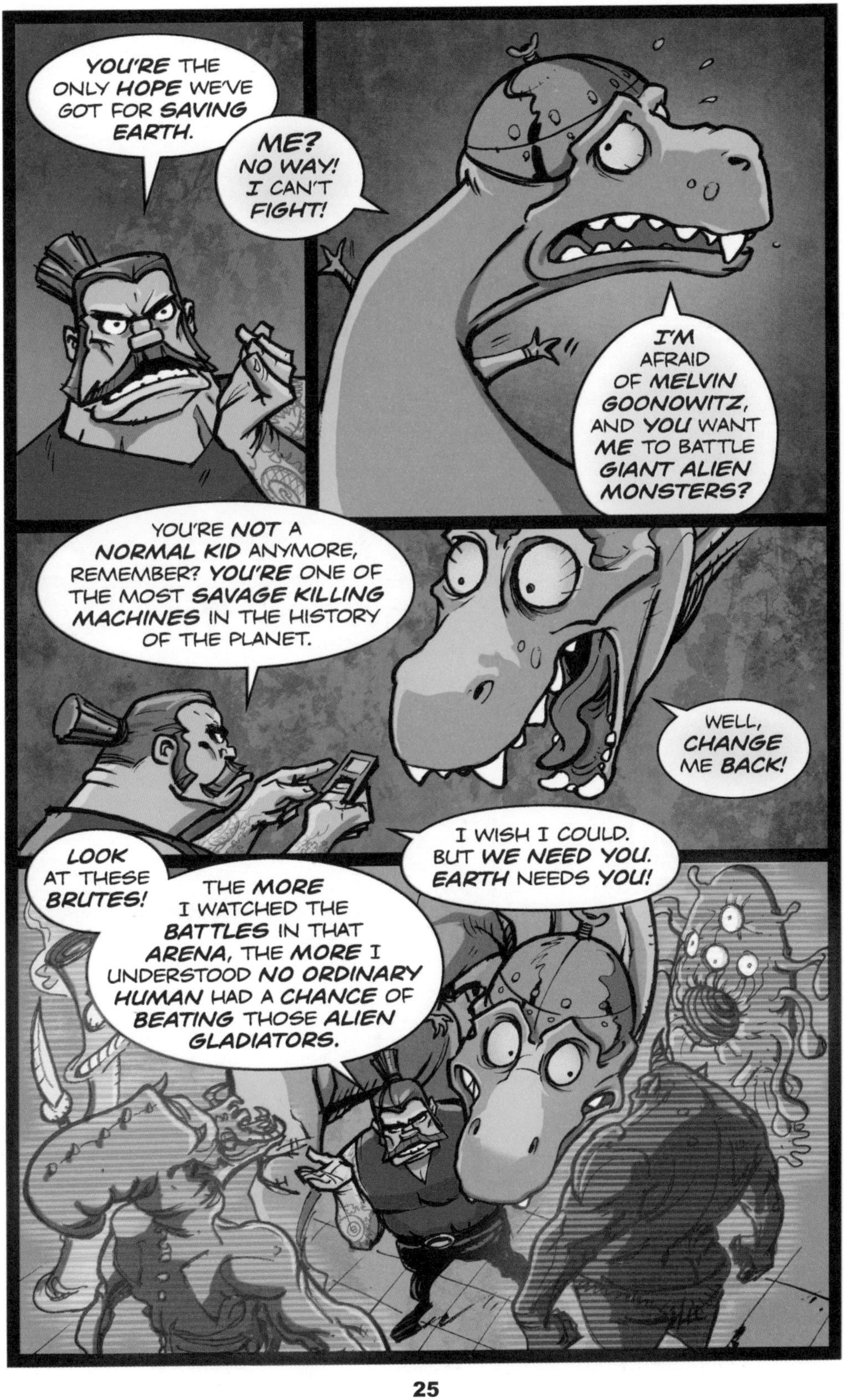
YOU'RE THE ONLY HOPE WE'VE GOT FOR SAVING EARTH.
ME? NO WAY! I CAN'T FIGHT!
I'M AFRAID OF MELVIN GOONOWITZ, AND YOU WANT ME TO BATTLE GIANT ALIEN MONSTERS?
YOU'RE NOT A NORMAL KID ANYMORE, REMEMBER? YOU'RE ONE OF THE MOST SAVAGE KILLING MACHINES IN THE HISTORY OF THE PLANET.
WELL, CHANGE ME BACK!
I WISH I COULD. BUT WE NEED YOU. EARTH NEEDS YOU!
LOOK AT THESE BRUTES!
THE MORE I WATCHED THE BATTLES IN THAT ARENA, THE MORE I UNDERSTOOD NO ORDINARY HUMAN HAD A CHANCE OF BEATING THOSE ALIEN GLADIATORS.

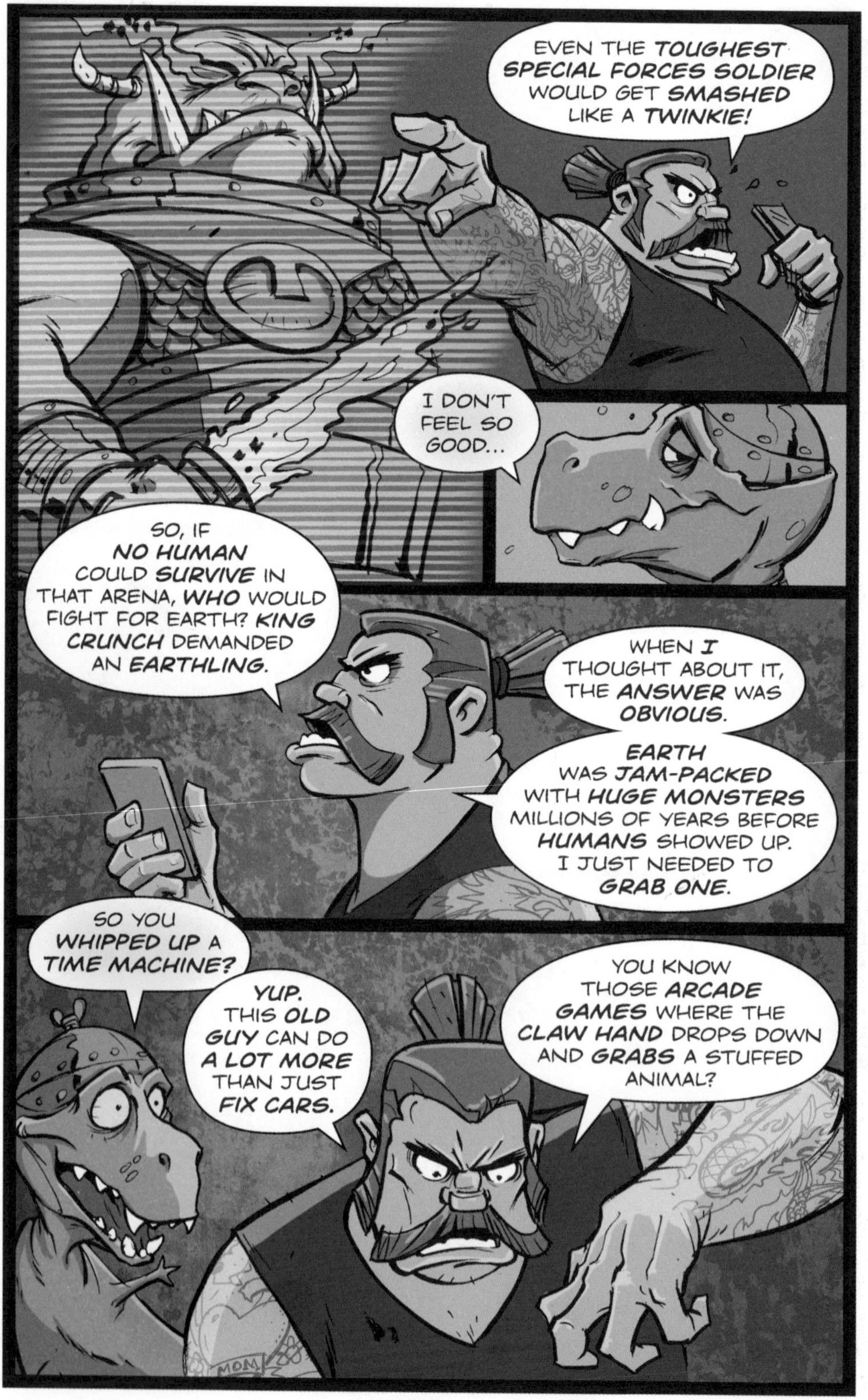
EVEN THE TOUGHEST SPECIAL FORCES SOLDIER WOULD GET SMASHED LIKE A TWINKIE!
I DON'T FEEL SO GOOD...
SO, IF NO HUMAN COULD SURVIVE IN THAT ARENA, WHO WOULD FIGHT FOR EARTH? KING CRUNCH DEMANDED AN EARTHLING.
WHEN I THOUGHT ABOUT IT, THE ANSWER WAS OBVIOUS.
EARTH WAS JAM-PACKED WITH HUGE MONSTERS MILLIONS OF YEARS BEFORE HUMANS SHOWED UP. I JUST NEEDED TO GRAB ONE.
SO YOU WHIPPED UP A TIME MACHINE?
YUP. THIS OLD GUY CAN DO A LOT MORE THAN JUST FIX CARS.
YOU KNOW THOSE ARCADE GAMES WHERE THE CLAW HAND DROPS DOWN AND GRABS A STUFFED ANIMAL?
MOM

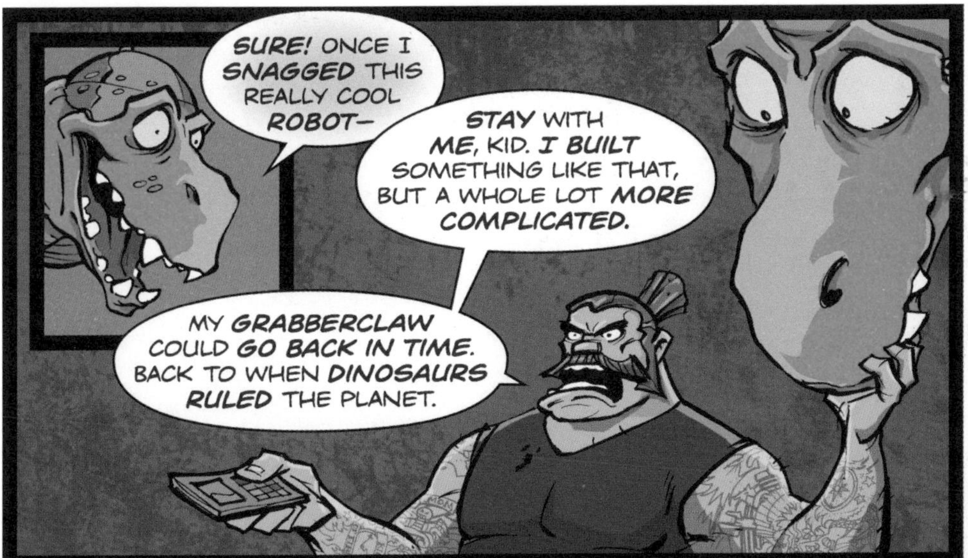
SURE! ONCE I SNAGGED THIS REALLY COOL ROBOT—
STAY WITH ME, KID. I BUILT SOMETHING LIKE THAT, BUT A WHOLE LOT MORE COMPLICATED.
MY GRABBERCLAW COULD GO BACK IN TIME. BACK TO WHEN DINOSAURS RULED THE PLANET.

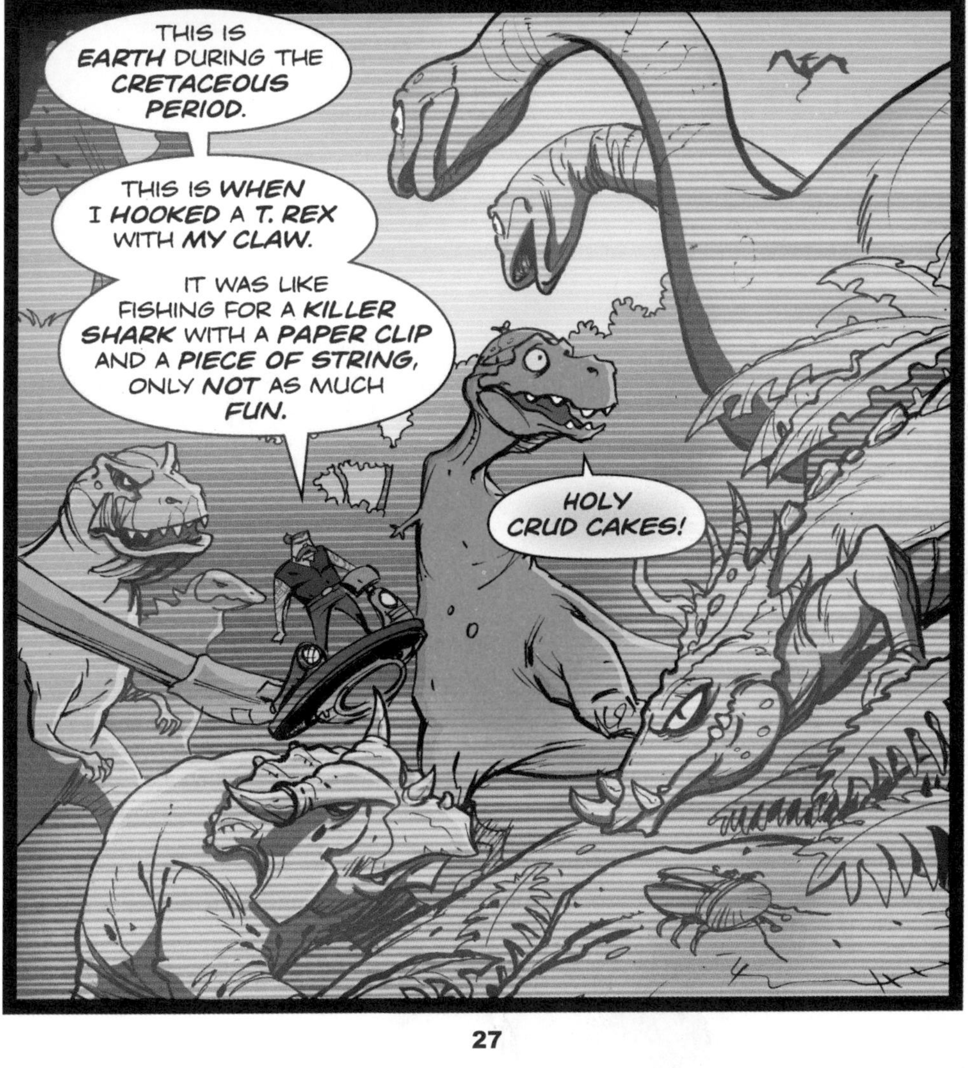
THIS IS EARTH DURING THE CRETACEOUS PERIOD.
THIS IS WHEN I HOOKED A T. REX WITH MY CLAW.
IT WAS LIKE FISHING FOR A KILLER SHARK WITH A PAPER CLIP AND A PIECE OF STRING, ONLY NOT AS MUCH FUN.
HOLY CRUD CAKES!

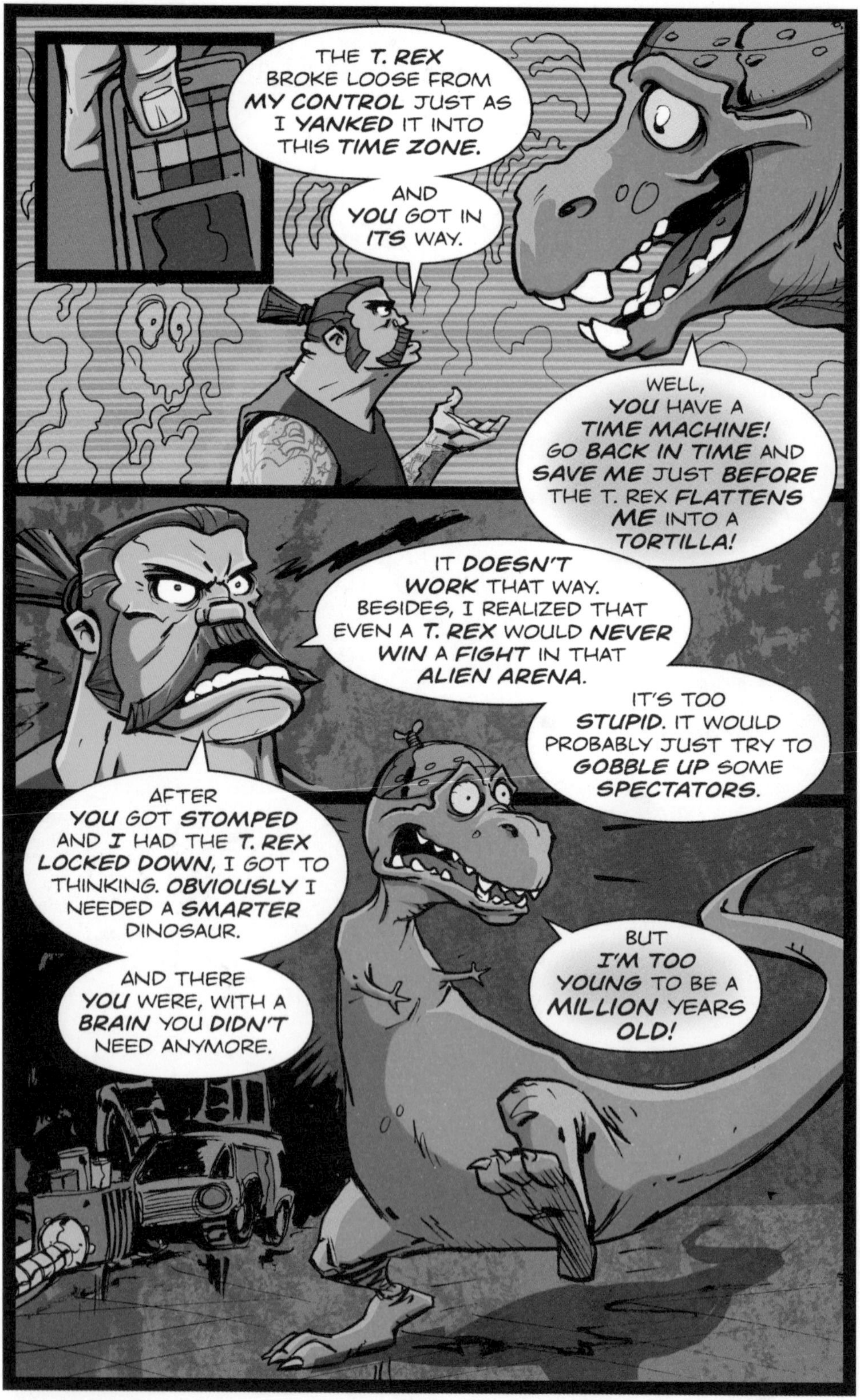
THE T. REX BROKE LOOSE FROM MY CONTROL JUST AS I YANKED IT INTO THIS TIME ZONE.
AND YOU GOT IN ITS WAY.
WELL, YOU HAVE A TIME MACHINE! GO BACK IN TIME AND SAVE ME JUST BEFORE THE T. REX FLATTENS ME INTO A TORTILLA!
IT DOESN'T WORK THAT WAY. BESIDES, I REALIZED THAT EVEN A T. REX WOULD NEVER WIN A FIGHT IN THAT ALIEN ARENA.
IT'S TOO STUPID. IT WOULD PROBABLY JUST TRY TO GOBBLE UP SOME SPECTATORS.
AFTER YOU GOT STOMPED AND I HAD THE T. REX LOCKED DOWN, I GOT TO THINKING. OBVIOUSLY I NEEDED A SMARTER DINOSAUR.
AND THERE YOU WERE, WITH A BRAIN YOU DIDN'T NEED ANYMORE.
BUT I'M TOO YOUNG TO BE A MILLION YEARS OLD!

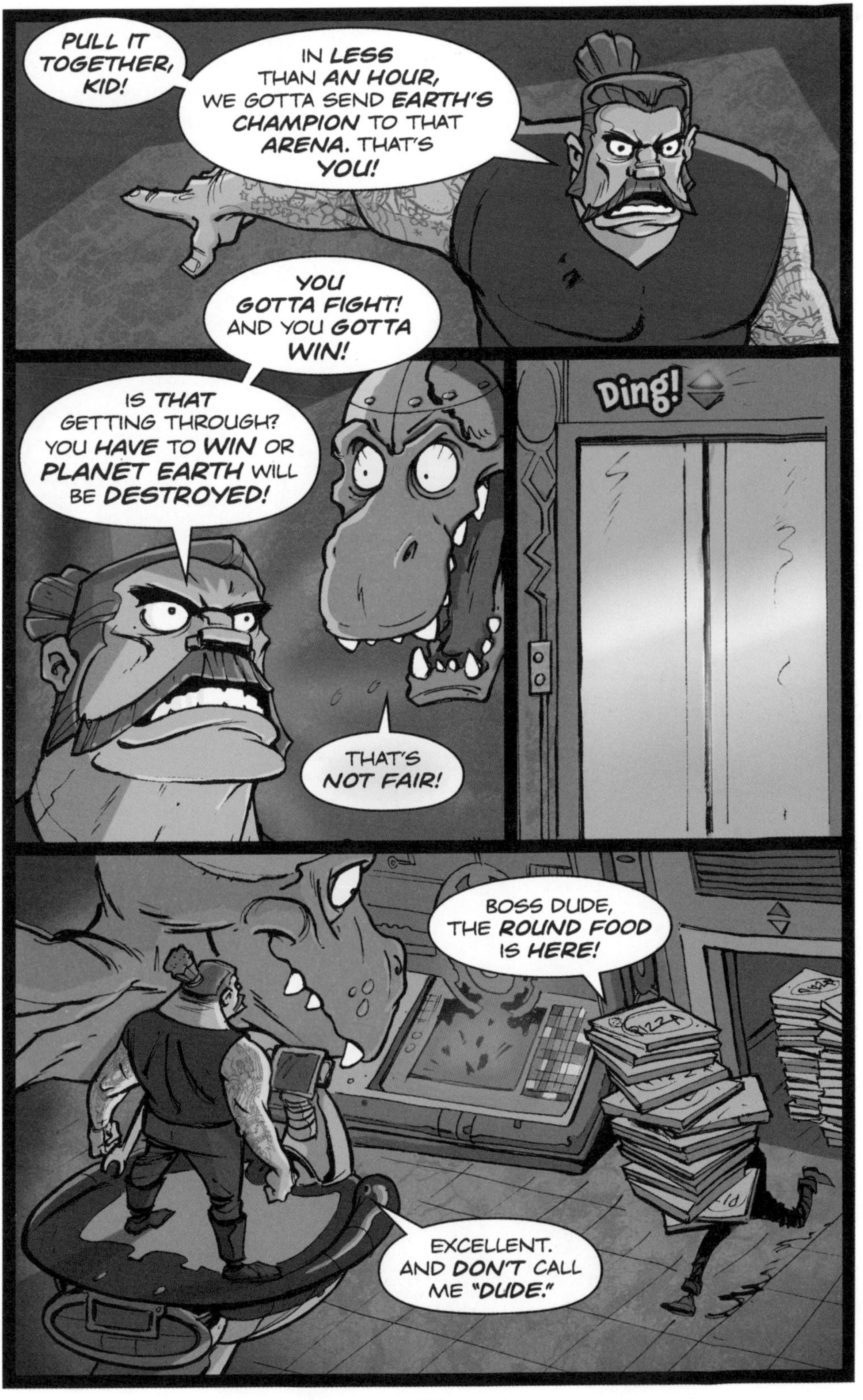
PULL IT TOGETHER, KID!
IN LESS THAN AN HOUR, WE GOTTA SEND EARTH'S CHAMPION TO THAT ARENA. THAT'S YOU!
YOU GOTTA FIGHT! AND YOU GOTTA WIN!
IS THAT GETTING THROUGH? YOU HAVE TO WIN OR PLANET EARTH WILL BE DESTROYED!
THAT'S NOT FAIR!
Ding!
BOSS DUDE, THE ROUND FOOD IS HERE!
EXCELLENT. AND DON'T CALL ME "DUDE."

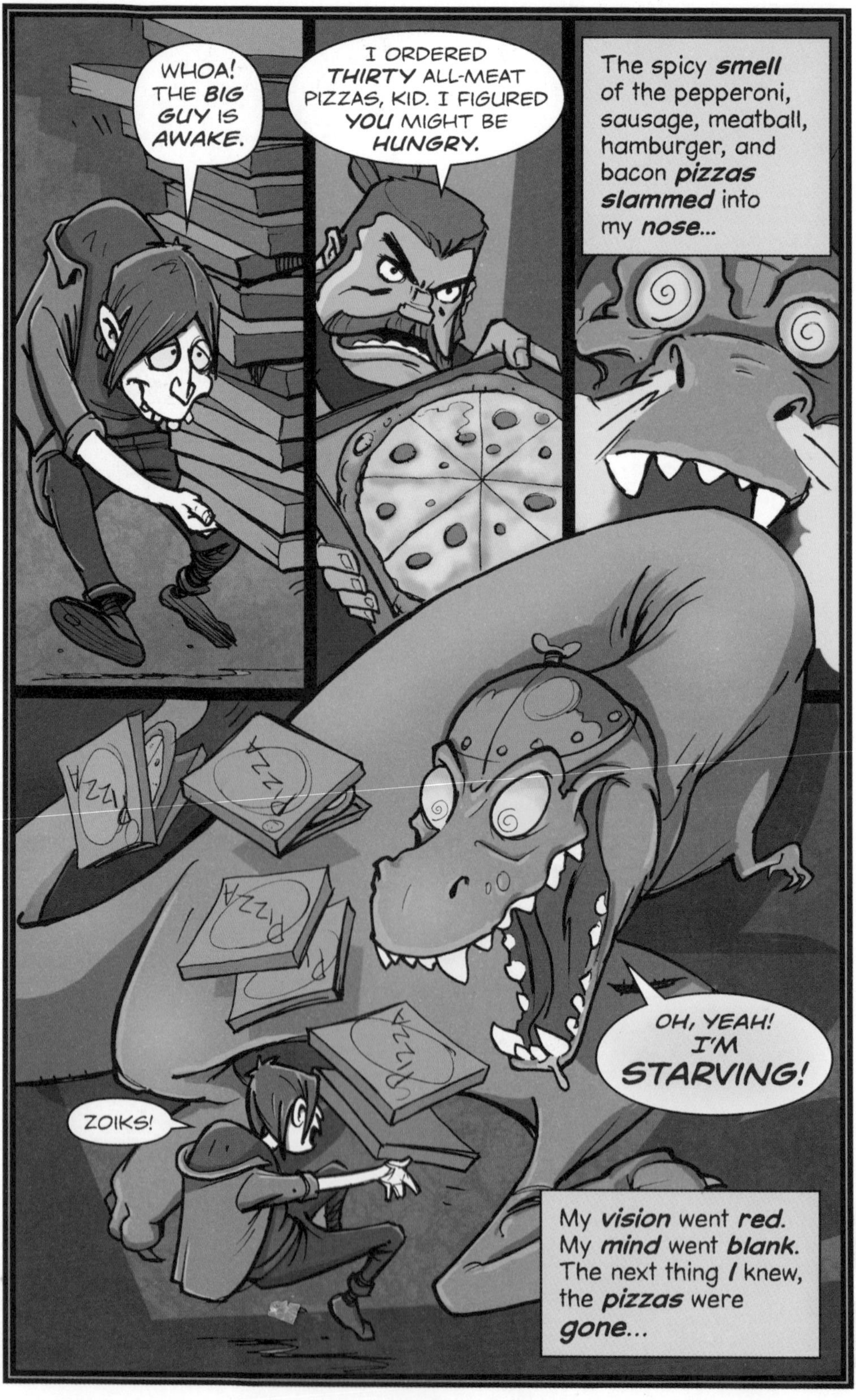
WHOA! THE BIG GUY IS AWAKE.
I ORDERED THIRTY ALL-MEAT PIZZAS, KID. I FIGURED YOU MIGHT BE HUNGRY.
The spicy smell of the pepperoni, sausage, meatball, hamburger, and bacon pizzas slammed into my nose...
PIZZA
OH, YEAH! I'M STARVING!
ZOIKS!
My vision went red. My mind went blank. The next thing I knew, the pizzas were gone...

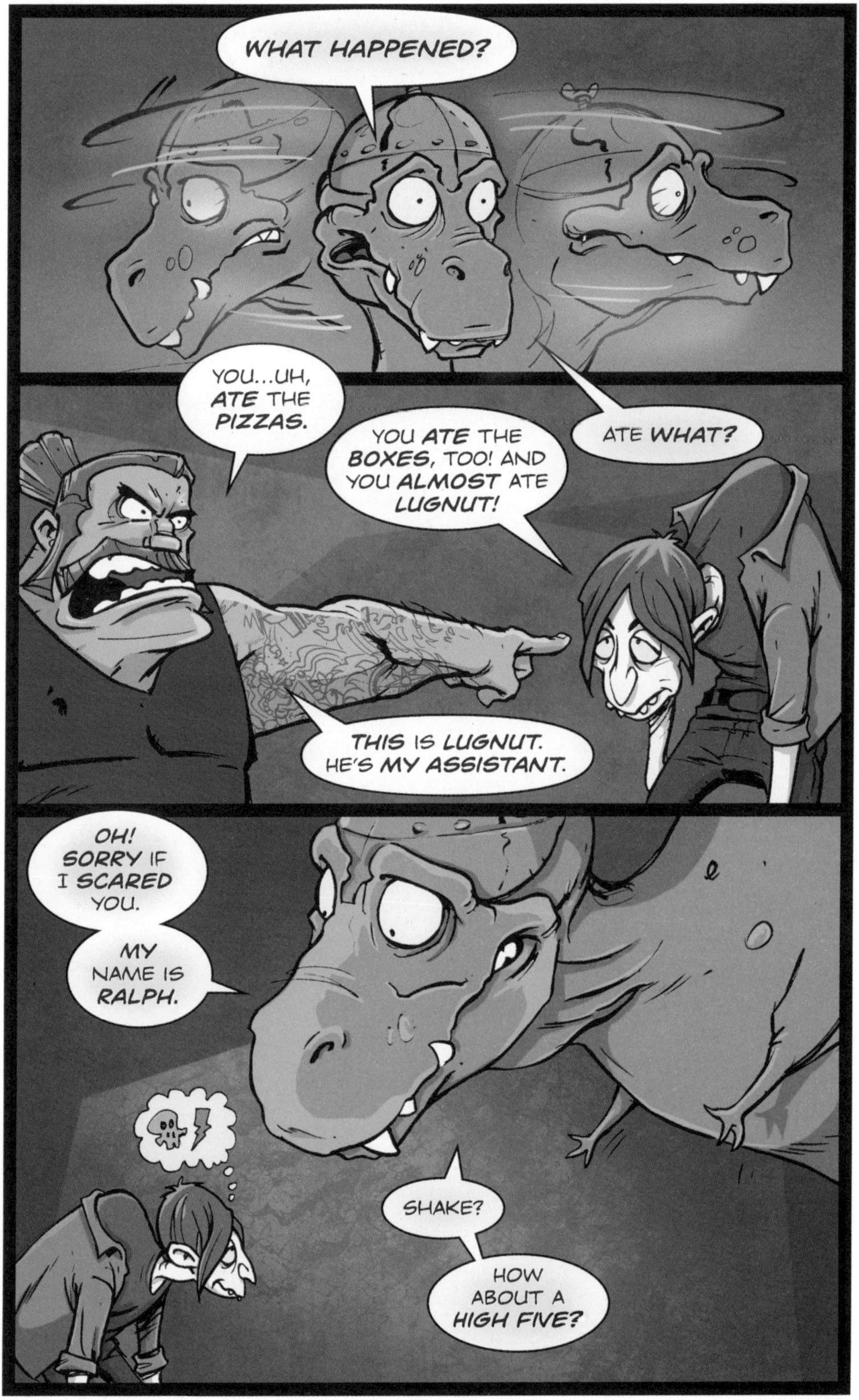
WHAT HAPPENED?
YOU...UH, ATE THE PIZZAS.
YOU ATE THE BOXES, TOO! AND YOU ALMOST ATE LUGNUT!
ATE WHAT?
THIS IS LUGNUT. HE'S MY ASSISTANT.
OH! SORRY IF I SCARED YOU.
MY NAME IS RALPH.
SHAKE?
HOW ABOUT A HIGH FIVE?

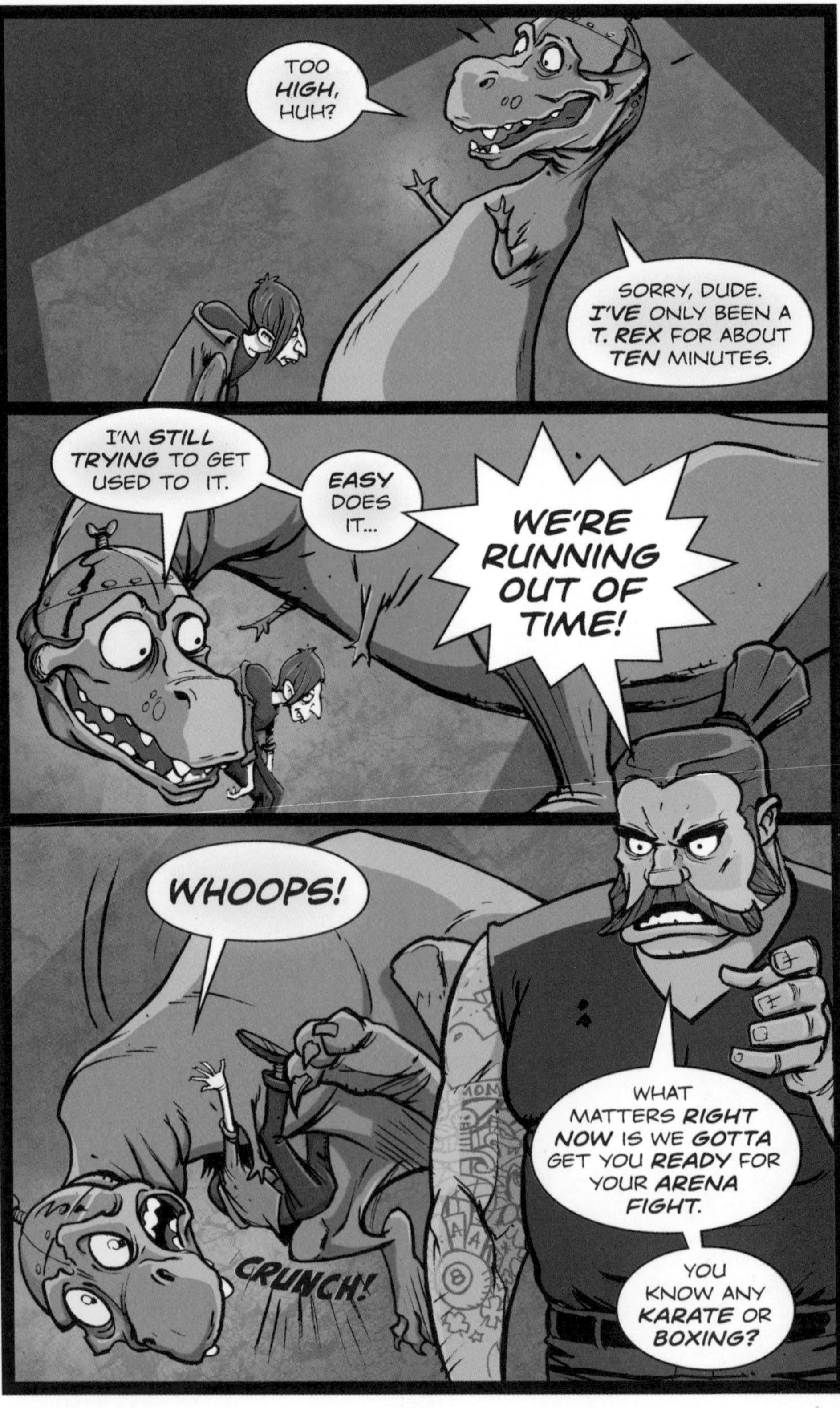
TOO HIGH, HUH?
SORRY, DUDE. I'VE ONLY BEEN A T. REX FOR ABOUT TEN MINUTES.
I'M STILL TRYING TO GET USED TO IT.
EASY DOES IT...
WE'RE RUNNING OUT OF TIME!
WHOOPS!
CRUNCH!
WHAT MATTERS RIGHT NOW IS WE GOTTA GET YOU READY FOR YOUR ARENA FIGHT.
YOU KNOW ANY KARATE OR BOXING?

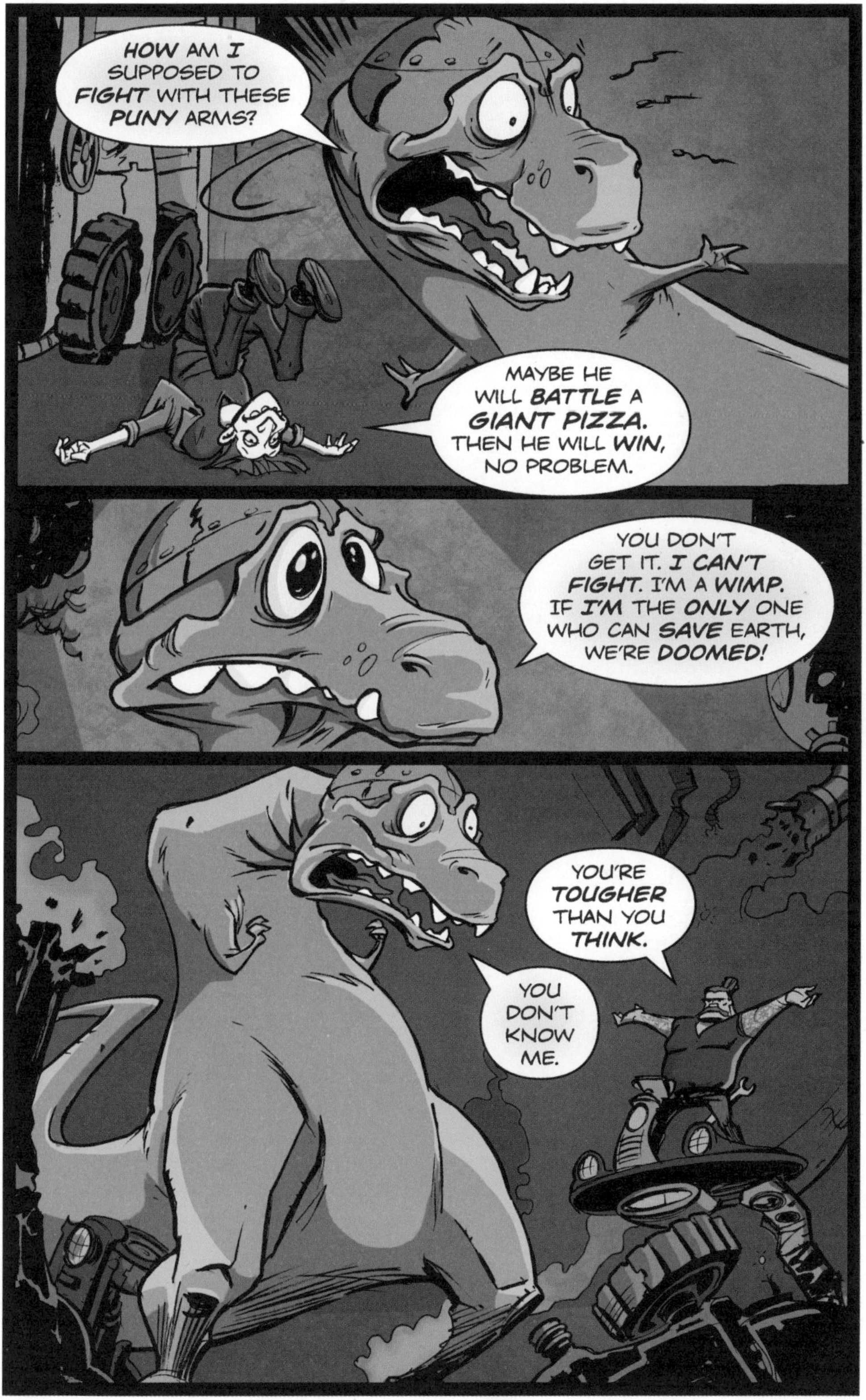
HOW AM I SUPPOSED TO FIGHT WITH THESE PUNY ARMS?
MAYBE HE WILL BATTLE A GIANT PIZZA. THEN HE WILL WIN, NO PROBLEM.
YOU DON'T GET IT. I CAN'T FIGHT. I'M A WIMP. IF I'M THE ONLY ONE WHO CAN SAVE EARTH, WE'RE DOOMED!
YOU'RE TOUGHER THAN YOU THINK.
YOU DON'T KNOW ME.

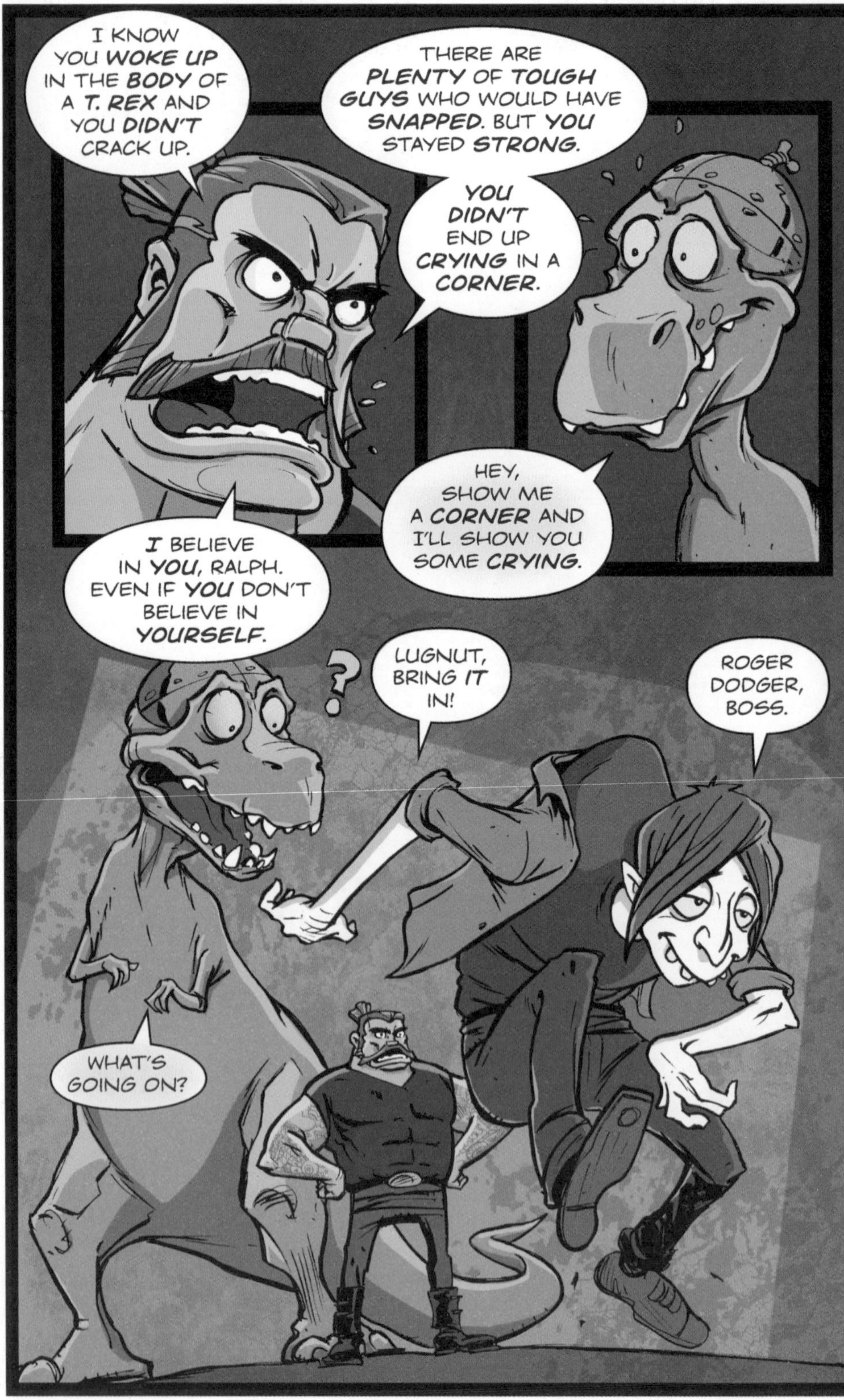
I KNOW YOU WOKE UP IN THE BODY OF A T. REX AND YOU DIDN'T CRACK UP.
THERE ARE PLENTY OF TOUGH GUYS WHO WOULD HAVE SNAPPED. BUT YOU STAYED STRONG.
YOU DIDN'T END UP CRYING IN A CORNER.
HEY, SHOW ME A CORNER AND I'LL SHOW YOU SOME CRYING.
I BELIEVE IN YOU, RALPH. EVEN IF YOU DON'T BELIEVE IN YOURSELF.
?
LUGNUT, BRING IT IN!
ROGER DODGER, BOSS.
WHAT'S GOING ON?

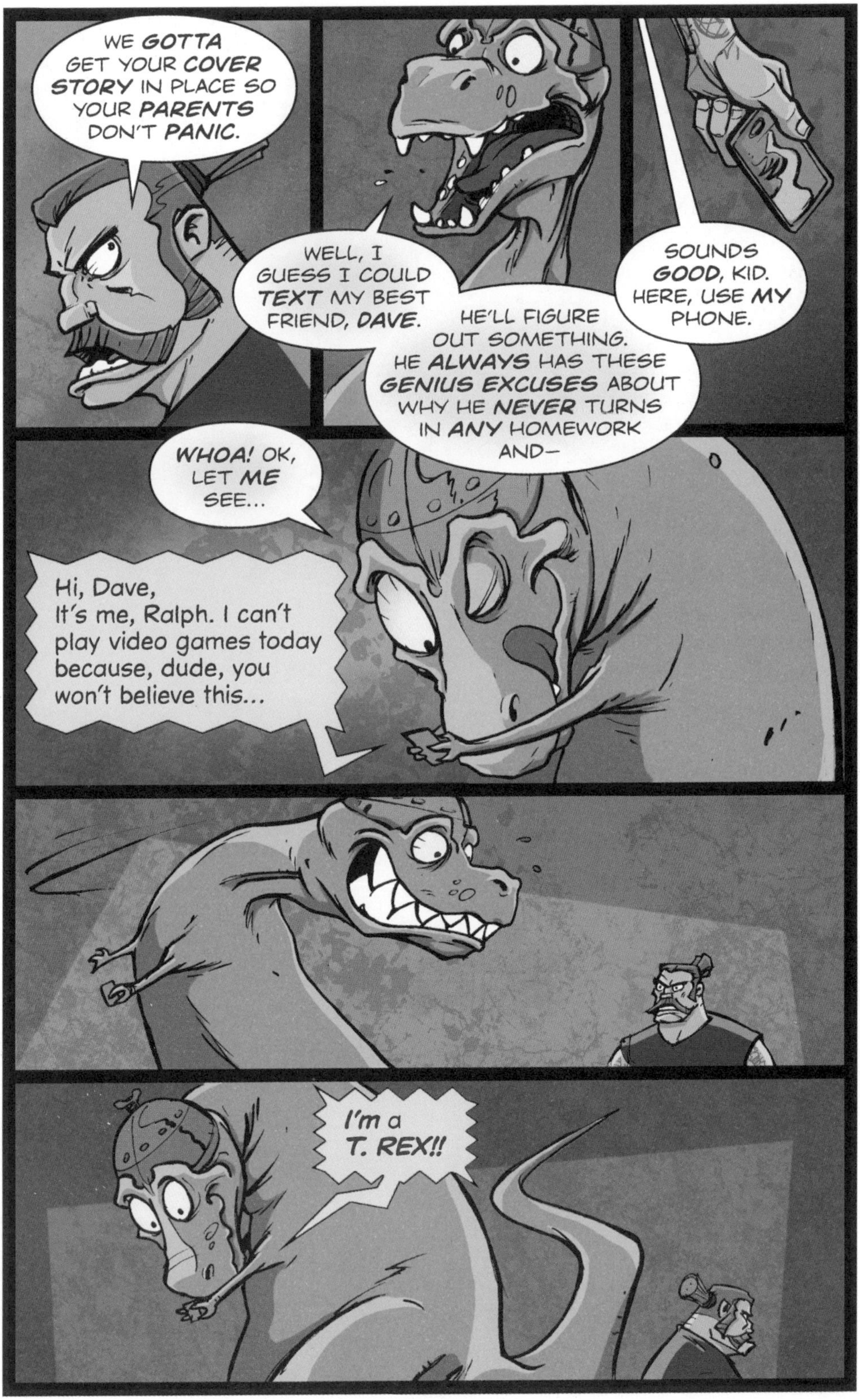
WE GOTTA GET YOUR COVER STORY IN PLACE SO YOUR PARENTS DON'T PANIC.
WELL, I GUESS I COULD TEXT MY BEST FRIEND, DAVE.
HE'LL FIGURE OUT SOMETHING. HE ALWAYS HAS THESE GENIUS EXCUSES ABOUT WHY HE NEVER TURNS IN ANY HOMEWORK AND—
SOUNDS GOOD, KID. HERE, USE MY PHONE.
WHOA! OK, LET ME SEE...
Hi, Dave, It's me, Ralph. I can't play video games today because, dude, you won't believe this...
I'm a T. REX!!

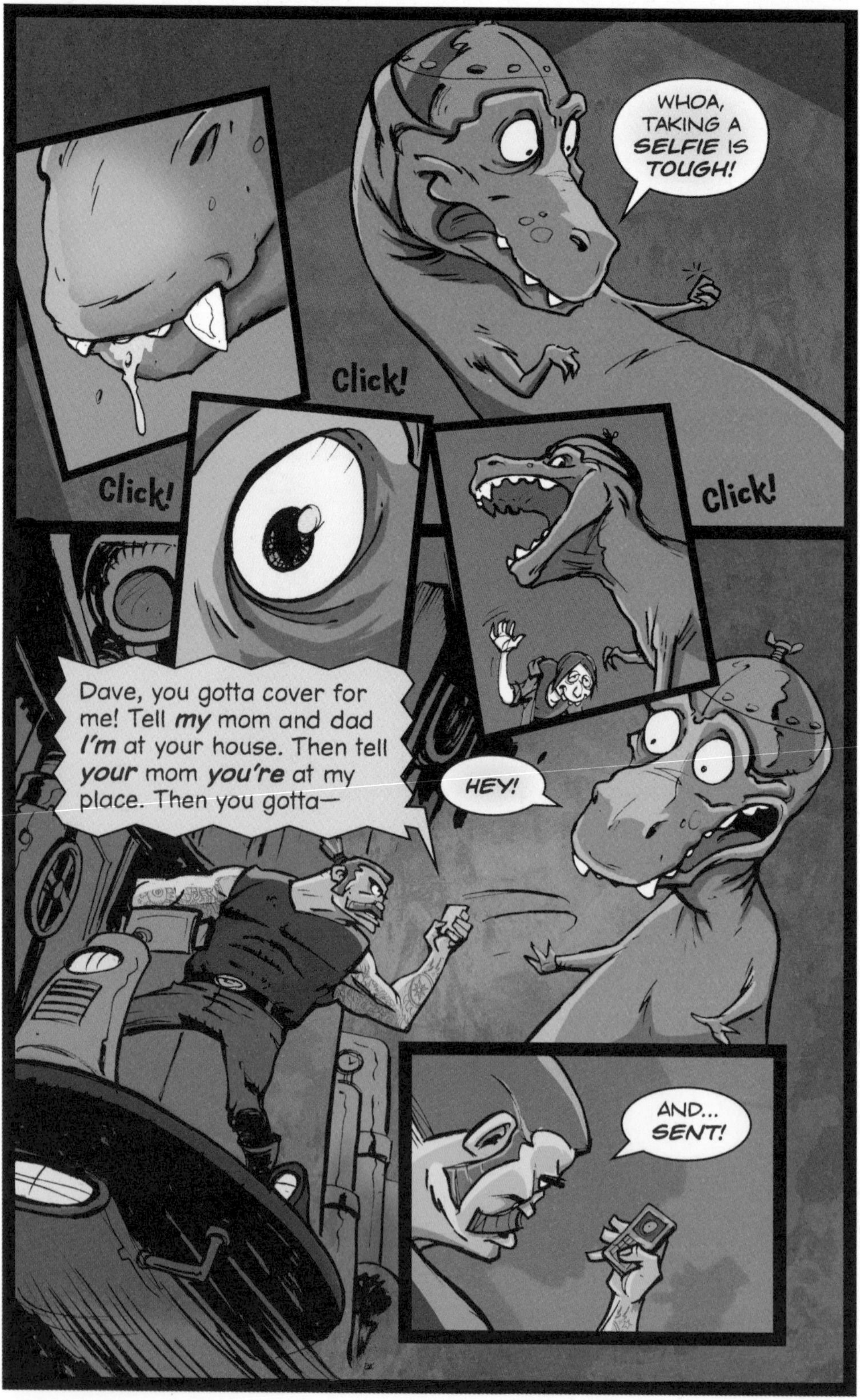
WHOA, TAKING A SELFIE IS TOUGH!
Click!
Click!
Click!
Dave, you gotta cover for me! Tell my mom and dad I'm at your house. Then tell your mom you're at my place. Then you gotta—
HEY!
AND... SENT!

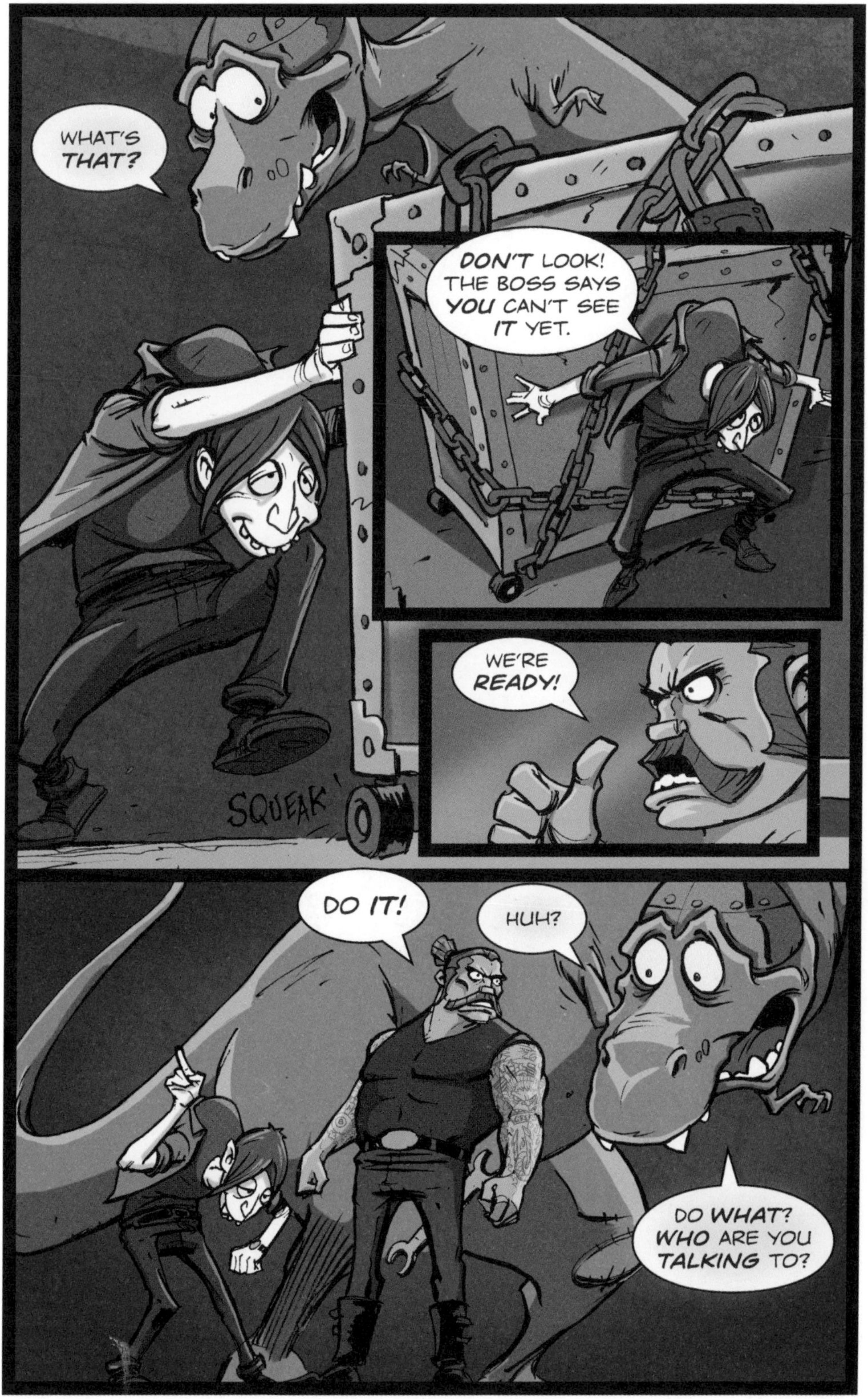
WHAT'S THAT?
DON'T LOOK! THE BOSS SAYS YOU CAN'T SEE IT YET.
SQUEAK
WE'RE READY!
DO IT!
HUH?
DO WHAT? WHO ARE YOU TALKING TO?

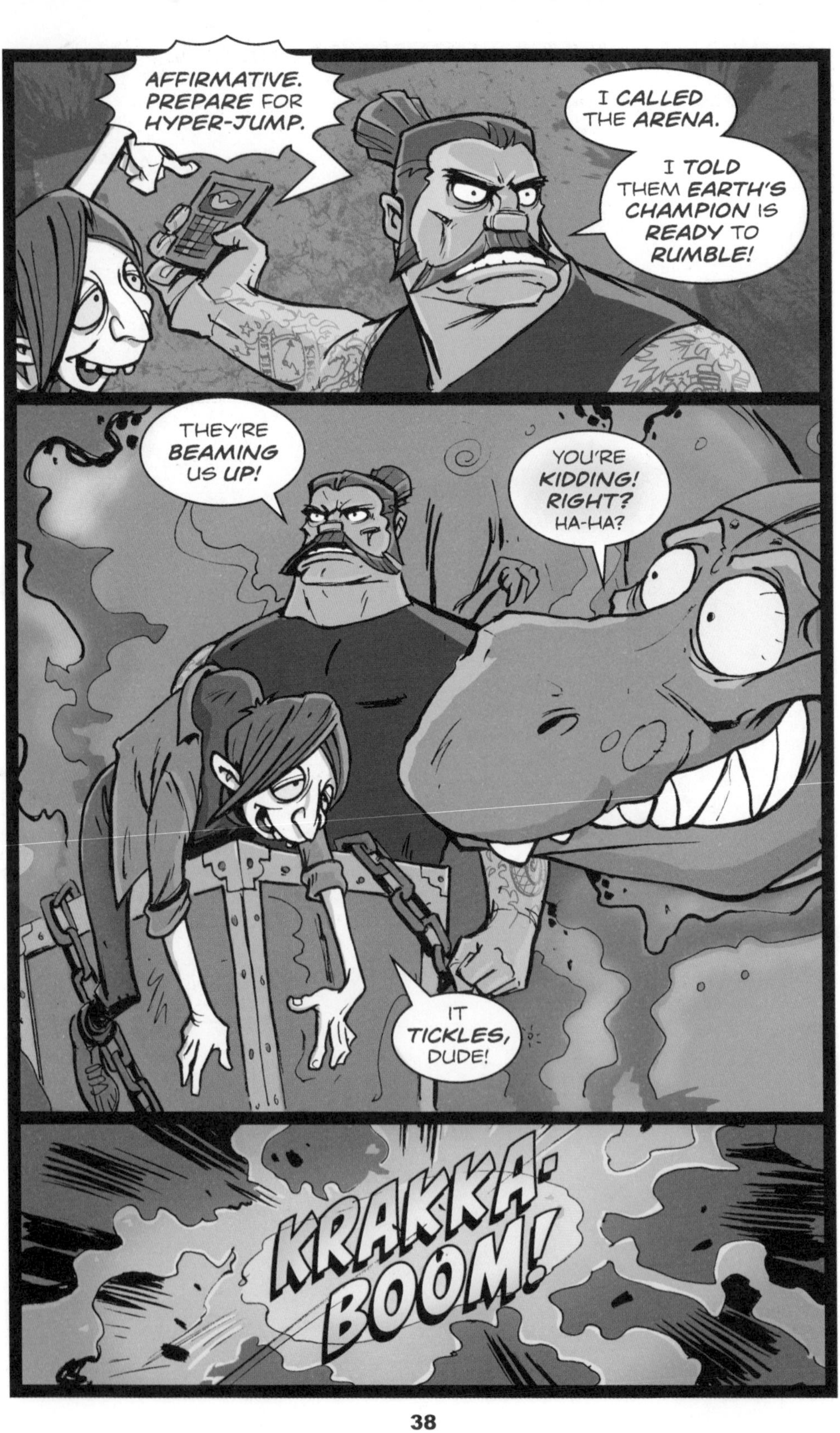
AFFIRMATIVE. PREPARE FOR HYPER-JUMP.
I CALLED THE ARENA.
I TOLD THEM EARTH'S CHAMPION IS READY TO RUMBLE!
THEY'RE BEAMING US UP!
YOU'RE KIDDING! RIGHT? HA-HA?
IT TICKLES, DUDE!
KRAKKA-BOOM!

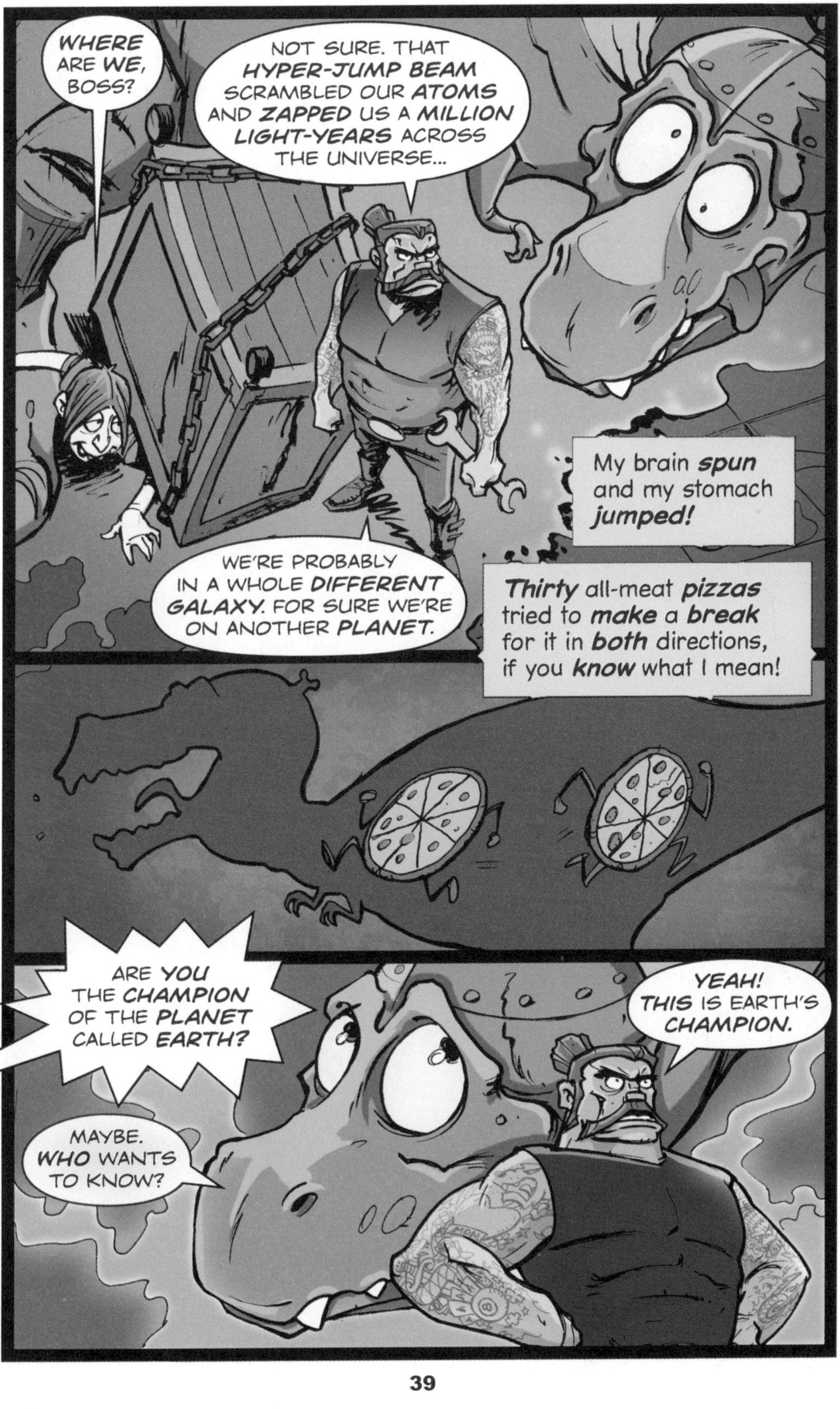
WHERE ARE WE, BOSS?
NOT SURE. THAT HYPER-JUMP BEAM SCRAMBLED OUR ATOMS AND ZAPPED US A MILLION LIGHT-YEARS ACROSS THE UNIVERSE...
My brain spun and my stomach jumped!
WE'RE PROBABLY IN A WHOLE DIFFERENT GALAXY. FOR SURE WE'RE ON ANOTHER PLANET.
Thirty all-meat pizzas tried to make a break for it in both directions, if you know what I mean!
ARE YOU THE CHAMPION OF THE PLANET CALLED EARTH?
YEAH! THIS IS EARTH'S CHAMPION.
MAYBE. WHO WANTS TO KNOW?

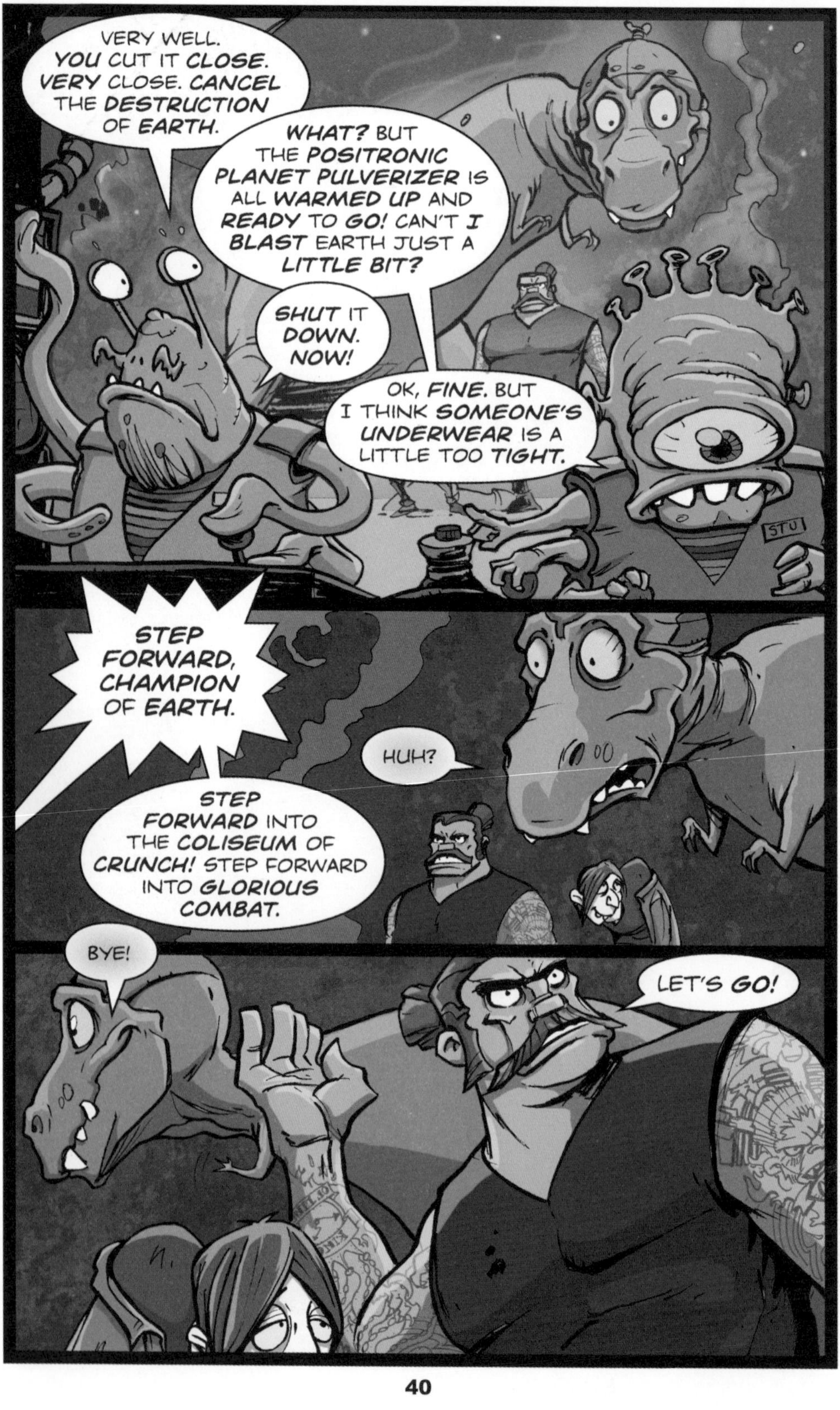
VERY WELL. YOU CUT IT CLOSE. VERY CLOSE. CANCEL THE DESTRUCTION OF EARTH.
WHAT? BUT THE POSITRONIC PLANET PULVERIZER IS ALL WARMED UP AND READY TO GO! CAN'T I BLAST EARTH JUST A LITTLE BIT?
SHUT IT DOWN. NOW!
OK, FINE. BUT I THINK SOMEONE'S UNDERWEAR IS A LITTLE TOO TIGHT.
STU
STEP FORWARD, CHAMPION OF EARTH.
HUH?
STEP FORWARD INTO THE COLISEUM OF CRUNCH! STEP FORWARD INTO GLORIOUS COMBAT.
BYE!
LET'S GO!

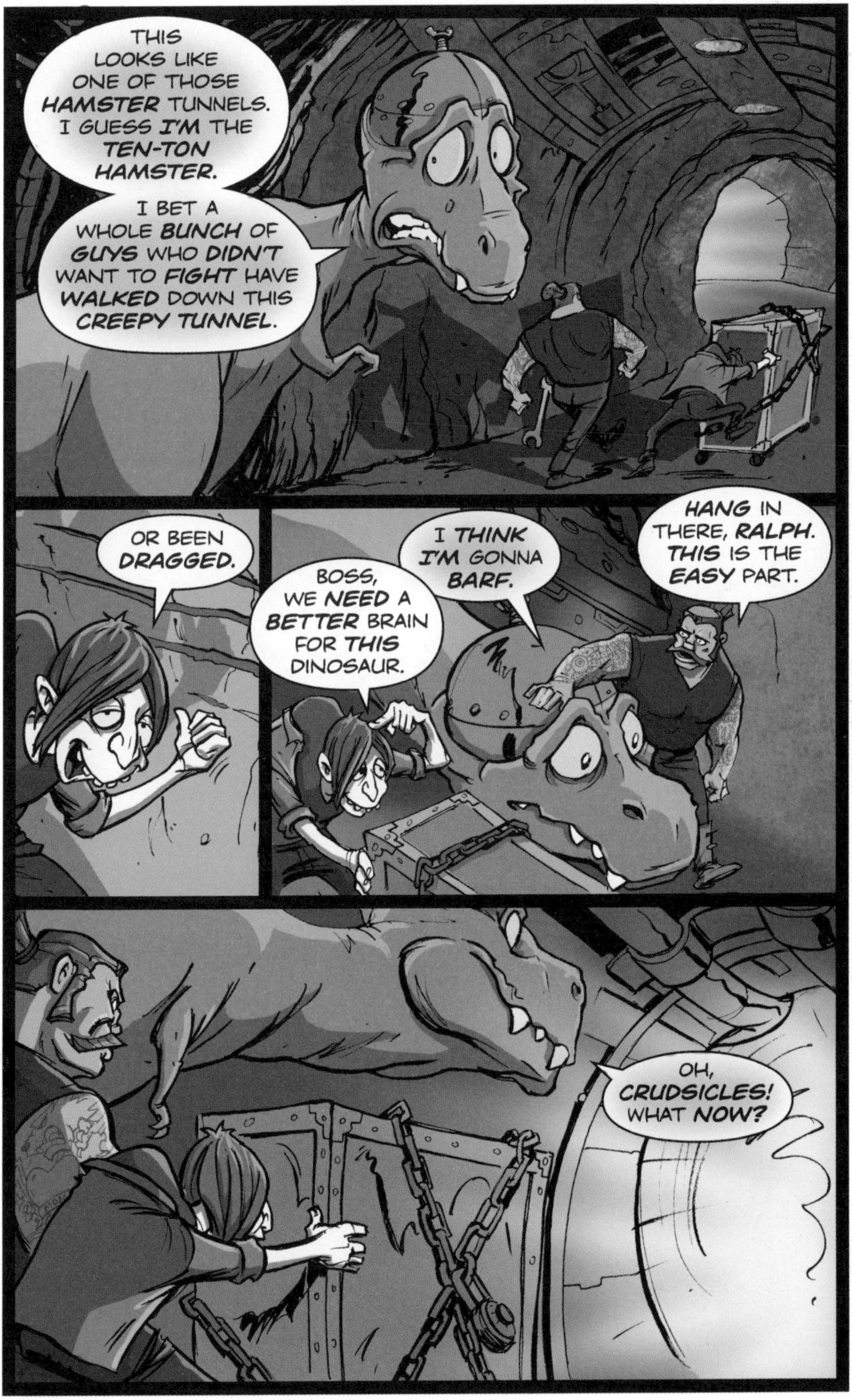
THIS LOOKS LIKE ONE OF THOSE HAMSTER TUNNELS. I GUESS I'M THE TEN-TON HAMSTER.
I BET A WHOLE BUNCH OF GUYS WHO DIDN'T WANT TO FIGHT HAVE WALKED DOWN THIS CREEPY TUNNEL.
OR BEEN DRAGGED.
I THINK I'M GONNA BARF.
BOSS, WE NEED A BETTER BRAIN FOR THIS DINOSAUR.
HANG IN THERE, RALPH. THIS IS THE EASY PART.
OH, CRUDSICLES! WHAT NOW?

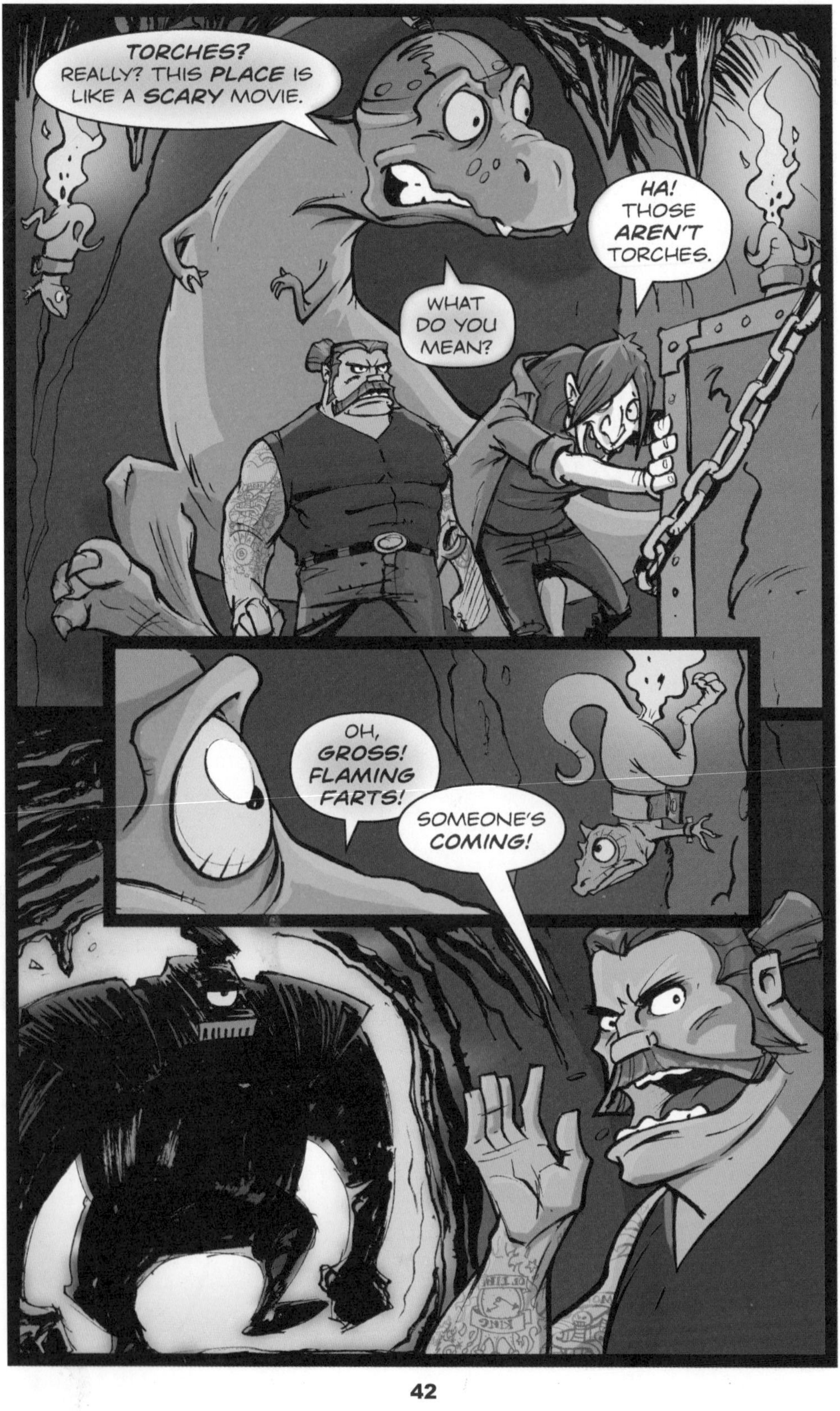
TORCHES? REALLY? THIS PLACE IS LIKE A SCARY MOVIE.
WHAT DO YOU MEAN?
HA! THOSE AREN'T TORCHES.
OH, GROSS! FLAMING FARTS!
SOMEONE'S COMING!

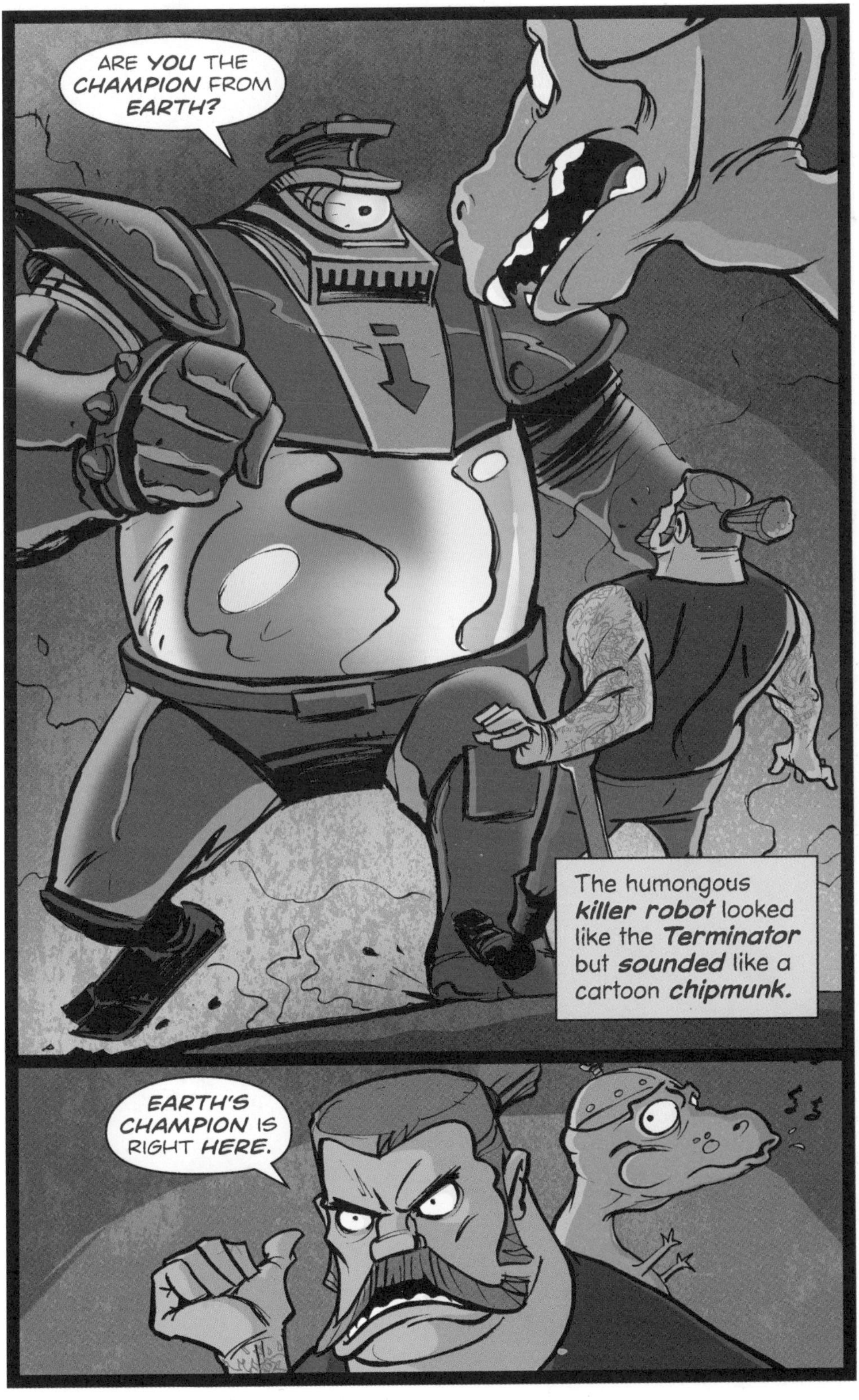
ARE YOU THE CHAMPION FROM EARTH?
The humongous killer robot looked like the Terminator but sounded like a cartoon chipmunk.
EARTH'S CHAMPION IS RIGHT HERE.

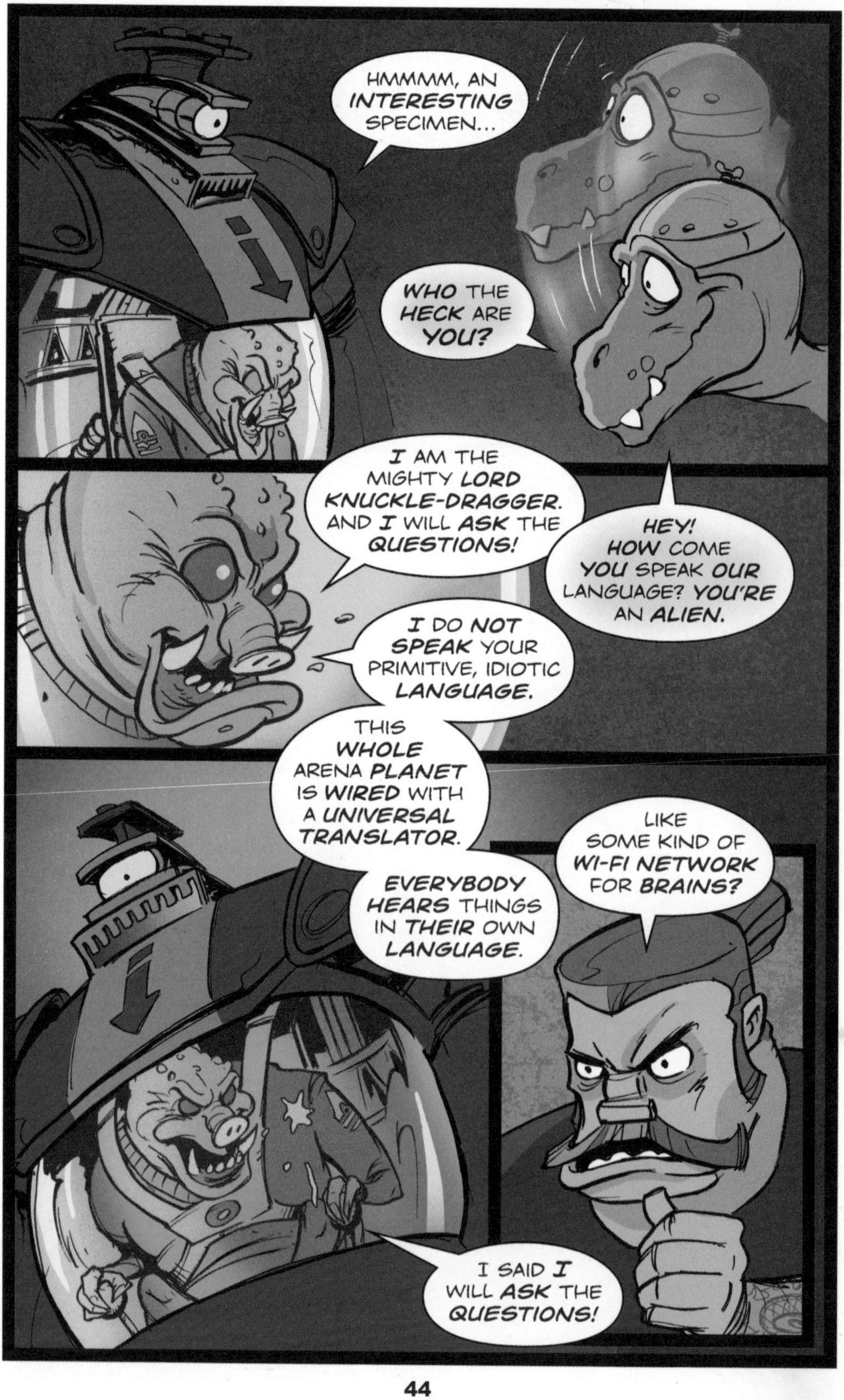

HMMMM, AN INTERESTING SPECIMEN...
WHO THE HECK ARE YOU?
I AM THE MIGHTY LORD KNUCKLE-DRAGGER. AND I WILL ASK THE QUESTIONS!
HEY! HOW COME YOU SPEAK OUR LANGUAGE? YOU'RE AN ALIEN.
I DO NOT SPEAK YOUR PRIMITIVE, IDIOTIC LANGUAGE.
THIS WHOLE ARENA PLANET IS WIRED WITH A UNIVERSAL TRANSLATOR.
EVERYBODY HEARS THINGS IN THEIR OWN LANGUAGE.
LIKE SOME KIND OF WI-FI NETWORK FOR BRAINS?
I SAID I WILL ASK THE QUESTIONS!

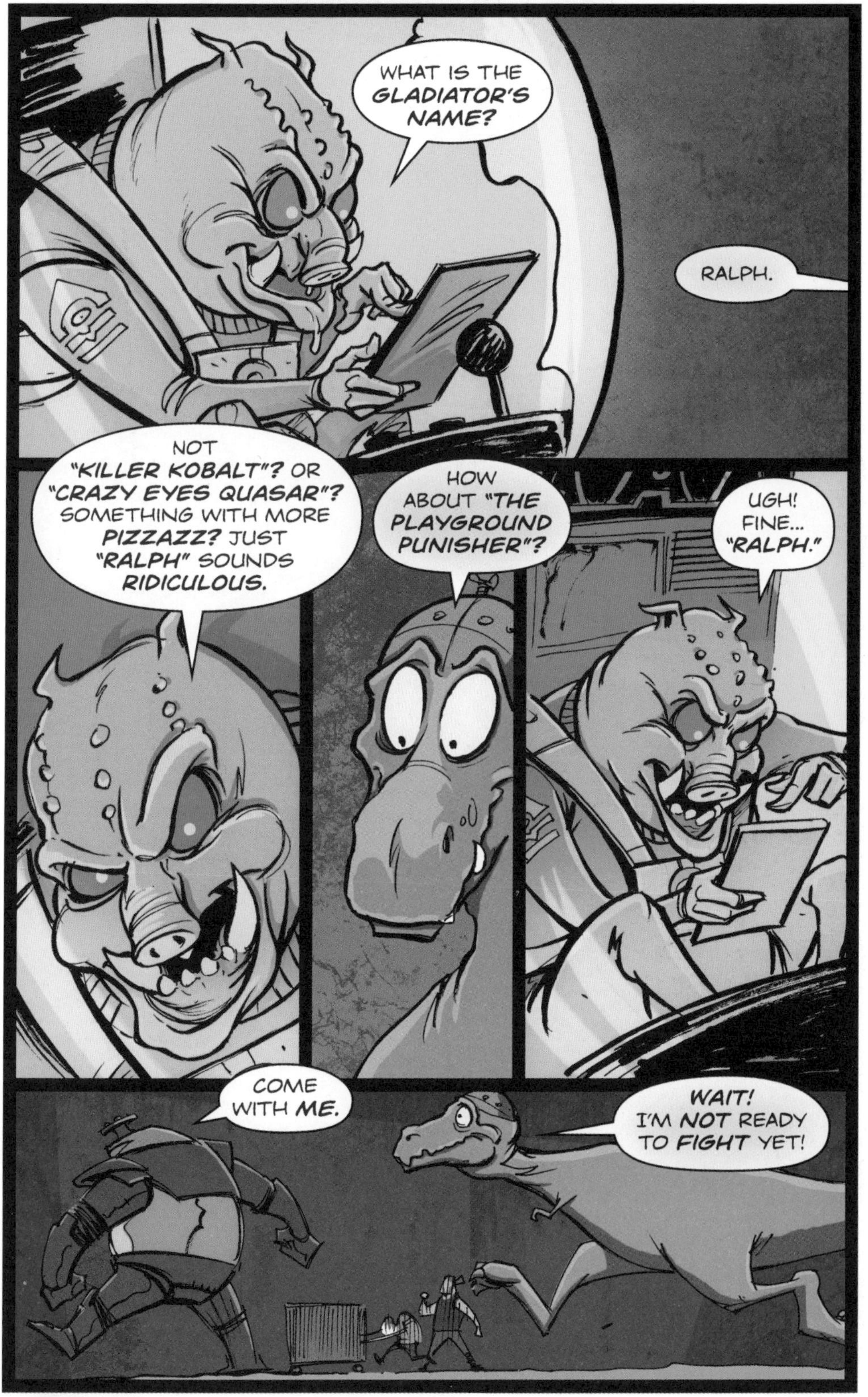
WHAT IS THE GLADIATOR'S NAME?
RALPH.
NOT "KILLER KOBALT"? OR "CRAZY EYES QUASAR"? SOMETHING WITH MORE PIZZAZZ? JUST "RALPH" SOUNDS RIDICULOUS.
HOW ABOUT "THE PLAYGROUND PUNISHER"?
UGH! FINE... "RALPH."
COME WITH ME.
WAIT! I'M NOT READY TO FIGHT YET!

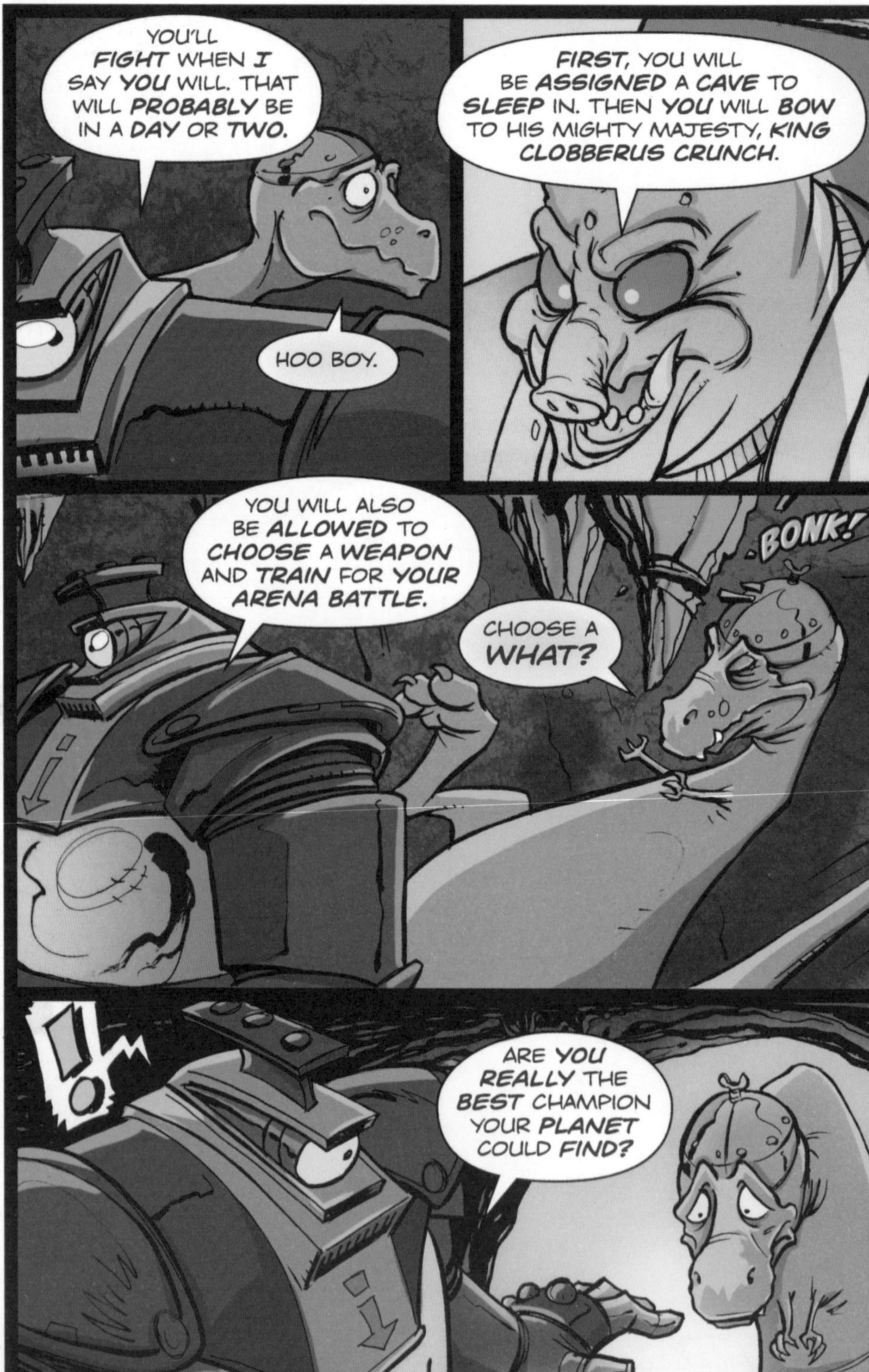
YOU'LL FIGHT WHEN I SAY YOU WILL. THAT WILL PROBABLY BE IN A DAY OR TWO.
HOO BOY.
FIRST, YOU WILL BE ASSIGNED A CAVE TO SLEEP IN. THEN YOU WILL BOW TO HIS MIGHTY MAJESTY, KING CLOBBERUS CRUNCH.
YOU WILL ALSO BE ALLOWED TO CHOOSE A WEAPON AND TRAIN FOR YOUR ARENA BATTLE.
BONK!
CHOOSE A WHAT?
!
ARE YOU REALLY THE BEST CHAMPION YOUR PLANET COULD FIND?

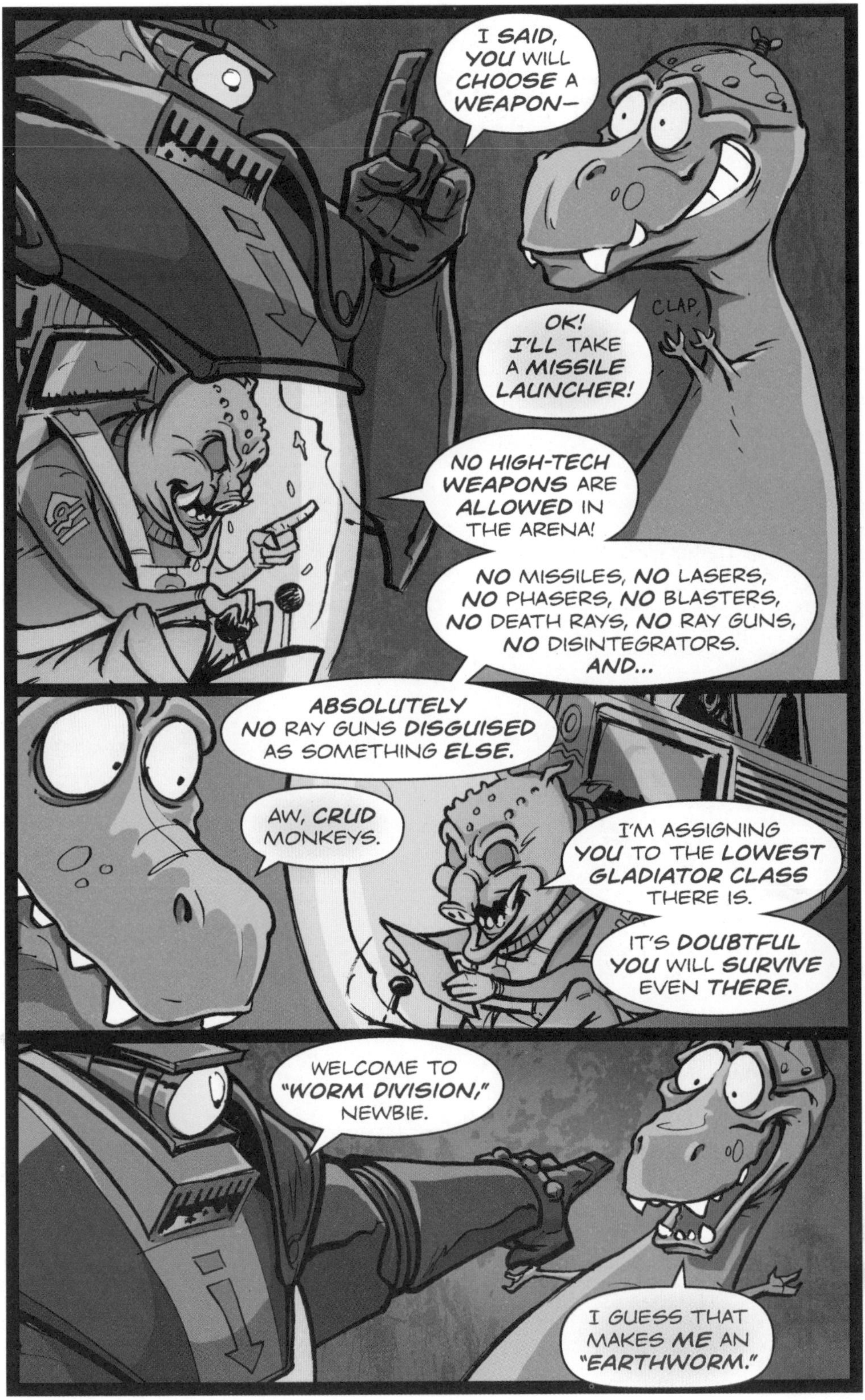
I SAID, YOU WILL CHOOSE A WEAPON—
OK! I'LL TAKE A MISSILE LAUNCHER!
CLAP,
NO HIGH-TECH WEAPONS ARE ALLOWED IN THE ARENA!
NO MISSILES, NO LASERS, NO PHASERS, NO BLASTERS, NO DEATH RAYS, NO RAY GUNS, NO DISINTEGRATORS. AND...
ABSOLUTELY NO RAY GUNS DISGUISED AS SOMETHING ELSE.
AW, CRUD MONKEYS.
I'M ASSIGNING YOU TO THE LOWEST GLADIATOR CLASS THERE IS.
IT'S DOUBTFUL YOU WILL SURVIVE EVEN THERE.
WELCOME TO "WORM DIVISION," NEWBIE.
I GUESS THAT MAKES ME AN "EARTHWORM."

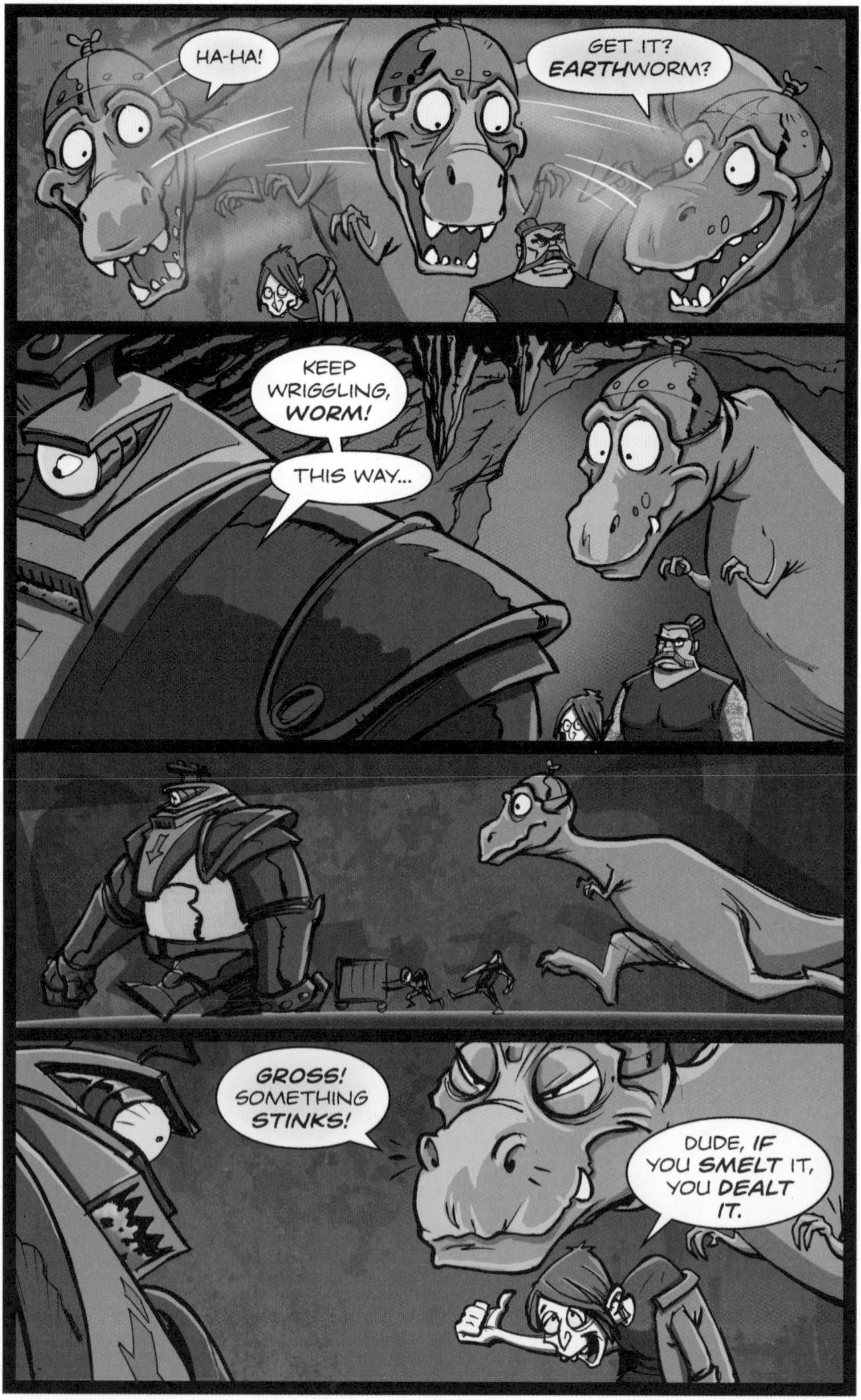
HA-HA!
GET IT? EARTHWORM?
KEEP WRIGGLING, WORM!
THIS WAY...
GROSS! SOMETHING STINKS!
DUDE, IF YOU SMELT IT, YOU DEALT IT.

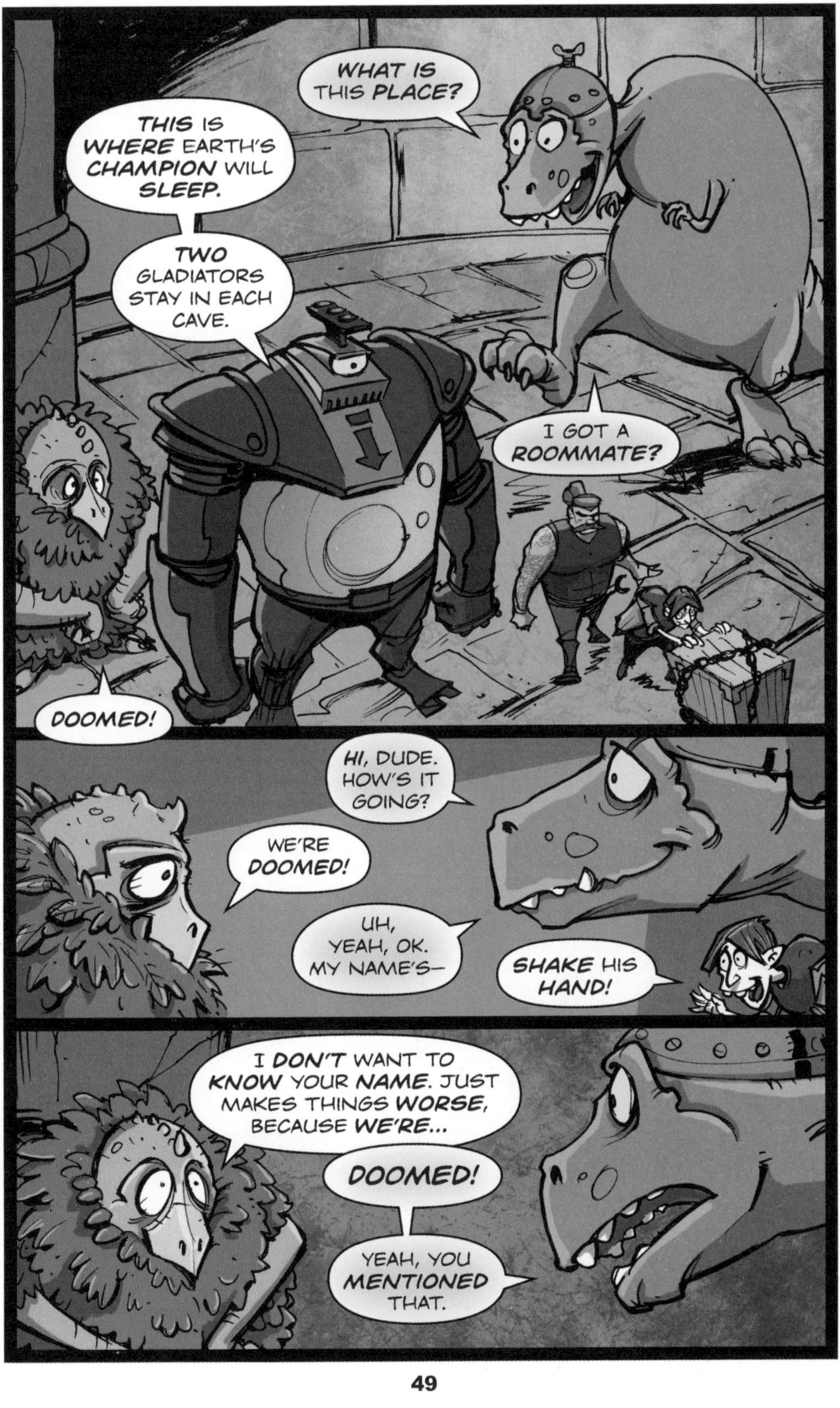
WHAT IS THIS PLACE?
THIS IS WHERE EARTH'S CHAMPION WILL SLEEP.
TWO GLADIATORS STAY IN EACH CAVE.
I GOT A ROOMMATE?
DOOMED!
HI, DUDE. HOW'S IT GOING?
WE'RE DOOMED!
UH, YEAH, OK. MY NAME'S—
SHAKE HIS HAND!
I DON'T WANT TO KNOW YOUR NAME. JUST MAKES THINGS WORSE, BECAUSE WE'RE...
DOOMED!
YEAH, YOU MENTIONED THAT.

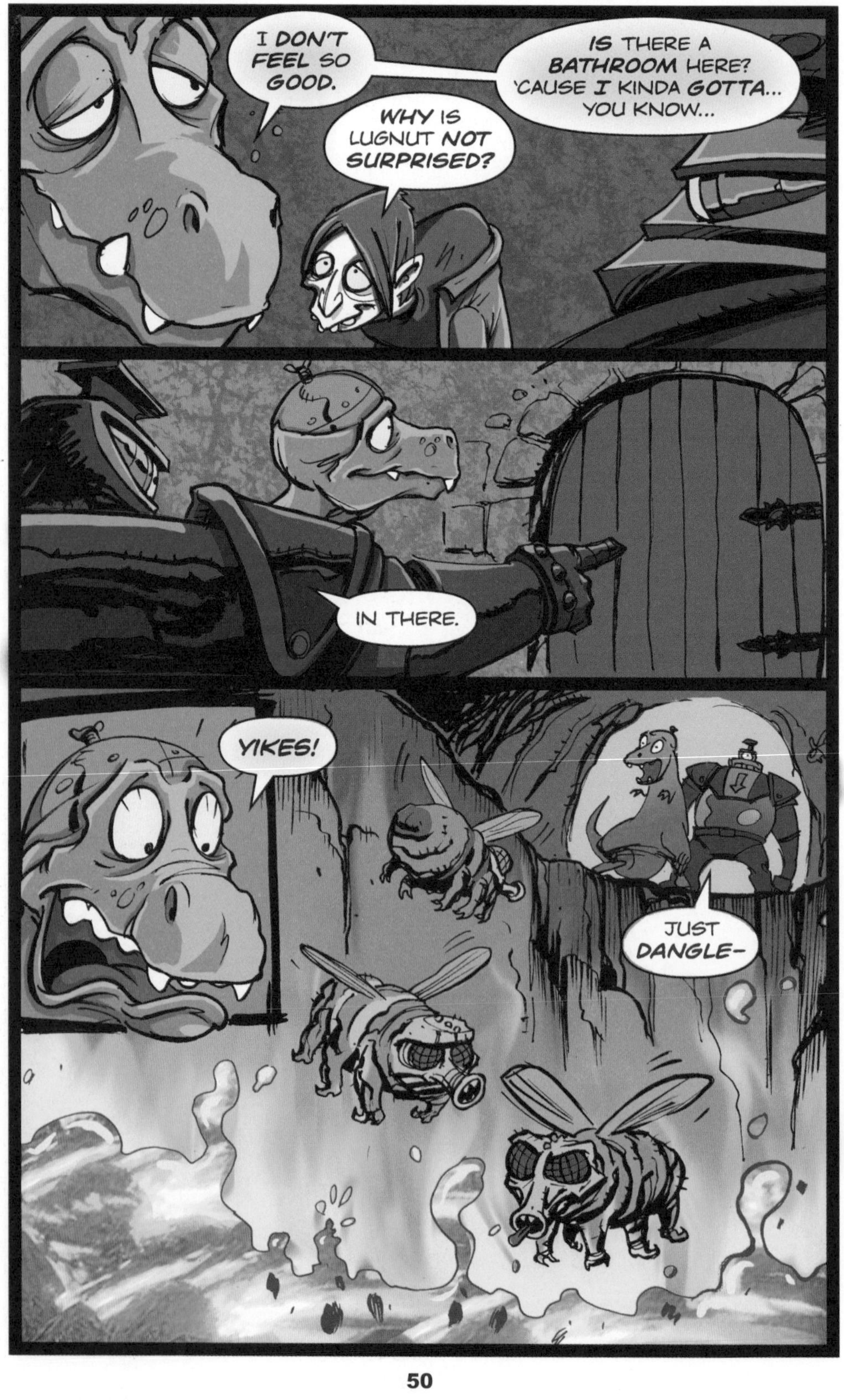
I DON'T FEEL SO GOOD.
IS THERE A BATHROOM HERE? 'CAUSE I KINDA GOTTA... YOU KNOW...
WHY IS LUGNUT NOT SURPRISED?
IN THERE.
YIKES!
JUST DANGLE-

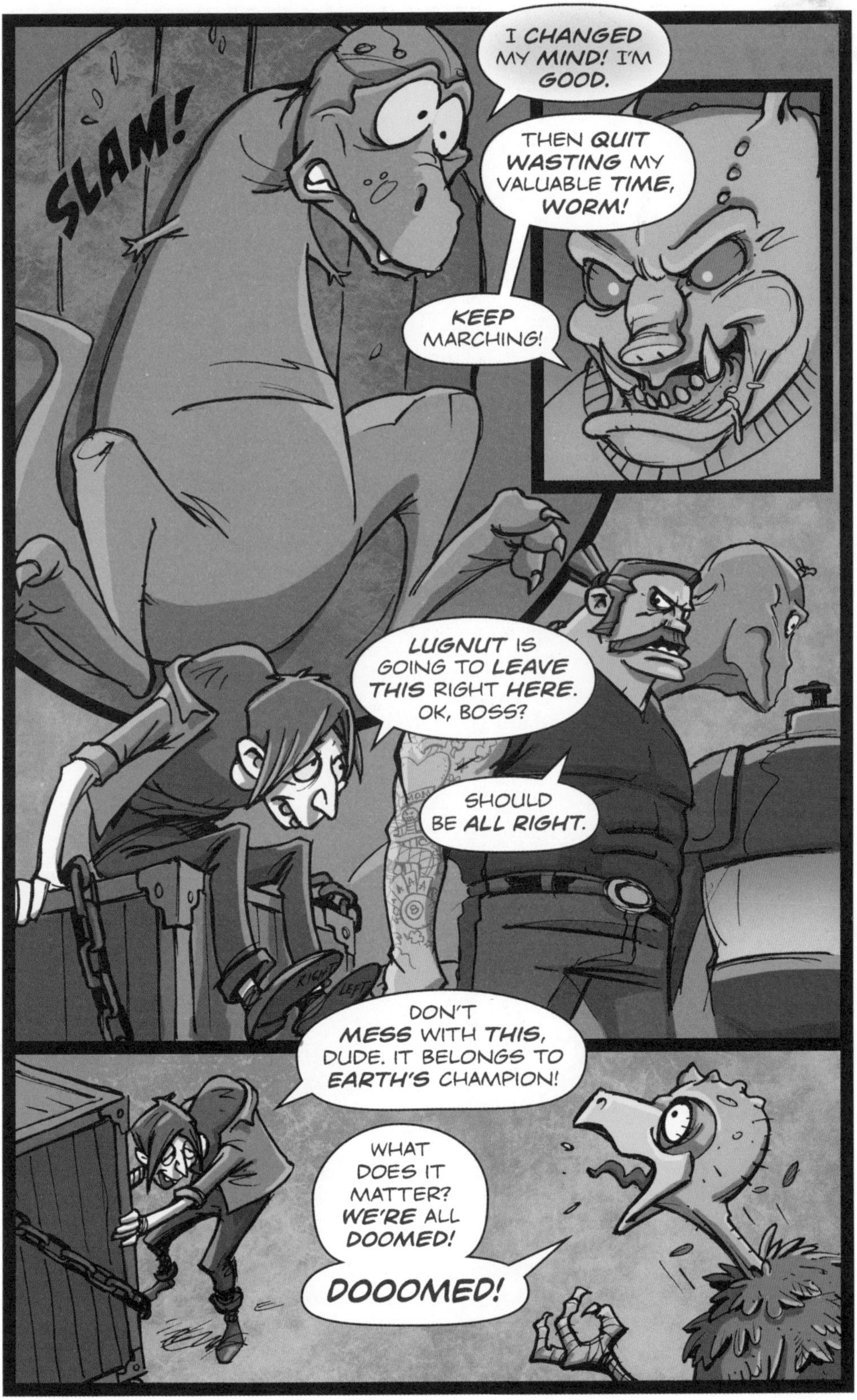

SLAM!
I CHANGED MY MIND! I'M GOOD.
THEN QUIT WASTING MY VALUABLE TIME, WORM!
KEEP MARCHING!
LUGNUT IS GOING TO LEAVE THIS RIGHT HERE. OK, BOSS?
SHOULD BE ALL RIGHT.
RIGHT
LEFT
DON'T MESS WITH THIS, DUDE. IT BELONGS TO EARTH'S CHAMPION!
WHAT DOES IT MATTER? WE'RE ALL DOOMED!
DOOOMED!

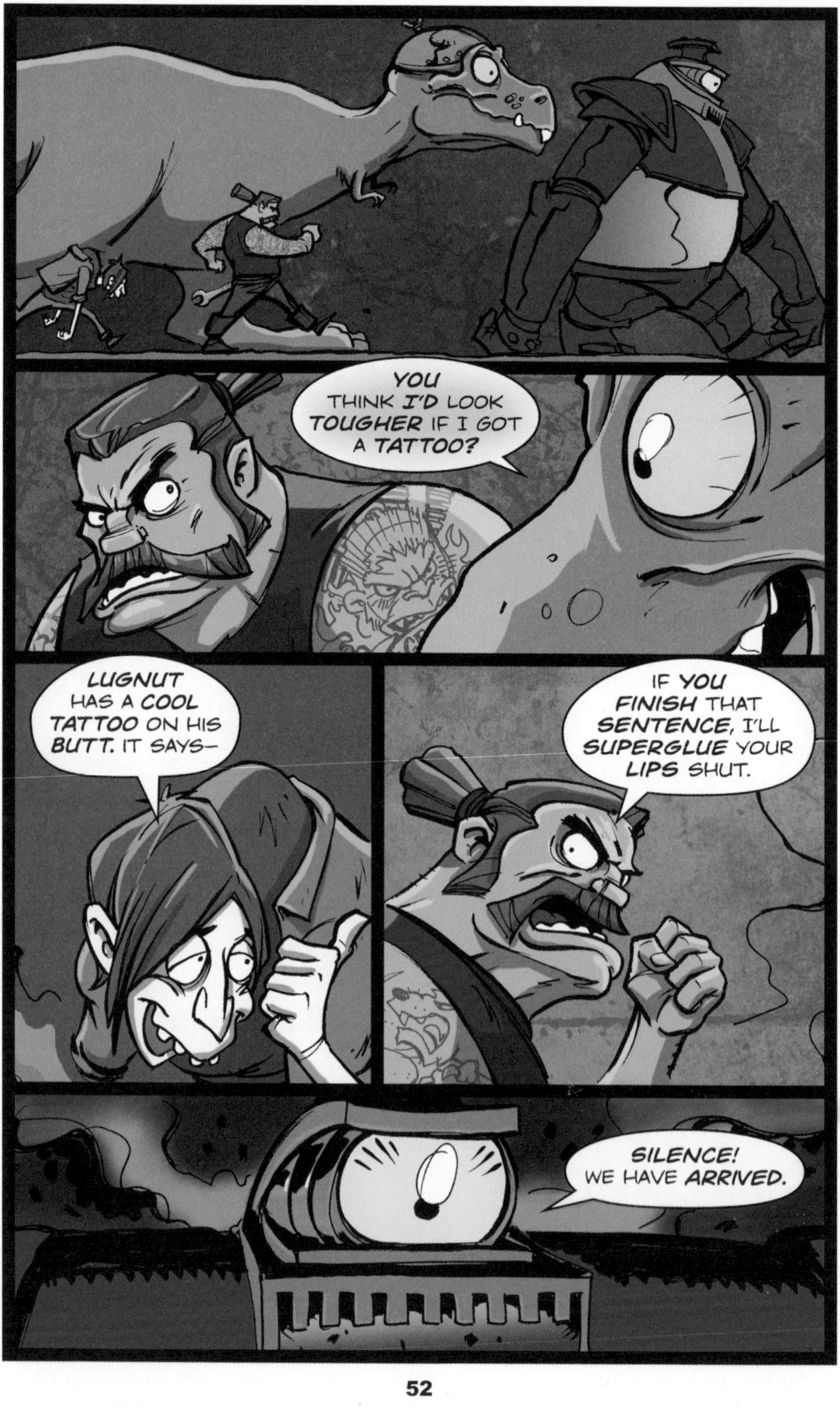

YOU THINK I'D LOOK TOUGHER IF I GOT A TATTOO?
LUGNUT HAS A COOL TATTOO ON HIS BUTT. IT SAYS—
IF YOU FINISH THAT SENTENCE, I'LL SUPERGLUE YOUR LIPS SHUT.
SILENCE! WE HAVE ARRIVED.

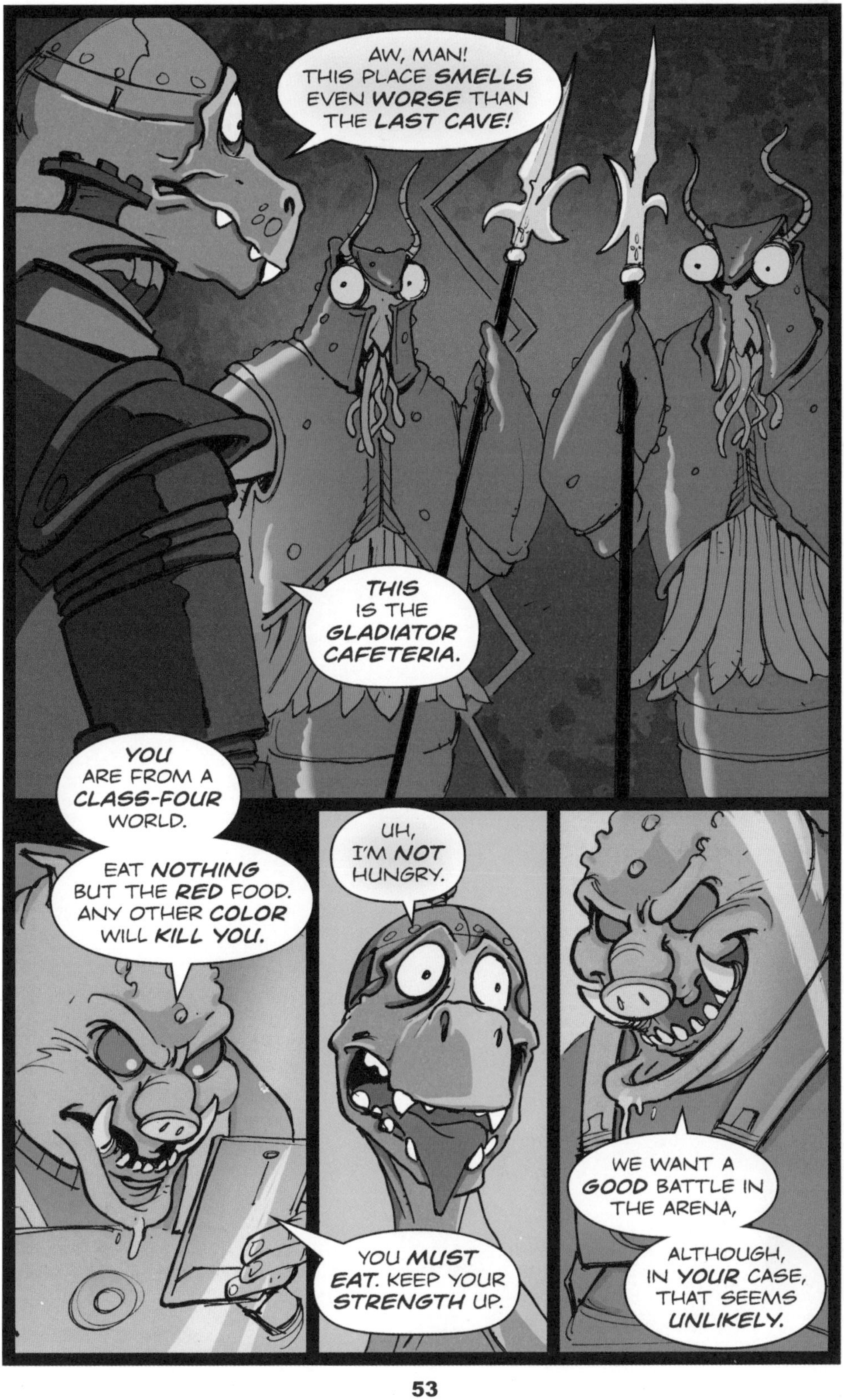
AW, MAN! THIS PLACE SMELLS EVEN WORSE THAN THE LAST CAVE!
THIS IS THE GLADIATOR CAFETERIA.
YOU ARE FROM A CLASS-FOUR WORLD.
EAT NOTHING BUT THE RED FOOD. ANY OTHER COLOR WILL KILL YOU.
UH, I'M NOT HUNGRY.
YOU MUST EAT. KEEP YOUR STRENGTH UP.
WE WANT A GOOD BATTLE IN THE ARENA,
ALTHOUGH, IN YOUR CASE, THAT SEEMS UNLIKELY.

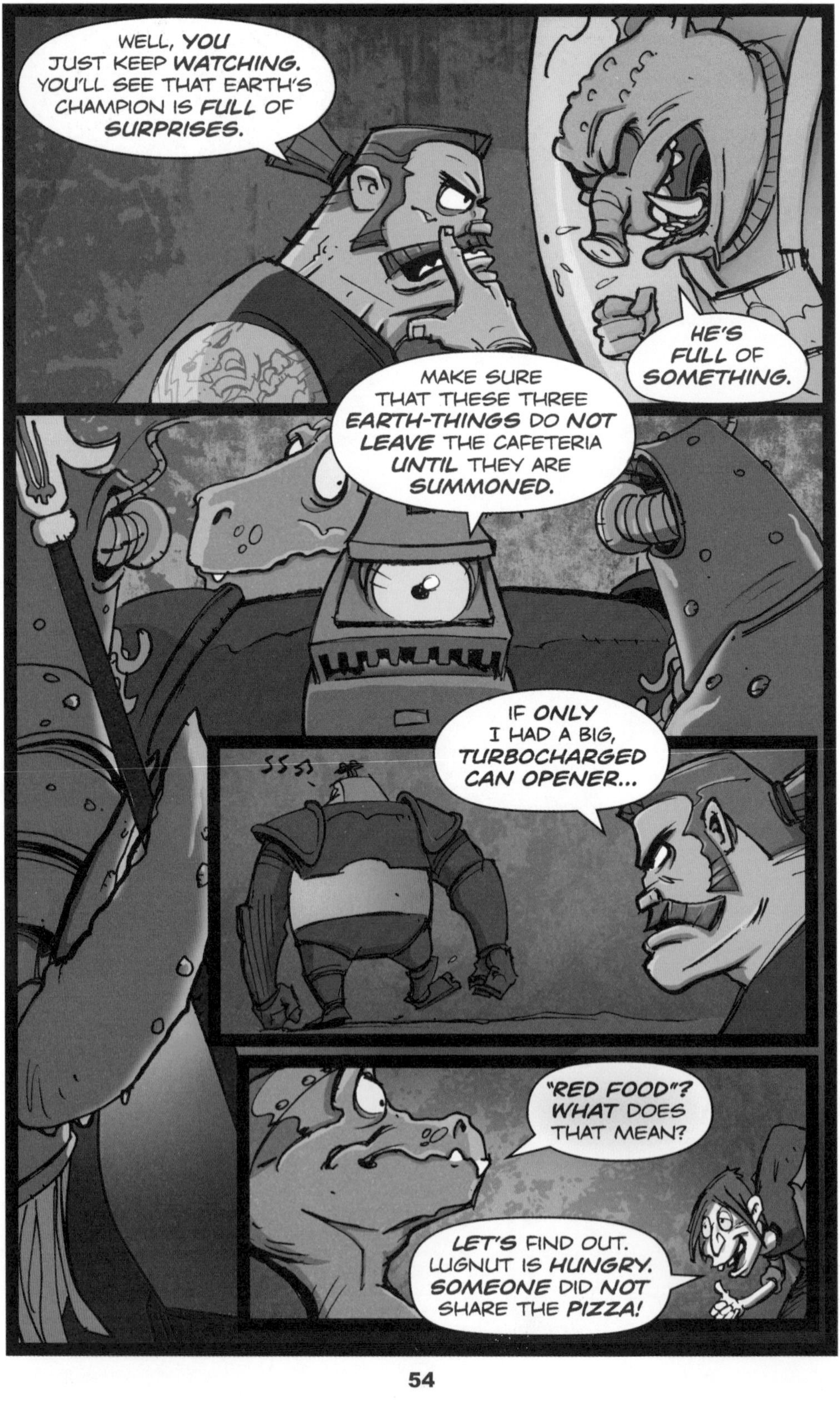
WELL, YOU JUST KEEP WATCHING. YOU'LL SEE THAT EARTH'S CHAMPION IS FULL OF SURPRISES.
HE'S FULL OF SOMETHING.
MAKE SURE THAT THESE THREE EARTH-THINGS DO NOT LEAVE THE CAFETERIA UNTIL THEY ARE SUMMONED.
IF ONLY I HAD A BIG, TURBOCHARGED CAN OPENER...
"RED FOOD"? WHAT DOES THAT MEAN?
LET'S FIND OUT. LUGNUT IS HUNGRY. SOMEONE DID NOT SHARE THE PIZZA!

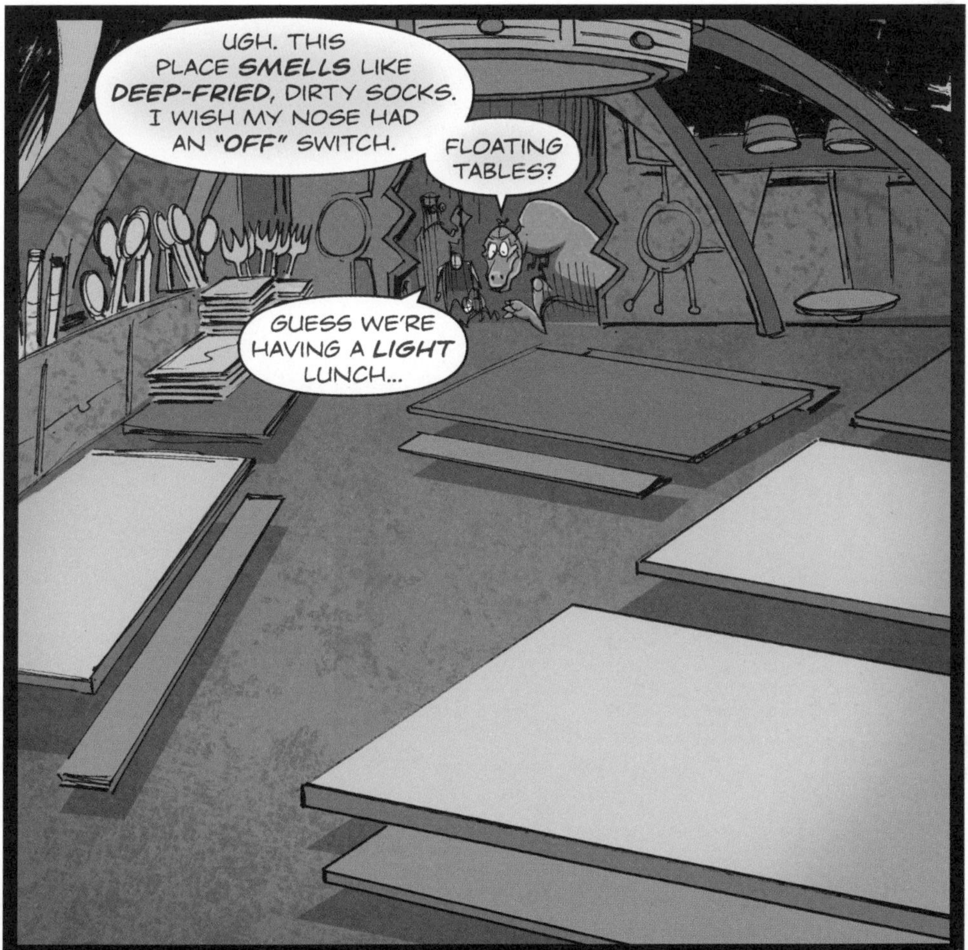
UGH. THIS PLACE SMELLS LIKE DEEP-FRIED, DIRTY SOCKS. I WISH MY NOSE HAD AN "OFF" SWITCH.
FLOATING TABLES?
GUESS WE'RE HAVING A LIGHT LUNCH...

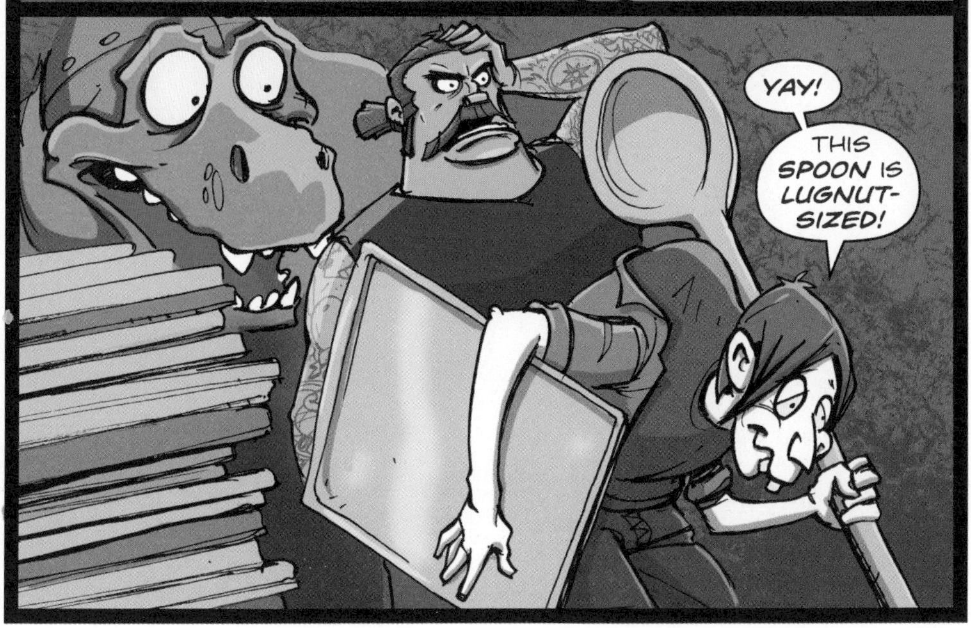
YAY!
THIS SPOON IS LUGNUT-SIZED!

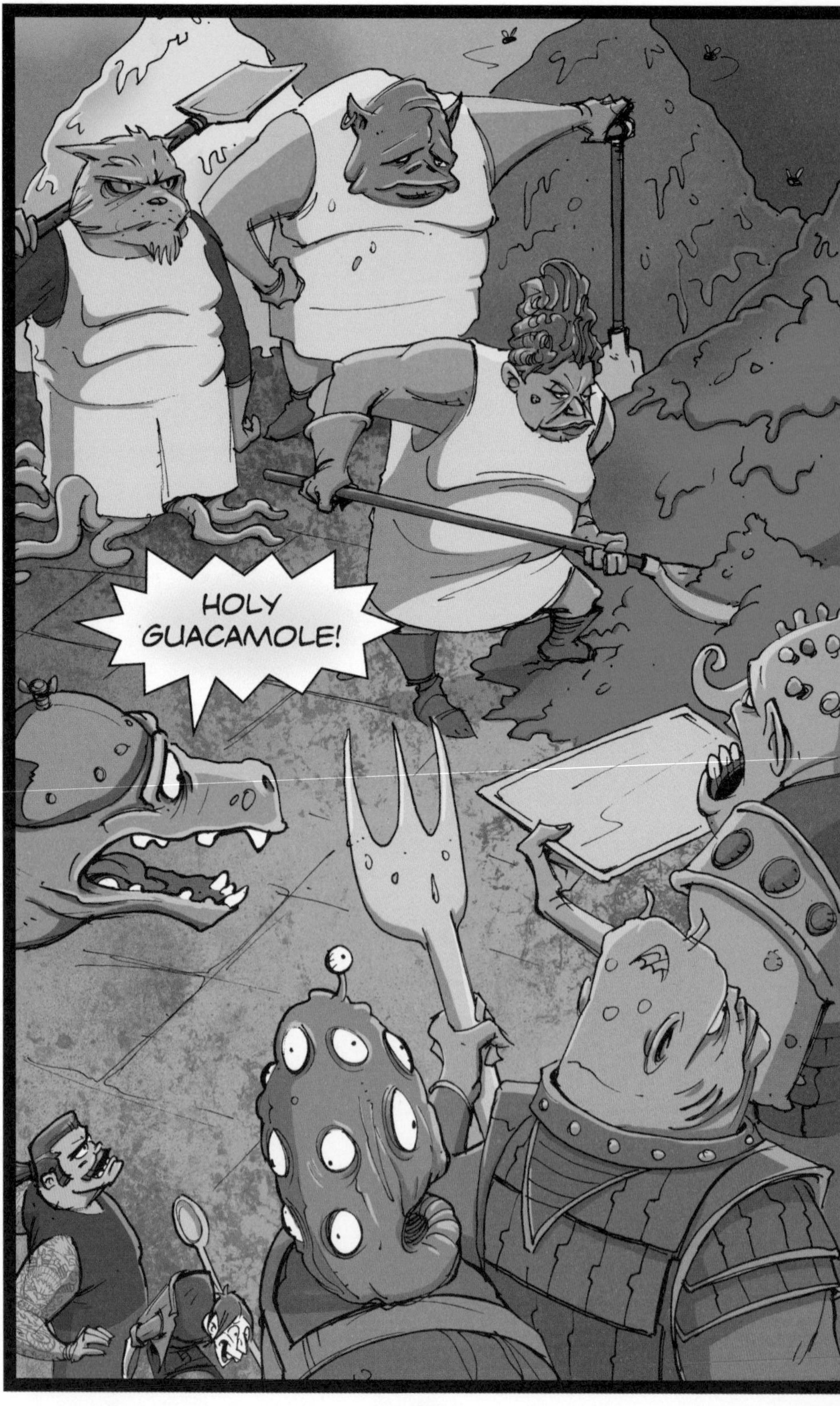
HOLY GUACAMOLE!

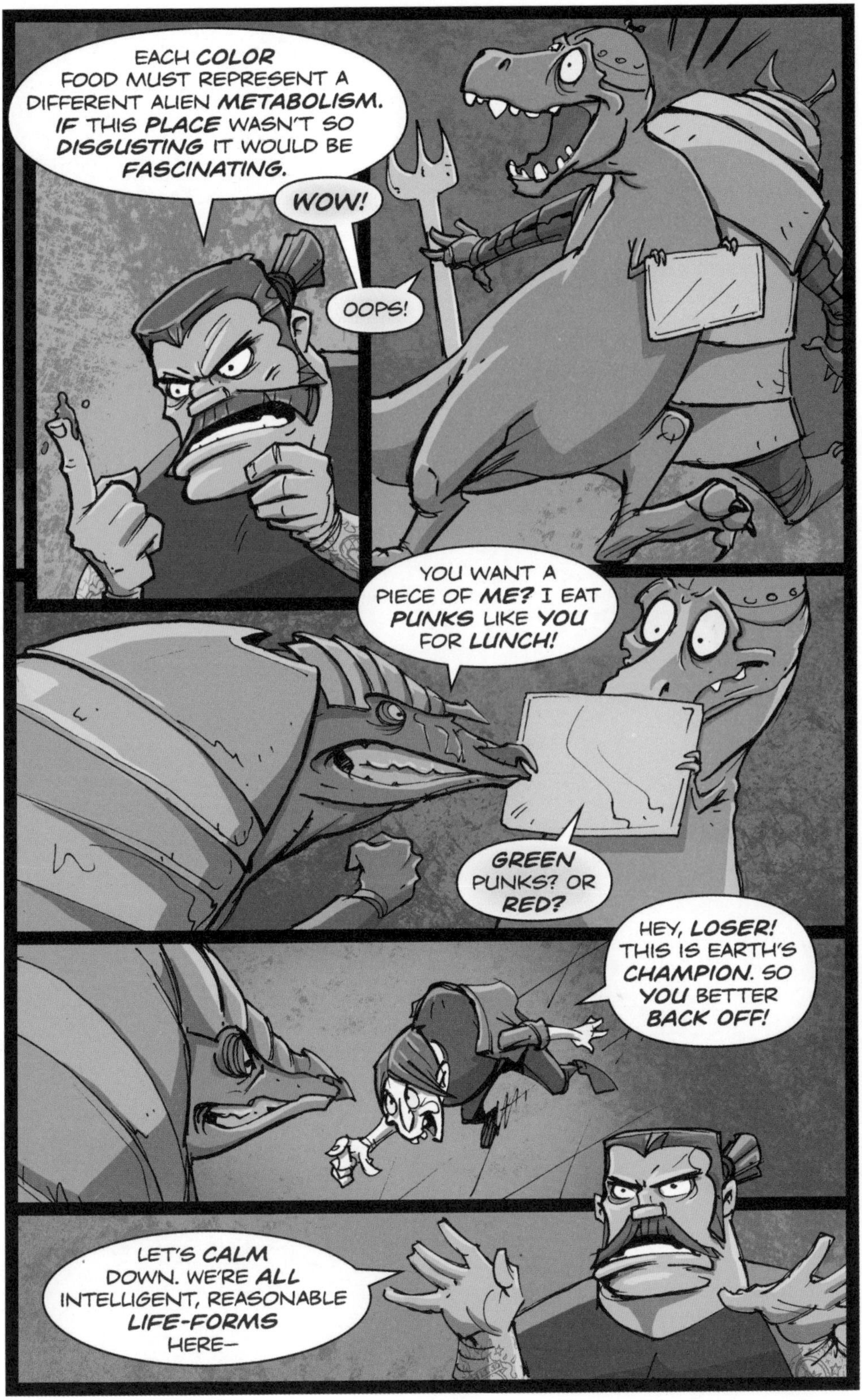
EACH COLOR FOOD MUST REPRESENT A DIFFERENT ALIEN METABOLISM. IF THIS PLACE WASN'T SO DISGUSTING IT WOULD BE FASCINATING.
WOW!
OOPS!
YOU WANT A PIECE OF ME? I EAT PUNKS LIKE YOU FOR LUNCH!
GREEN PUNKS? OR RED?
HEY, LOSER! THIS IS EARTH'S CHAMPION. SO YOU BETTER BACK OFF!
LET'S CALM DOWN. WE'RE ALL INTELLIGENT, REASONABLE LIFE-FORMS HERE–

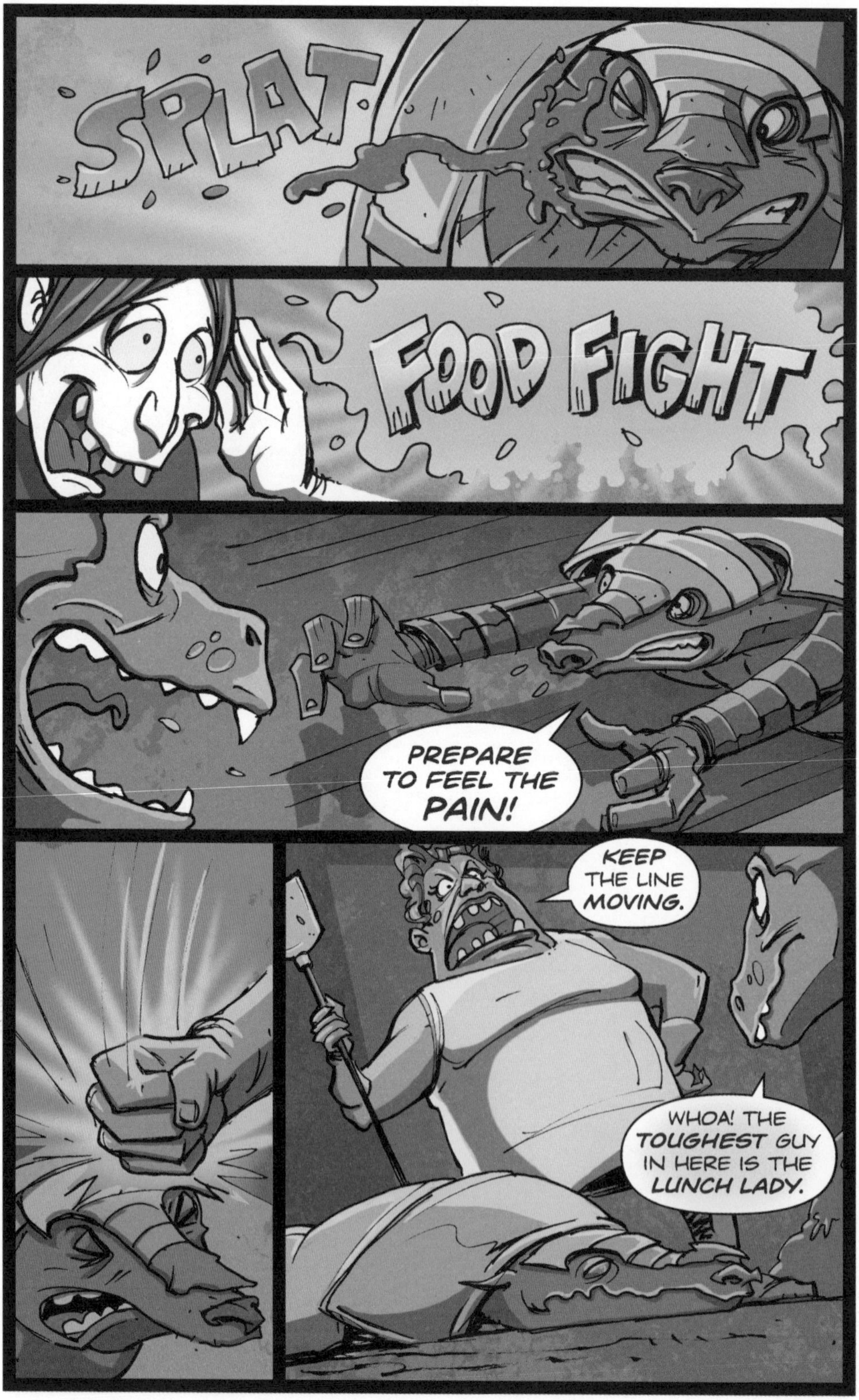
SPLAT
FOOD FIGHT
PREPARE TO FEEL THE PAIN!
KEEP THE LINE MOVING.
WHOA! THE TOUGHEST GUY IN HERE IS THE LUNCH LADY.

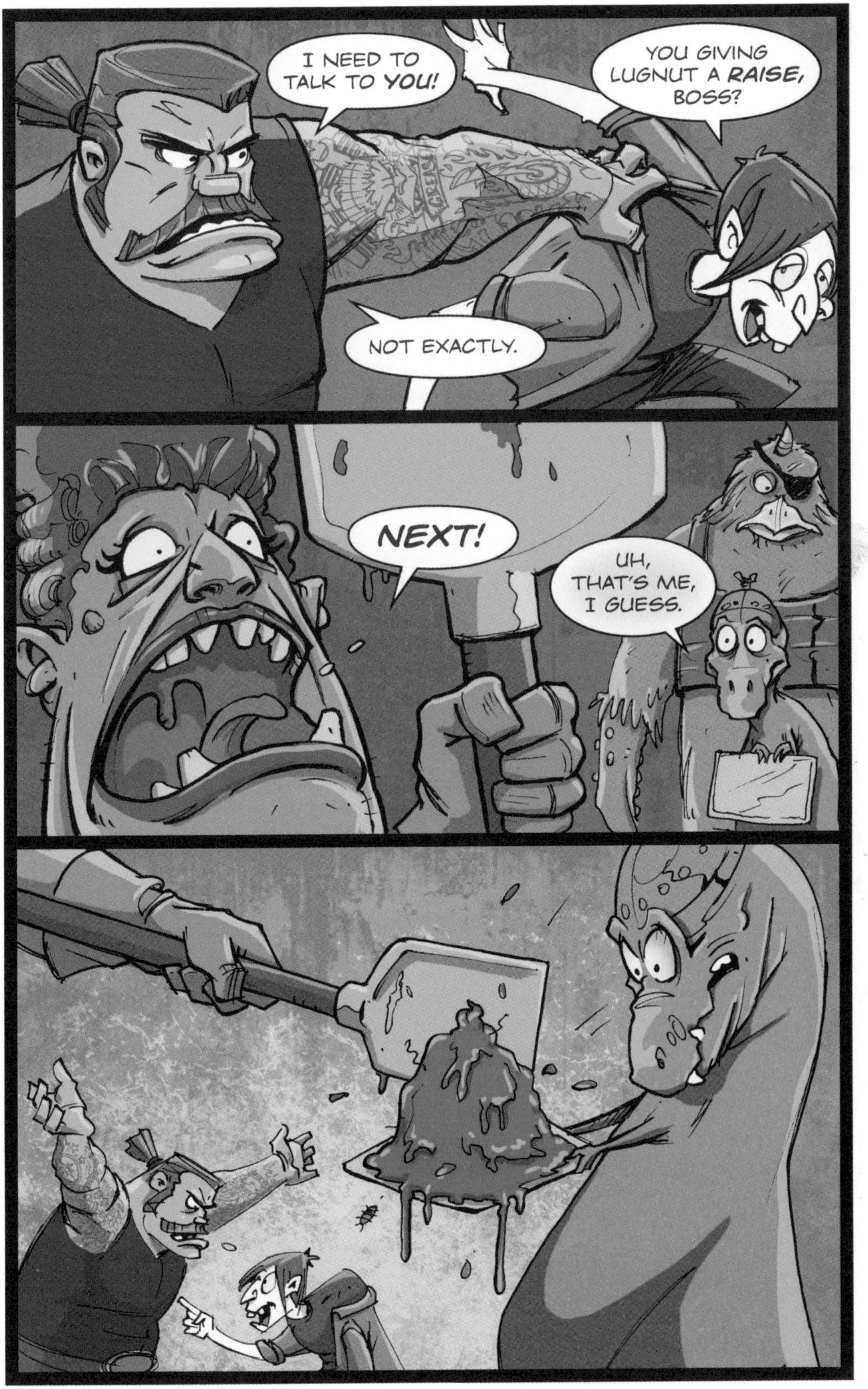
I NEED TO TALK TO YOU!
YOU GIVING LUGNUT A RAISE, BOSS?
NOT EXACTLY.
NEXT!
UH, THAT'S ME, I GUESS.

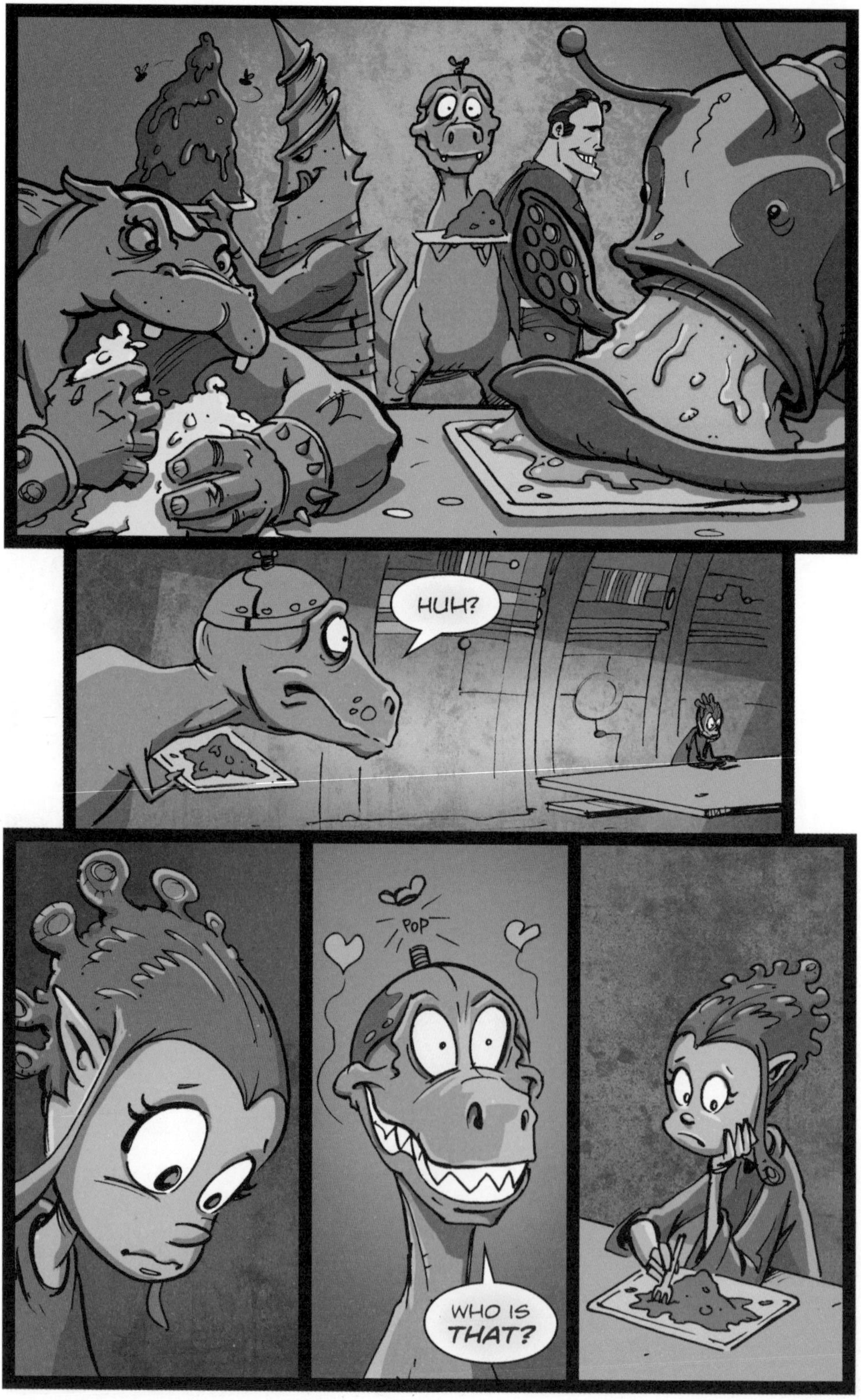
HUH?
POP
WHO IS THAT?

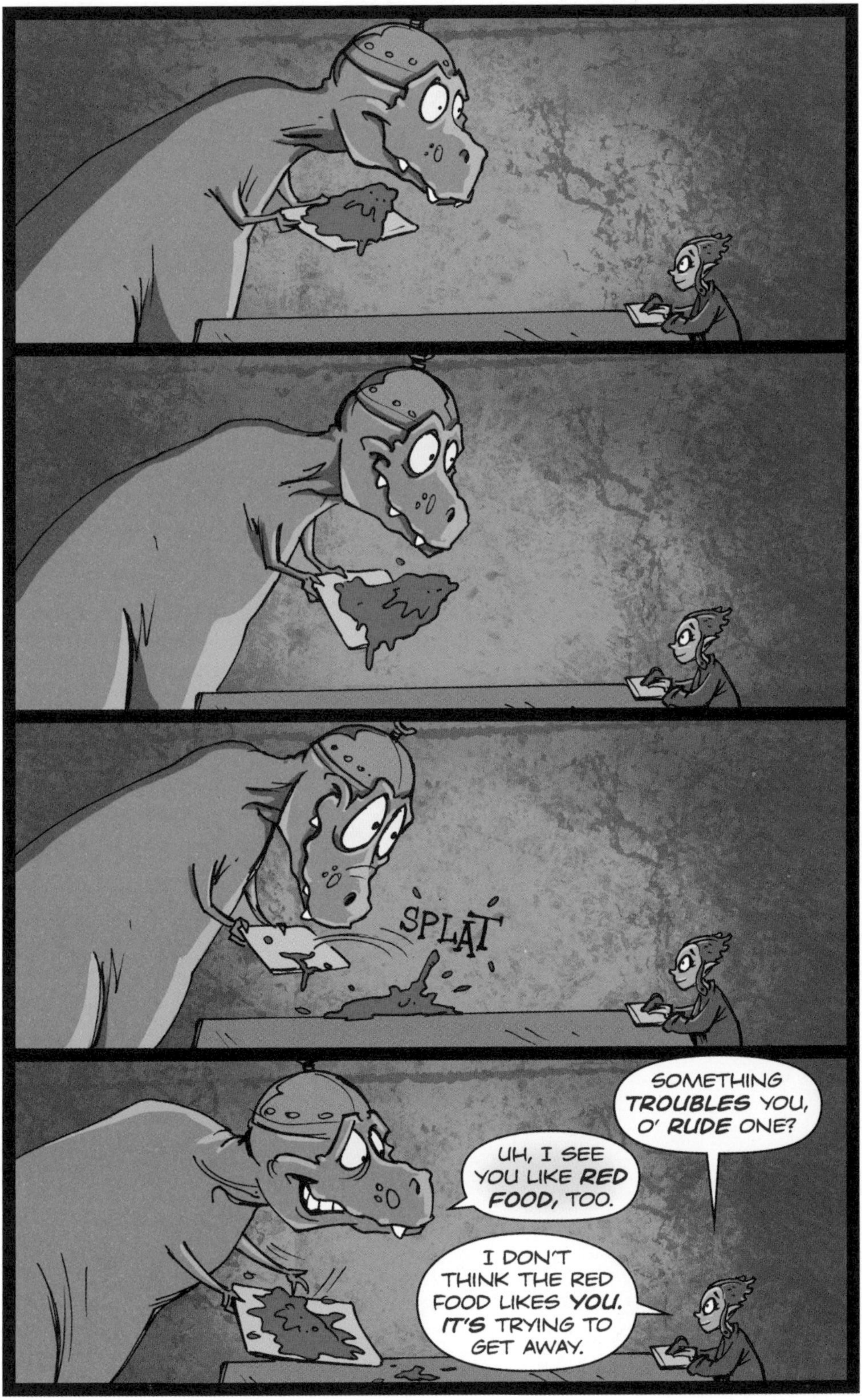
SPLAT
SOMETHING TROUBLES YOU, O' RUDE ONE?
UH, I SEE YOU LIKE RED FOOD, TOO.
I DON'T THINK THE RED FOOD LIKES YOU. IT'S TRYING TO GET AWAY.

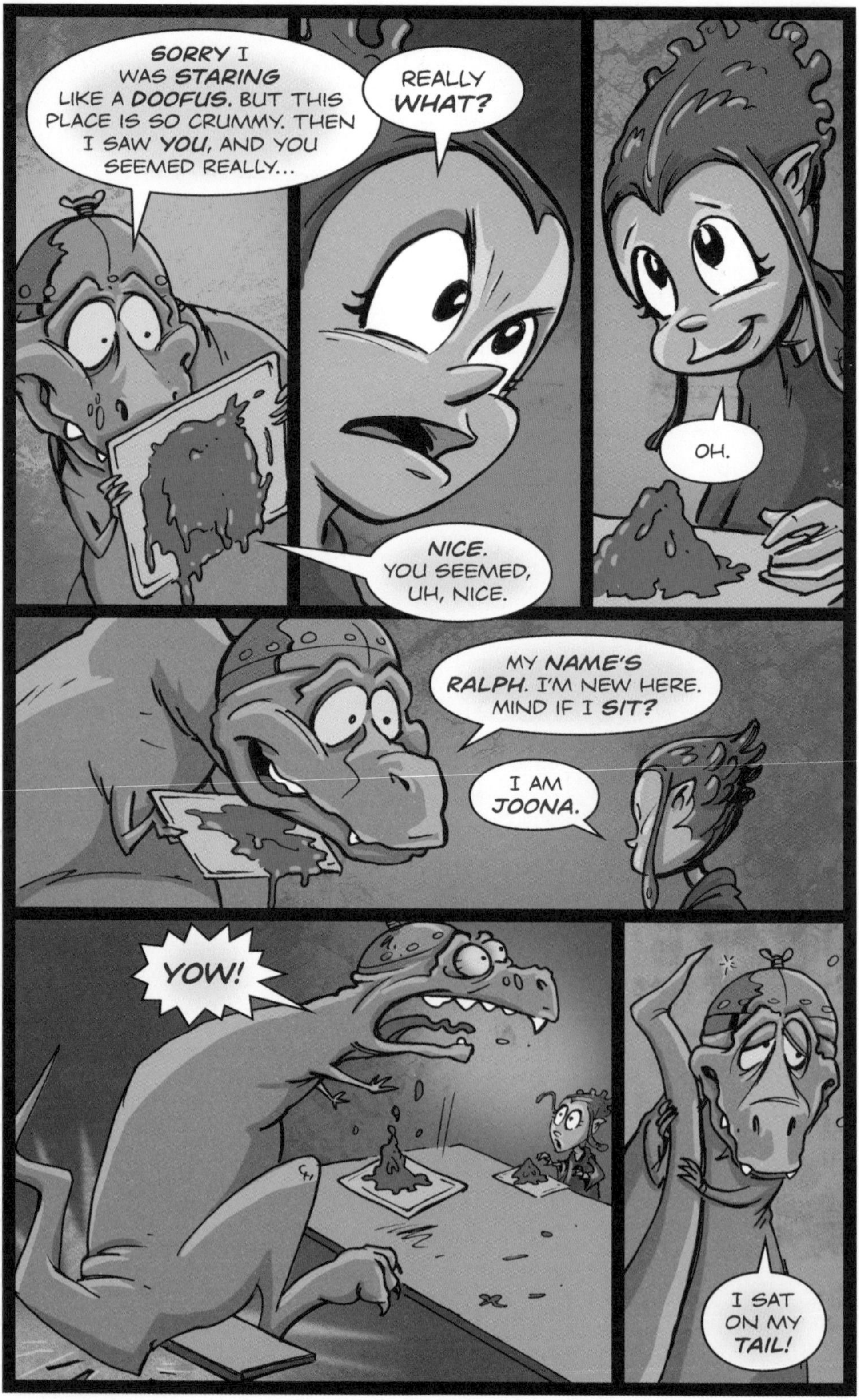
SORRY I WAS STARING LIKE A DOOFUS. BUT THIS PLACE IS SO CRUMMY. THEN I SAW YOU, AND YOU SEEMED REALLY...
REALLY WHAT?
NICE. YOU SEEMED, UH, NICE.
OH.
MY NAME'S RALPH. I'M NEW HERE. MIND IF I SIT?
I AM JOONA.
YOW!
I SAT ON MY TAIL!

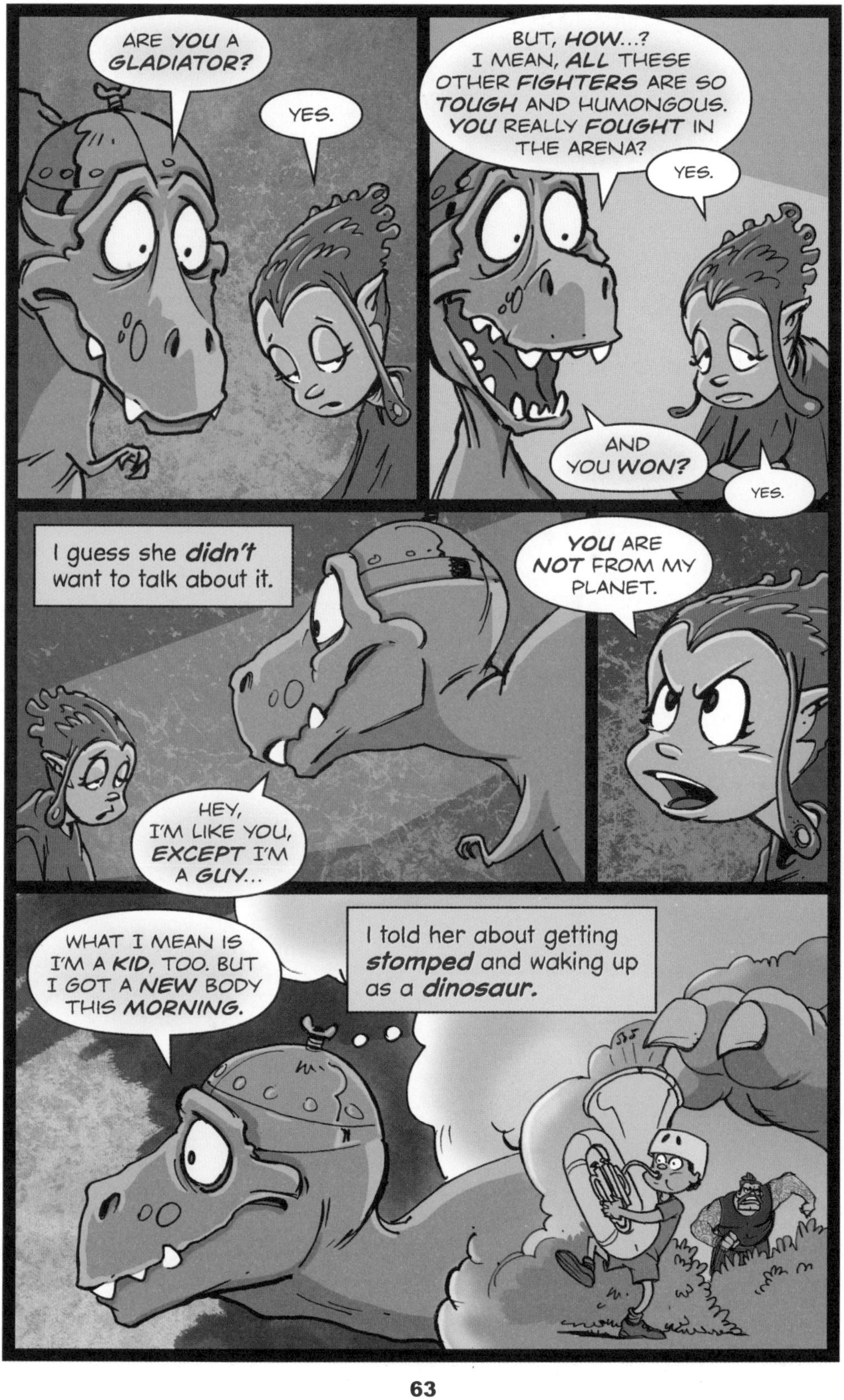
ARE YOU A GLADIATOR?
YES.
BUT, HOW...? I MEAN, ALL THESE OTHER FIGHTERS ARE SO TOUGH AND HUMONGOUS. YOU REALLY FOUGHT IN THE ARENA?
YES.
AND YOU WON?
YES.
I guess she didn't want to talk about it.
YOU ARE NOT FROM MY PLANET.
HEY, I'M LIKE YOU, EXCEPT I'M A GUY...
WHAT I MEAN IS I'M A KID, TOO. BUT I GOT A NEW BODY THIS MORNING.
I told her about getting stomped and waking up as a dinosaur.

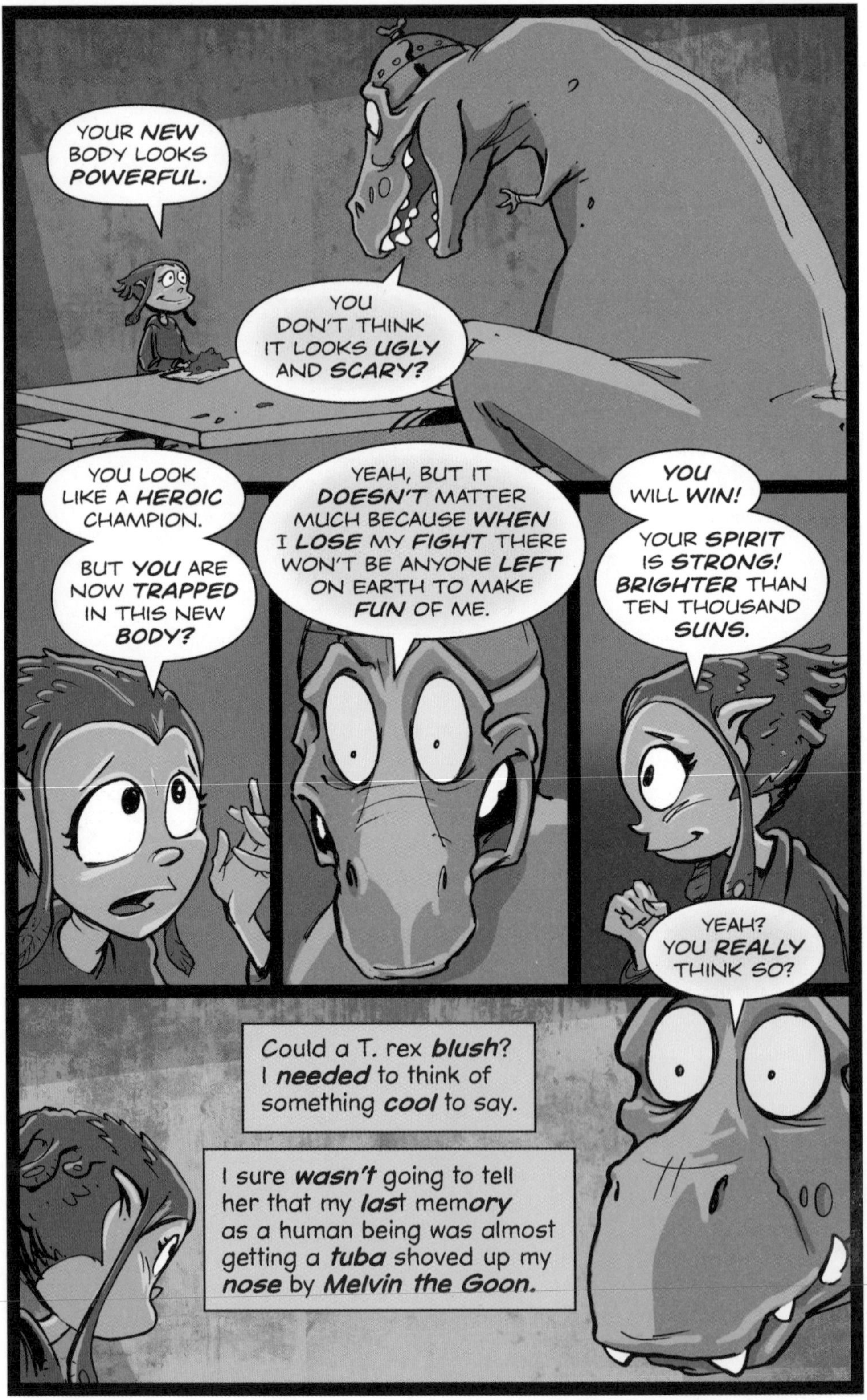
YOUR NEW BODY LOOKS POWERFUL.
YOU DON'T THINK IT LOOKS UGLY AND SCARY?
YOU LOOK LIKE A HEROIC CHAMPION.
BUT YOU ARE NOW TRAPPED IN THIS NEW BODY?
YEAH, BUT IT DOESN'T MATTER MUCH BECAUSE WHEN I LOSE MY FIGHT THERE WON'T BE ANYONE LEFT ON EARTH TO MAKE FUN OF ME.
YOU WILL WIN!
YOUR SPIRIT IS STRONG! BRIGHTER THAN TEN THOUSAND SUNS.
YEAH? YOU REALLY THINK SO?
Could a T. rex blush? I needed to think of something cool to say.
I sure wasn't going to tell her that my last memory as a human being was almost getting a tuba shoved up my nose by Melvin the Goon.

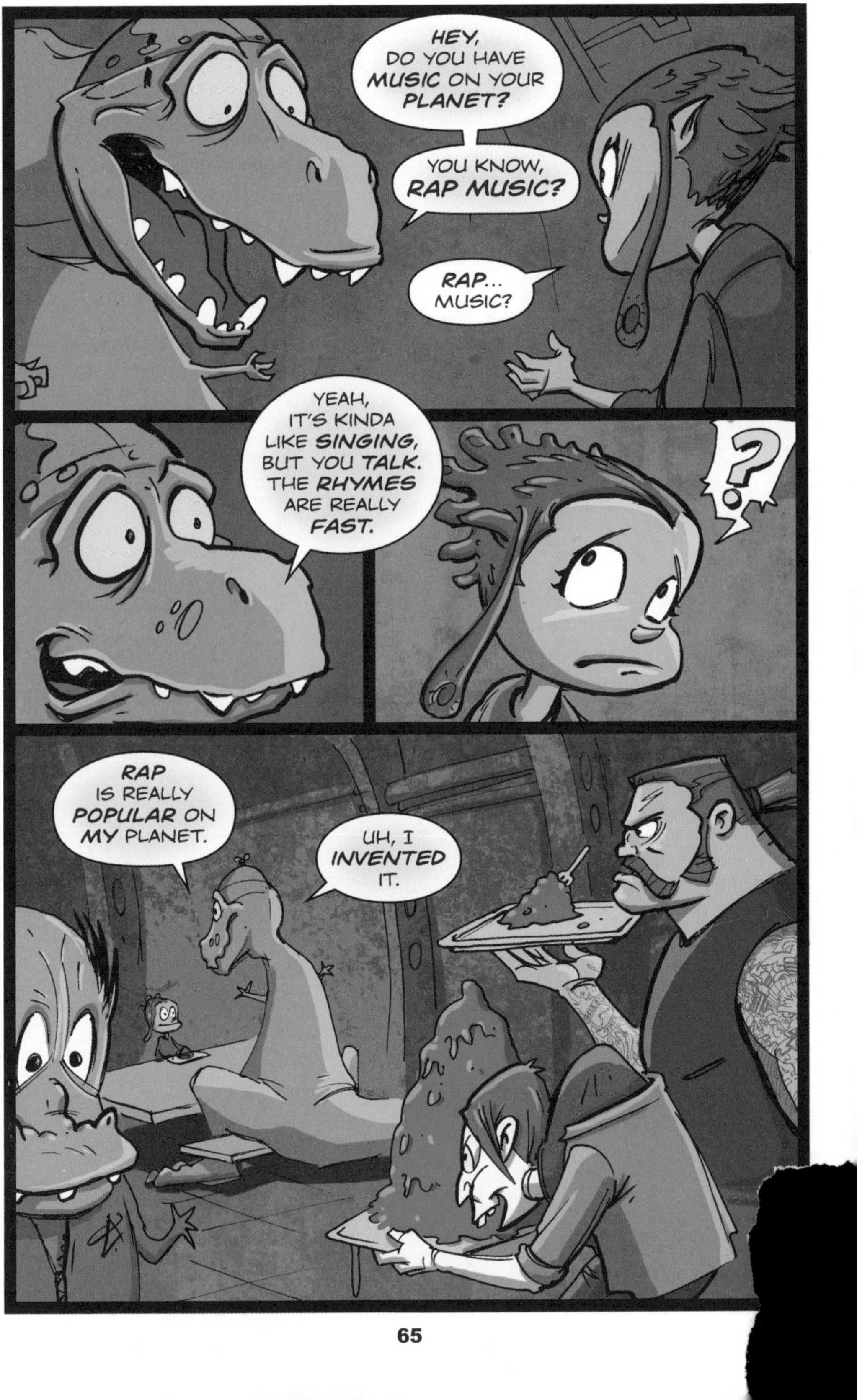
HEY, DO YOU HAVE MUSIC ON YOUR PLANET?
YOU KNOW, RAP MUSIC?
RAP... MUSIC?
YEAH, IT'S KINDA LIKE SINGING, BUT YOU TALK. THE RHYMES ARE REALLY FAST.
?
RAP IS REALLY POPULAR ON MY PLANET.
UH, I INVENTED IT.

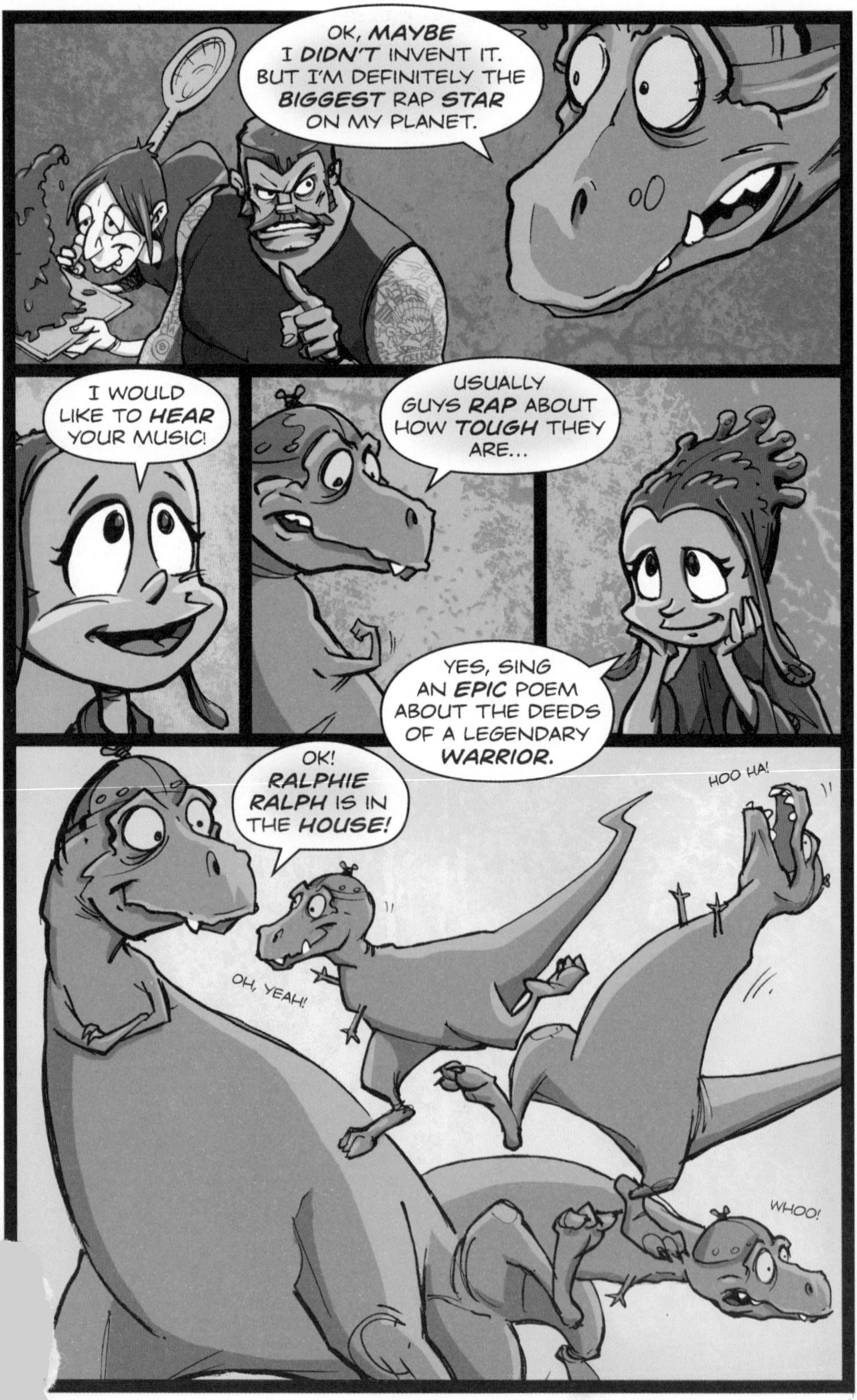
OK, MAYBE I DIDN'T INVENT IT. BUT I'M DEFINITELY THE BIGGEST RAP STAR ON MY PLANET.
I WOULD LIKE TO HEAR YOUR MUSIC!
USUALLY GUYS RAP ABOUT HOW TOUGH THEY ARE...
YES, SING AN EPIC POEM ABOUT THE DEEDS OF A LEGENDARY WARRIOR.
OK! RALPHIE RALPH IS IN THE HOUSE!
HOO HA!
OH, YEAH!
WHOO!

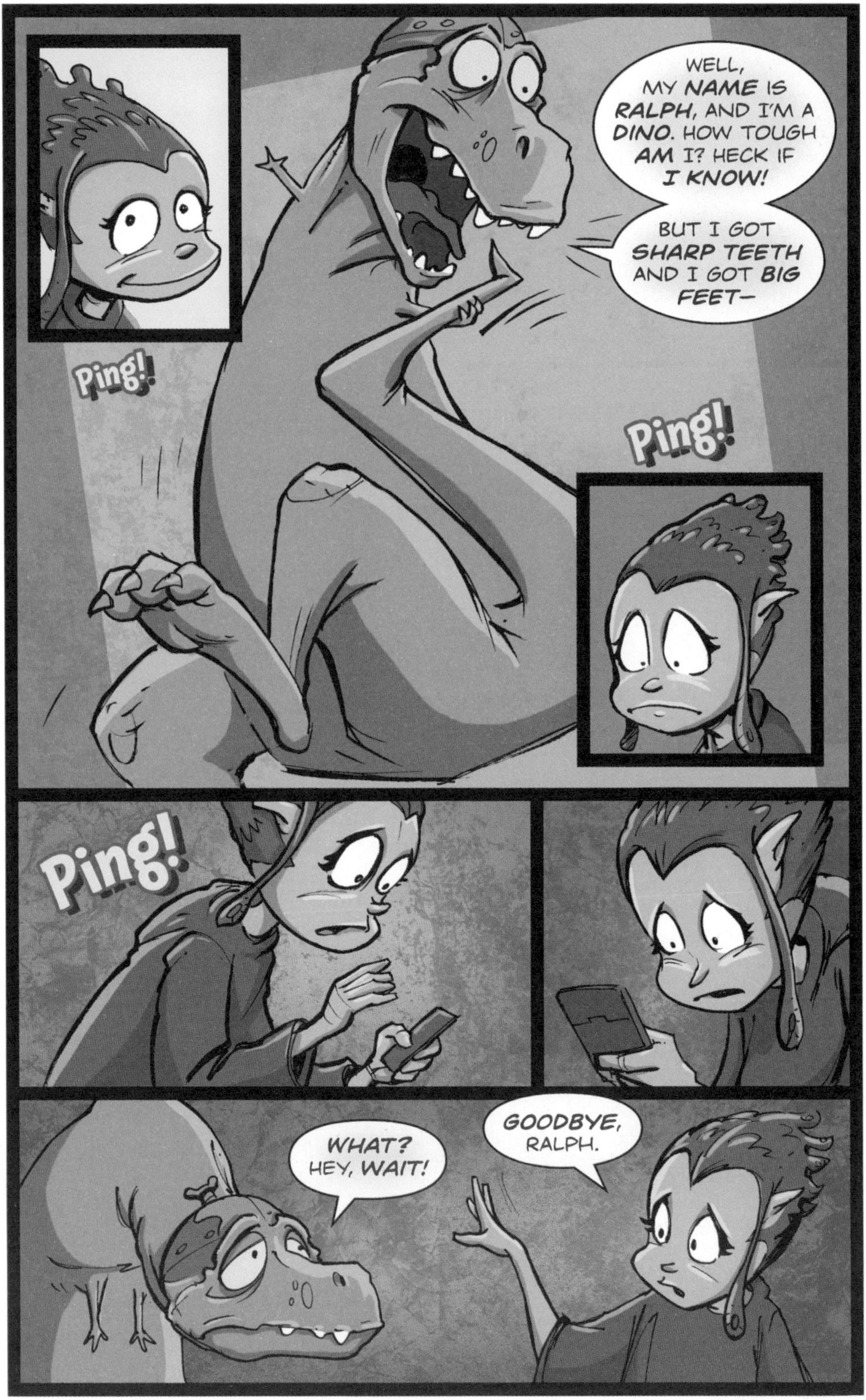
WELL, MY NAME IS RALPH, AND I'M A DINO. HOW TOUGH AM I? HECK IF I KNOW!
BUT I GOT SHARP TEETH AND I GOT BIG FEET—
Ping!
Ping!
Ping!
WHAT? HEY, WAIT!
GOODBYE, RALPH.

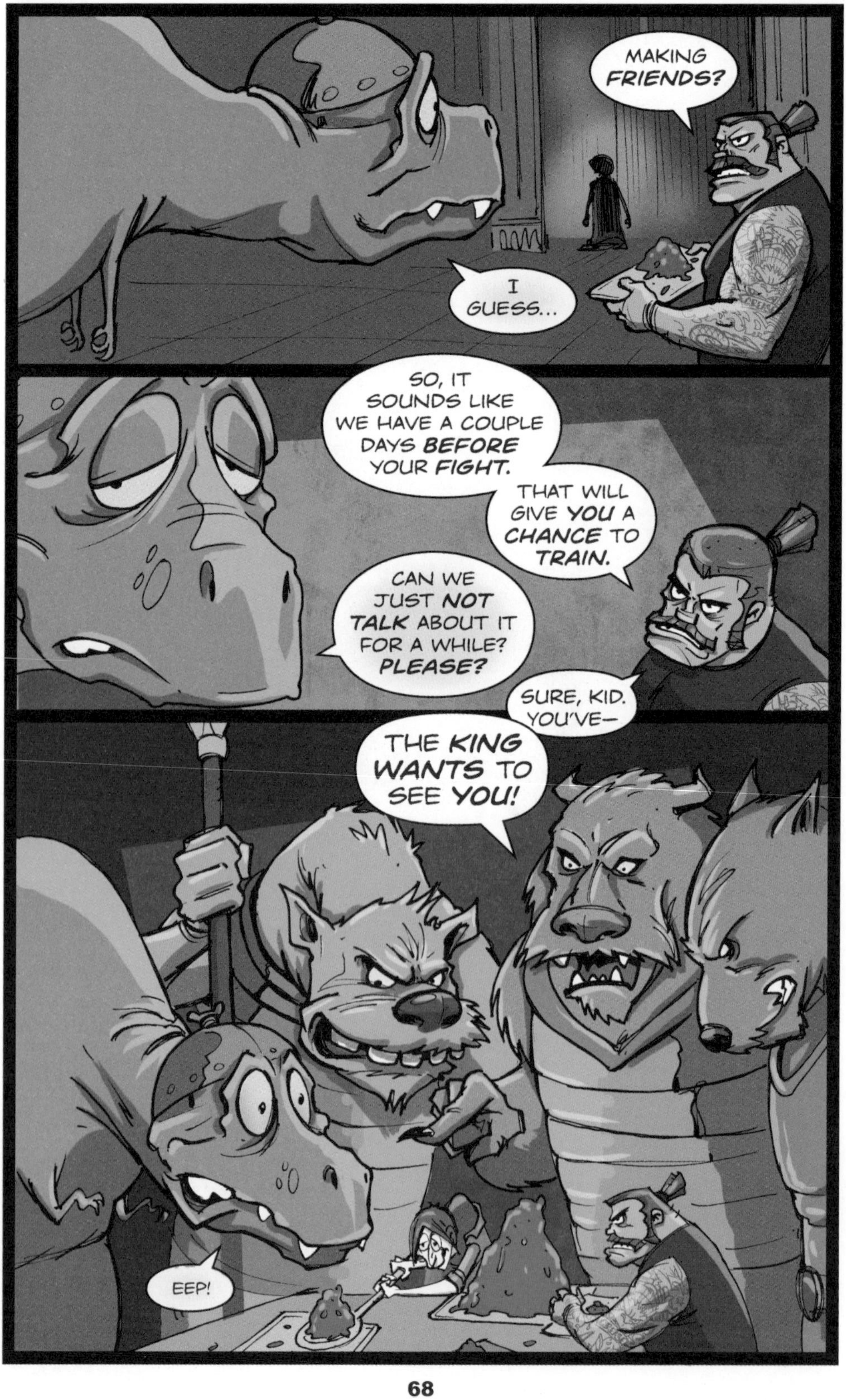
MAKING FRIENDS?
I GUESS...
SO, IT SOUNDS LIKE WE HAVE A COUPLE DAYS BEFORE YOUR FIGHT.
THAT WILL GIVE YOU A CHANCE TO TRAIN.
CAN WE JUST NOT TALK ABOUT IT FOR A WHILE? PLEASE?
SURE, KID. YOU'VE—
THE KING WANTS TO SEE YOU!
EEP!

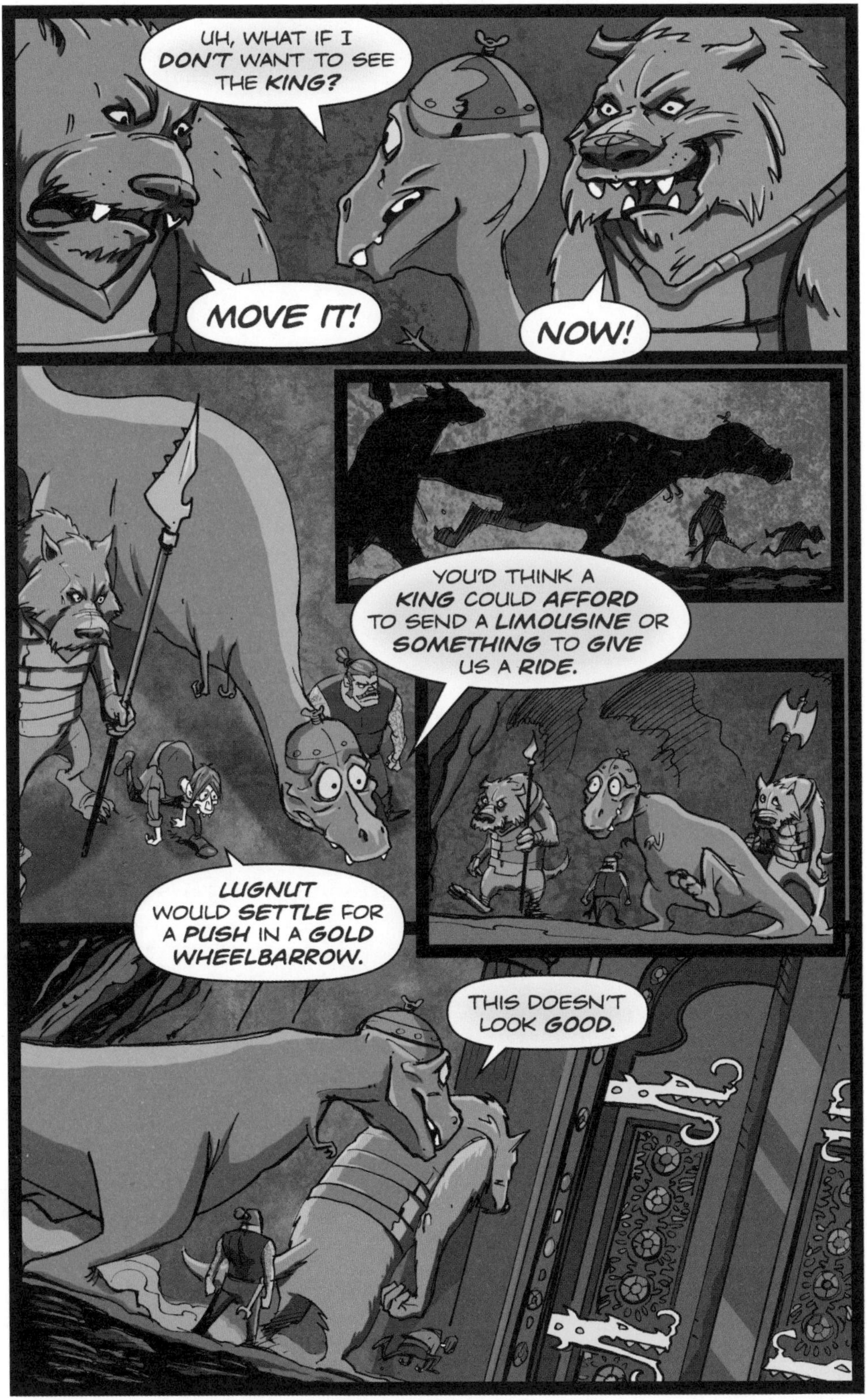
UH, WHAT IF I DON'T WANT TO SEE THE KING?
MOVE IT!
NOW!
YOU'D THINK A KING COULD AFFORD TO SEND A LIMOUSINE OR SOMETHING TO GIVE US A RIDE.
LUGNUT WOULD SETTLE FOR A PUSH IN A GOLD WHEELBARROW.
THIS DOESN'T LOOK GOOD.

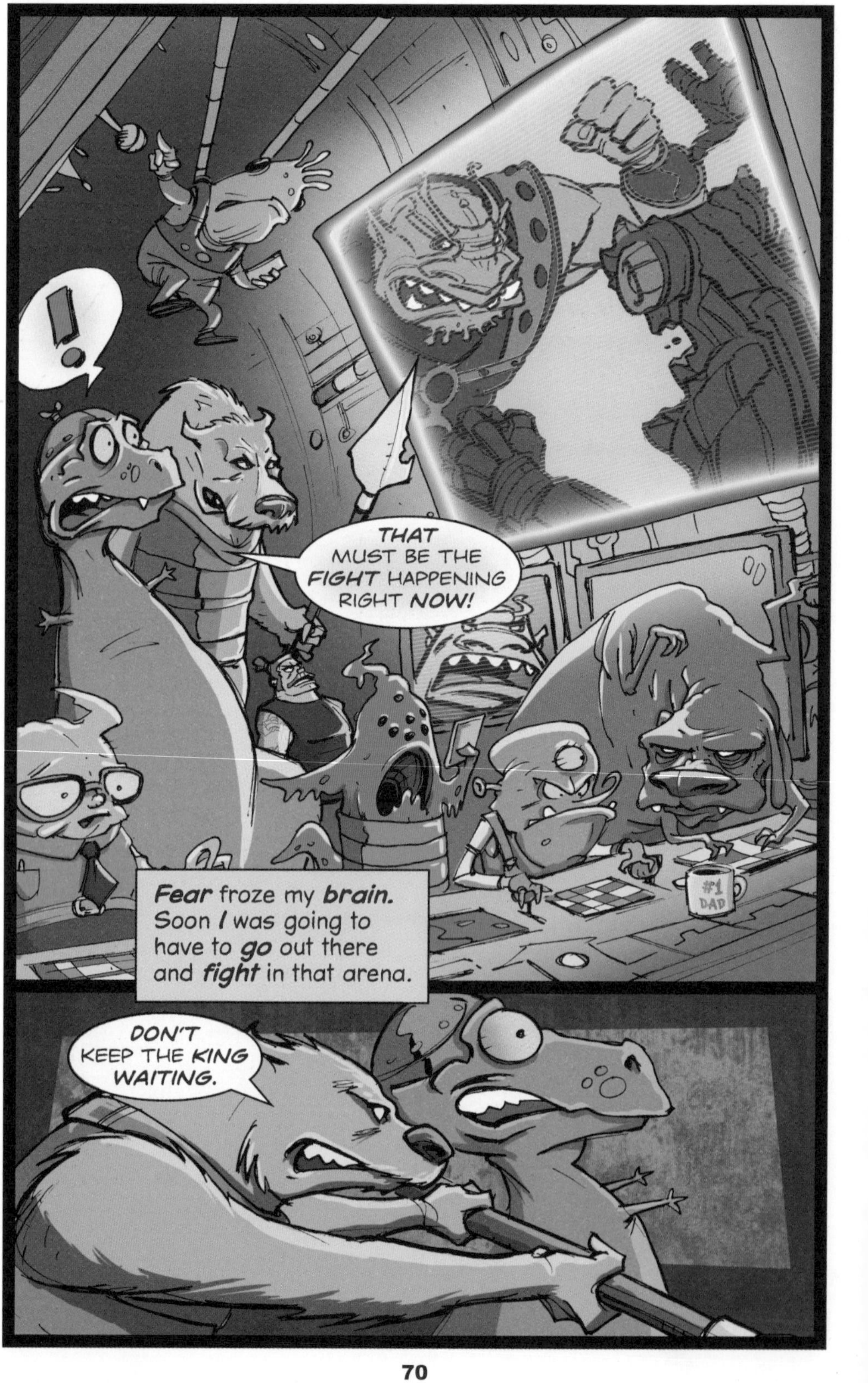
!
THAT MUST BE THE FIGHT HAPPENING RIGHT NOW!
Fear froze my brain. Soon I was going to have to go out there and fight in that arena.
#1 DAD
DON'T KEEP THE KING WAITING.

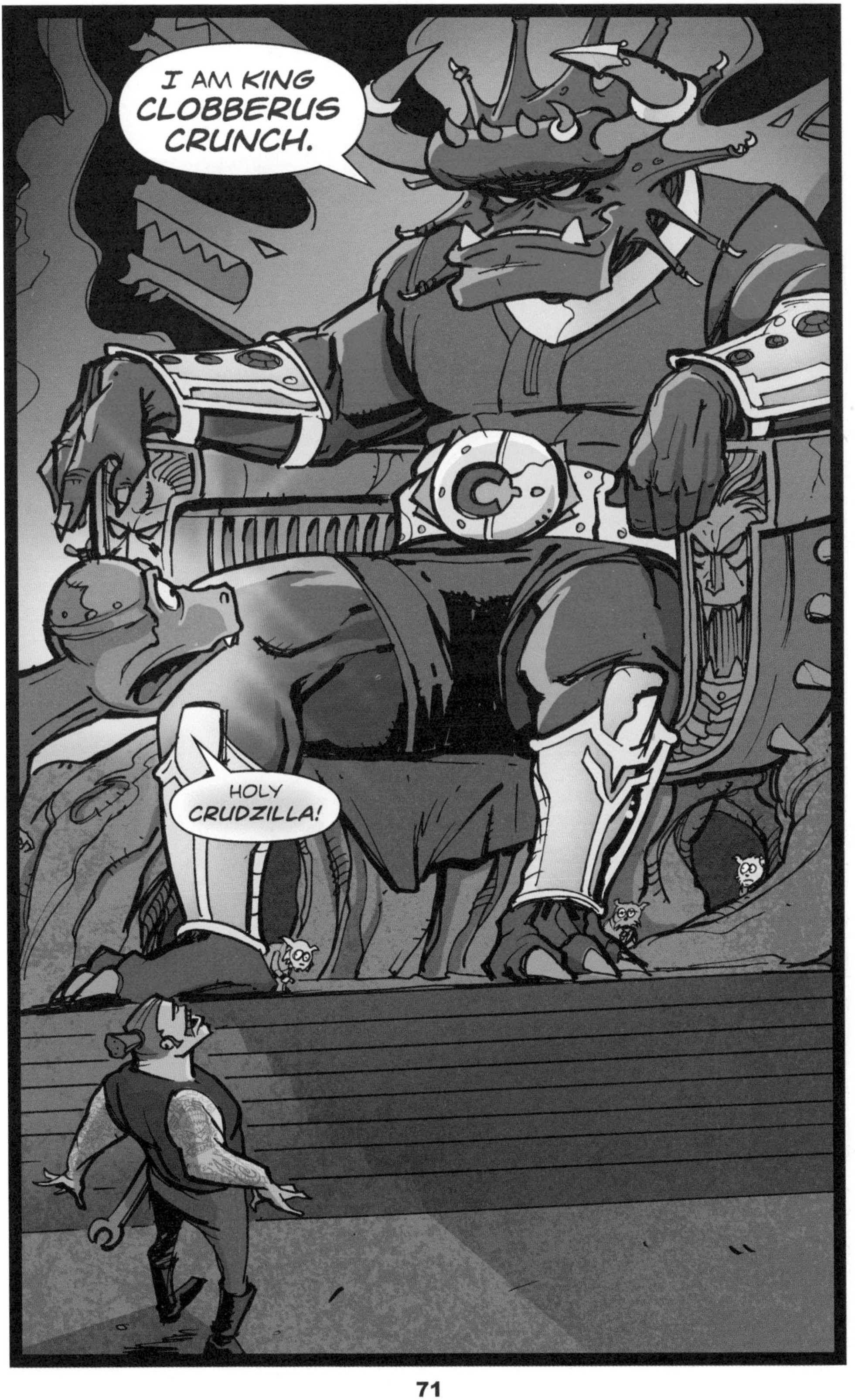
I AM KING CLOBBERUS CRUNCH.
HOLY CRUDZILLA!

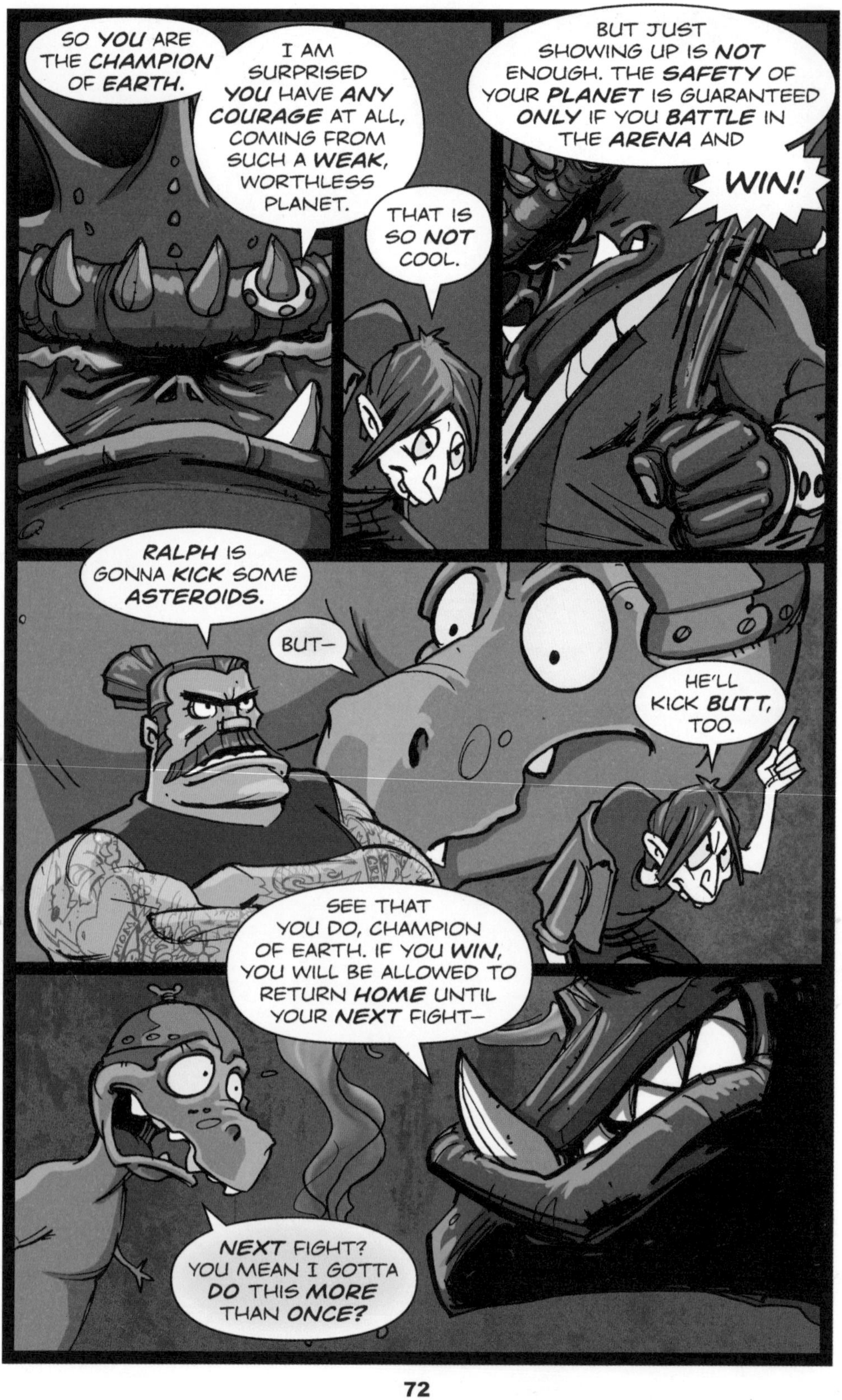
SO YOU ARE THE CHAMPION OF EARTH.
I AM SURPRISED YOU HAVE ANY COURAGE AT ALL, COMING FROM SUCH A WEAK, WORTHLESS PLANET.
THAT IS SO NOT COOL.
BUT JUST SHOWING UP IS NOT ENOUGH. THE SAFETY OF YOUR PLANET IS GUARANTEED ONLY IF YOU BATTLE IN THE ARENA AND
WIN!
RALPH IS GONNA KICK SOME ASTEROIDS.
BUT–
HE'LL KICK BUTT, TOO.
SEE THAT YOU DO, CHAMPION OF EARTH. IF YOU WIN, YOU WILL BE ALLOWED TO RETURN HOME UNTIL YOUR NEXT FIGHT–
NEXT FIGHT? YOU MEAN I GOTTA DO THIS MORE THAN ONCE?

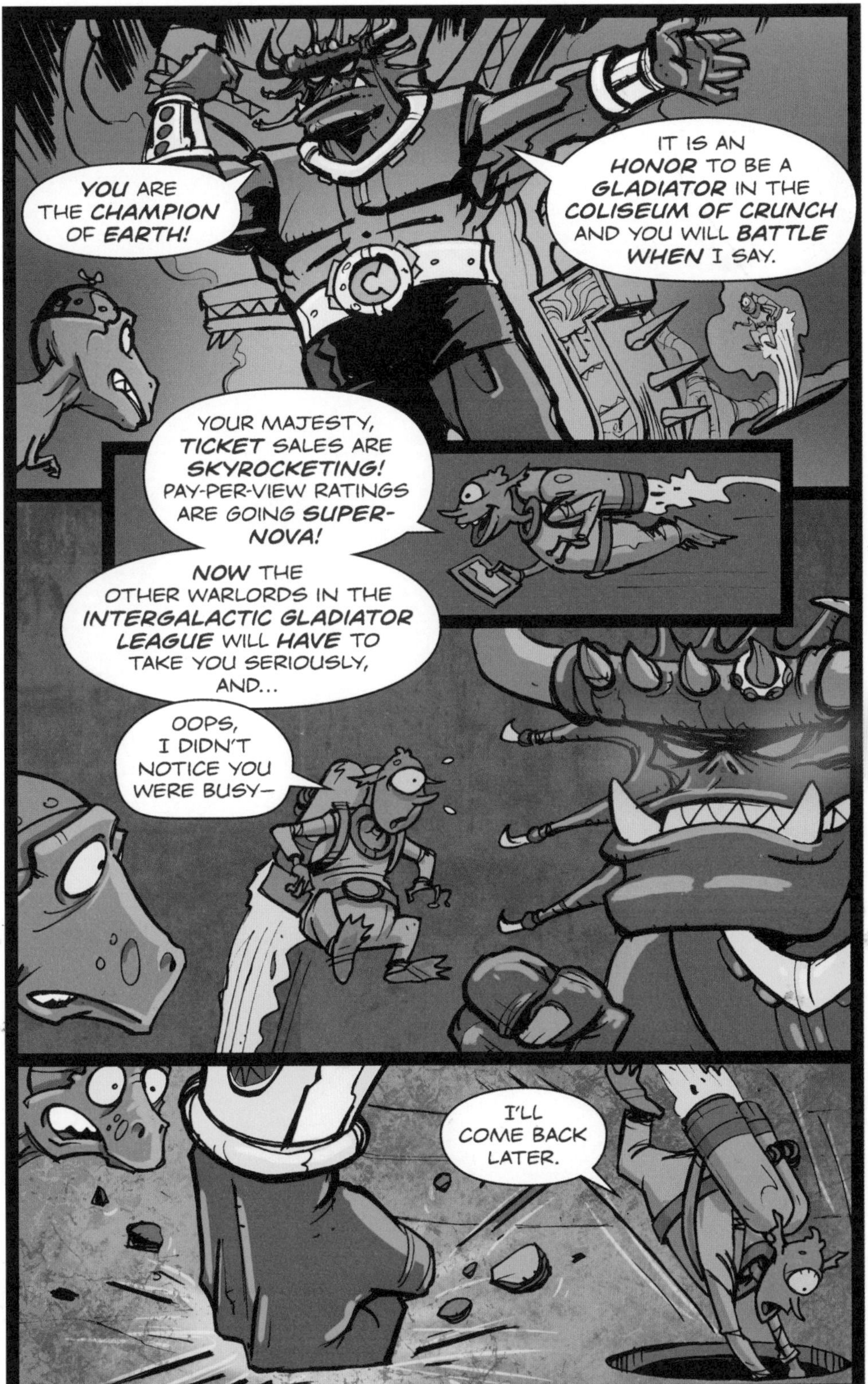
YOU ARE THE CHAMPION OF EARTH!
IT IS AN HONOR TO BE A GLADIATOR IN THE COLISEUM OF CRUNCH AND YOU WILL BATTLE WHEN I SAY.
YOUR MAJESTY, TICKET SALES ARE SKYROCKETING! PAY-PER-VIEW RATINGS ARE GOING SUPER-NOVA!
NOW THE OTHER WARLORDS IN THE INTERGALACTIC GLADIATOR LEAGUE WILL HAVE TO TAKE YOU SERIOUSLY, AND...
OOPS, I DIDN'T NOTICE YOU WERE BUSY—
I'LL COME BACK LATER.

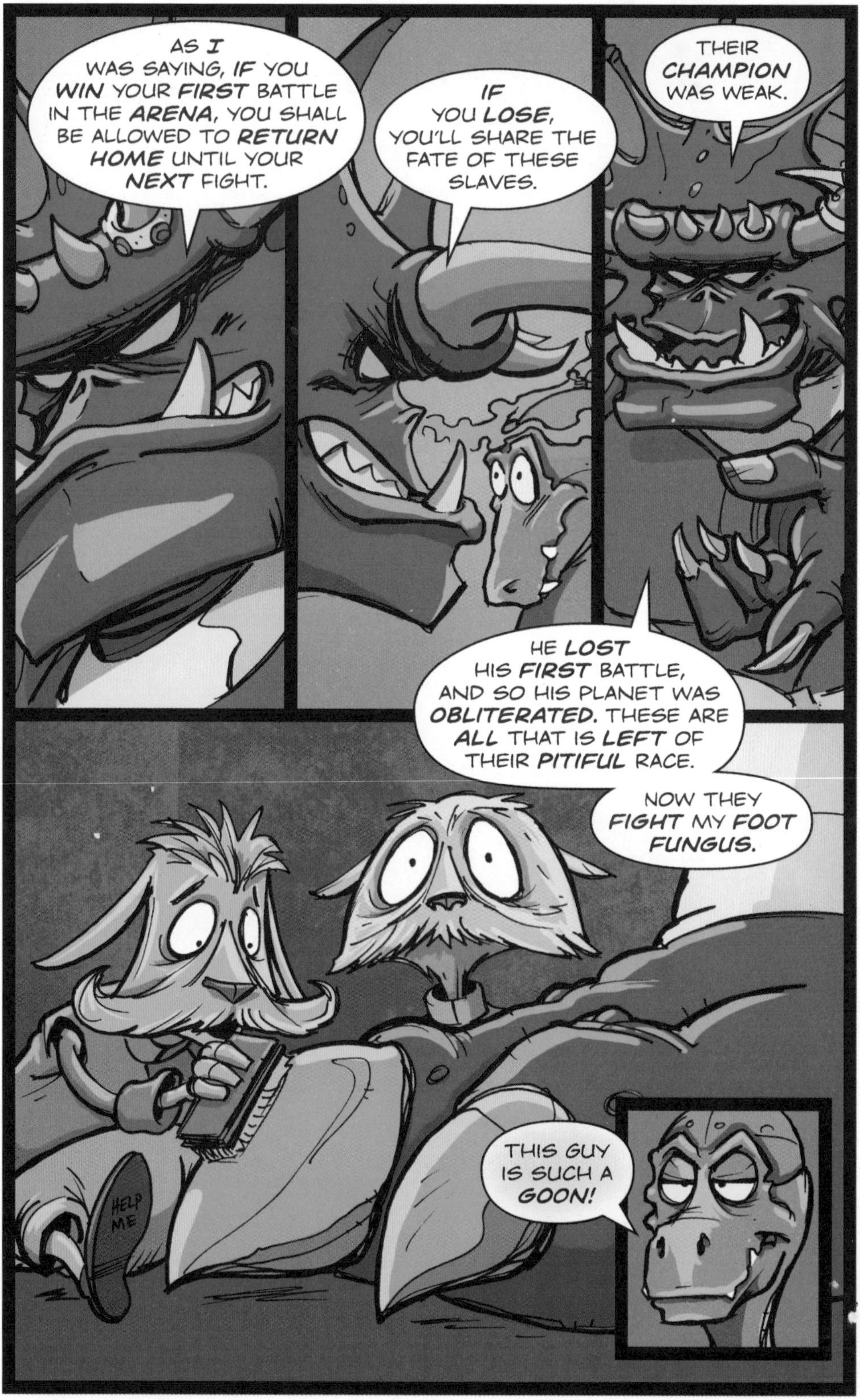
AS I WAS SAYING, IF YOU WIN YOUR FIRST BATTLE IN THE ARENA, YOU SHALL BE ALLOWED TO RETURN HOME UNTIL YOUR NEXT FIGHT.
IF YOU LOSE, YOU'LL SHARE THE FATE OF THESE SLAVES.
THEIR CHAMPION WAS WEAK.
HE LOST HIS FIRST BATTLE, AND SO HIS PLANET WAS OBLITERATED. THESE ARE ALL THAT IS LEFT OF THEIR PITIFUL RACE.
NOW THEY FIGHT MY FOOT FUNGUS.
HELP ME
THIS GUY IS SUCH A GOON!

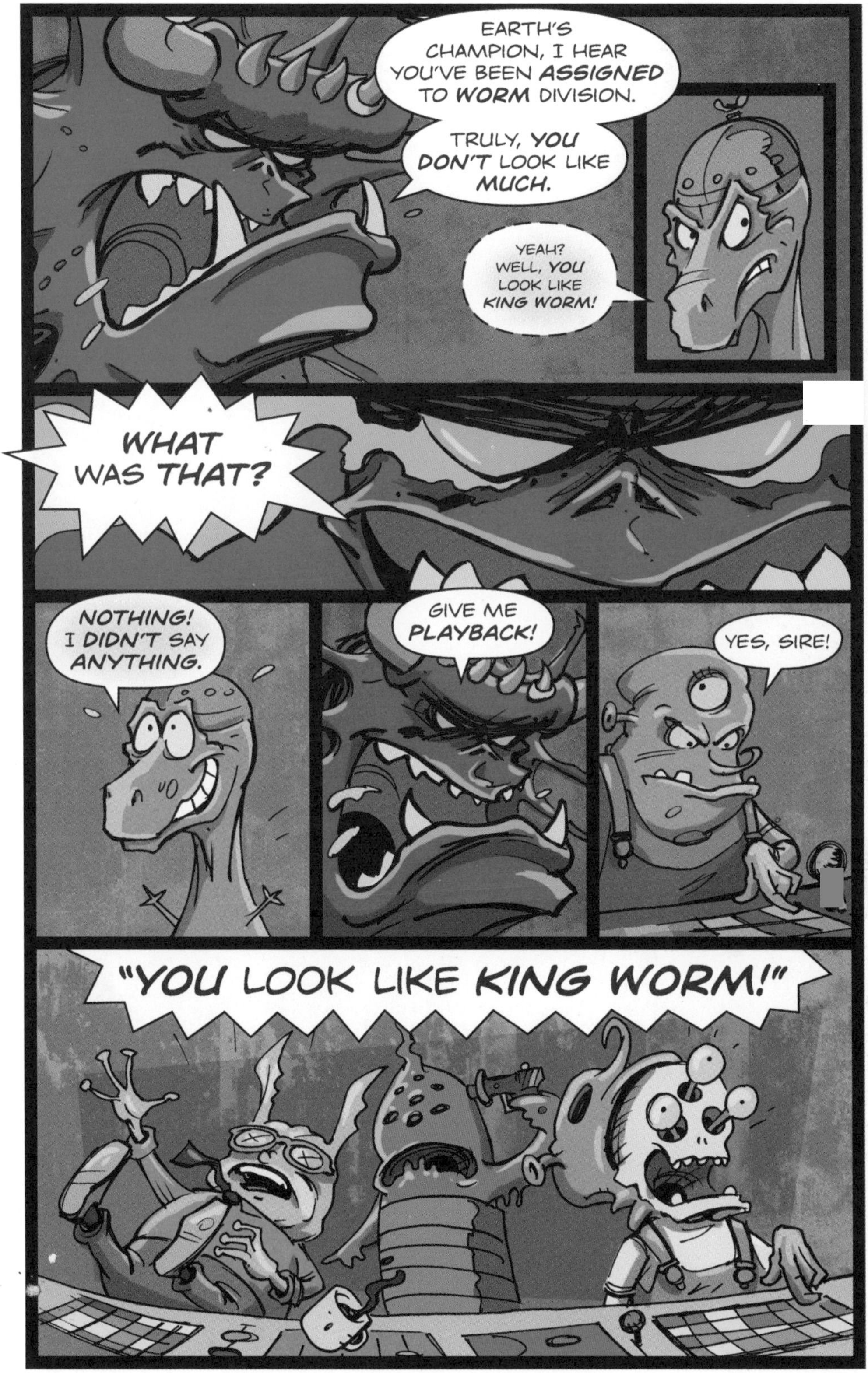
EARTH'S CHAMPION, I HEAR YOU'VE BEEN ASSIGNED TO WORM DIVISION.
TRULY, YOU DON'T LOOK LIKE MUCH.
YEAH? WELL, YOU LOOK LIKE KING WORM!
WHAT WAS THAT?
NOTHING! I DIDN'T SAY ANYTHING.
GIVE ME PLAYBACK!
YES, SIRE!
"YOU LOOK LIKE KING WORM!"

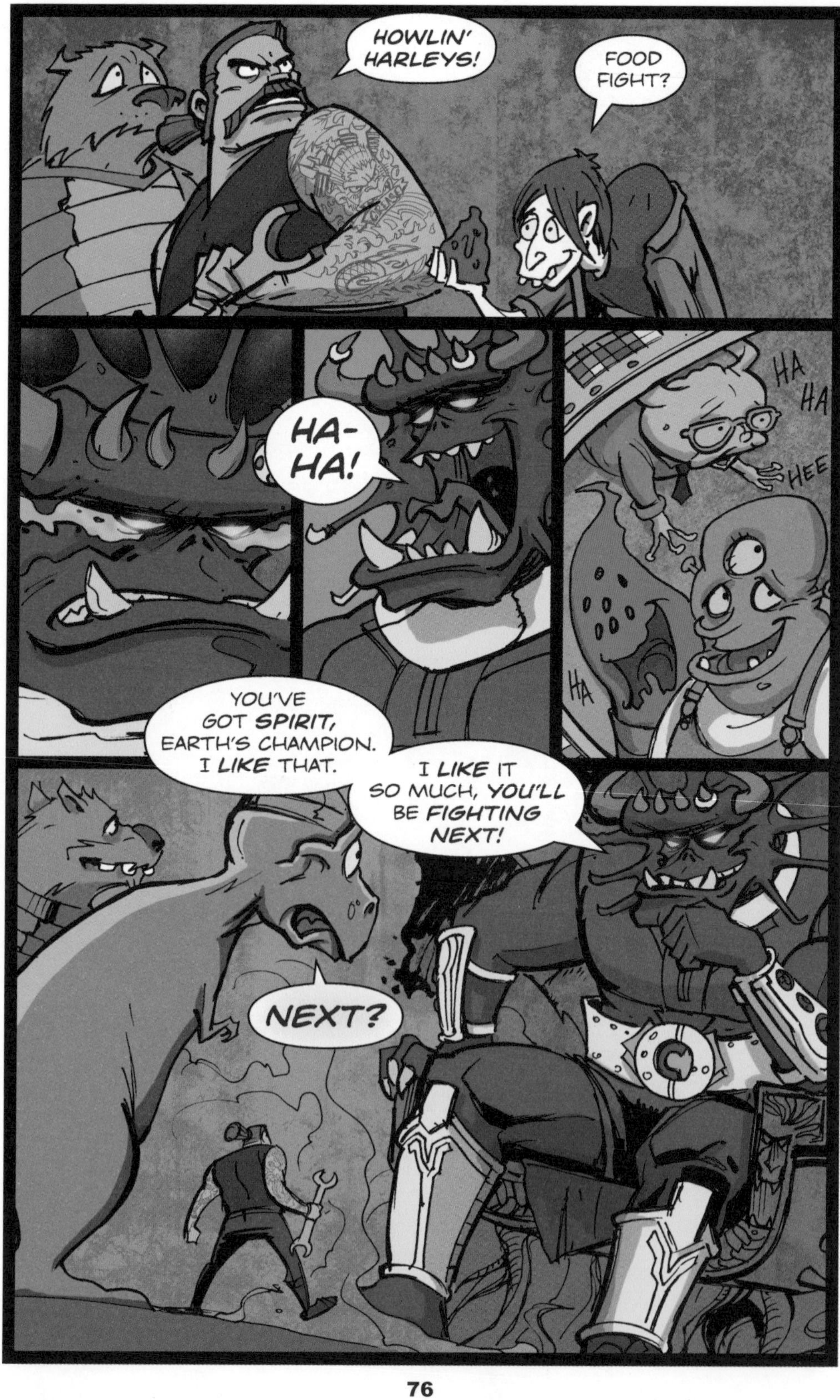
HOWLIN' HARLEYS!
FOOD FIGHT?
HA-HA!
HA HA
HEE
HA
YOU'VE GOT SPIRIT, EARTH'S CHAMPION. I LIKE THAT.
I LIKE IT SO MUCH, YOU'LL BE FIGHTING NEXT!
NEXT?

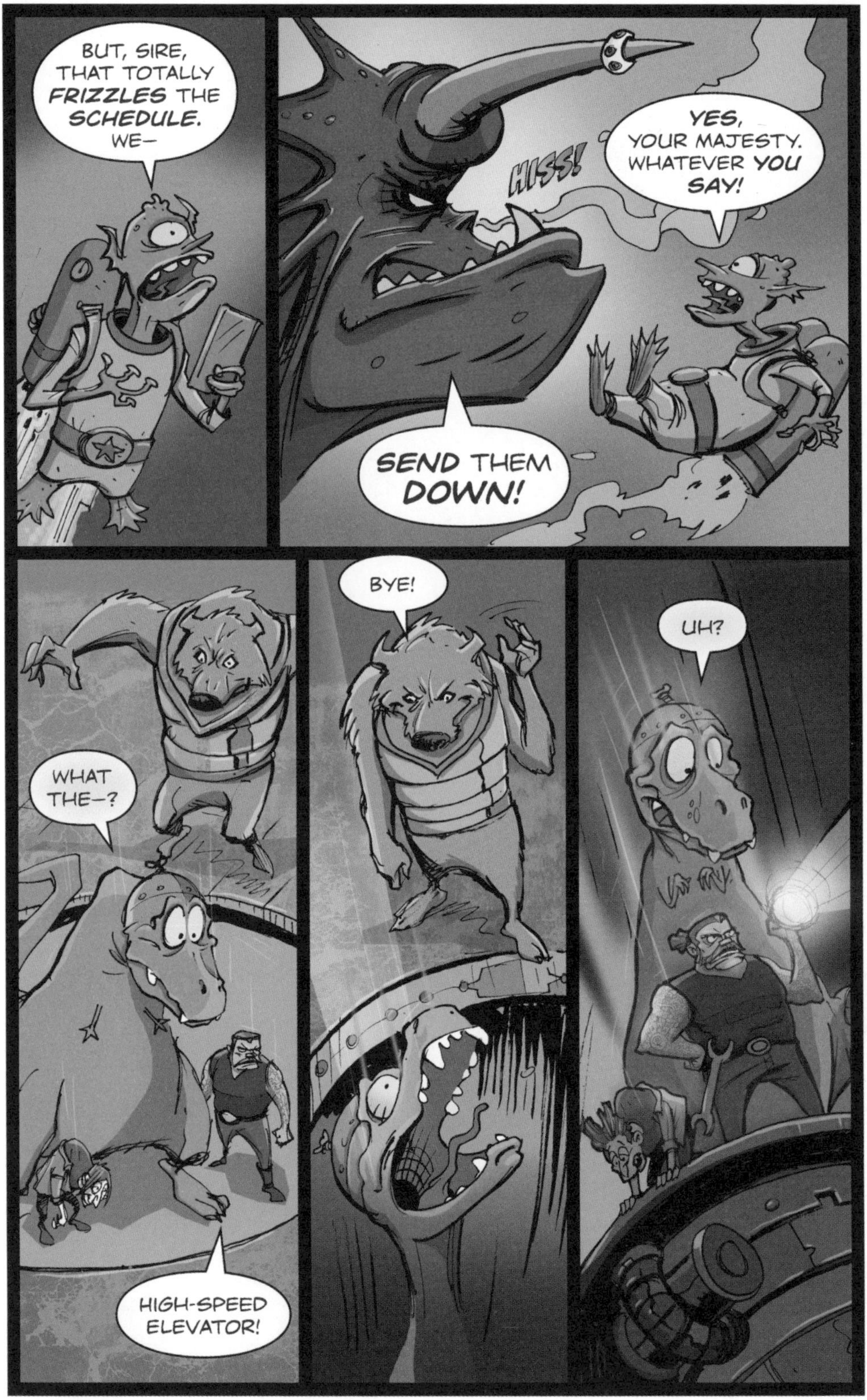
BUT, SIRE, THAT TOTALLY FRIZZLES THE SCHEDULE. WE–
HISS!
YES, YOUR MAJESTY. WHATEVER YOU SAY!
SEND THEM DOWN!
WHAT THE–?
HIGH-SPEED ELEVATOR!
BYE!
UH?

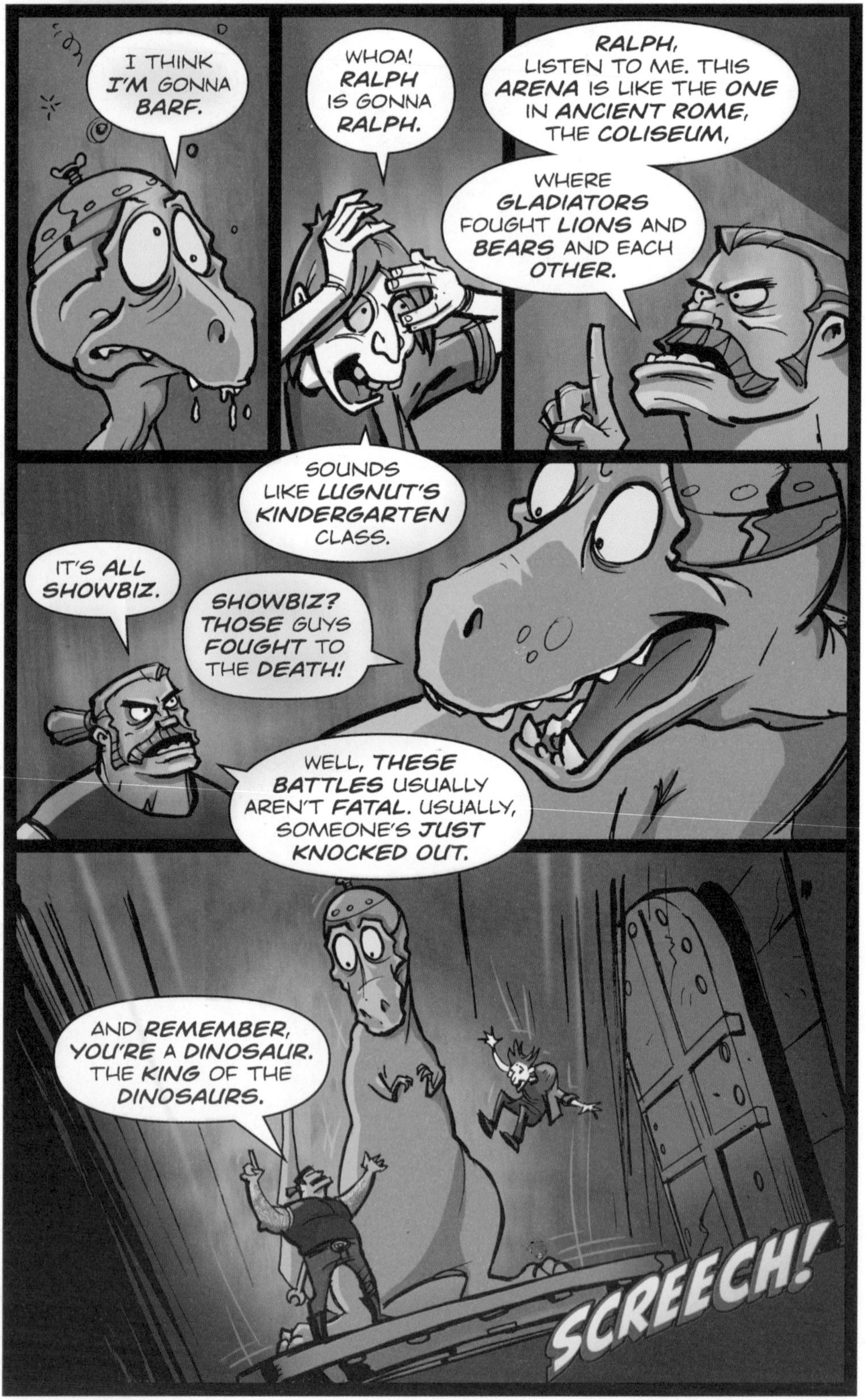

I THINK I'M GONNA BARF.
WHOA! RALPH IS GONNA RALPH.
RALPH, LISTEN TO ME. THIS ARENA IS LIKE THE ONE IN ANCIENT ROME, THE COLISEUM,
WHERE GLADIATORS FOUGHT LIONS AND BEARS AND EACH OTHER.
SOUNDS LIKE LUGNUT'S KINDERGARTEN CLASS.
IT'S ALL SHOWBIZ.
SHOWBIZ? THOSE GUYS FOUGHT TO THE DEATH!
WELL, THESE BATTLES USUALLY AREN'T FATAL. USUALLY, SOMEONE'S JUST KNOCKED OUT.
AND REMEMBER, YOU'RE A DINOSAUR. THE KING OF THE DINOSAURS.
SCREECH!

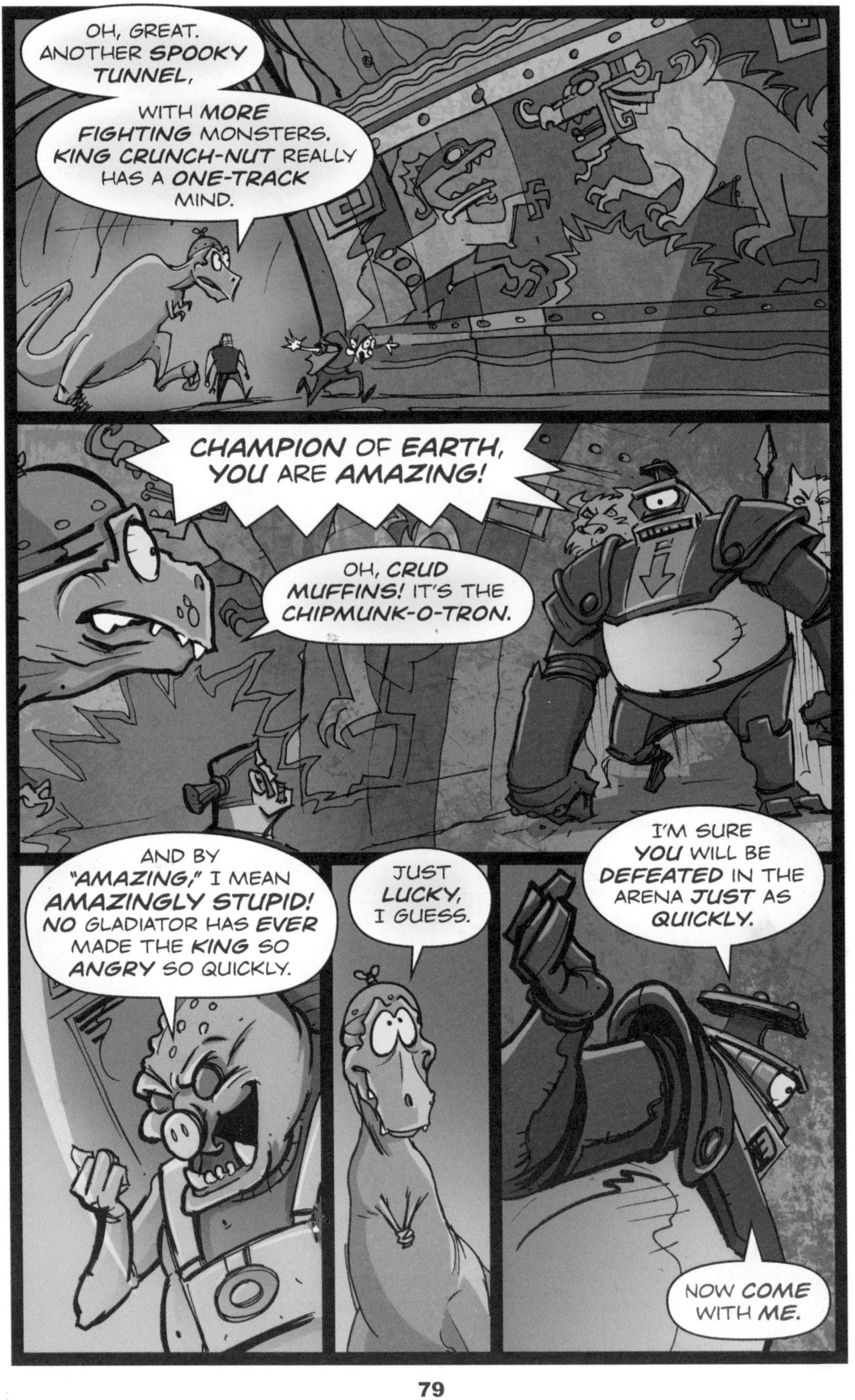
OH, GREAT. ANOTHER SPOOKY TUNNEL,
WITH MORE FIGHTING MONSTERS. KING CRUNCH-NUT REALLY HAS A ONE-TRACK MIND.
CHAMPION OF EARTH, YOU ARE AMAZING!
OH, CRUD MUFFINS! IT'S THE CHIPMUNK-O-TRON.
AND BY "AMAZING," I MEAN AMAZINGLY STUPID! NO GLADIATOR HAS EVER MADE THE KING SO ANGRY SO QUICKLY.
JUST LUCKY, I GUESS.
I'M SURE YOU WILL BE DEFEATED IN THE ARENA JUST AS QUICKLY.
NOW COME WITH ME.

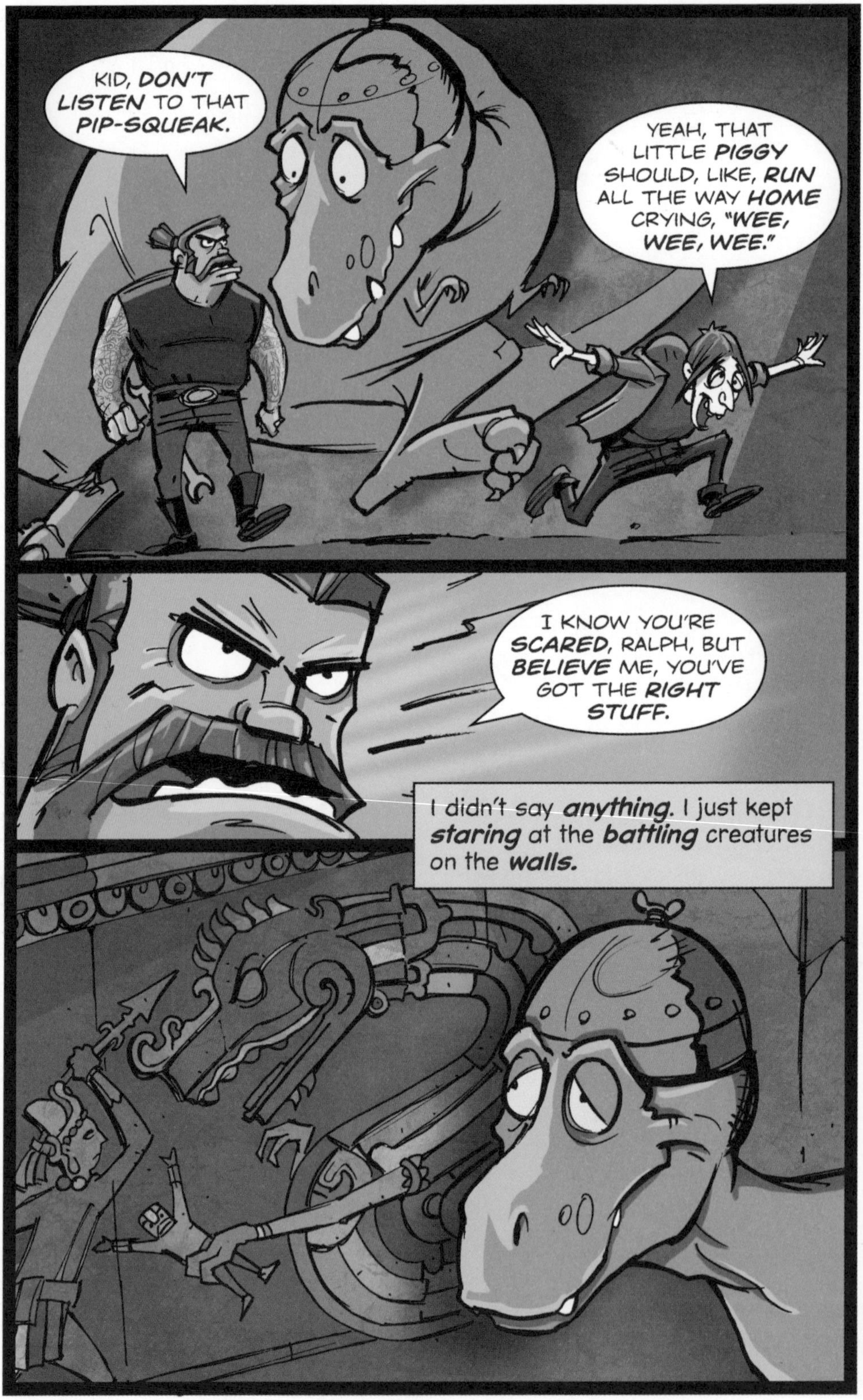
KID, DON'T LISTEN TO THAT PIP-SQUEAK.
YEAH, THAT LITTLE PIGGY SHOULD, LIKE, RUN ALL THE WAY HOME CRYING, "WEE, WEE, WEE."
I KNOW YOU'RE SCARED, RALPH, BUT BELIEVE ME, YOU'VE GOT THE RIGHT STUFF.
I didn't say anything. I just kept staring at the battling creatures on the walls.

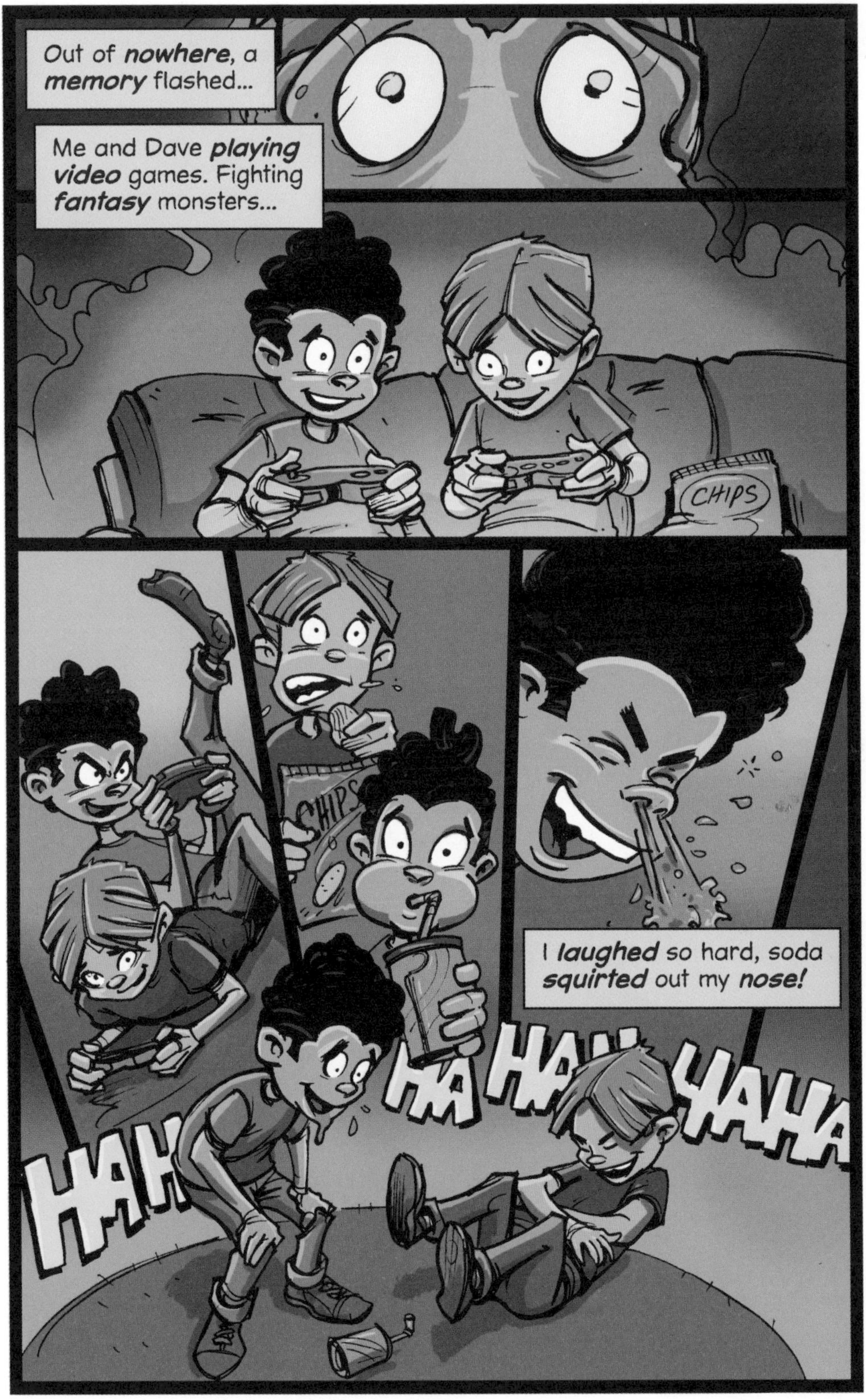
Out of nowhere, a memory flashed...
Me and Dave playing video games. Fighting fantasy monsters...
CHIPS
CHIPS
I laughed so hard, soda squirted out my nose!
HAH
HA HAH
YAHA

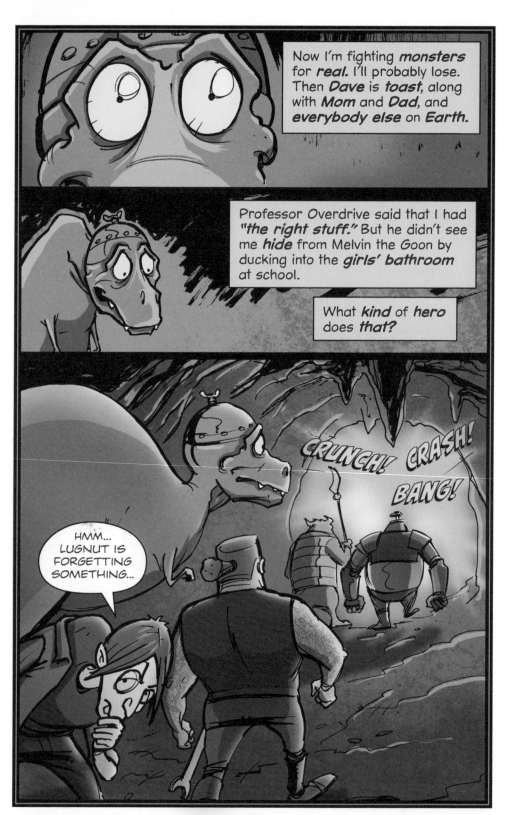

Now I'm fighting **monsters** for **real.** I'll probably lose. Then **Dave** is **toast**, along with **Mom** and **Dad**, and **everybody else** on **Earth.**

Professor Overdrive said that I had **"the right stuff."** But he didn't see me **hide** from Melvin the Goon by ducking into the **girls' bathroom** at school.

What **kind** of **hero** does **that?**

CRUNCH! CRASH! BANG!

HMM... LUGNUT IS FORGETTING SOMETHING...

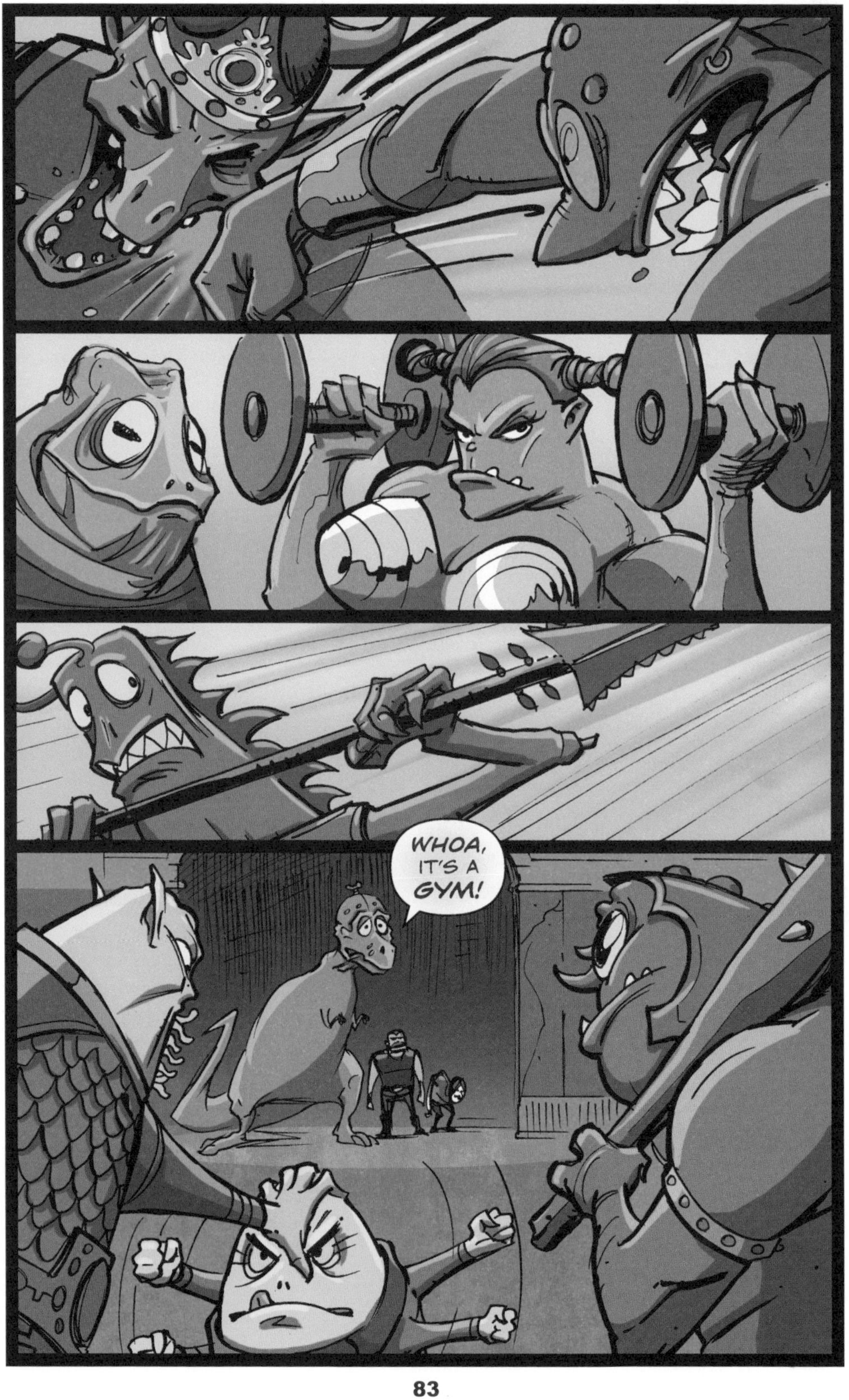
WHOA, IT'S A GYM!

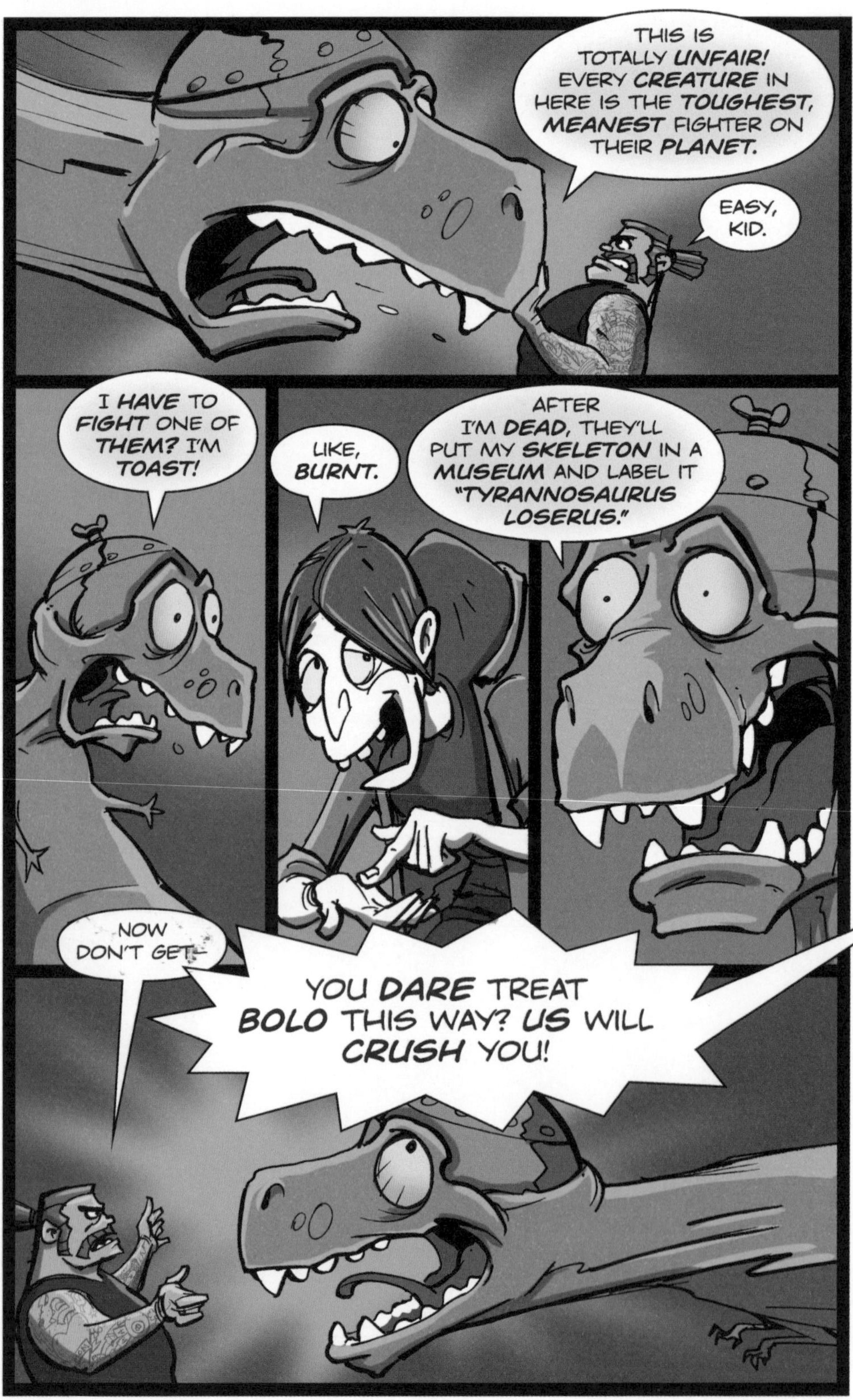
THIS IS TOTALLY UNFAIR! EVERY CREATURE IN HERE IS THE TOUGHEST, MEANEST FIGHTER ON THEIR PLANET.
EASY, KID.
I HAVE TO FIGHT ONE OF THEM? I'M TOAST!
LIKE, BURNT.
AFTER I'M DEAD, THEY'LL PUT MY SKELETON IN A MUSEUM AND LABEL IT "TYRANNOSAURUS LOSERUS."
NOW DON'T GET—
YOU DARE TREAT BOLO THIS WAY? US WILL CRUSH YOU!

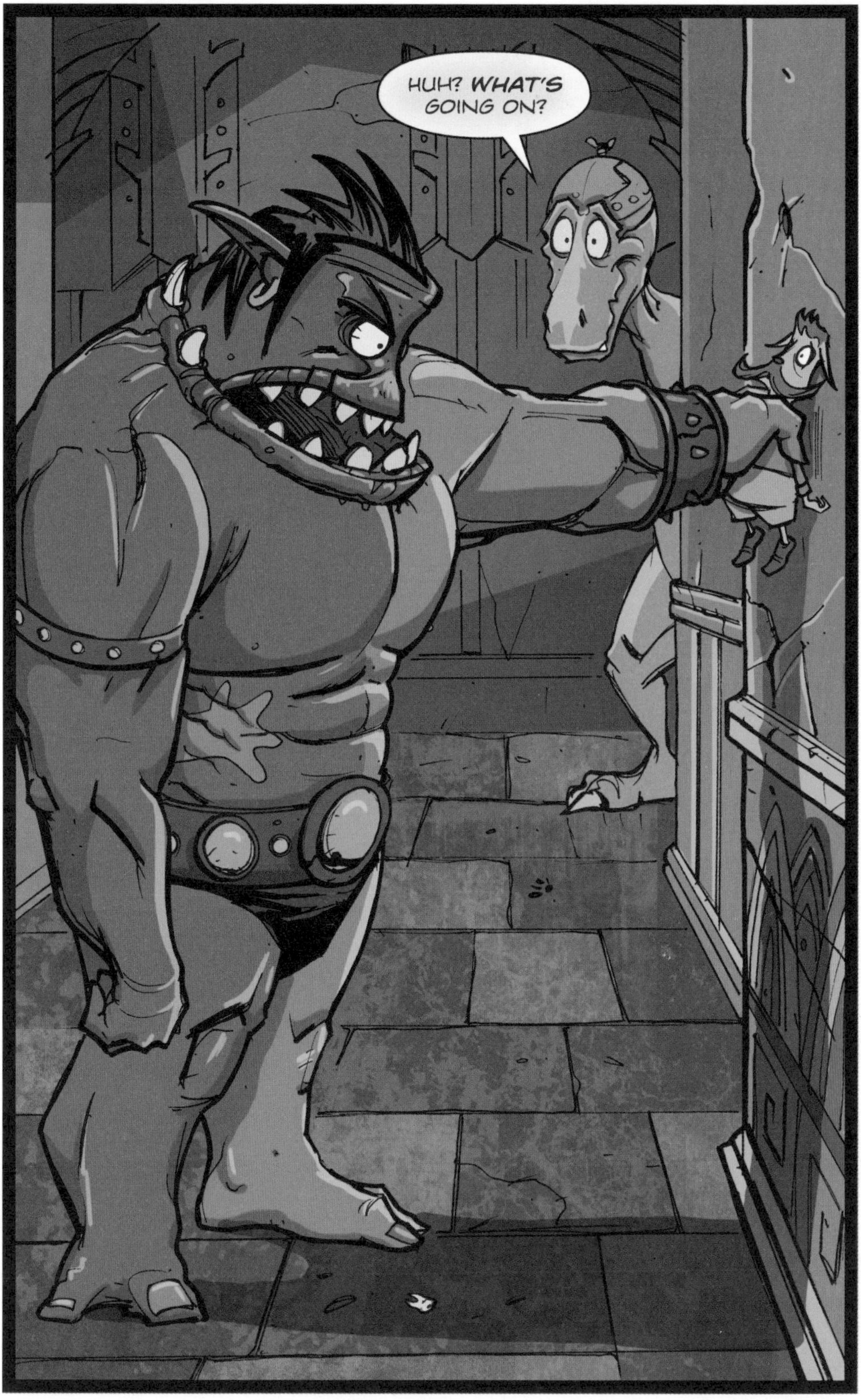
HUH? WHAT'S GOING ON?

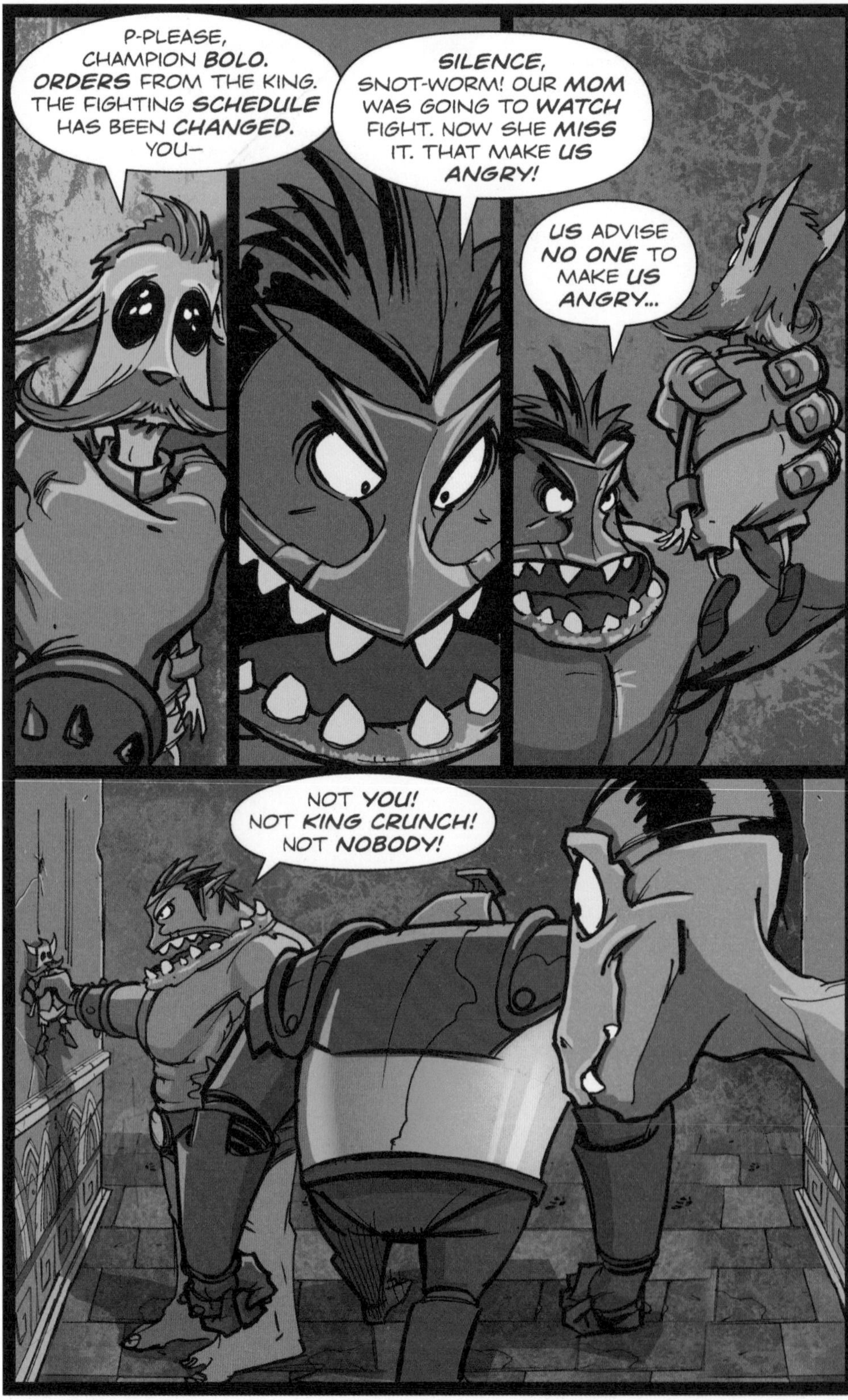
P-PLEASE, CHAMPION BOLO. ORDERS FROM THE KING. THE FIGHTING SCHEDULE HAS BEEN CHANGED. YOU–
SILENCE, SNOT-WORM! OUR MOM WAS GOING TO WATCH FIGHT. NOW SHE MISS IT. THAT MAKE US ANGRY!
US ADVISE NO ONE TO MAKE US ANGRY...
NOT YOU! NOT KING CRUNCH! NOT NOBODY!

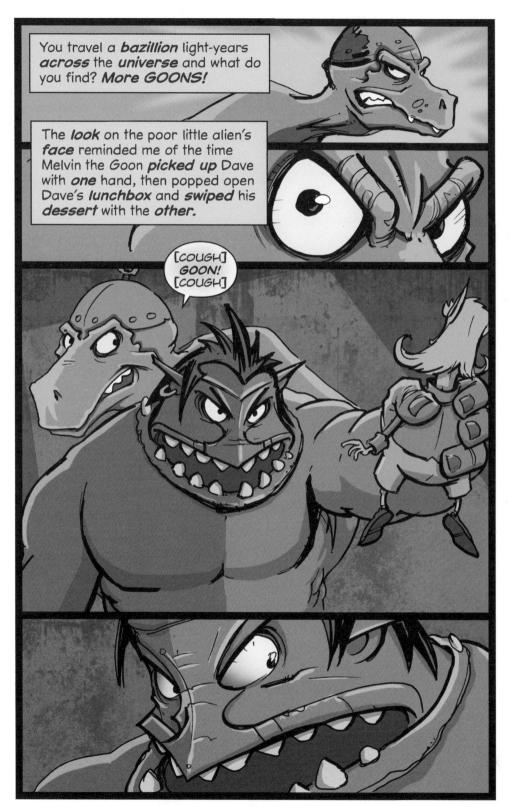

You travel a *bazillion* light-years *across* the *universe* and what do you find? *More GOONS!*

The *look* on the poor little alien's *face* reminded me of the time Melvin the Goon *picked up* Dave with *one* hand, then popped open Dave's *lunchbox* and *swiped* his *dessert* with the *other*.

[COUGH] GOON! [COUGH]

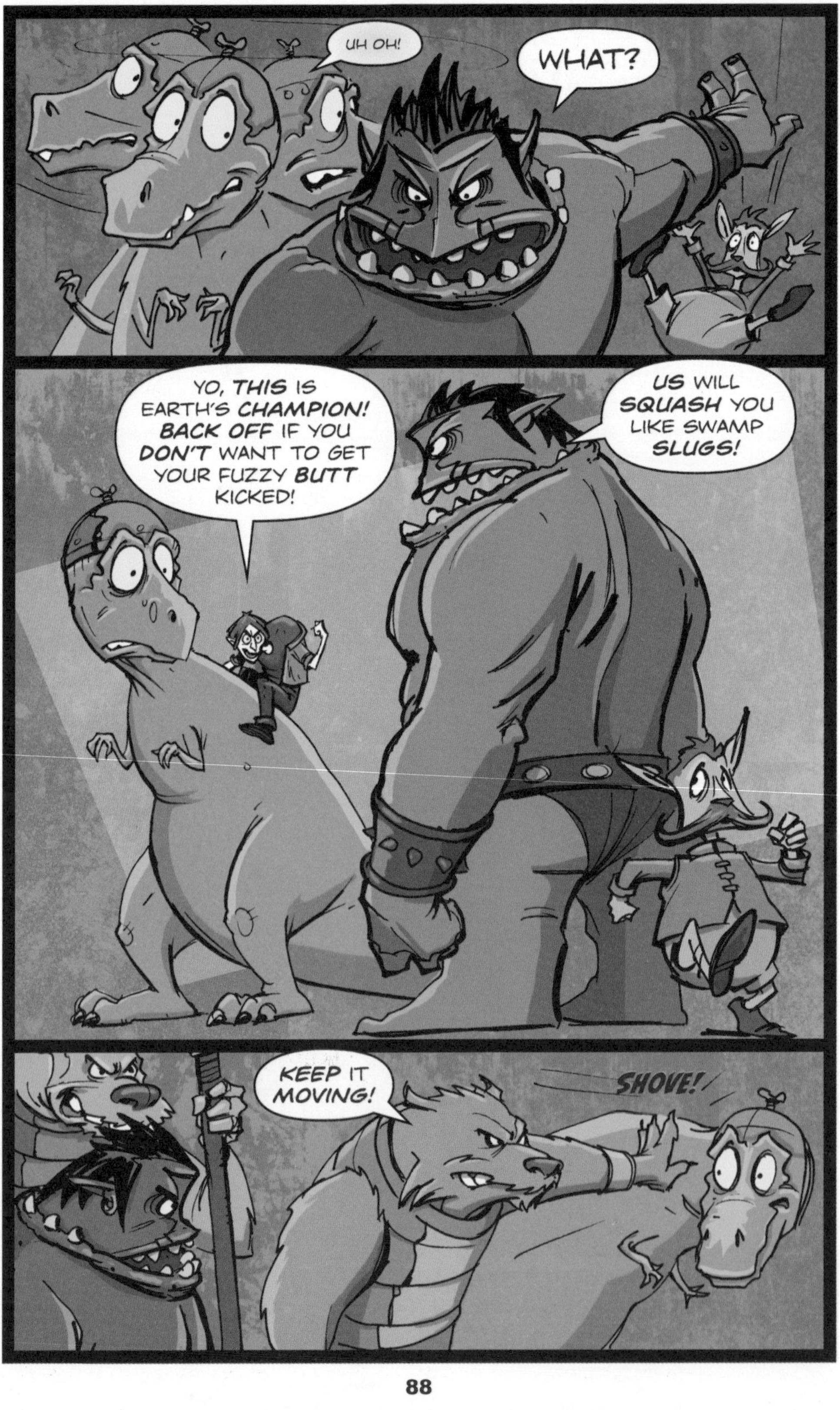
UH OH!
WHAT?
YO, THIS IS EARTH'S CHAMPION! BACK OFF IF YOU DON'T WANT TO GET YOUR FUZZY BUTT KICKED!
US WILL SQUASH YOU LIKE SWAMP SLUGS!
KEEP IT MOVING!
SHOVE!

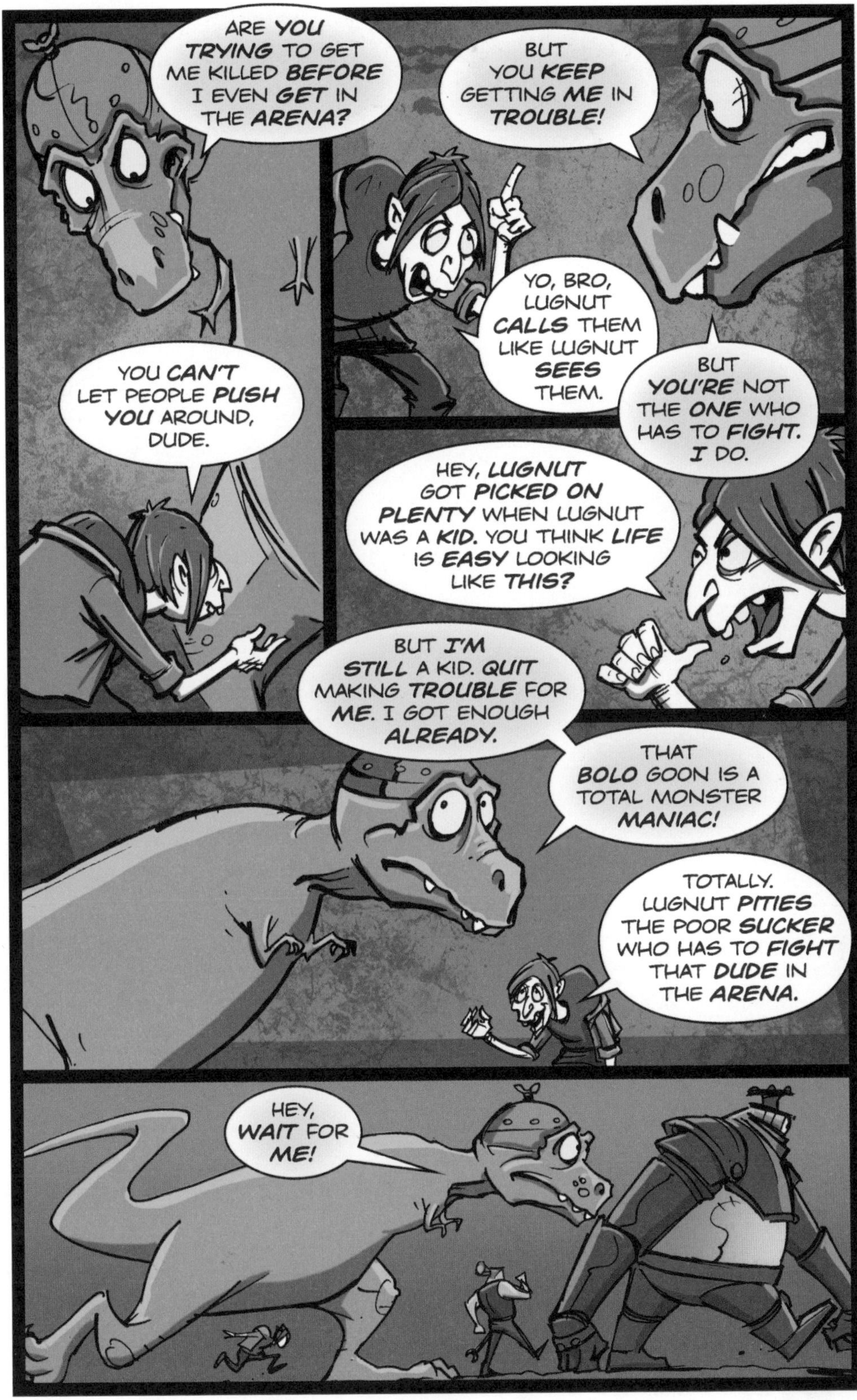
ARE YOU TRYING TO GET ME KILLED BEFORE I EVEN GET IN THE ARENA?
BUT YOU KEEP GETTING ME IN TROUBLE!
YO, BRO, LUGNUT CALLS THEM LIKE LUGNUT SEES THEM.
YOU CAN'T LET PEOPLE PUSH YOU AROUND, DUDE.
BUT YOU'RE NOT THE ONE WHO HAS TO FIGHT. I DO.
HEY, LUGNUT GOT PICKED ON PLENTY WHEN LUGNUT WAS A KID. YOU THINK LIFE IS EASY LOOKING LIKE THIS?
BUT I'M STILL A KID. QUIT MAKING TROUBLE FOR ME. I GOT ENOUGH ALREADY.
THAT BOLO GOON IS A TOTAL MONSTER MANIAC!
TOTALLY. LUGNUT PITIES THE POOR SUCKER WHO HAS TO FIGHT THAT DUDE IN THE ARENA.
HEY, WAIT FOR ME!

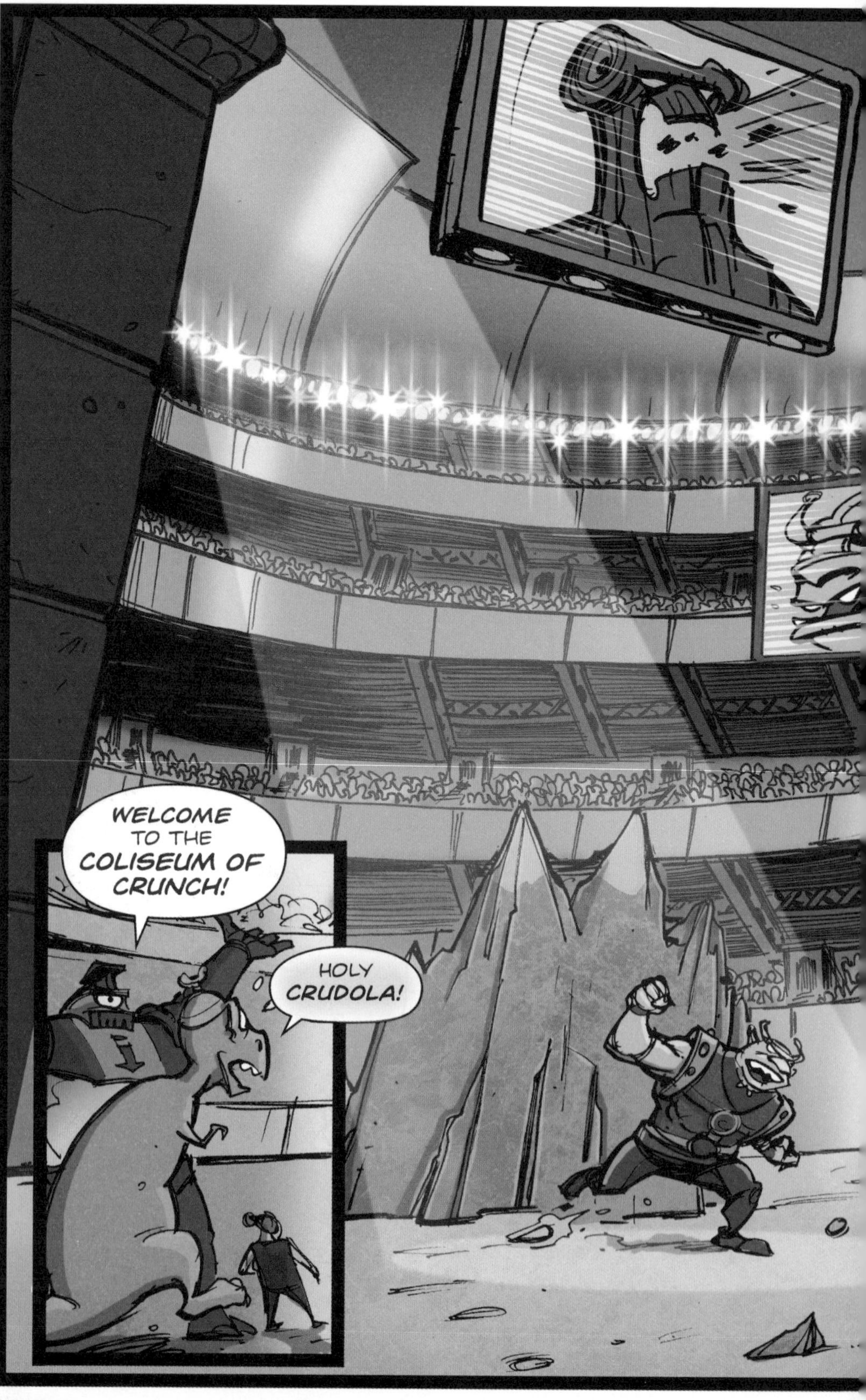
WELCOME TO THE COLISEUM OF CRUNCH!
HOLY CRUDOLA!

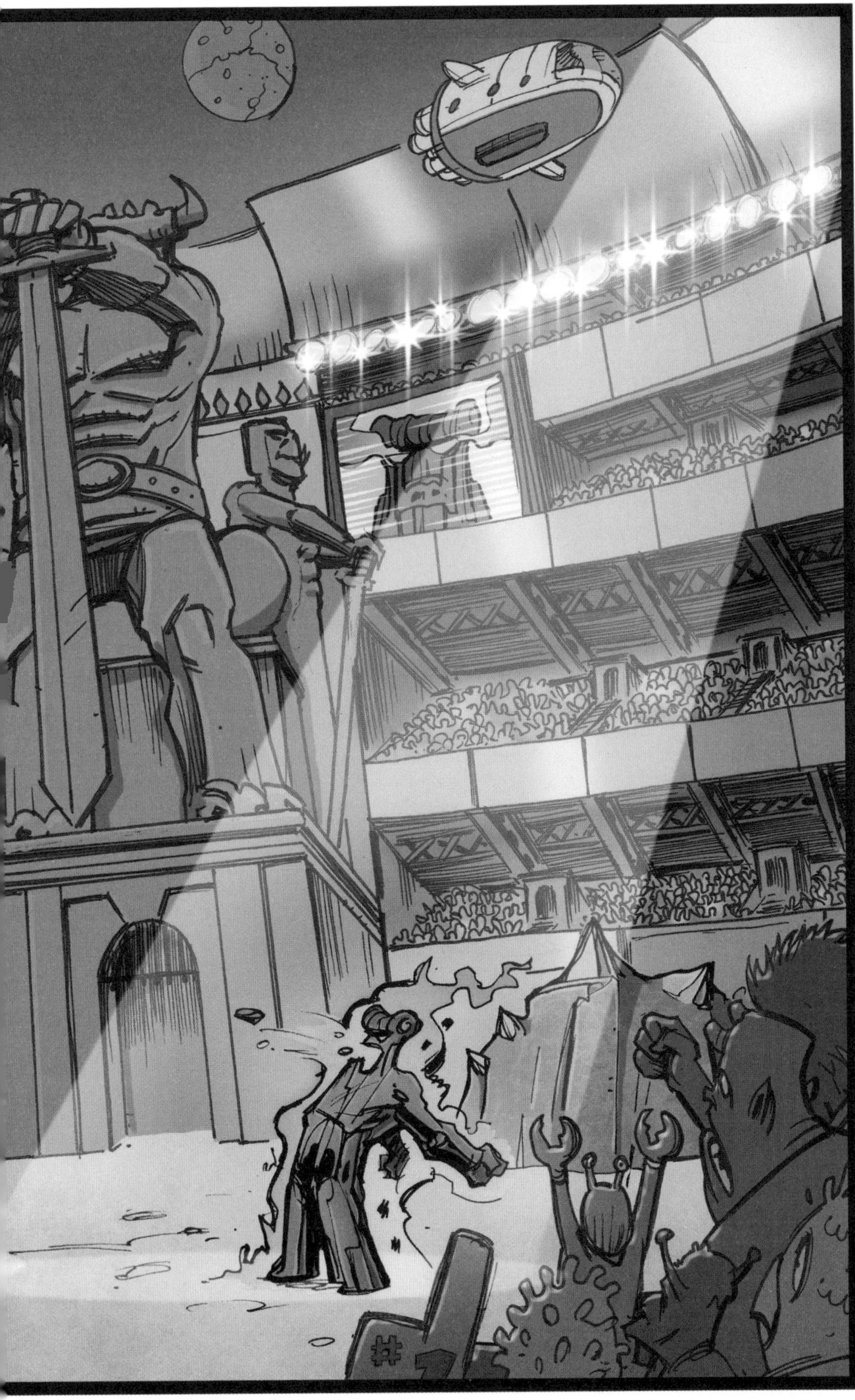

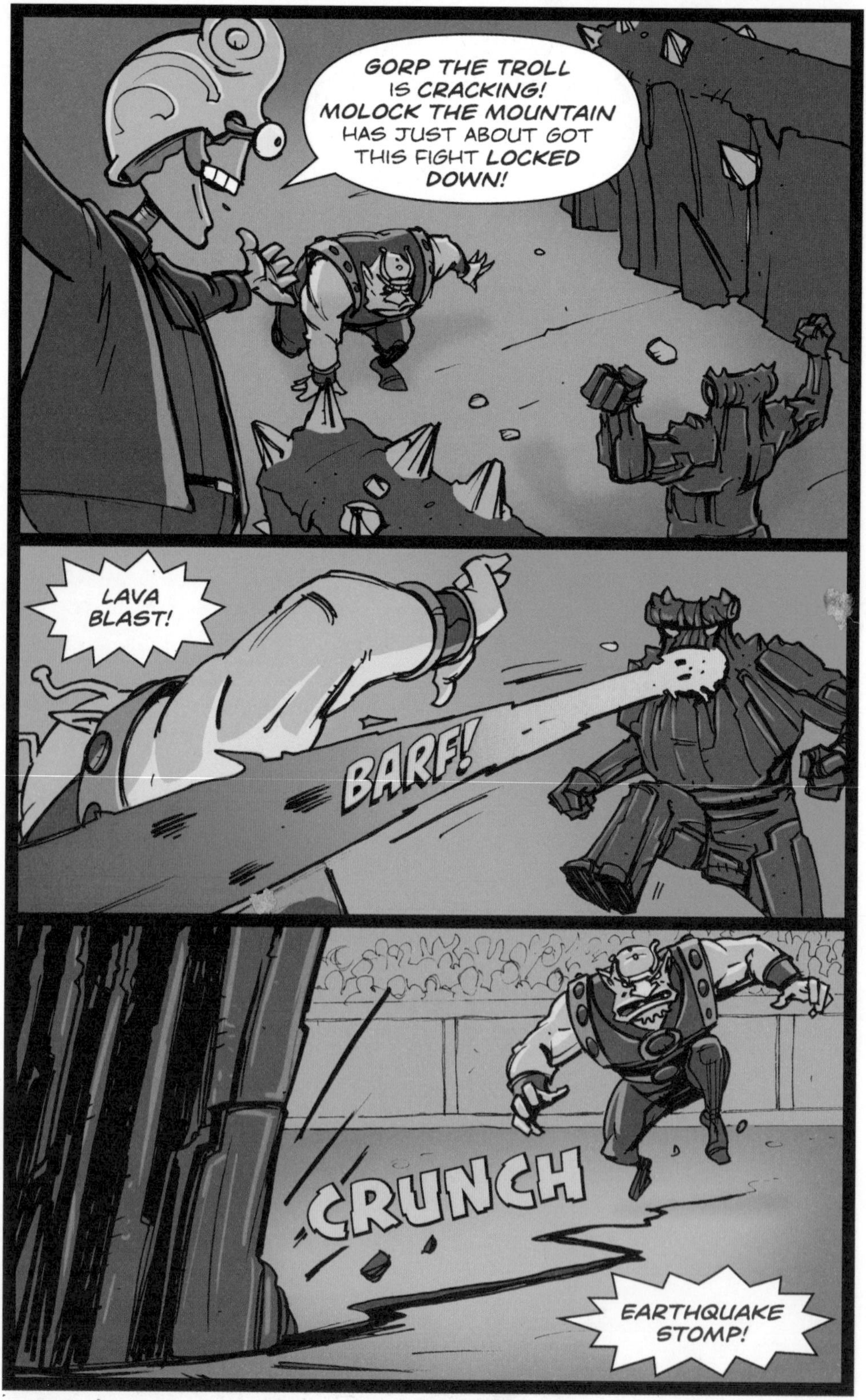
GORP THE TROLL IS CRACKING! MOLOCK THE MOUNTAIN HAS JUST ABOUT GOT THIS FIGHT LOCKED DOWN!
LAVA BLAST!
BARF!
CRUNCH
EARTHQUAKE STOMP!

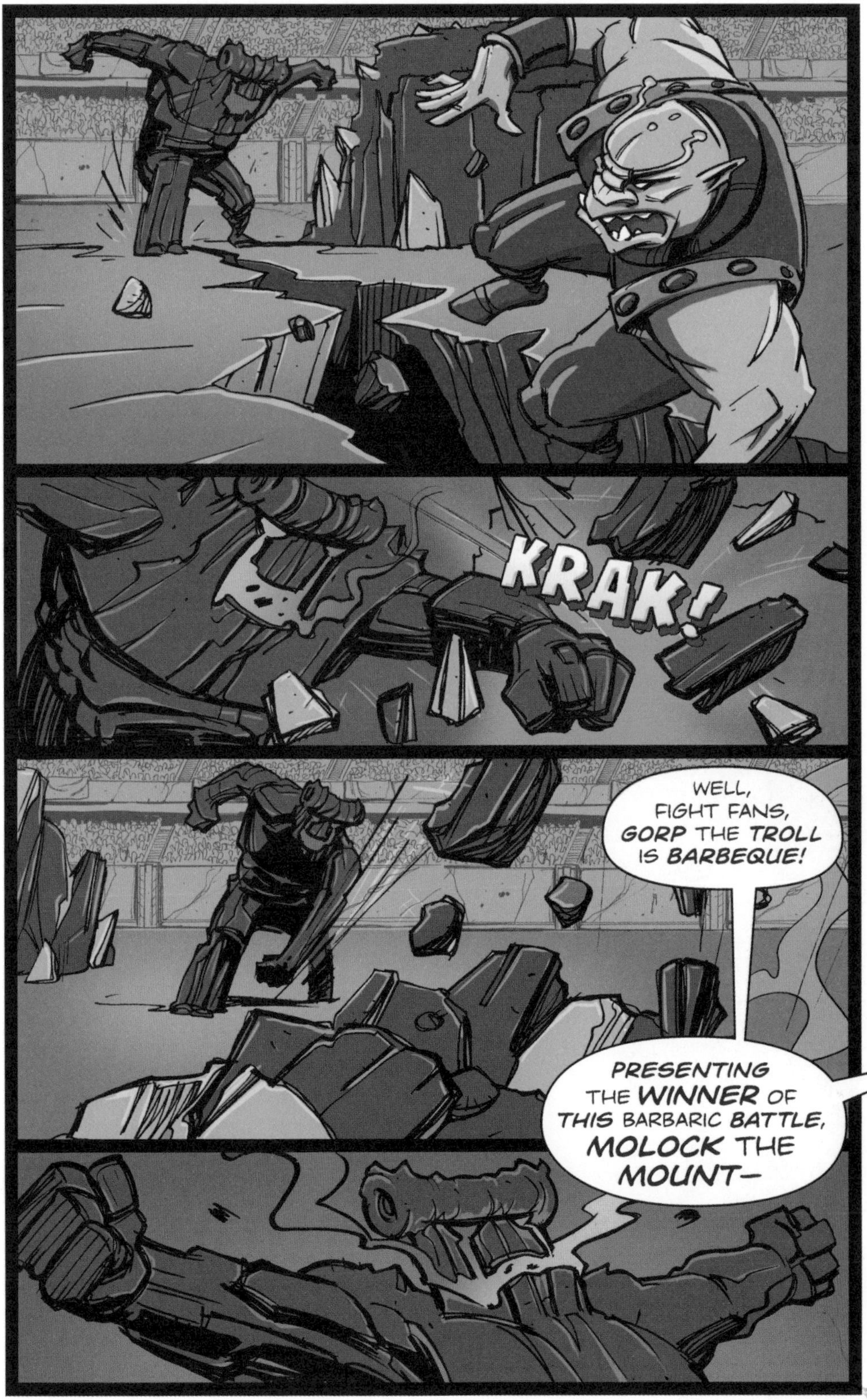
KRAK!
WELL, FIGHT FANS, GORP THE TROLL IS BARBEQUE!
PRESENTING THE WINNER OF THIS BARBARIC BATTLE, MOLOCK THE MOUNT–

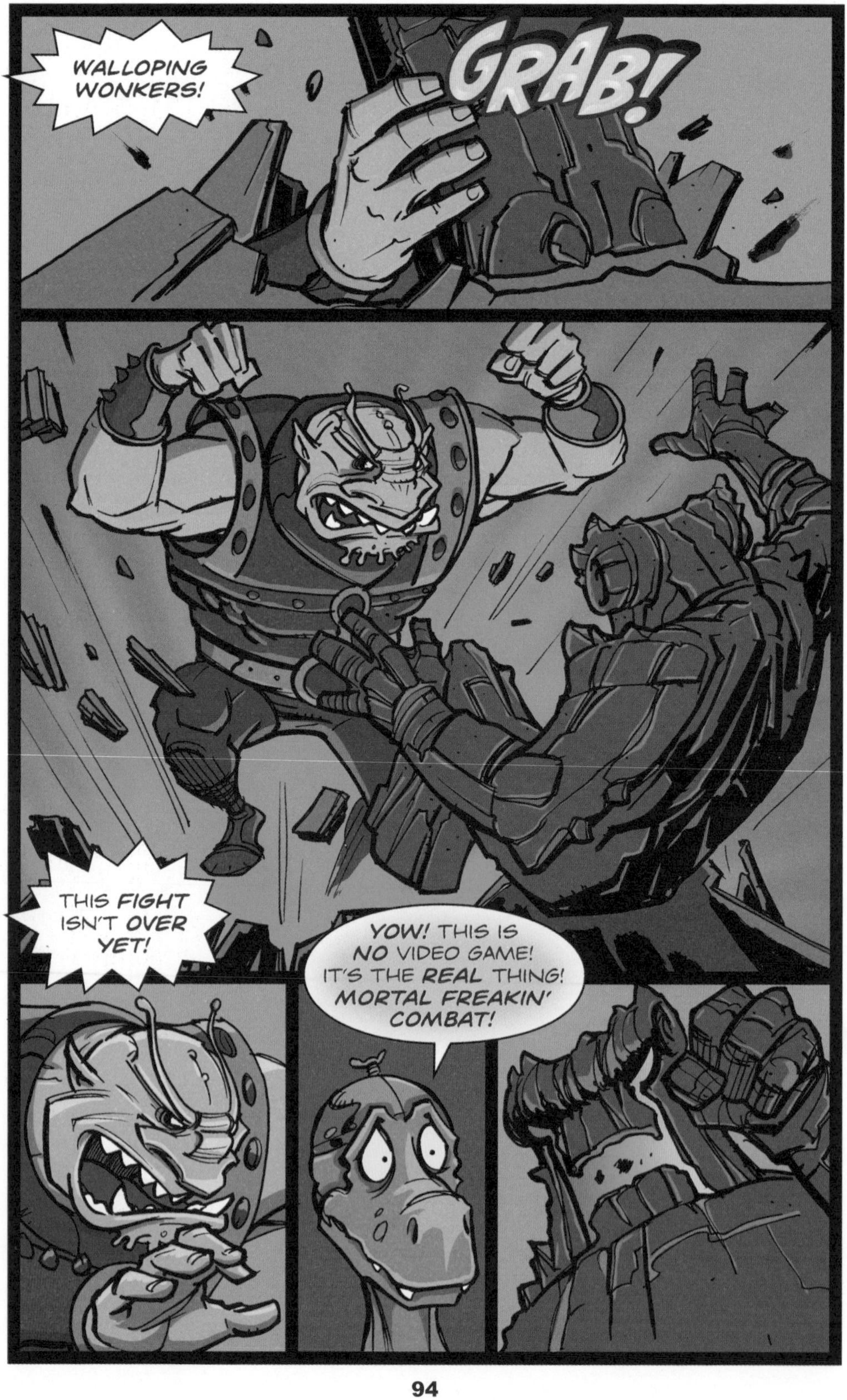
WALLOPING WONKERS!
GRAB!
THIS FIGHT ISN'T OVER YET!
YOW! THIS IS NO VIDEO GAME! IT'S THE REAL THING! MORTAL FREAKIN' COMBAT!

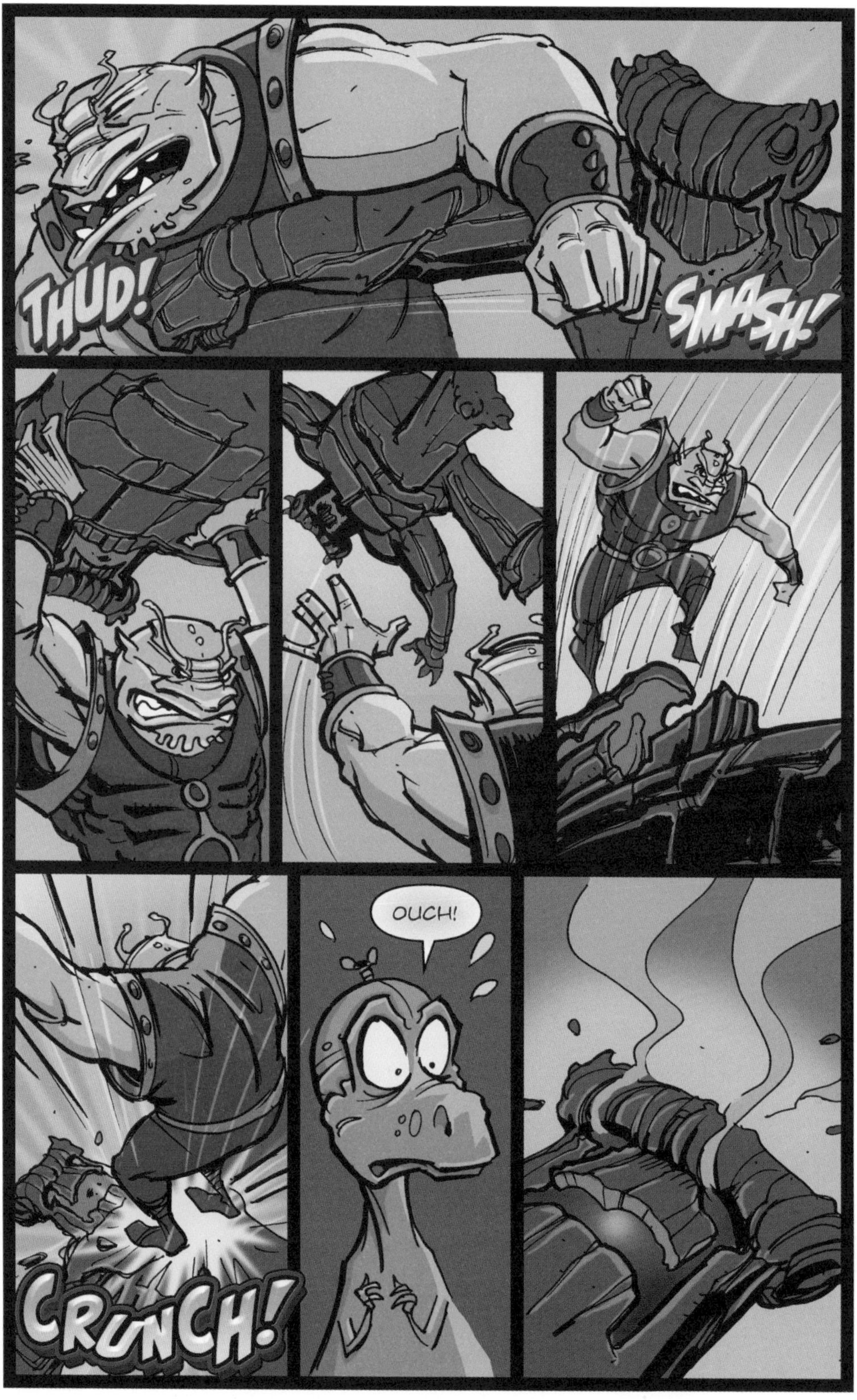
THUD!
SMASH!
CRUNCH!
OUCH!

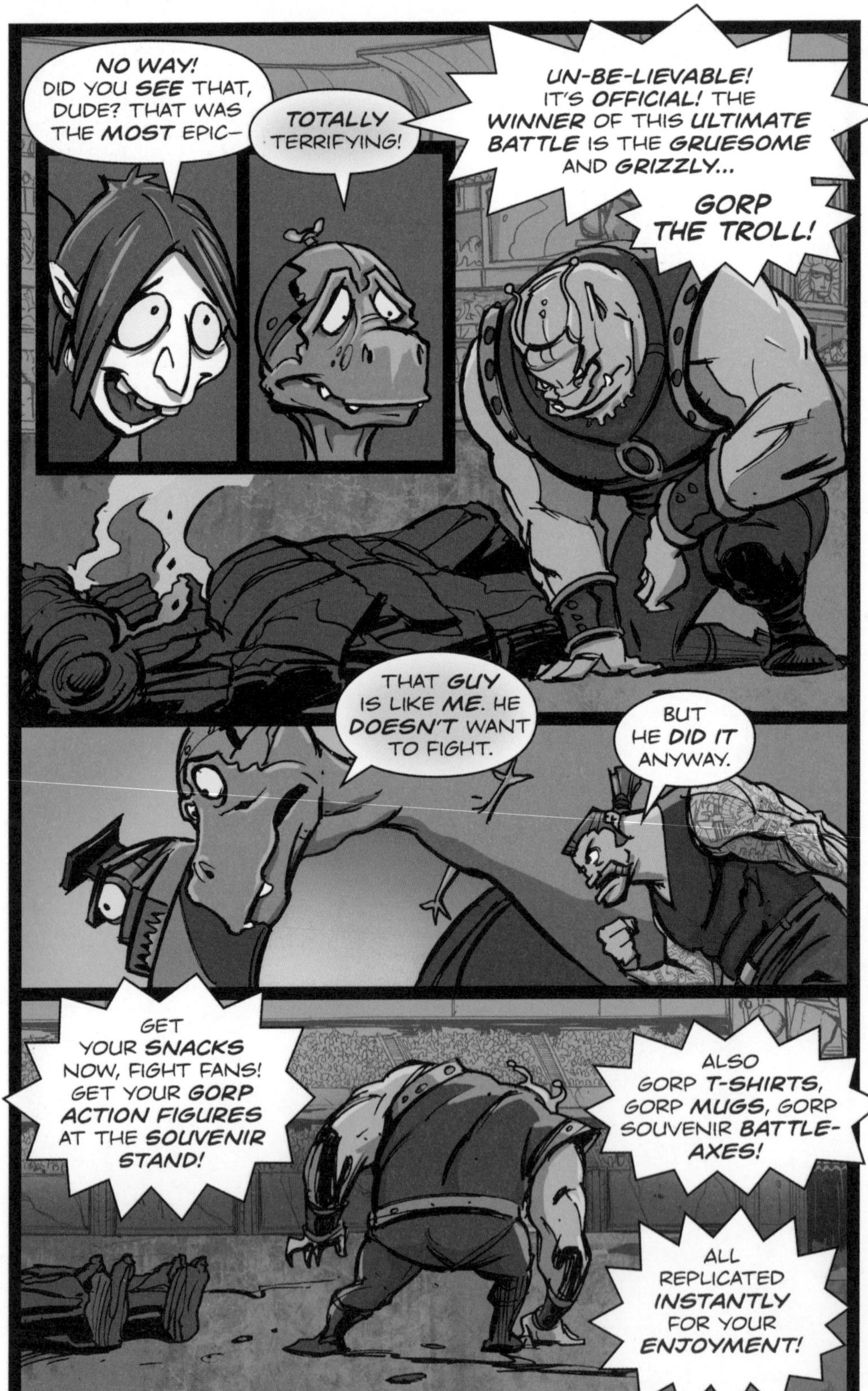
NO WAY! DID YOU SEE THAT, DUDE? THAT WAS THE MOST EPIC—
TOTALLY TERRIFYING!
UN-BE-LIEVABLE! IT'S OFFICIAL! THE WINNER OF THIS ULTIMATE BATTLE IS THE GRUESOME AND GRIZZLY...
GORP THE TROLL!
THAT GUY IS LIKE ME. HE DOESN'T WANT TO FIGHT.
BUT HE DID IT ANYWAY.
GET YOUR SNACKS NOW, FIGHT FANS! GET YOUR GORP ACTION FIGURES AT THE SOUVENIR STAND!
ALSO GORP T-SHIRTS, GORP MUGS, GORP SOUVENIR BATTLE-AXES!
ALL REPLICATED INSTANTLY FOR YOUR ENJOYMENT!

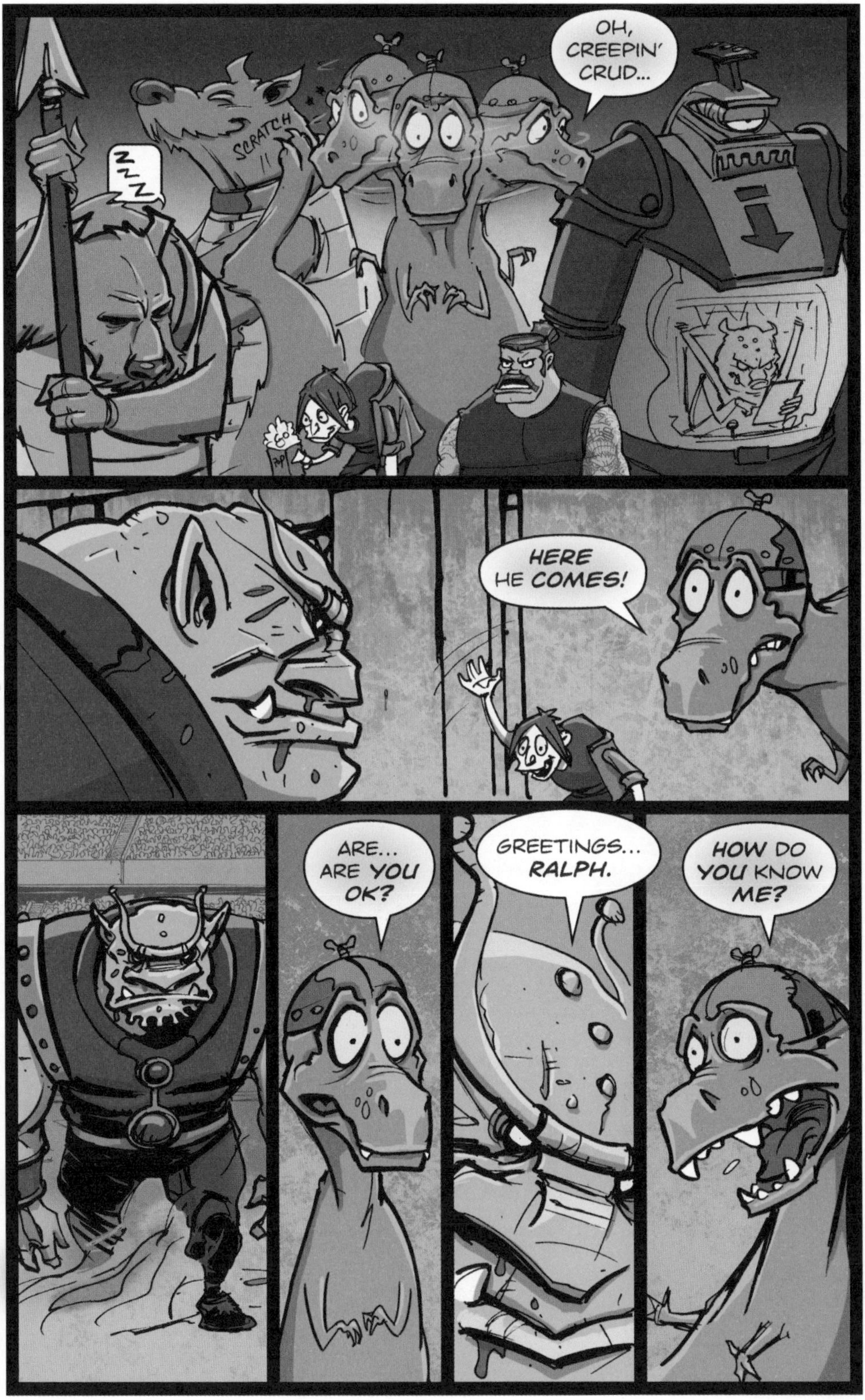

OH, CREEPIN' CRUD...
Z Z Z
SCRATCH
HERE HE COMES!
ARE... ARE YOU OK?
GREETINGS... RALPH.
HOW DO YOU KNOW ME?

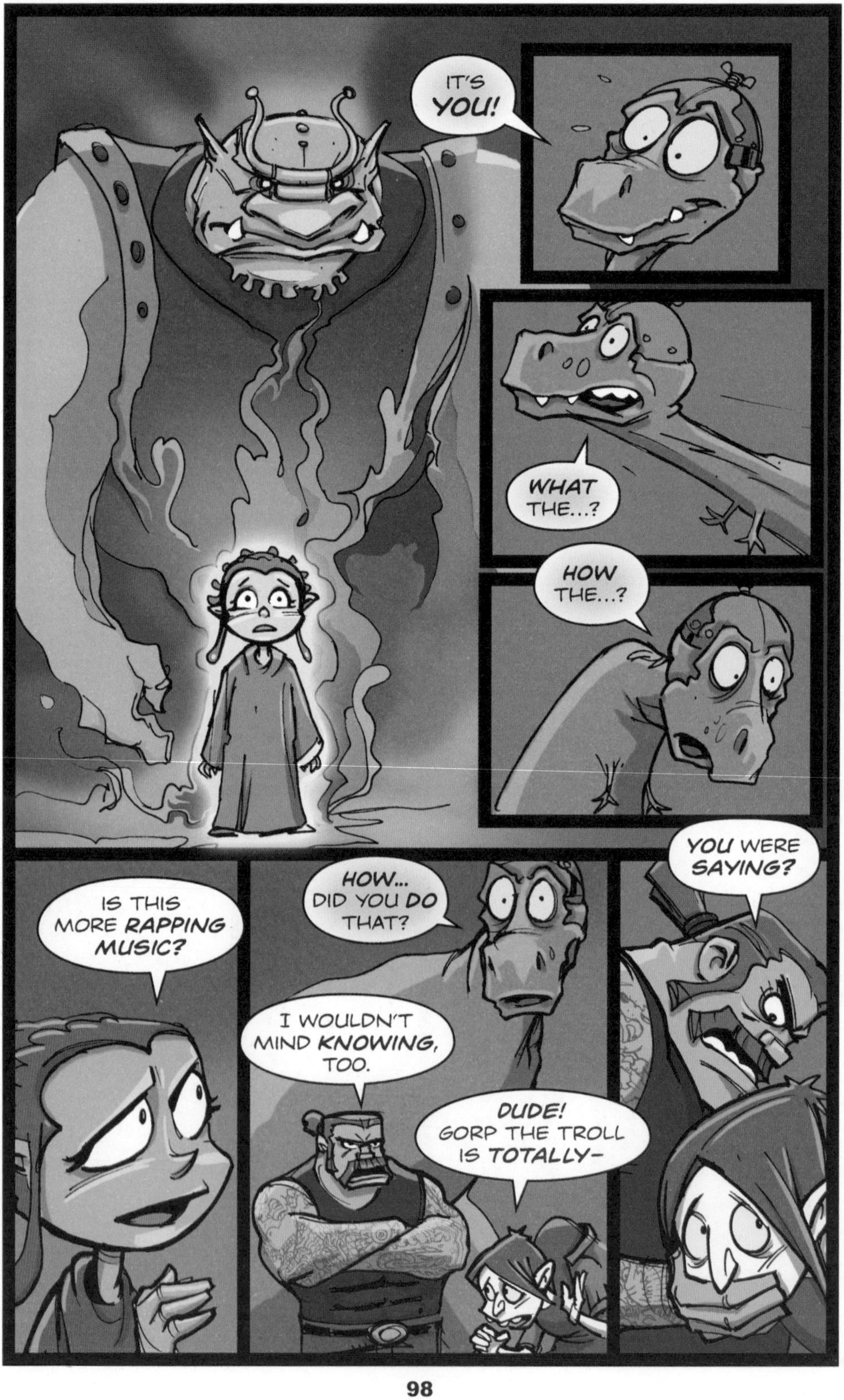
IT'S YOU!
WHAT THE...?
HOW THE...?
IS THIS MORE RAPPING MUSIC?
HOW... DID YOU DO THAT?
I WOULDN'T MIND KNOWING, TOO.
DUDE! GORP THE TROLL IS TOTALLY–
YOU WERE SAYING?

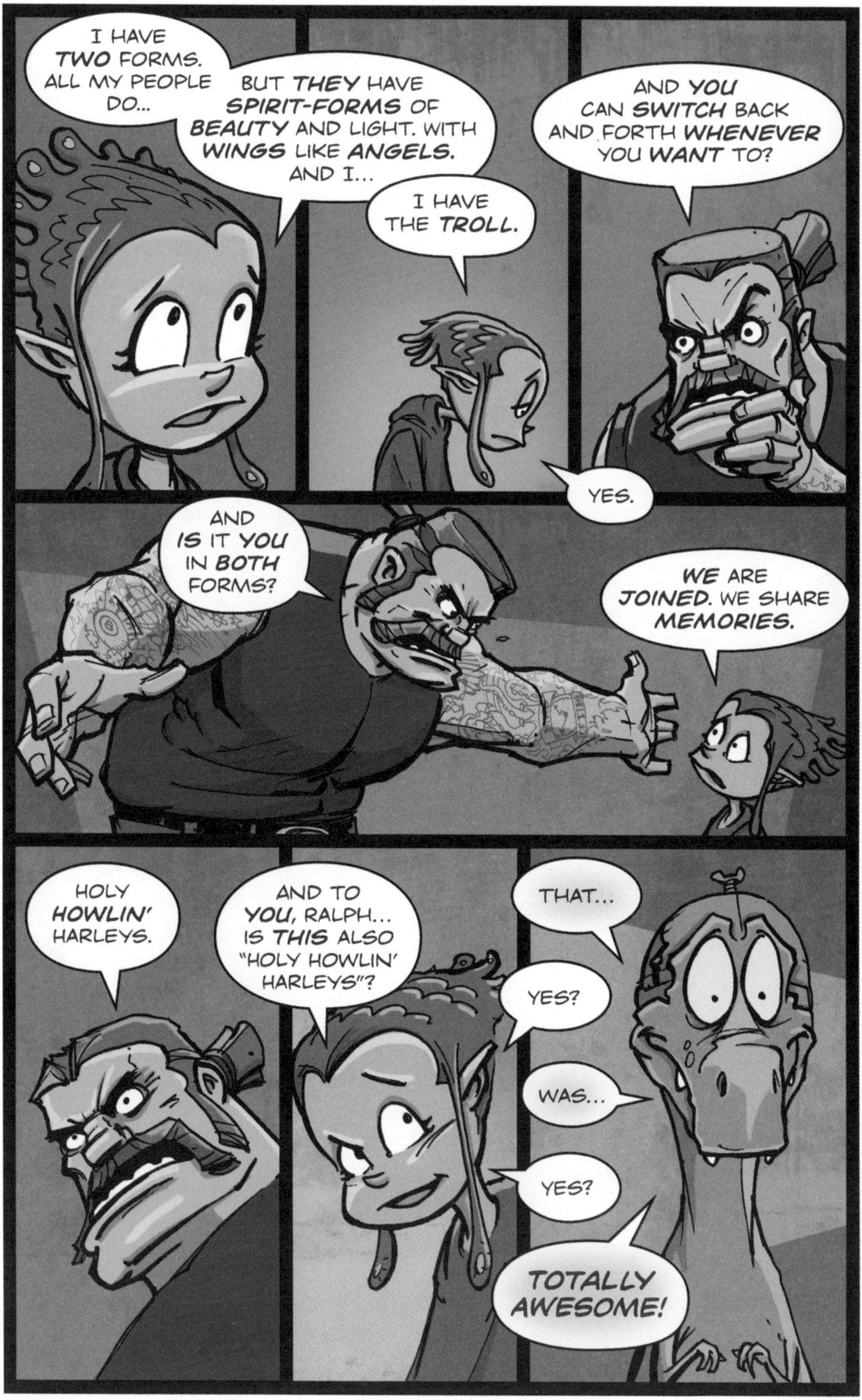
I HAVE TWO FORMS. ALL MY PEOPLE DO...
BUT THEY HAVE SPIRIT-FORMS OF BEAUTY AND LIGHT. WITH WINGS LIKE ANGELS. AND I...
I HAVE THE TROLL.
AND YOU CAN SWITCH BACK AND FORTH WHENEVER YOU WANT TO?
YES.
AND IS IT YOU IN BOTH FORMS?
WE ARE JOINED. WE SHARE MEMORIES.
HOLY HOWLIN' HARLEYS.
AND TO YOU, RALPH... IS THIS ALSO "HOLY HOWLIN' HARLEYS"?
THAT...
YES?
WAS...
YES?
TOTALLY AWESOME!

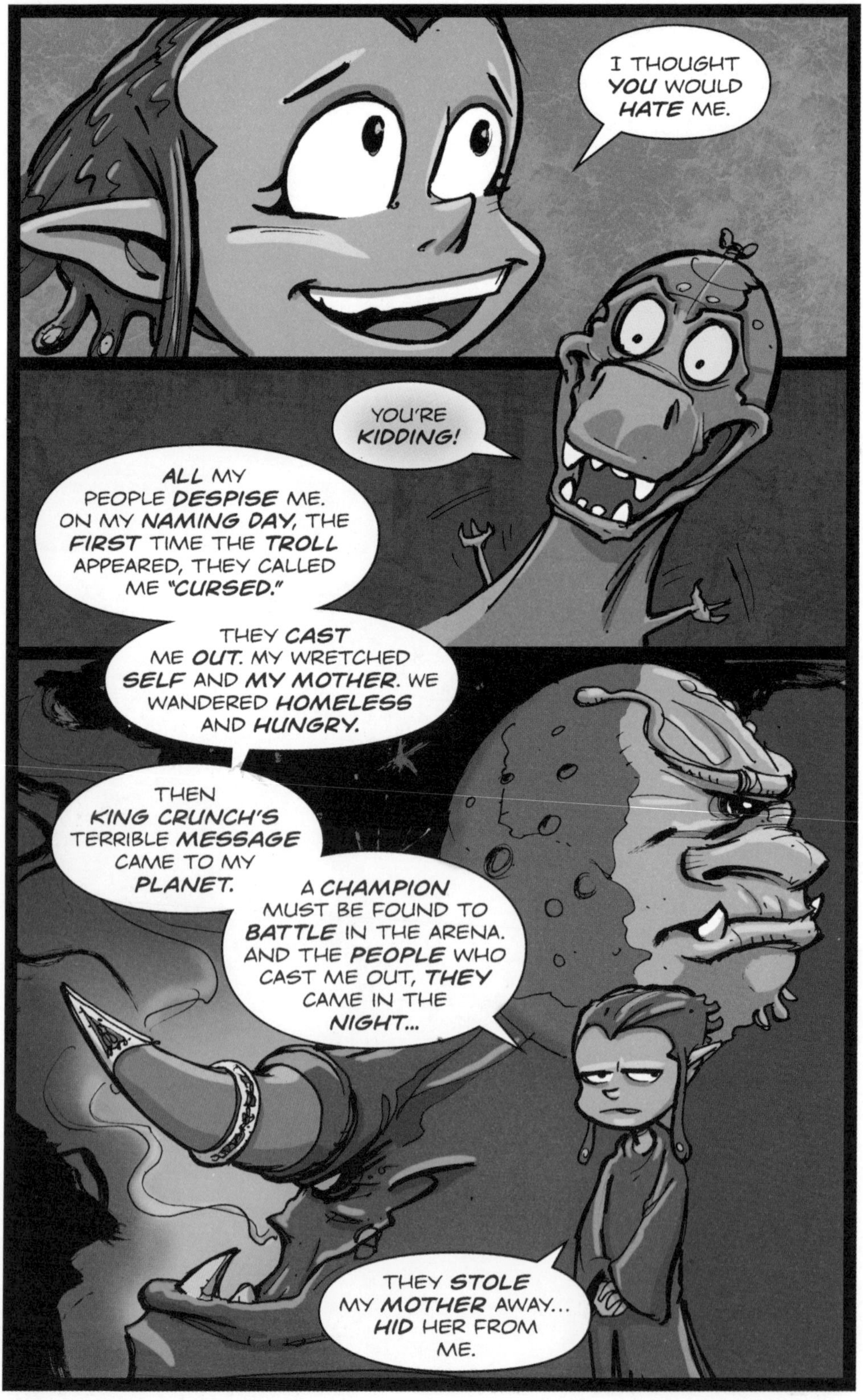
I THOUGHT YOU WOULD HATE ME.
YOU'RE KIDDING!
ALL MY PEOPLE DESPISE ME. ON MY NAMING DAY, THE FIRST TIME THE TROLL APPEARED, THEY CALLED ME "CURSED."
THEY CAST ME OUT. MY WRETCHED SELF AND MY MOTHER. WE WANDERED HOMELESS AND HUNGRY.
THEN KING CRUNCH'S TERRIBLE MESSAGE CAME TO MY PLANET.
A CHAMPION MUST BE FOUND TO BATTLE IN THE ARENA. AND THE PEOPLE WHO CAST ME OUT, THEY CAME IN THE NIGHT...
THEY STOLE MY MOTHER AWAY... HID HER FROM ME.

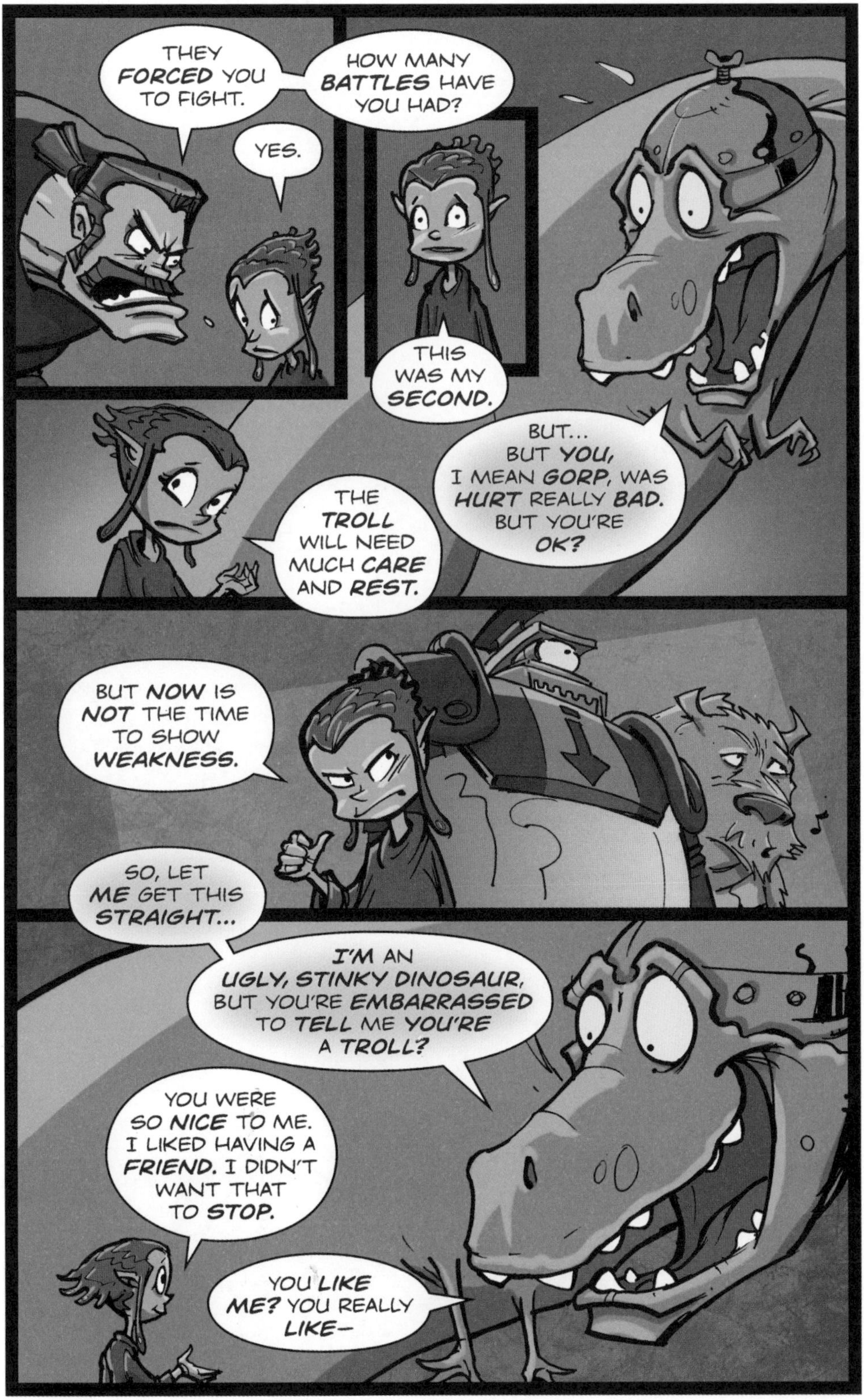
THEY FORCED YOU TO FIGHT.
HOW MANY BATTLES HAVE YOU HAD?
YES.
THIS WAS MY SECOND.
BUT... BUT YOU, I MEAN GORP, WAS HURT REALLY BAD. BUT YOU'RE OK?
THE TROLL WILL NEED MUCH CARE AND REST.
BUT NOW IS NOT THE TIME TO SHOW WEAKNESS.
SO, LET ME GET THIS STRAIGHT...
I'M AN UGLY, STINKY DINOSAUR, BUT YOU'RE EMBARRASSED TO TELL ME YOU'RE A TROLL?
YOU WERE SO NICE TO ME. I LIKED HAVING A FRIEND. I DIDN'T WANT THAT TO STOP.
YOU LIKE ME? YOU REALLY LIKE–

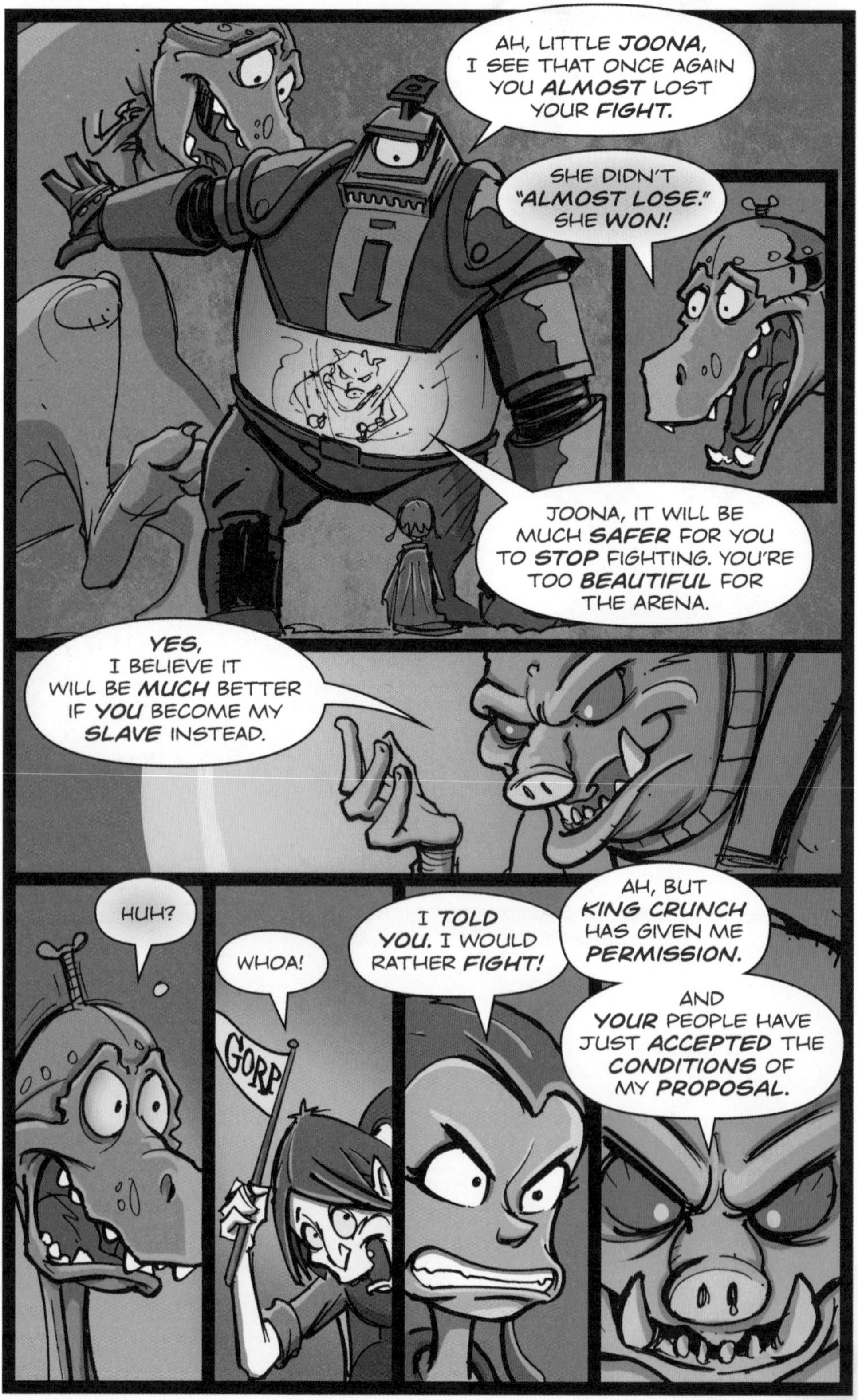
AH, LITTLE JOONA, I SEE THAT ONCE AGAIN YOU ALMOST LOST YOUR FIGHT.
SHE DIDN'T "ALMOST LOSE." SHE WON!
JOONA, IT WILL BE MUCH SAFER FOR YOU TO STOP FIGHTING. YOU'RE TOO BEAUTIFUL FOR THE ARENA.
YES, I BELIEVE IT WILL BE MUCH BETTER IF YOU BECOME MY SLAVE INSTEAD.
HUH?
WHOA!
GORP
I TOLD YOU. I WOULD RATHER FIGHT!
AH, BUT KING CRUNCH HAS GIVEN ME PERMISSION.
AND YOUR PEOPLE HAVE JUST ACCEPTED THE CONDITIONS OF MY PROPOSAL.

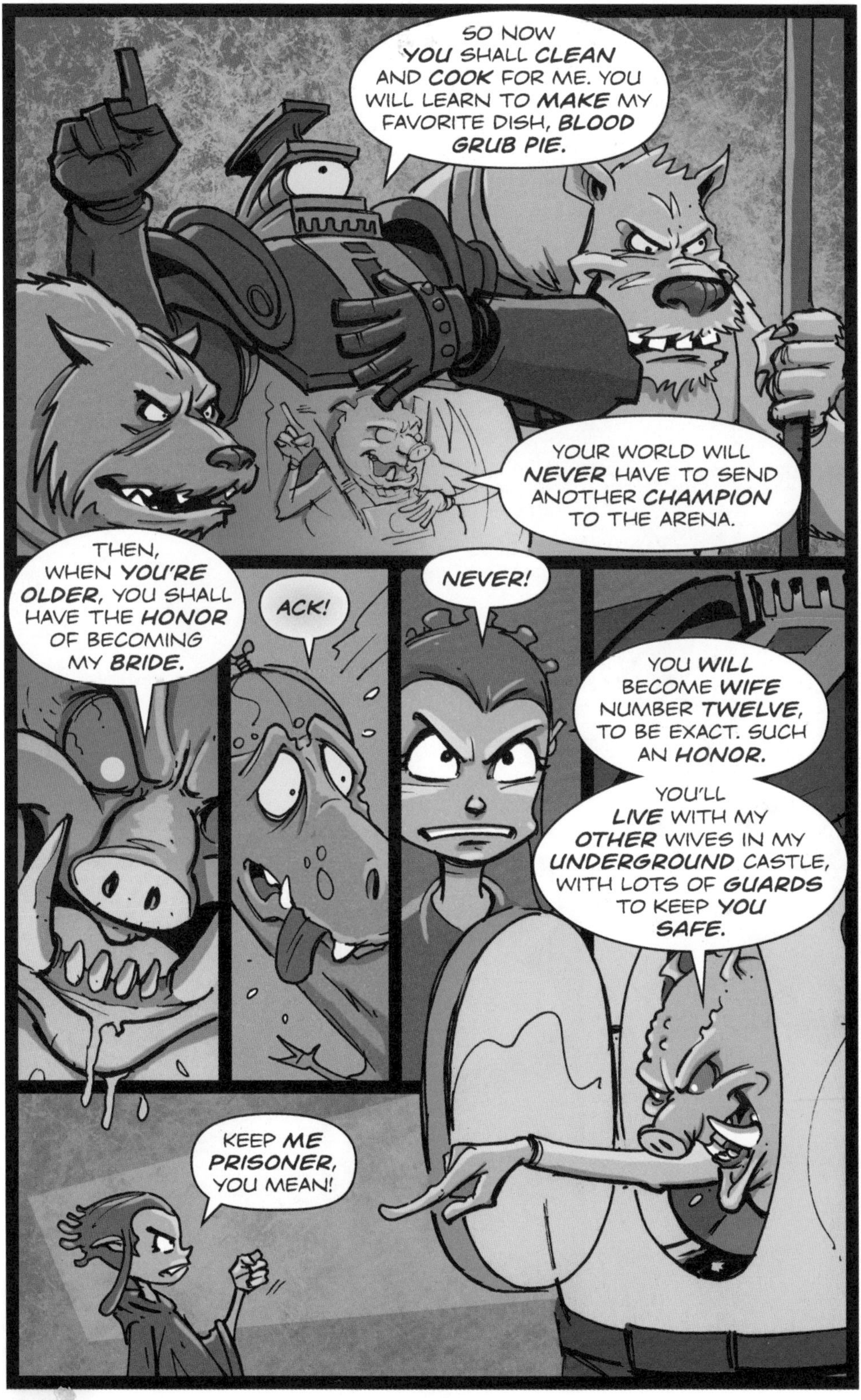

SO NOW YOU SHALL CLEAN AND COOK FOR ME. YOU WILL LEARN TO MAKE MY FAVORITE DISH, BLOOD GRUB PIE.
YOUR WORLD WILL NEVER HAVE TO SEND ANOTHER CHAMPION TO THE ARENA.
THEN, WHEN YOU'RE OLDER, YOU SHALL HAVE THE HONOR OF BECOMING MY BRIDE.
ACK!
NEVER!
YOU WILL BECOME WIFE NUMBER TWELVE, TO BE EXACT. SUCH AN HONOR.
YOU'LL LIVE WITH MY OTHER WIVES IN MY UNDERGROUND CASTLE, WITH LOTS OF GUARDS TO KEEP YOU SAFE.
KEEP ME PRISONER, YOU MEAN!

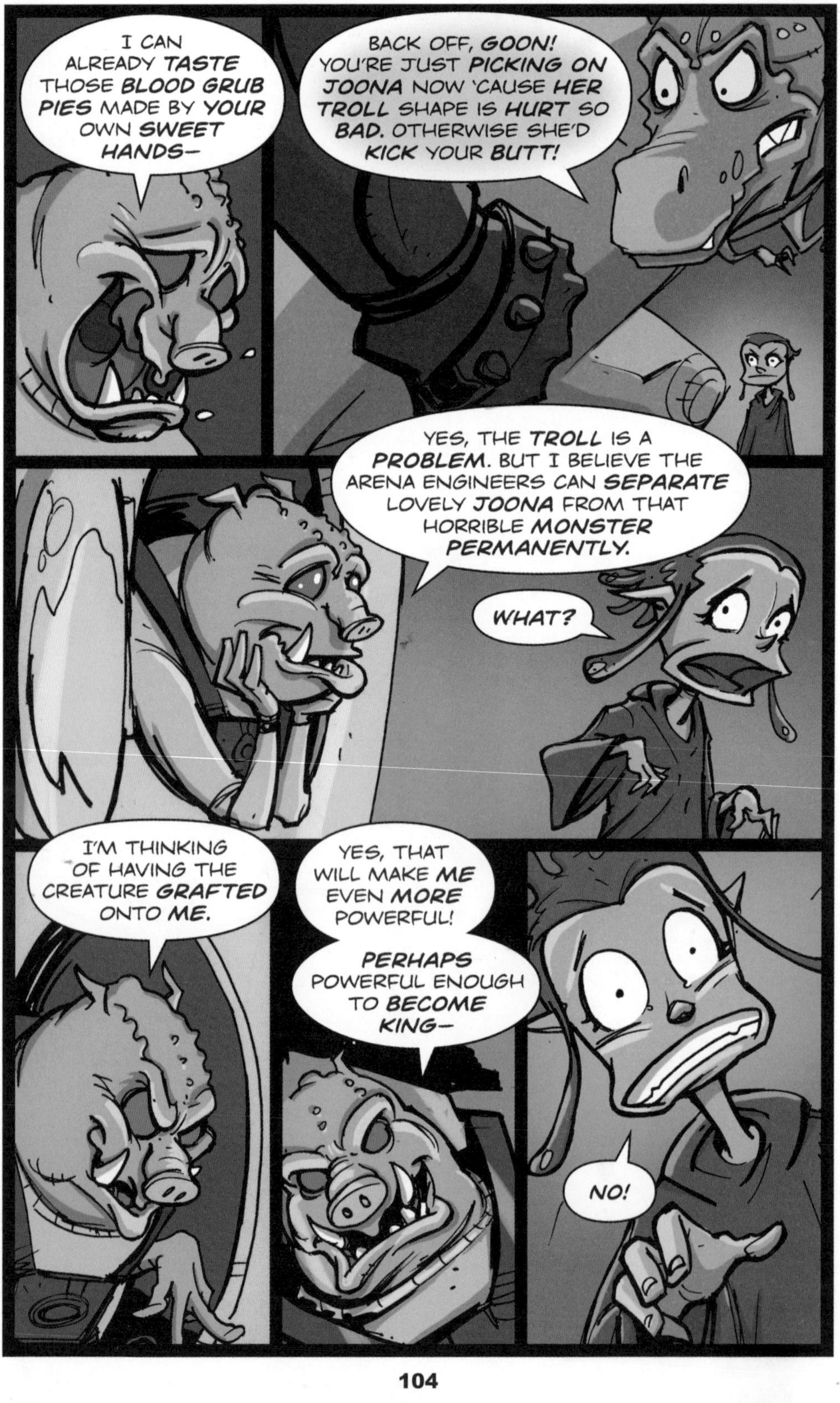
I CAN ALREADY TASTE THOSE BLOOD GRUB PIES MADE BY YOUR OWN SWEET HANDS–
BACK OFF, GOON! YOU'RE JUST PICKING ON JOONA NOW 'CAUSE HER TROLL SHAPE IS HURT SO BAD. OTHERWISE SHE'D KICK YOUR BUTT!
YES, THE TROLL IS A PROBLEM. BUT I BELIEVE THE ARENA ENGINEERS CAN SEPARATE LOVELY JOONA FROM THAT HORRIBLE MONSTER PERMANENTLY.
WHAT?
I'M THINKING OF HAVING THE CREATURE GRAFTED ONTO ME.
YES, THAT WILL MAKE ME EVEN MORE POWERFUL!
PERHAPS POWERFUL ENOUGH TO BECOME KING–
NO!

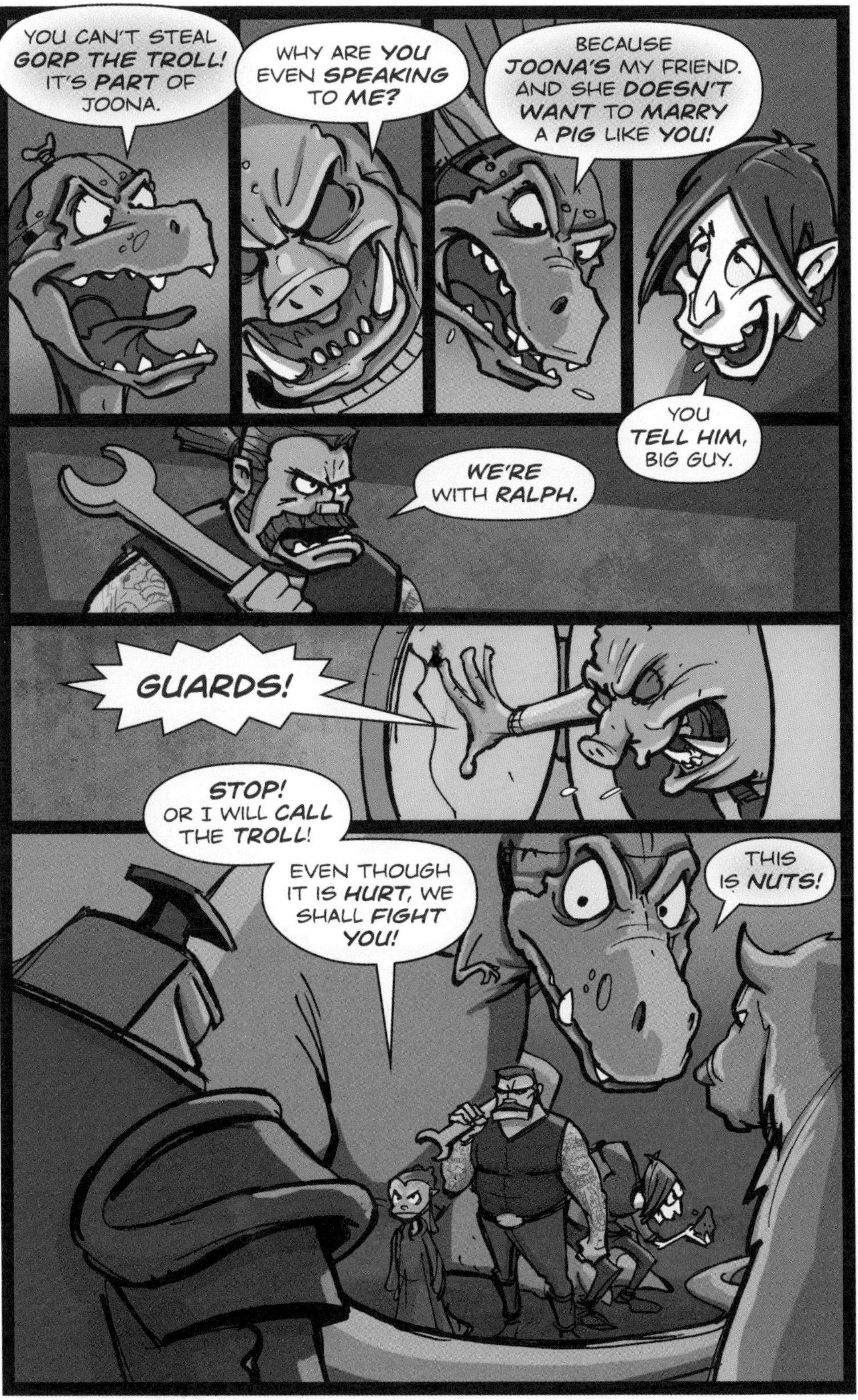
YOU CAN'T STEAL GORP THE TROLL! IT'S PART OF JOONA.
WHY ARE YOU EVEN SPEAKING TO ME?
BECAUSE JOONA'S MY FRIEND. AND SHE DOESN'T WANT TO MARRY A PIG LIKE YOU!
YOU TELL HIM, BIG GUY.
WE'RE WITH RALPH.
GUARDS!
STOP! OR I WILL CALL THE TROLL!
EVEN THOUGH IT IS HURT, WE SHALL FIGHT YOU!
THIS IS NUTS!

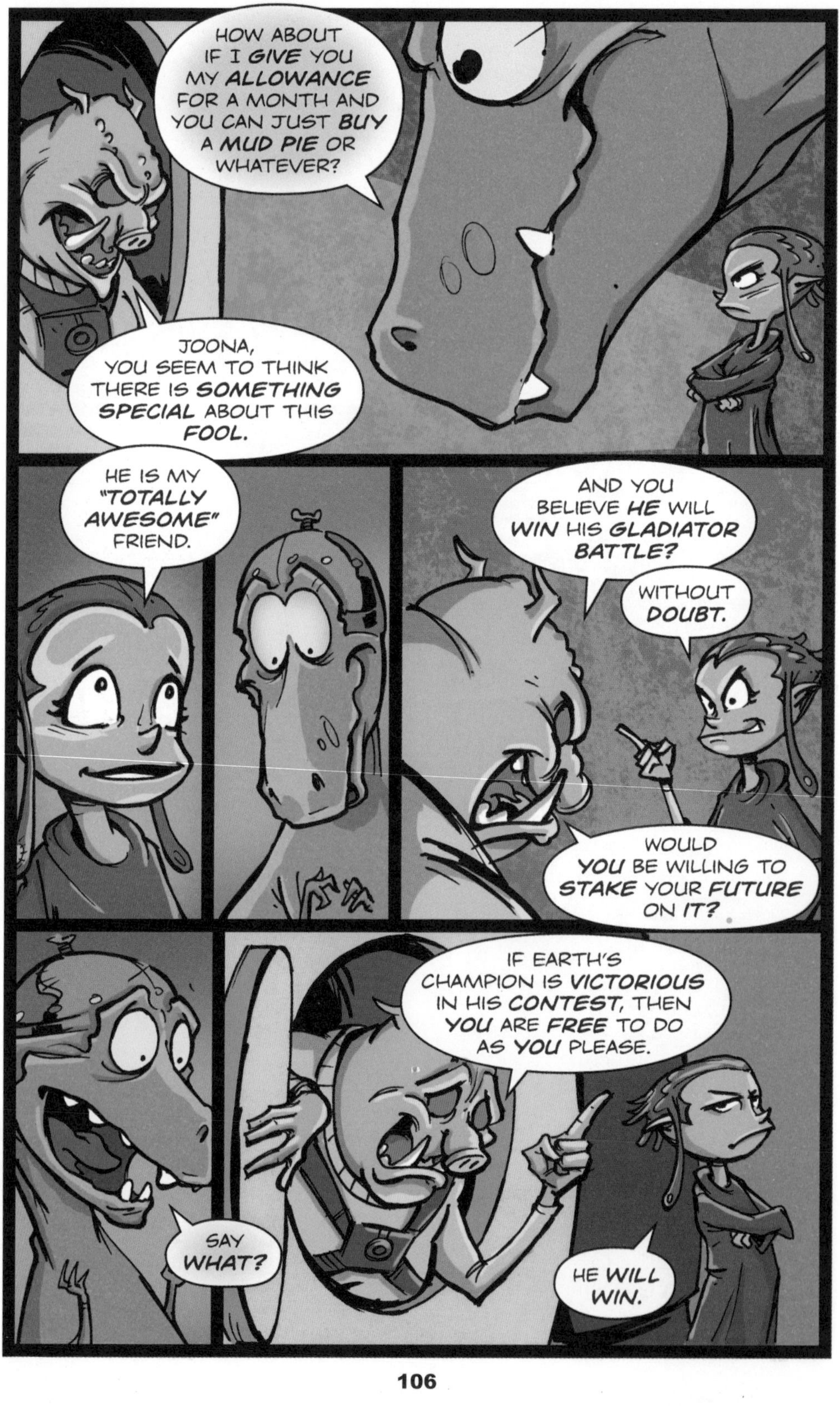
HOW ABOUT IF I GIVE YOU MY ALLOWANCE FOR A MONTH AND YOU CAN JUST BUY A MUD PIE OR WHATEVER?
JOONA, YOU SEEM TO THINK THERE IS SOMETHING SPECIAL ABOUT THIS FOOL.
HE IS MY "TOTALLY AWESOME" FRIEND.
AND YOU BELIEVE HE WILL WIN HIS GLADIATOR BATTLE?
WITHOUT DOUBT.
WOULD YOU BE WILLING TO STAKE YOUR FUTURE ON IT?
SAY WHAT?
IF EARTH'S CHAMPION IS VICTORIOUS IN HIS CONTEST, THEN YOU ARE FREE TO DO AS YOU PLEASE.
HE WILL WIN.

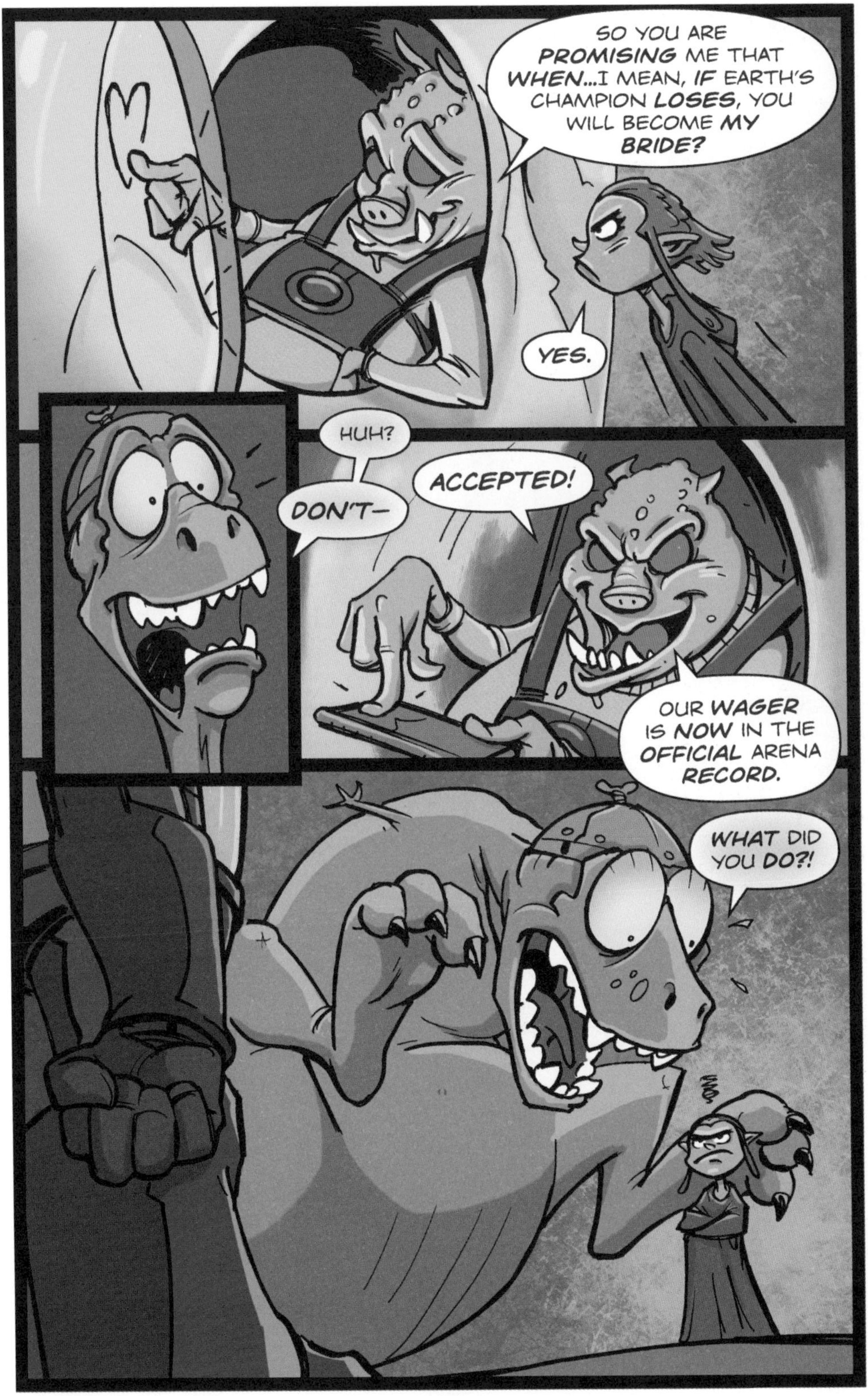
SO YOU ARE PROMISING ME THAT WHEN...I MEAN, IF EARTH'S CHAMPION LOSES, YOU WILL BECOME MY BRIDE?
YES.
HUH?
DON'T-
ACCEPTED!
OUR WAGER IS NOW IN THE OFFICIAL ARENA RECORD.
WHAT DID YOU DO?!

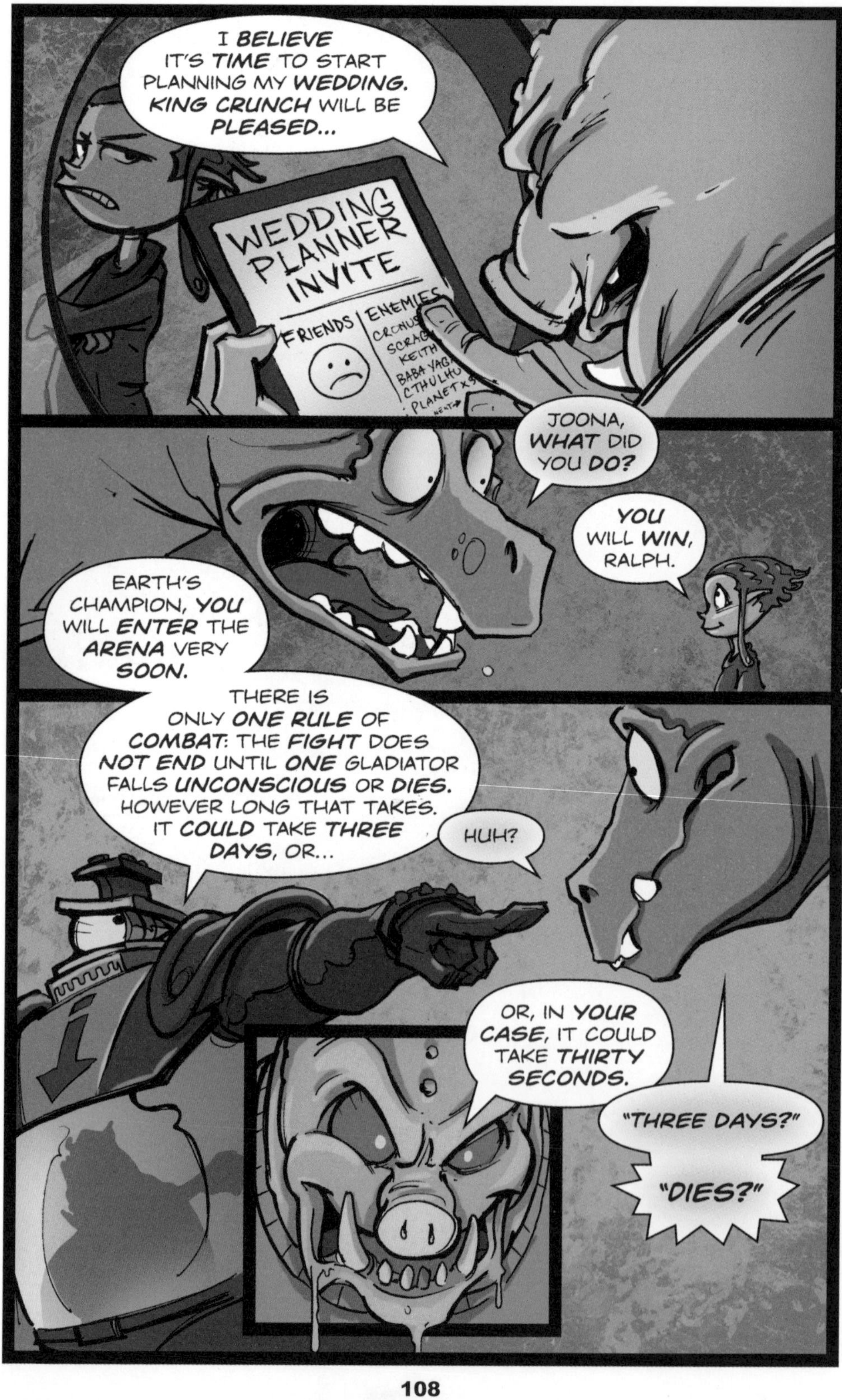
I BELIEVE IT'S TIME TO START PLANNING MY WEDDING. KING CRUNCH WILL BE PLEASED...
WEDDING PLANNER INVITE
FRIENDS
ENEMIES
CRONUS
KEITH
JOONA, WHAT DID YOU DO?
YOU WILL WIN, RALPH.
EARTH'S CHAMPION, YOU WILL ENTER THE ARENA VERY SOON.
THERE IS ONLY ONE RULE OF COMBAT: THE FIGHT DOES NOT END UNTIL ONE GLADIATOR FALLS UNCONSCIOUS OR DIES. HOWEVER LONG THAT TAKES. IT COULD TAKE THREE DAYS, OR...
HUH?
OR, IN YOUR CASE, IT COULD TAKE THIRTY SECONDS.
"THREE DAYS?"
"DIES?"

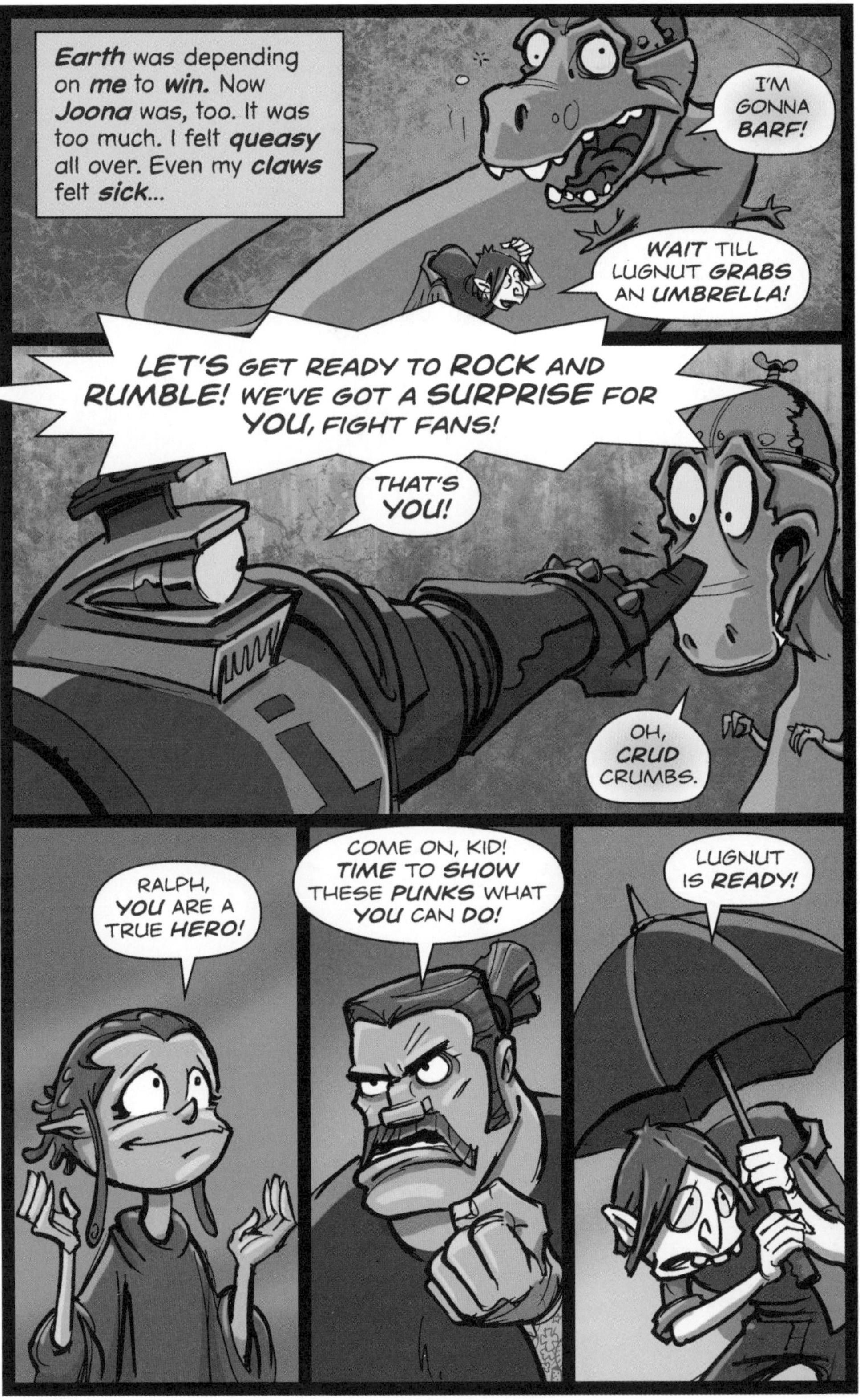
Earth was depending on me to win. Now Joona was, too. It was too much. I felt queasy all over. Even my claws felt sick...
I'M GONNA BARF!
WAIT TILL LUGNUT GRABS AN UMBRELLA!
LET'S GET READY TO ROCK AND RUMBLE! WE'VE GOT A SURPRISE FOR YOU, FIGHT FANS!
THAT'S YOU!
OH, CRUD CRUMBS.
RALPH, YOU ARE A TRUE HERO!
COME ON, KID! TIME TO SHOW THESE PUNKS WHAT YOU CAN DO!
LUGNUT IS READY!

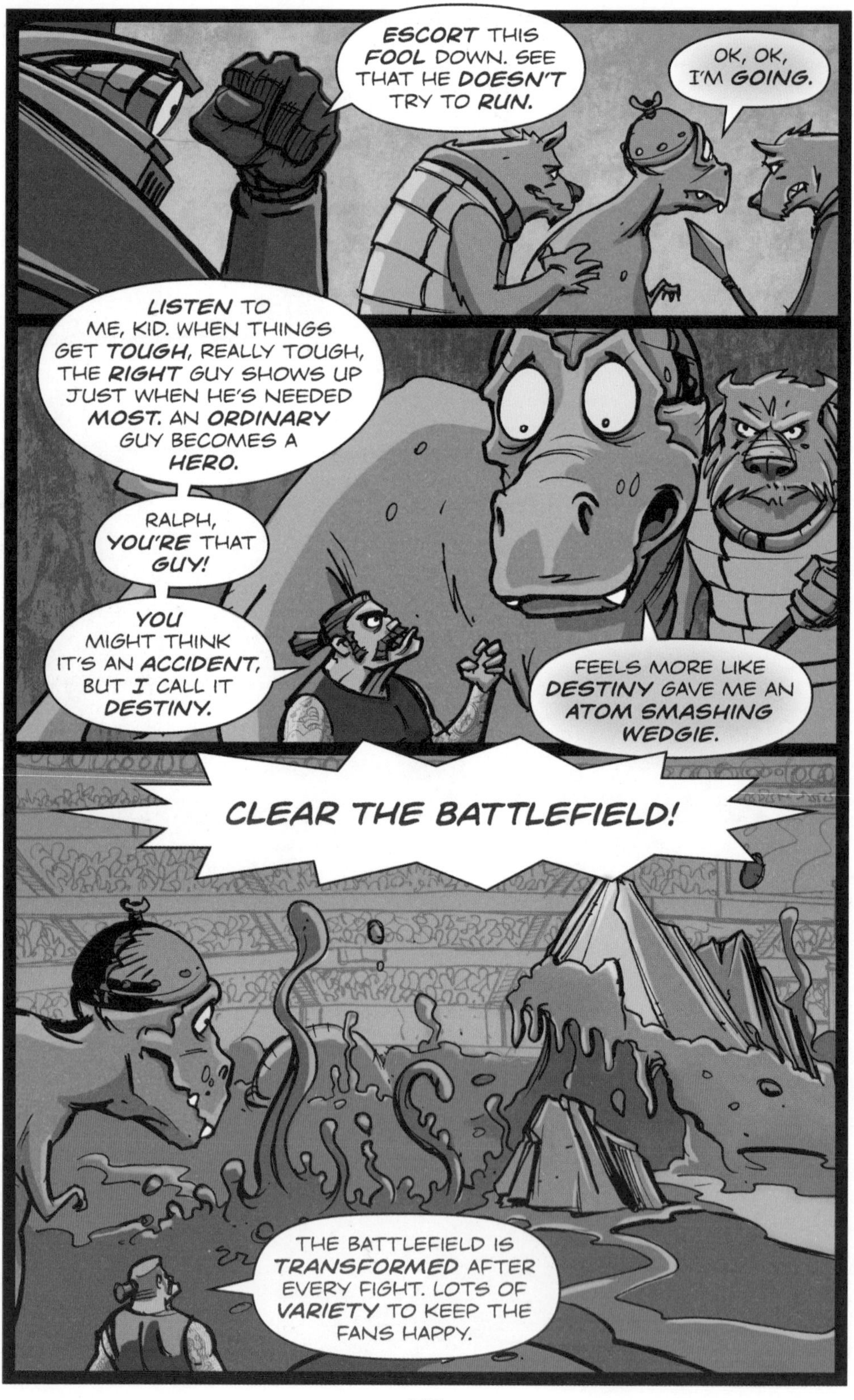
ESCORT THIS FOOL DOWN. SEE THAT HE DOESN'T TRY TO RUN.
OK, OK, I'M GOING.
LISTEN TO ME, KID. WHEN THINGS GET TOUGH, REALLY TOUGH, THE RIGHT GUY SHOWS UP JUST WHEN HE'S NEEDED MOST. AN ORDINARY GUY BECOMES A HERO.
RALPH, YOU'RE THAT GUY!
YOU MIGHT THINK IT'S AN ACCIDENT, BUT I CALL IT DESTINY.
FEELS MORE LIKE DESTINY GAVE ME AN ATOM SMASHING WEDGIE.
CLEAR THE BATTLEFIELD!
THE BATTLEFIELD IS TRANSFORMED AFTER EVERY FIGHT. LOTS OF VARIETY TO KEEP THE FANS HAPPY.

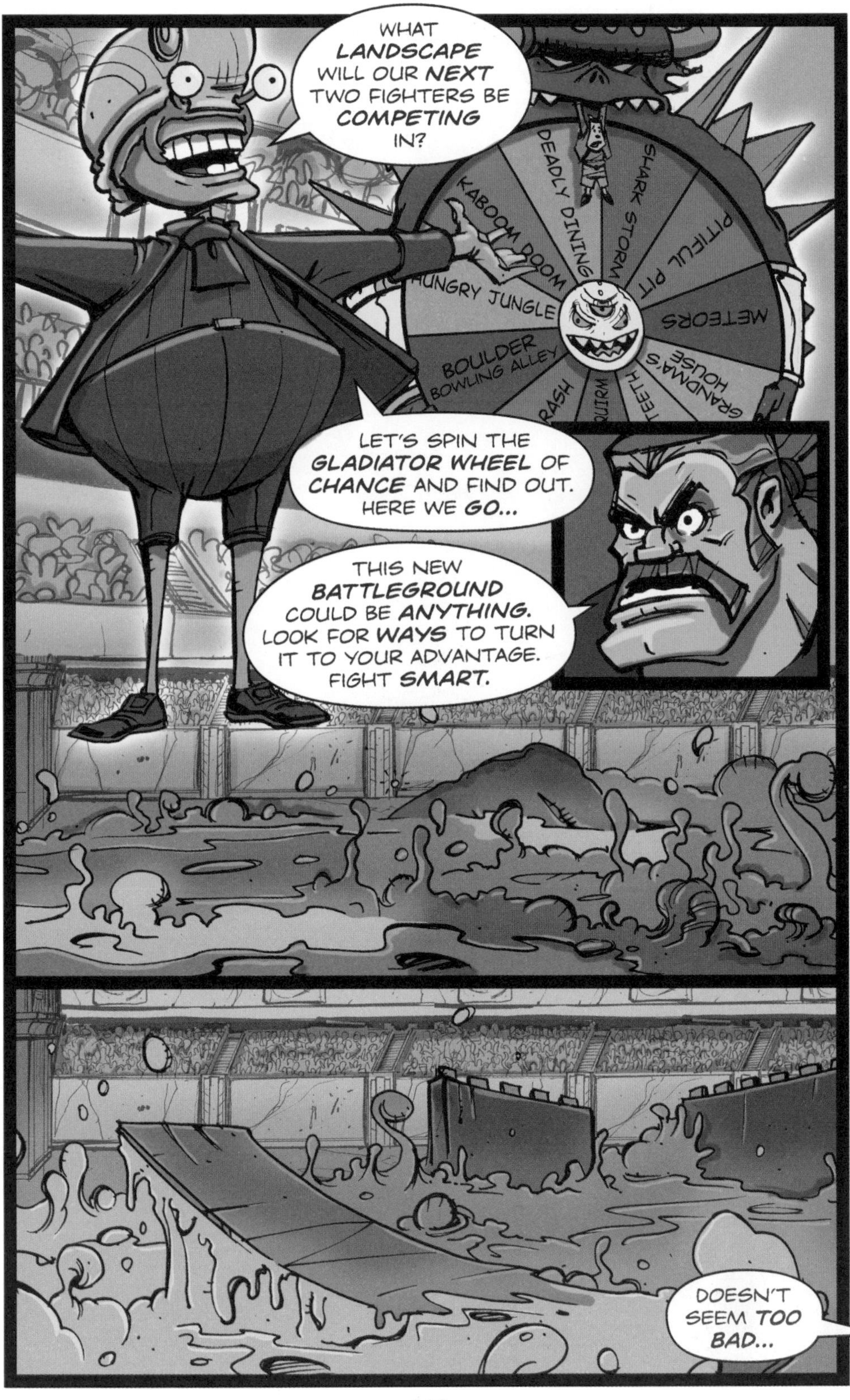
WHAT LANDSCAPE WILL OUR NEXT TWO FIGHTERS BE COMPETING IN?
SHARK STORM
DEADLY DINING
KABOOM DOOM
PITIFUL PIT
METEORS
GRANDMA'S HOUSE
HUNGRY JUNGLE
BOULDER BOWLING ALLEY
LET'S SPIN THE GLADIATOR WHEEL OF CHANCE AND FIND OUT. HERE WE GO...
THIS NEW BATTLEGROUND COULD BE ANYTHING. LOOK FOR WAYS TO TURN IT TO YOUR ADVANTAGE. FIGHT SMART.
DOESN'T SEEM TOO BAD...

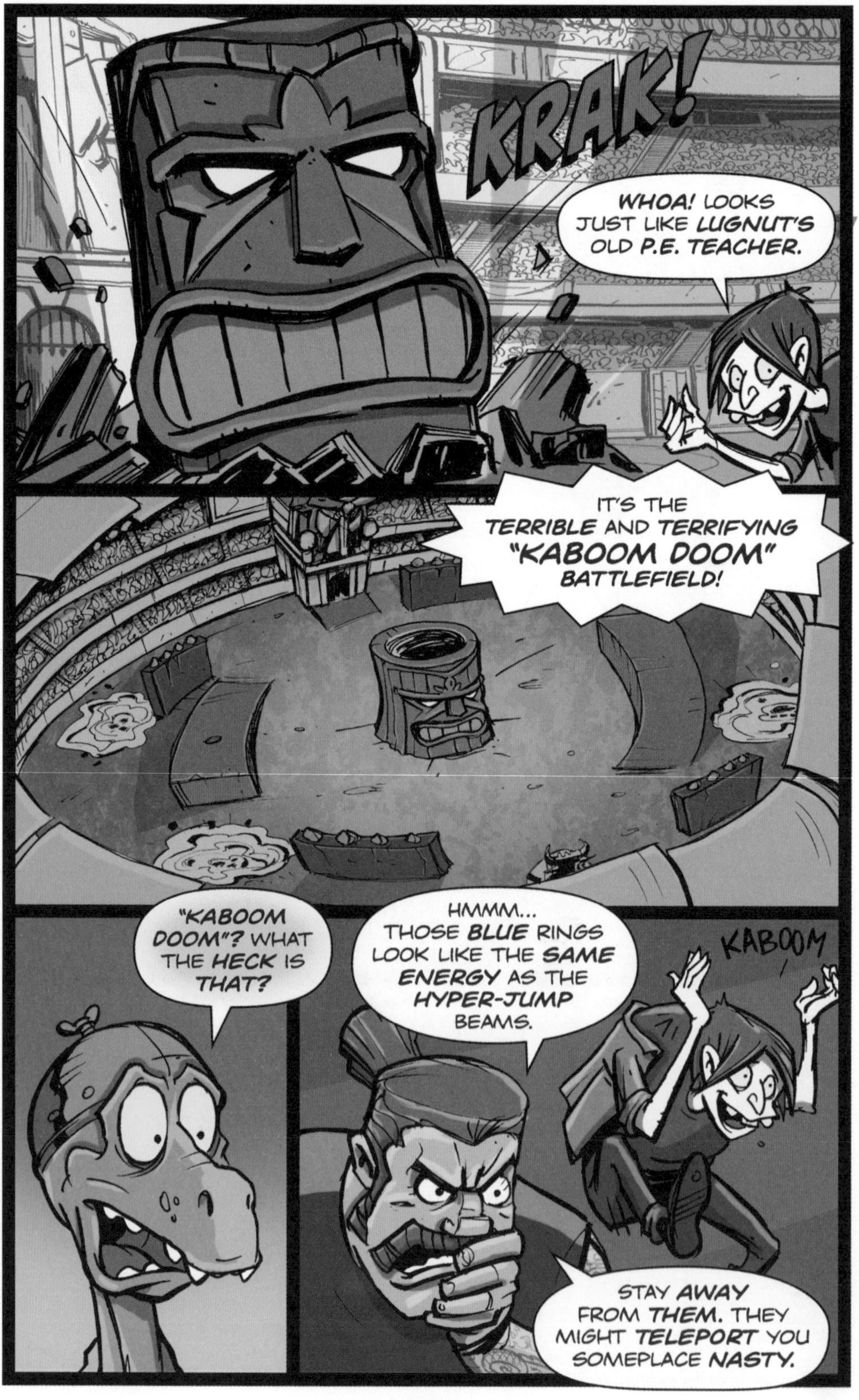
KRAK!
WHOA! LOOKS JUST LIKE LUGNUT'S OLD P.E. TEACHER.
IT'S THE TERRIBLE AND TERRIFYING "KABOOM DOOM" BATTLEFIELD!
"KABOOM DOOM"? WHAT THE HECK IS THAT?
HMMM... THOSE BLUE RINGS LOOK LIKE THE SAME ENERGY AS THE HYPER-JUMP BEAMS.
KABOOM
STAY AWAY FROM THEM. THEY MIGHT TELEPORT YOU SOMEPLACE NASTY.

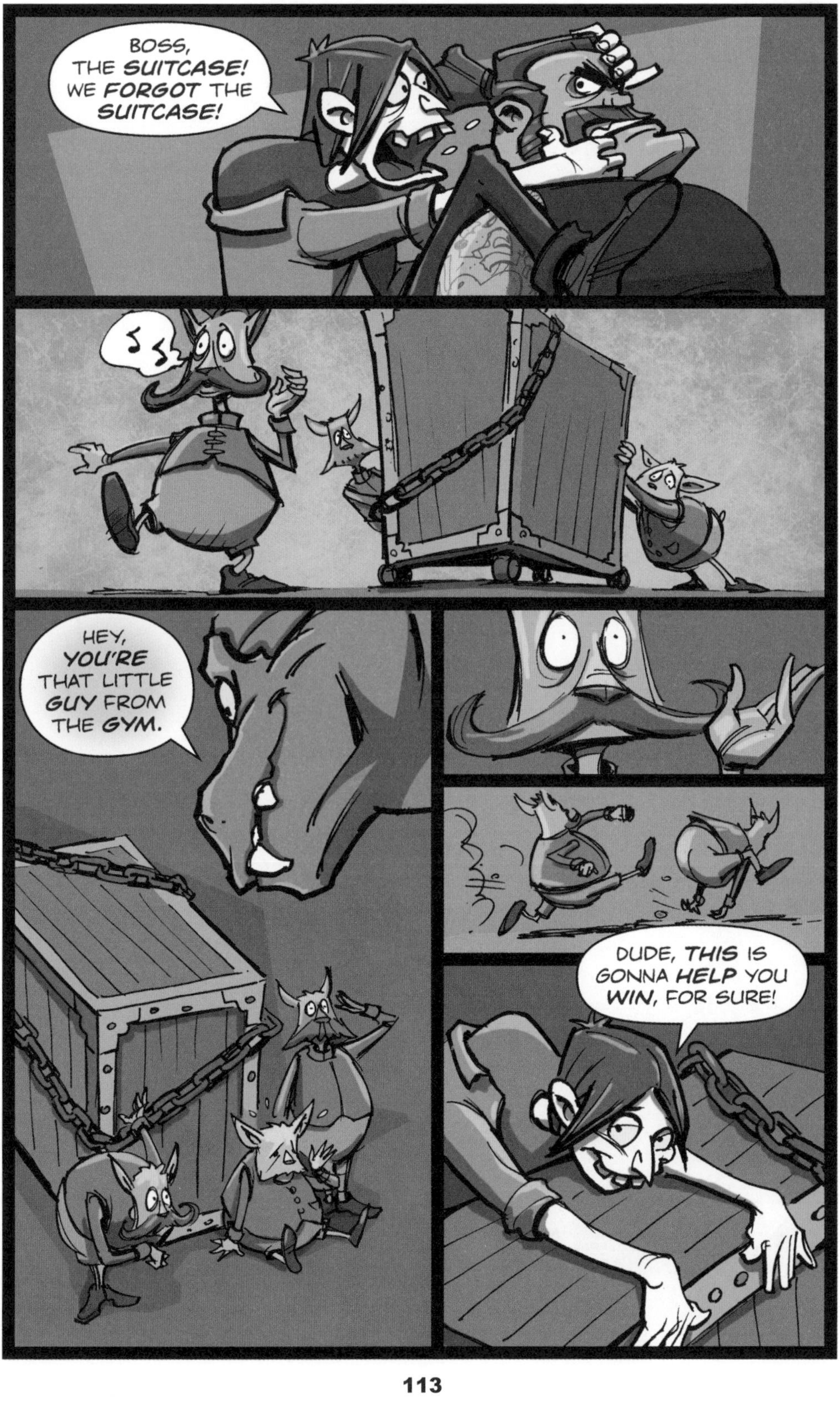
BOSS, THE SUITCASE! WE FORGOT THE SUITCASE!
HEY, YOU'RE THAT LITTLE GUY FROM THE GYM.
DUDE, THIS IS GONNA HELP YOU WIN, FOR SURE!

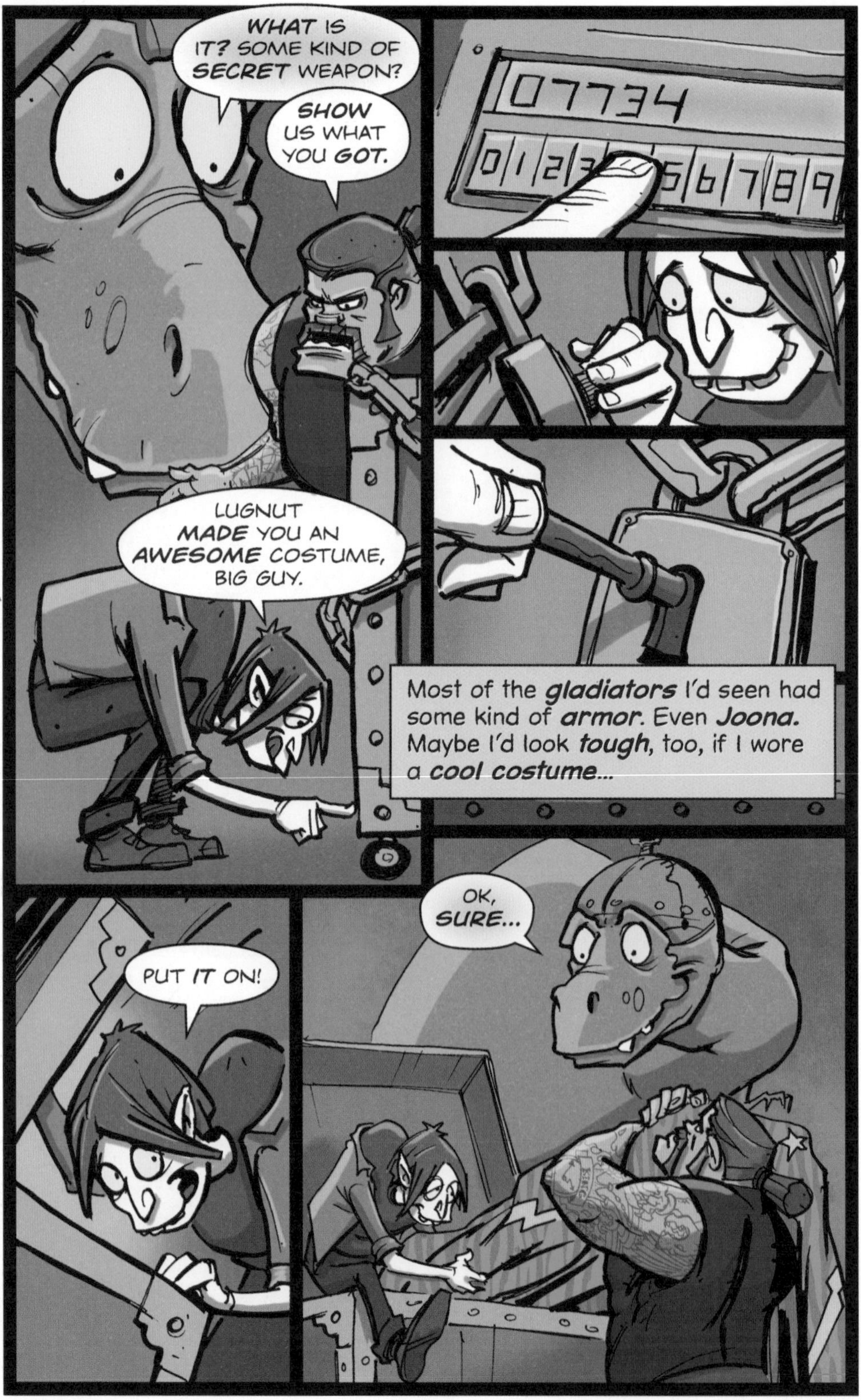
WHAT IS IT? SOME KIND OF SECRET WEAPON?
SHOW US WHAT YOU GOT.
07734
0 1 2 3 5 6 7 8 9
LUGNUT MADE YOU AN AWESOME COSTUME, BIG GUY.
Most of the gladiators I'd seen had some kind of armor. Even Joona. Maybe I'd look tough, too, if I wore a cool costume...
PUT IT ON!
OK, SURE...

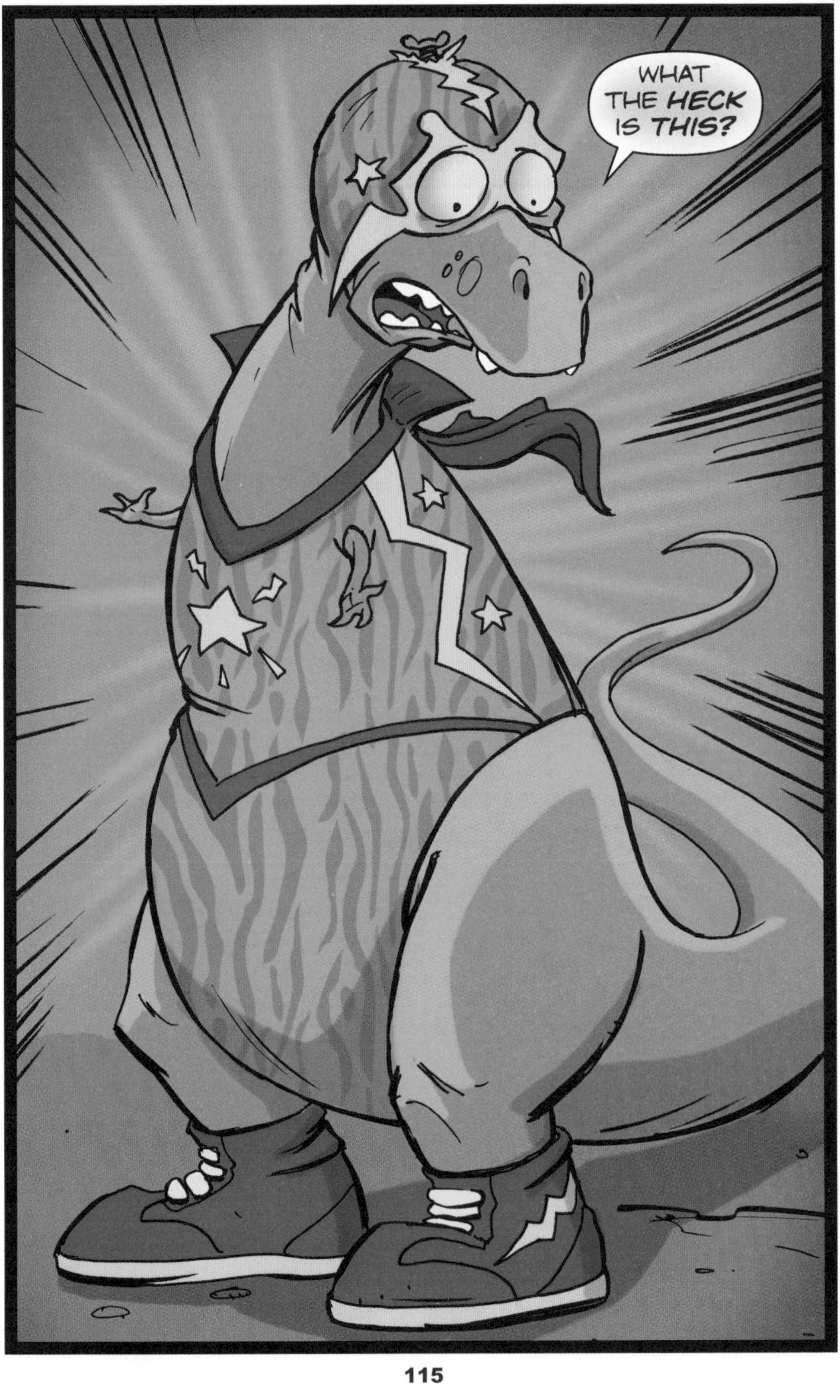
WHAT THE HECK IS THIS?

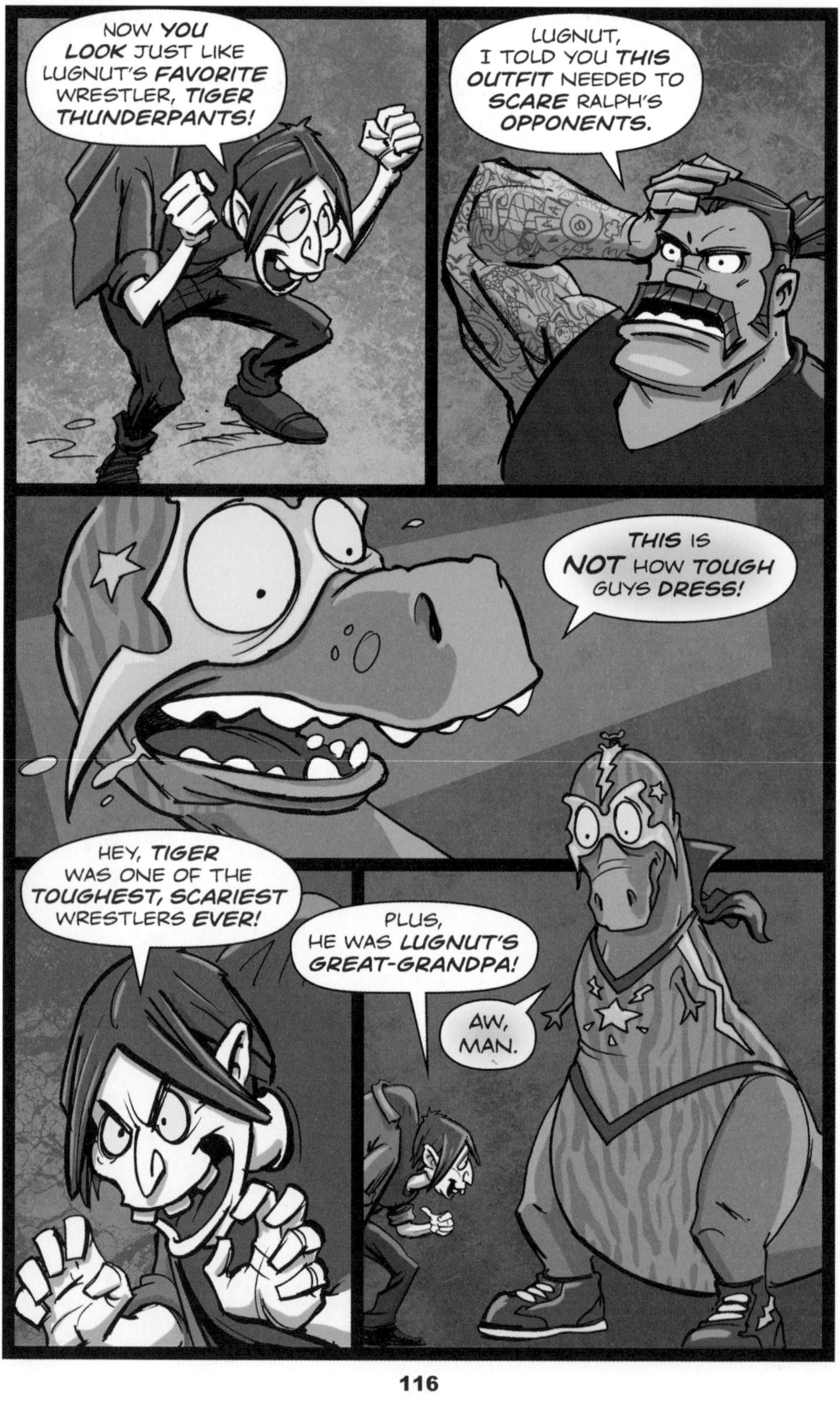
NOW YOU LOOK JUST LIKE LUGNUT'S FAVORITE WRESTLER, TIGER THUNDERPANTS!
LUGNUT, I TOLD YOU THIS OUTFIT NEEDED TO SCARE RALPH'S OPPONENTS.
THIS IS NOT HOW TOUGH GUYS DRESS!
HEY, TIGER WAS ONE OF THE TOUGHEST, SCARIEST WRESTLERS EVER!
PLUS, HE WAS LUGNUT'S GREAT-GRANDPA!
AW, MAN.

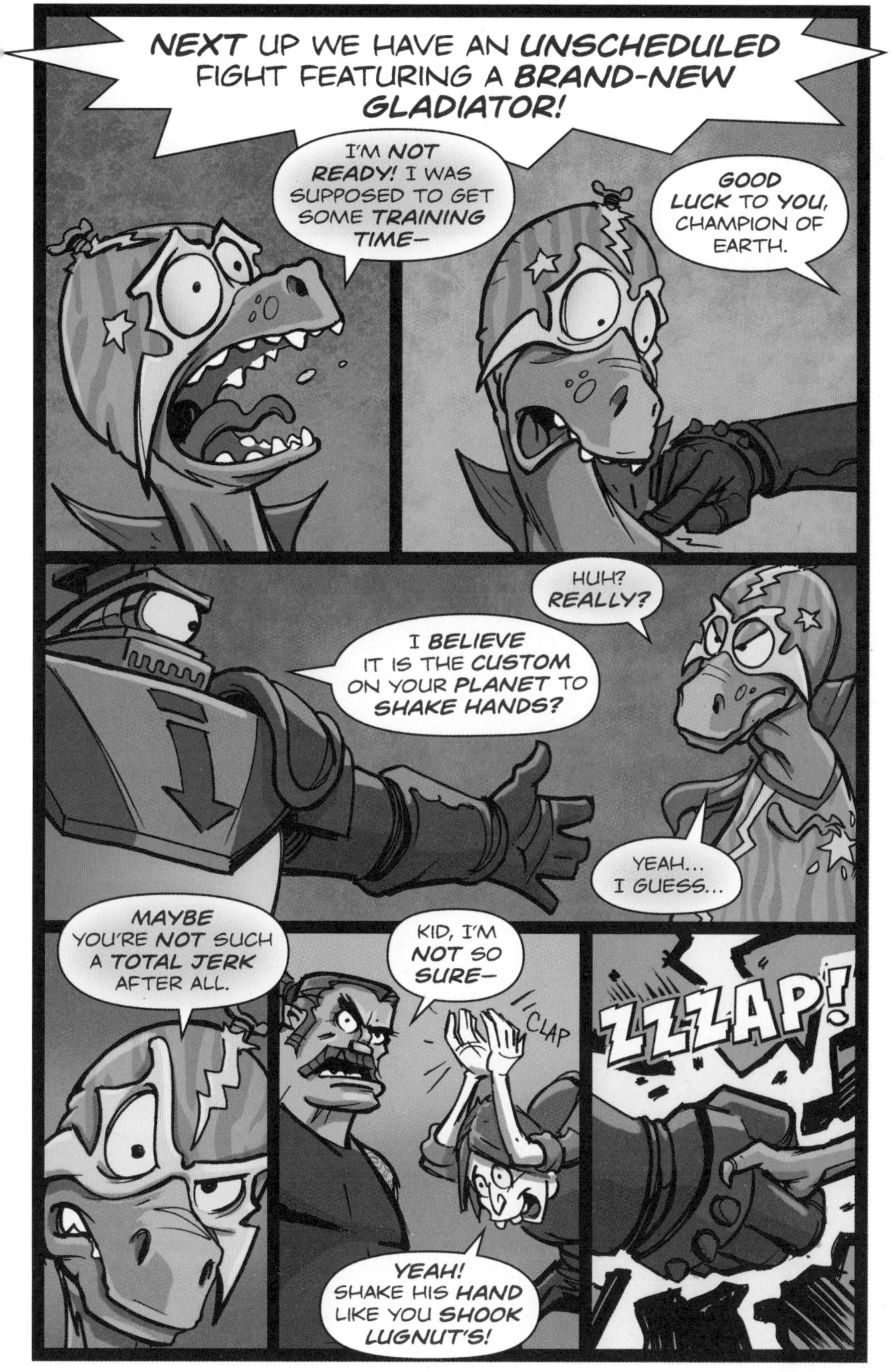
NEXT UP WE HAVE AN UNSCHEDULED FIGHT FEATURING A BRAND-NEW GLADIATOR!
I'M NOT READY! I WAS SUPPOSED TO GET SOME TRAINING TIME—
GOOD LUCK TO YOU, CHAMPION OF EARTH.
HUH? REALLY?
I BELIEVE IT IS THE CUSTOM ON YOUR PLANET TO SHAKE HANDS?
YEAH... I GUESS...
MAYBE YOU'RE NOT SUCH A TOTAL JERK AFTER ALL.
KID, I'M NOT SO SURE—
CLAP
YEAH! SHAKE HIS HAND LIKE YOU SHOOK LUGNUT'S!
ZZZZAP!

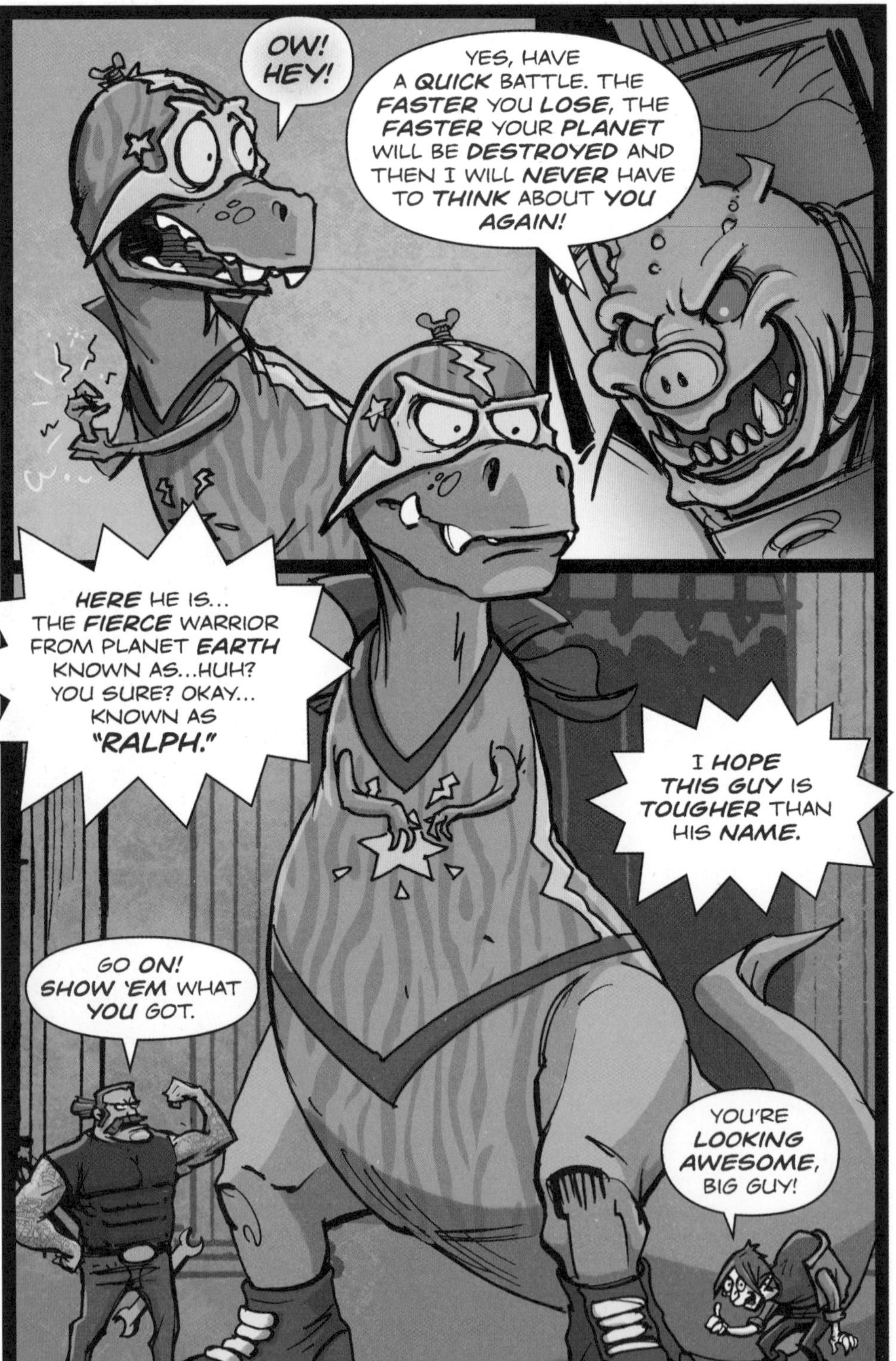
OW! HEY!
YES, HAVE A QUICK BATTLE. THE FASTER YOU LOSE, THE FASTER YOUR PLANET WILL BE DESTROYED AND THEN I WILL NEVER HAVE TO THINK ABOUT YOU AGAIN!
HERE HE IS... THE FIERCE WARRIOR FROM PLANET EARTH KNOWN AS...HUH? YOU SURE? OKAY... KNOWN AS "RALPH."
I HOPE THIS GUY IS TOUGHER THAN HIS NAME.
GO ON! SHOW 'EM WHAT YOU GOT.
YOU'RE LOOKING AWESOME, BIG GUY!

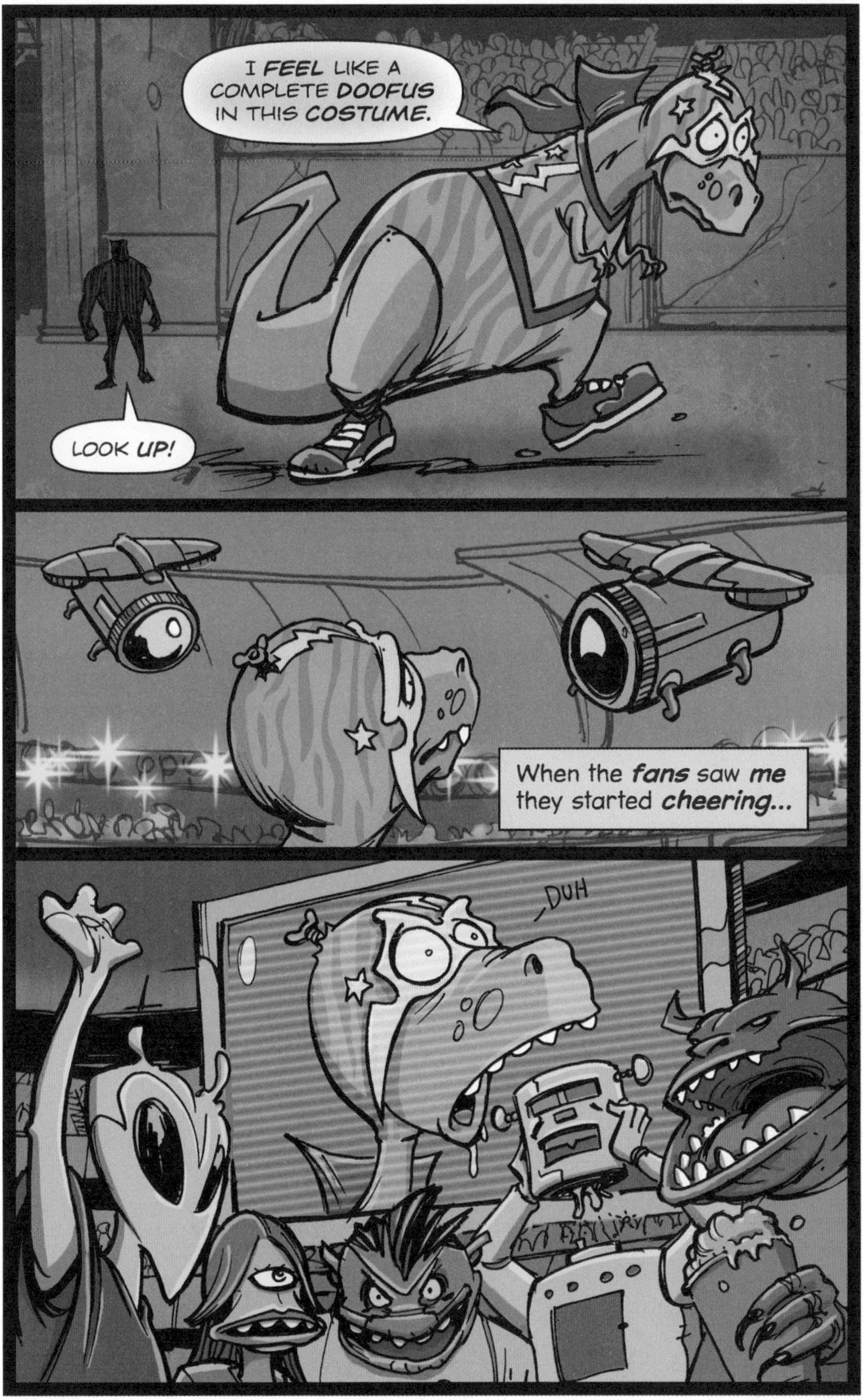
I FEEL LIKE A COMPLETE DOOFUS IN THIS COSTUME.
LOOK UP!
When the fans saw me they started cheering...
DUH

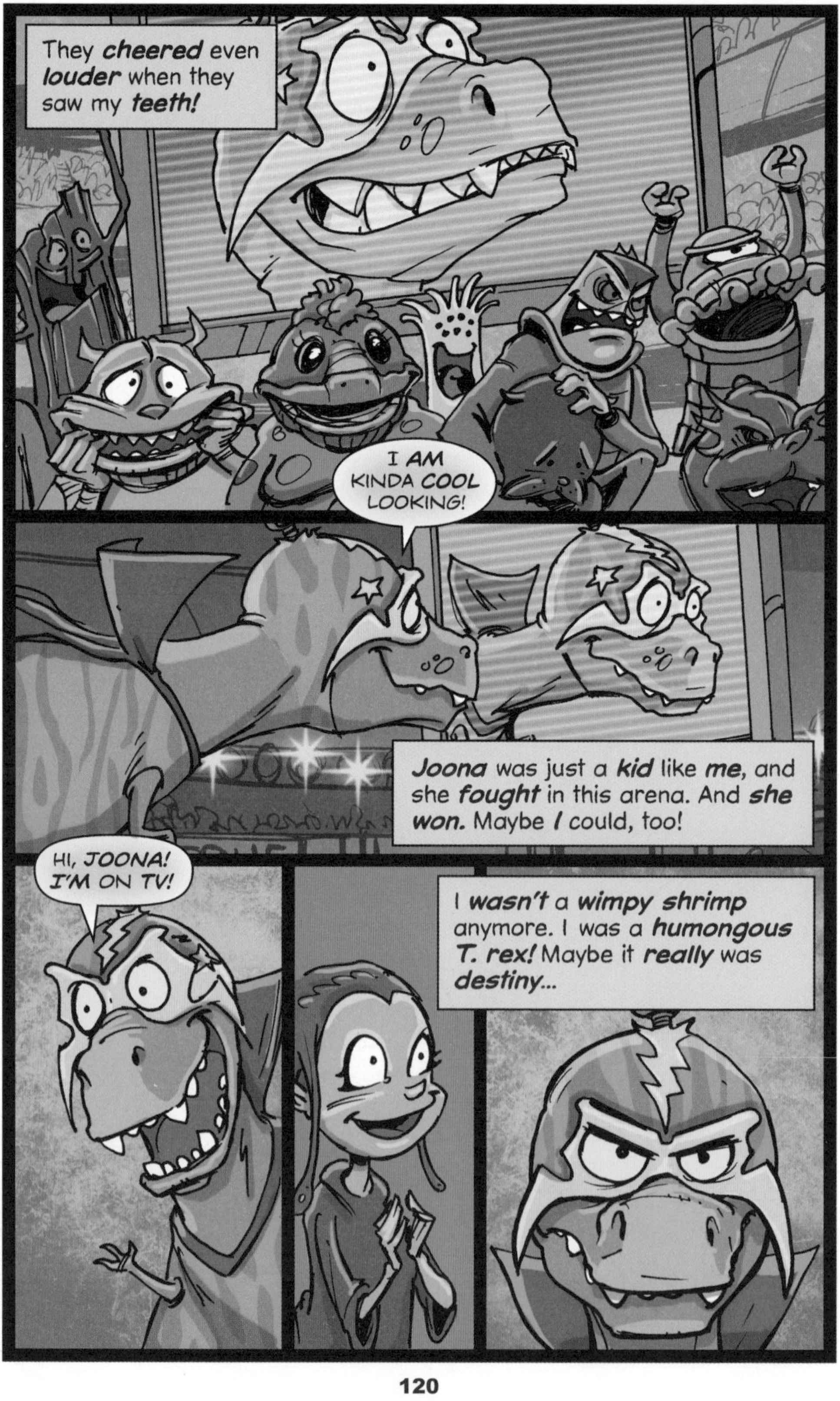
They cheered even louder when they saw my teeth!
I AM KINDA COOL LOOKING!
Joona was just a kid like me, and she fought in this arena. And she won. Maybe I could, too!
HI, JOONA! I'M ON TV!
I wasn't a wimpy shrimp anymore. I was a humongous T. rex! Maybe it really was destiny...

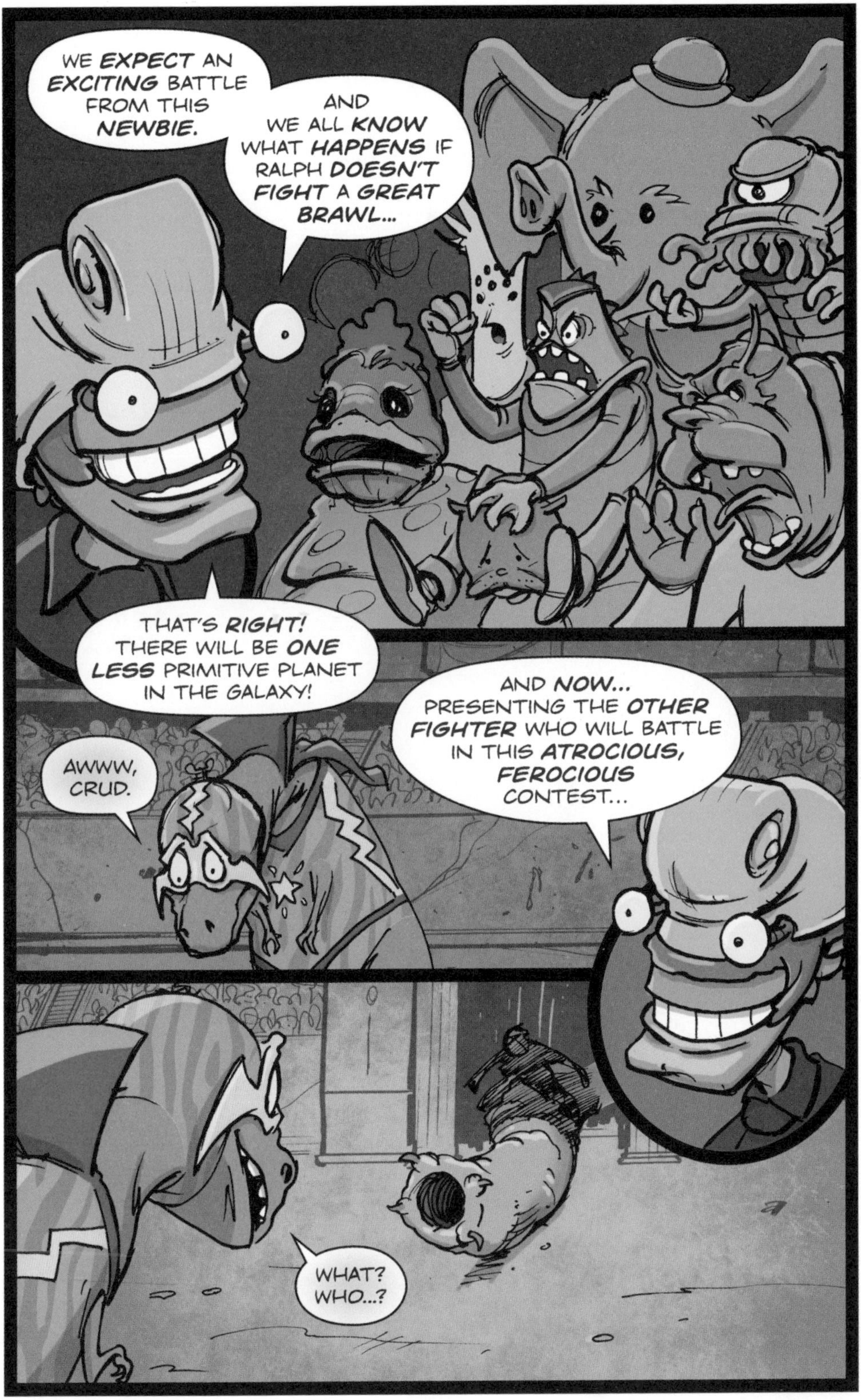
WE EXPECT AN EXCITING BATTLE FROM THIS NEWBIE.
AND WE ALL KNOW WHAT HAPPENS IF RALPH DOESN'T FIGHT A GREAT BRAWL...
THAT'S RIGHT! THERE WILL BE ONE LESS PRIMITIVE PLANET IN THE GALAXY!
AWWW, CRUD.
AND NOW... PRESENTING THE OTHER FIGHTER WHO WILL BATTLE IN THIS ATROCIOUS, FEROCIOUS CONTEST...
WHAT? WHO...?

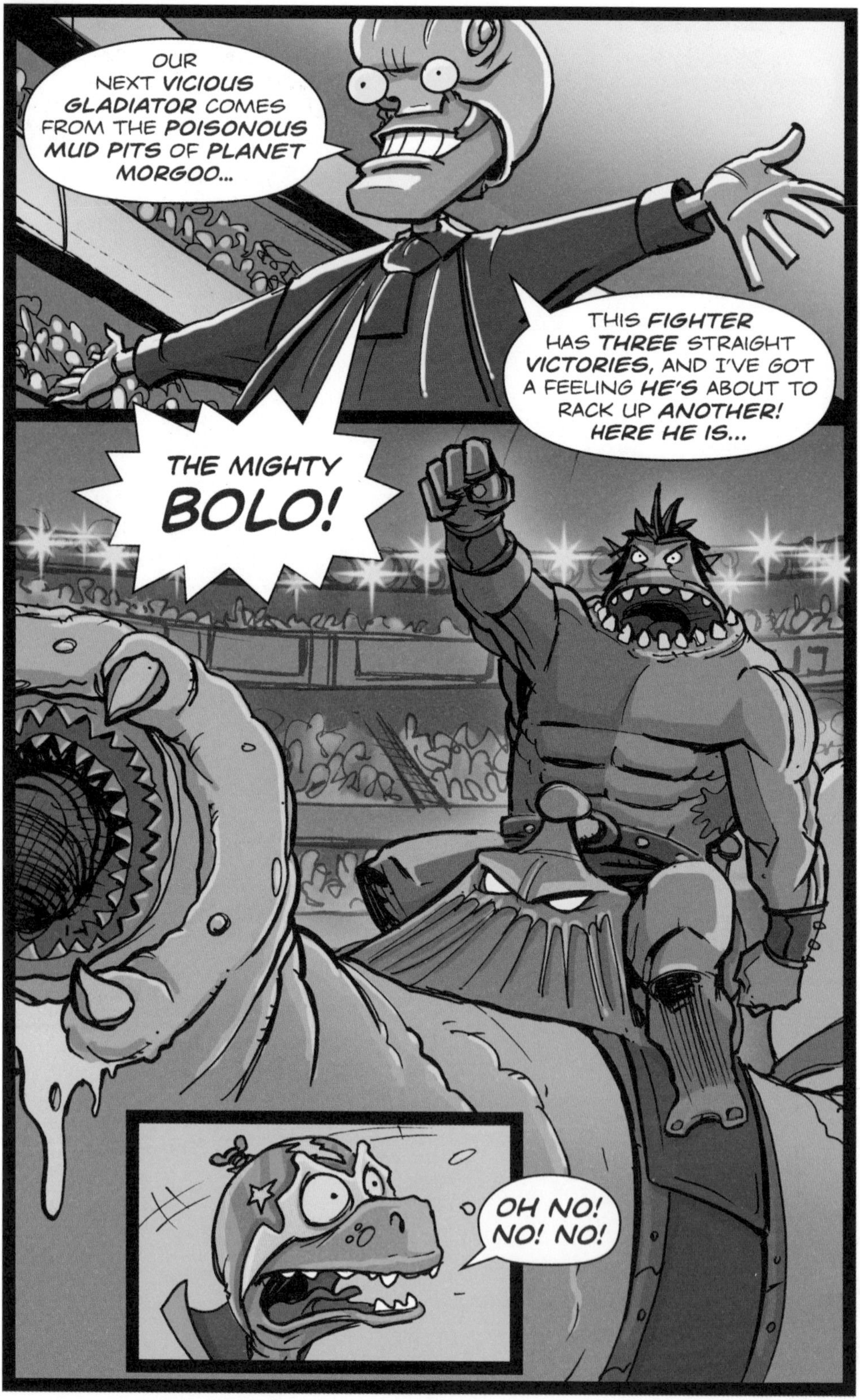
OUR NEXT VICIOUS GLADIATOR COMES FROM THE POISONOUS MUD PITS OF PLANET MORGOO...
THIS FIGHTER HAS THREE STRAIGHT VICTORIES, AND I'VE GOT A FEELING HE'S ABOUT TO RACK UP ANOTHER! HERE HE IS...
THE MIGHTY BOLO!
OH NO! NO! NO!

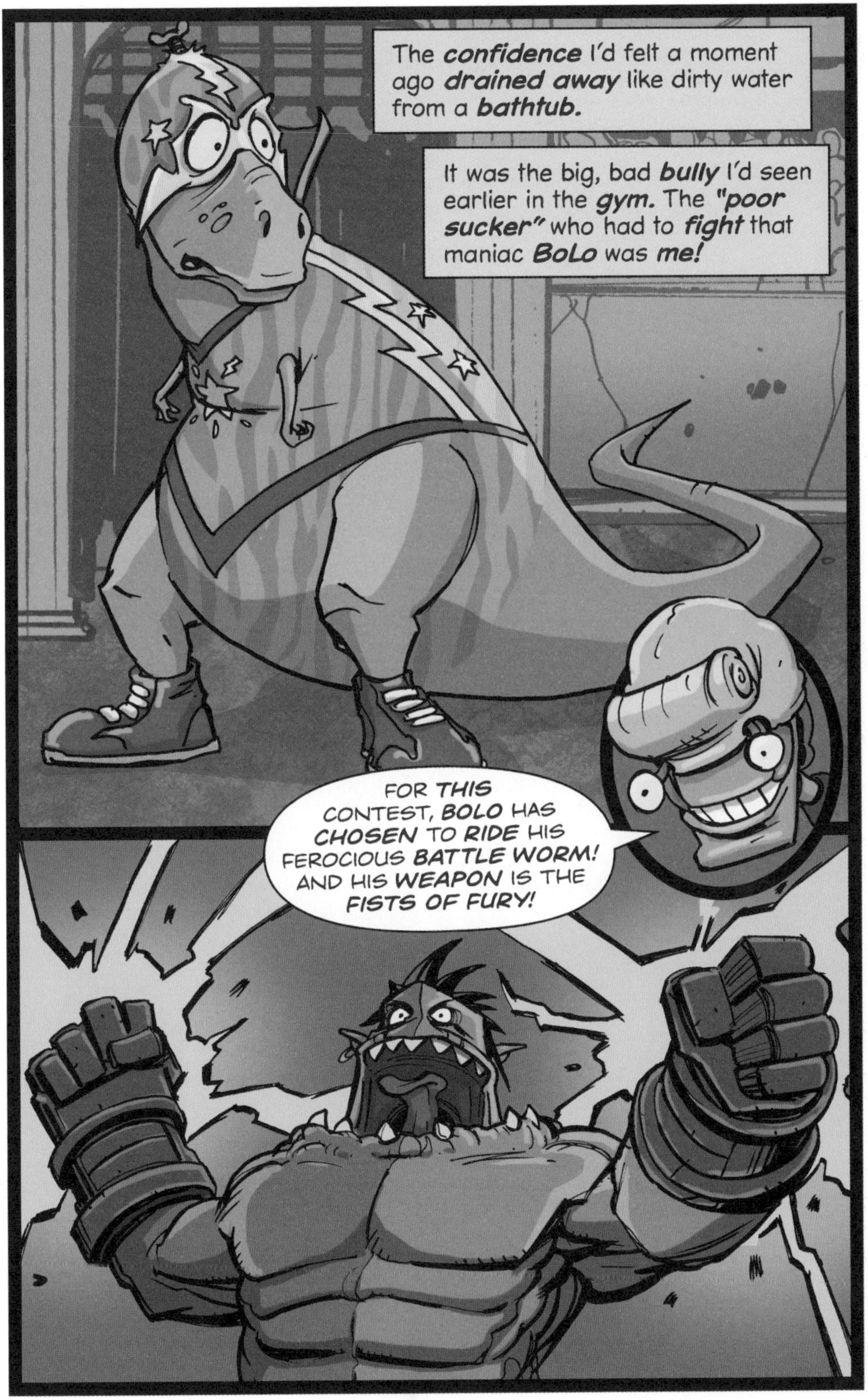
The confidence I'd felt a moment ago drained away like dirty water from a bathtub.
It was the big, bad bully I'd seen earlier in the gym. The "poor sucker" who had to fight that maniac BoLo was me!
FOR THIS CONTEST, BOLO HAS CHOSEN TO RIDE HIS FEROCIOUS BATTLE WORM! AND HIS WEAPON IS THE FISTS OF FURY!

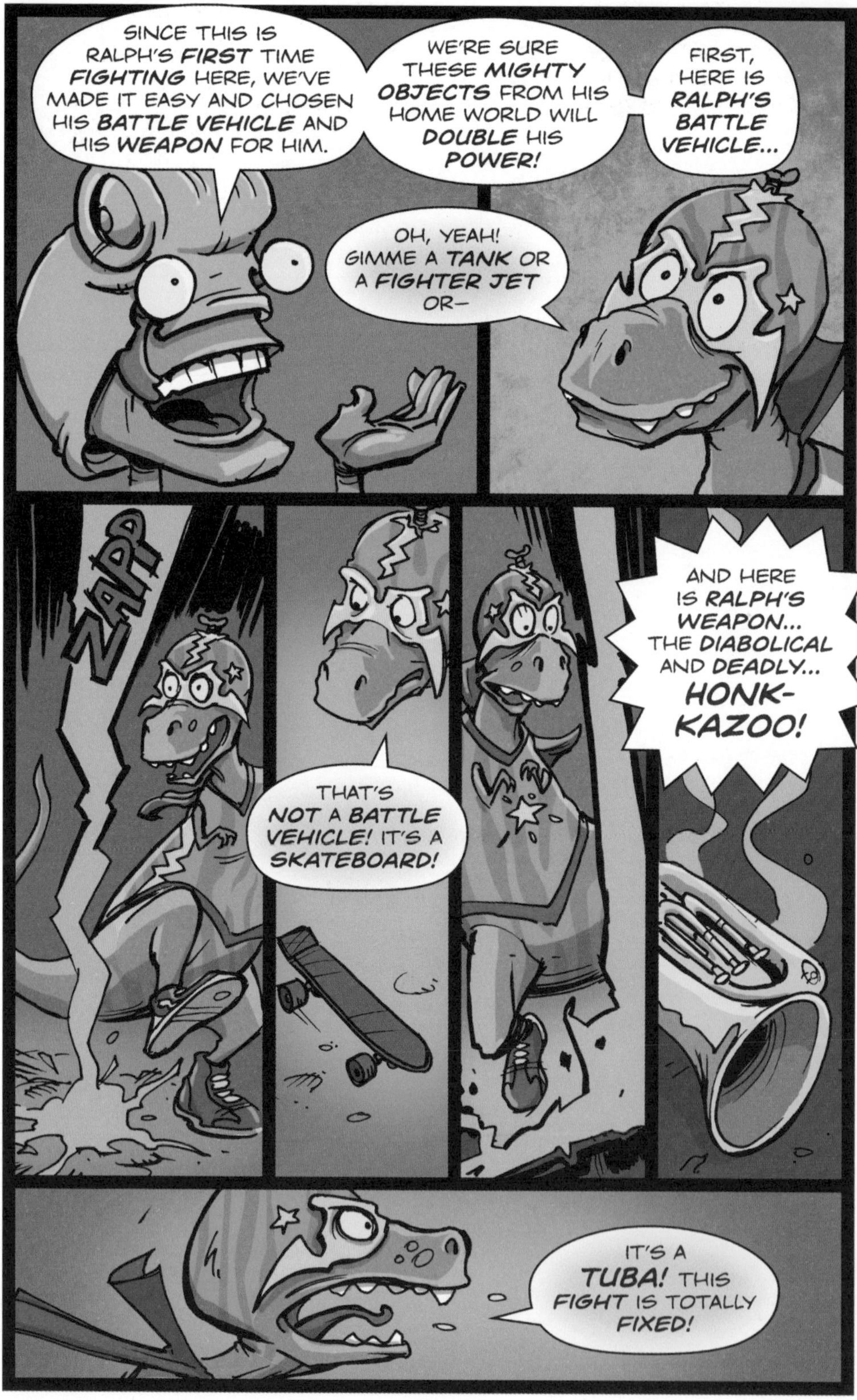
SINCE THIS IS RALPH'S FIRST TIME FIGHTING HERE, WE'VE MADE IT EASY AND CHOSEN HIS BATTLE VEHICLE AND HIS WEAPON FOR HIM.
WE'RE SURE THESE MIGHTY OBJECTS FROM HIS HOME WORLD WILL DOUBLE HIS POWER!
FIRST, HERE IS RALPH'S BATTLE VEHICLE...
OH, YEAH! GIMME A TANK OR A FIGHTER JET OR–
ZAPP
THAT'S NOT A BATTLE VEHICLE! IT'S A SKATEBOARD!
AND HERE IS RALPH'S WEAPON... THE DIABOLICAL AND DEADLY... HONK-KAZOO!
IT'S A TUBA! THIS FIGHT IS TOTALLY FIXED!

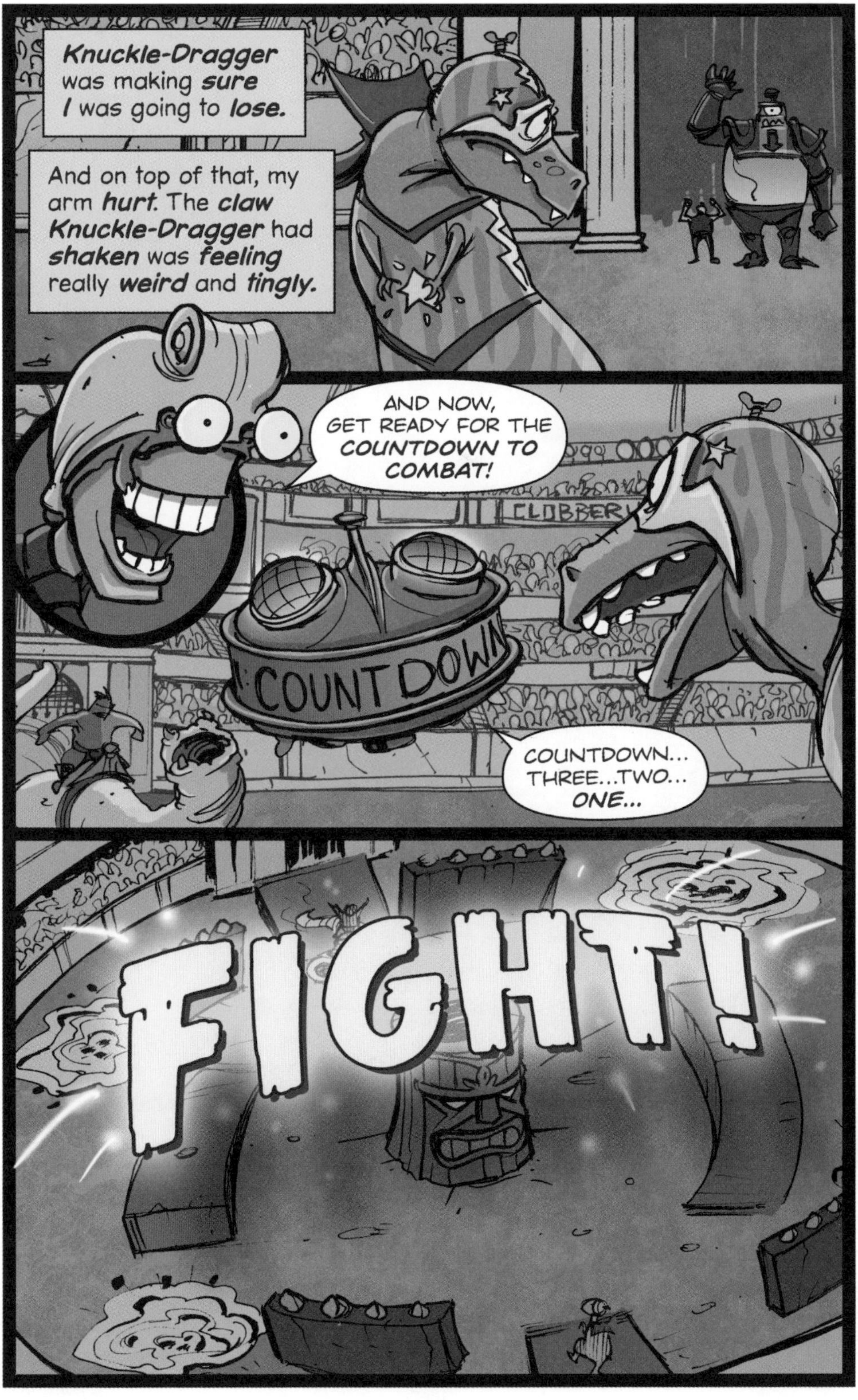
Knuckle-Dragger was making sure I was going to lose.
And on top of that, my arm hurt. The claw Knuckle-Dragger had shaken was feeling really weird and tingly.
AND NOW, GET READY FOR THE COUNTDOWN TO COMBAT!
CLOBBER
COUNTDOWN
COUNTDOWN... THREE...TWO... ONE...
FIGHT!

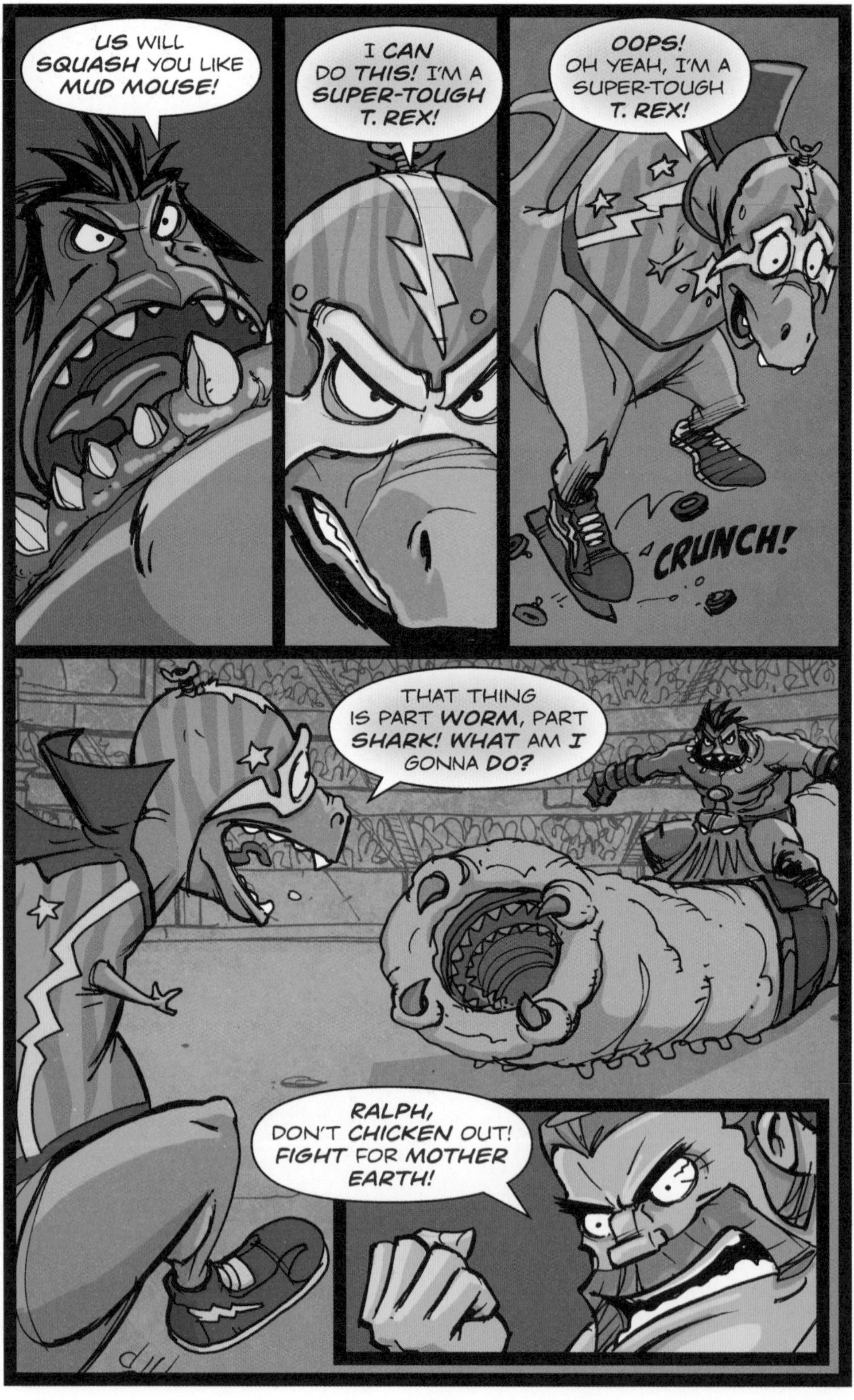
US WILL SQUASH YOU LIKE MUD MOUSE!
I CAN DO THIS! I'M A SUPER-TOUGH T. REX!
OOPS! OH YEAH, I'M A SUPER-TOUGH T. REX!
CRUNCH!
THAT THING IS PART WORM, PART SHARK! WHAT AM I GONNA DO?
RALPH, DON'T CHICKEN OUT! FIGHT FOR MOTHER EARTH!

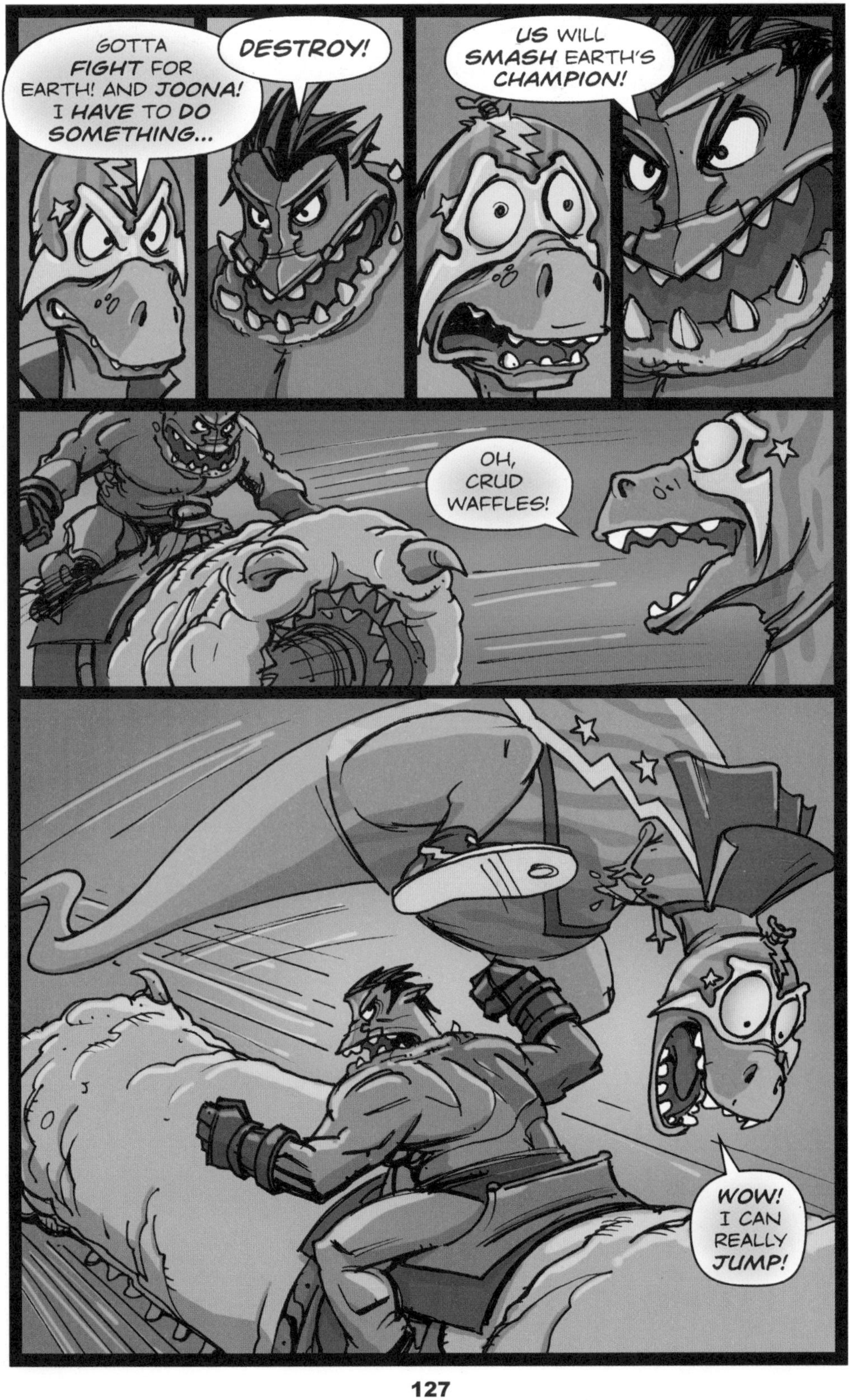
GOTTA FIGHT FOR EARTH! AND JOONA! I HAVE TO DO SOMETHING...
DESTROY!
US WILL SMASH EARTH'S CHAMPION!
OH, CRUD WAFFLES!
WOW! I CAN REALLY JUMP!

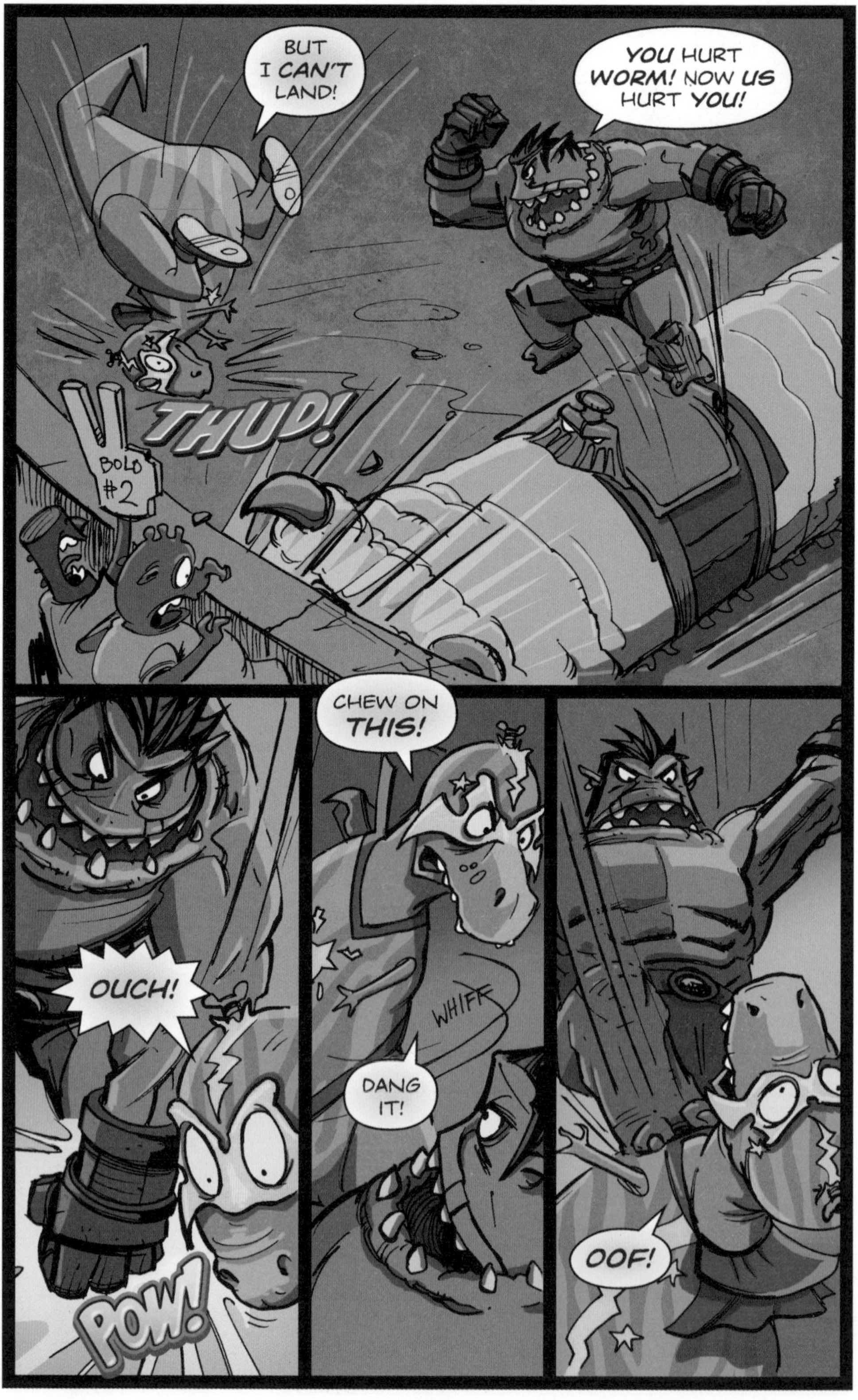
BUT I CAN'T LAND!
YOU HURT WORM! NOW US HURT YOU!
THUD!
BOLO #2
OUCH!
POW!
CHEW ON THIS!
WHIFF
DANG IT!
OOF!

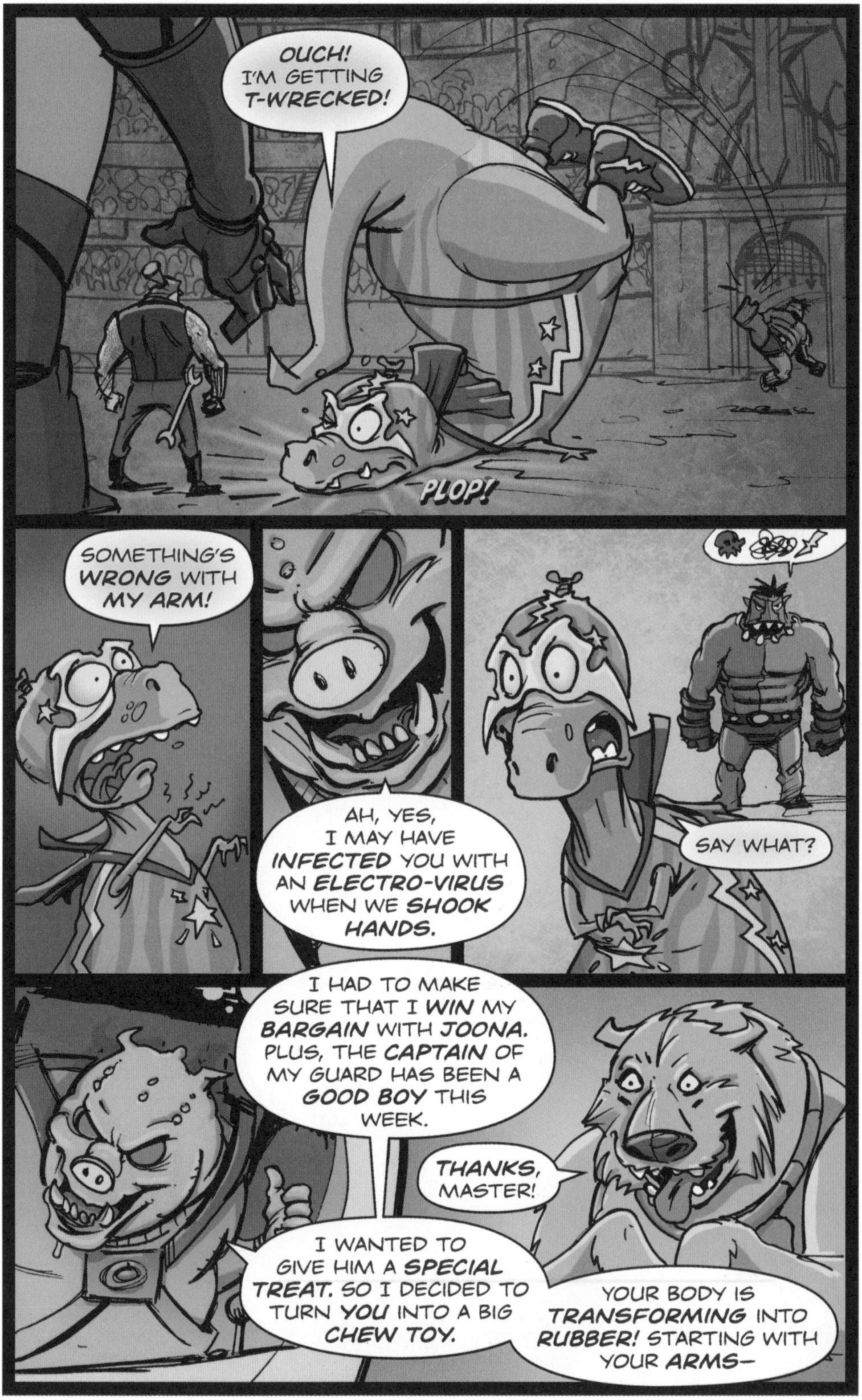
OUCH! I'M GETTING T-WRECKED!
PLOP!
SOMETHING'S WRONG WITH MY ARM!
AH, YES, I MAY HAVE INFECTED YOU WITH AN ELECTRO-VIRUS WHEN WE SHOOK HANDS.
SAY WHAT?
I HAD TO MAKE SURE THAT I WIN MY BARGAIN WITH JOONA. PLUS, THE CAPTAIN OF MY GUARD HAS BEEN A GOOD BOY THIS WEEK.
THANKS, MASTER!
I WANTED TO GIVE HIM A SPECIAL TREAT. SO I DECIDED TO TURN YOU INTO A BIG CHEW TOY.
YOUR BODY IS TRANSFORMING INTO RUBBER! STARTING WITH YOUR ARMS—

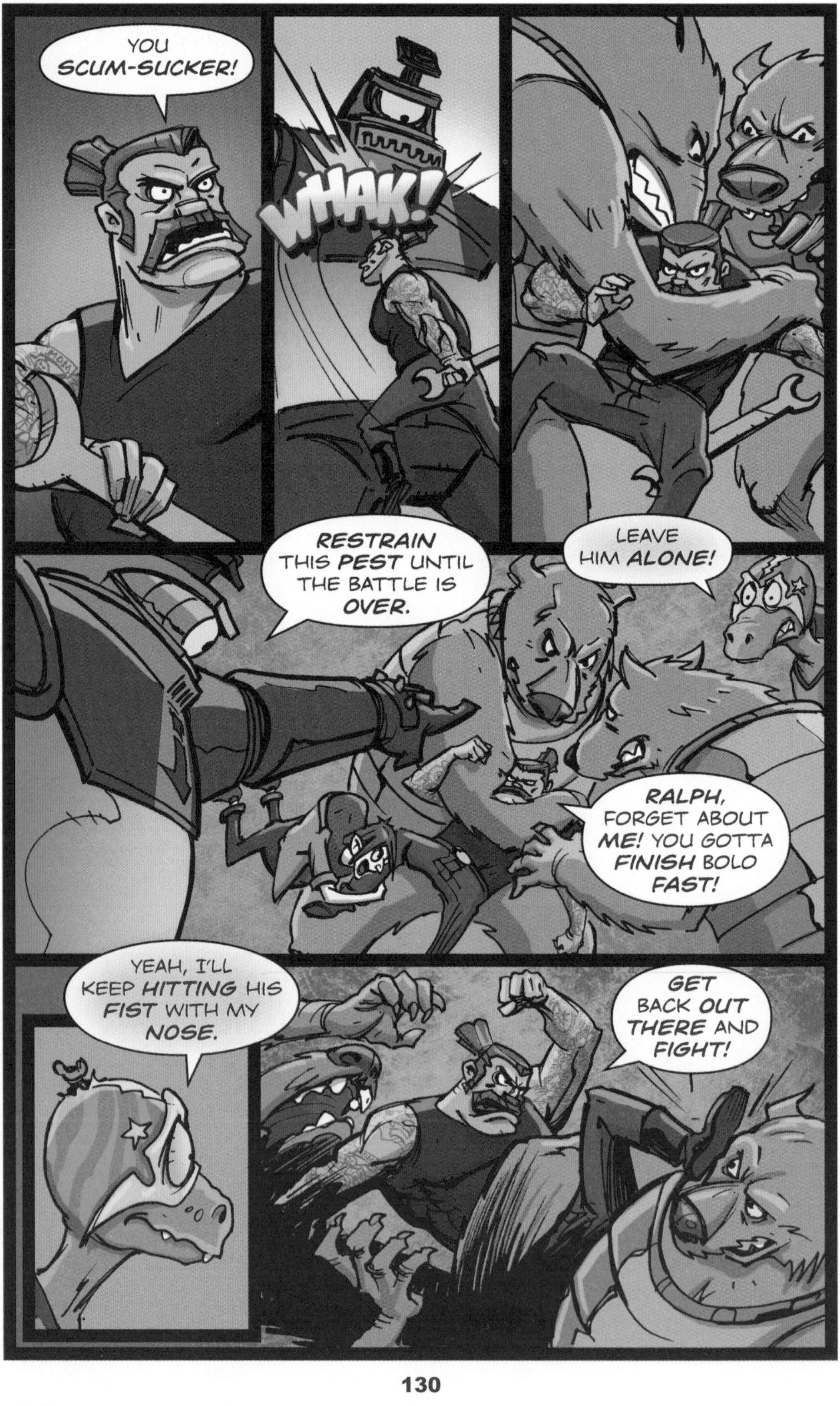

YOU SCUM-SUCKER!
WHAK!
RESTRAIN THIS PEST UNTIL THE BATTLE IS OVER.
LEAVE HIM ALONE!
RALPH, FORGET ABOUT ME! YOU GOTTA FINISH BOLO FAST!
YEAH, I'LL KEEP HITTING HIS FIST WITH MY NOSE.
GET BACK OUT THERE AND FIGHT!

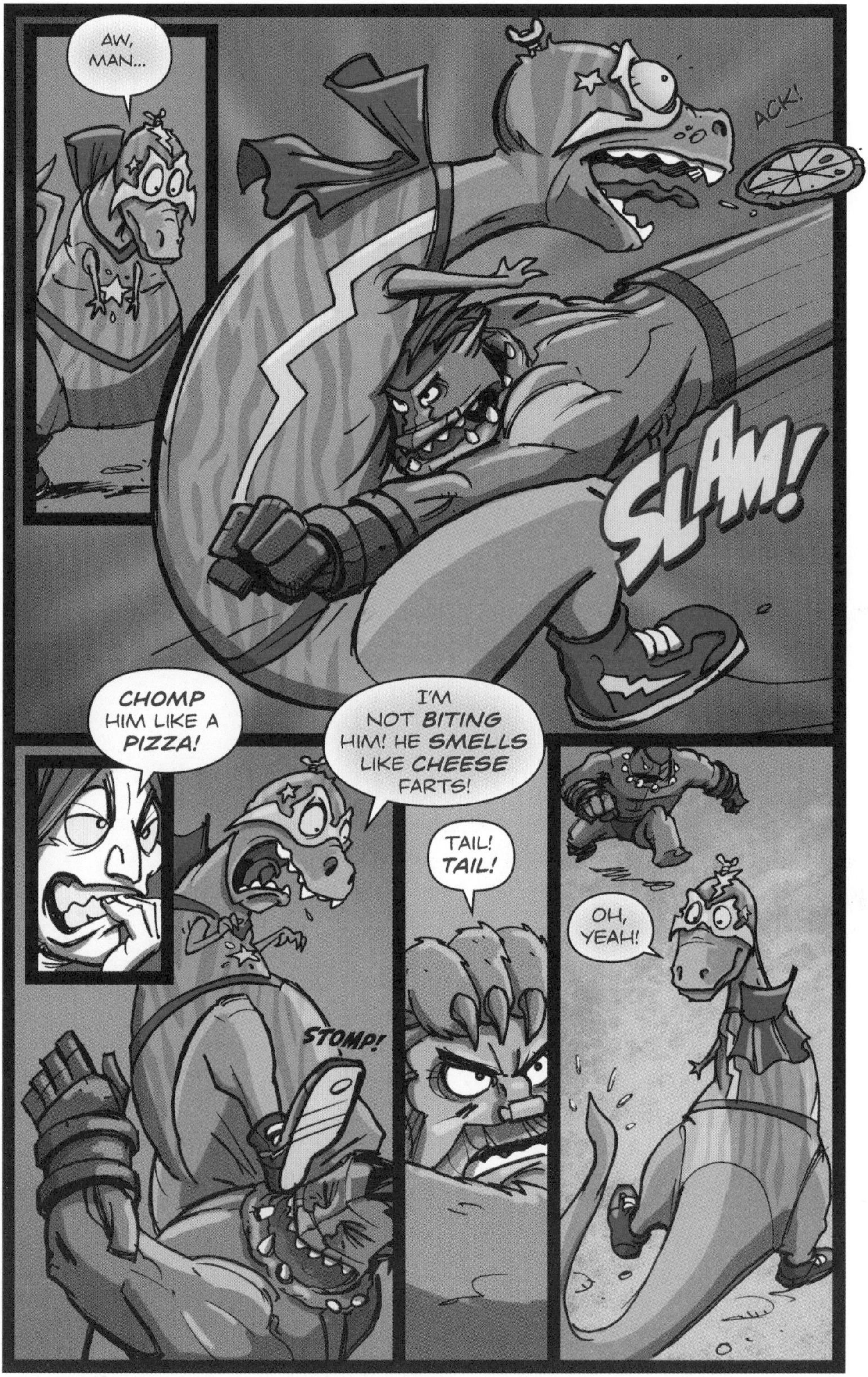
AW, MAN...
ACK!
SLAM!
CHOMP HIM LIKE A PIZZA!
I'M NOT BITING HIM! HE SMELLS LIKE CHEESE FARTS!
STOMP!
TAIL! TAIL!
OH, YEAH!

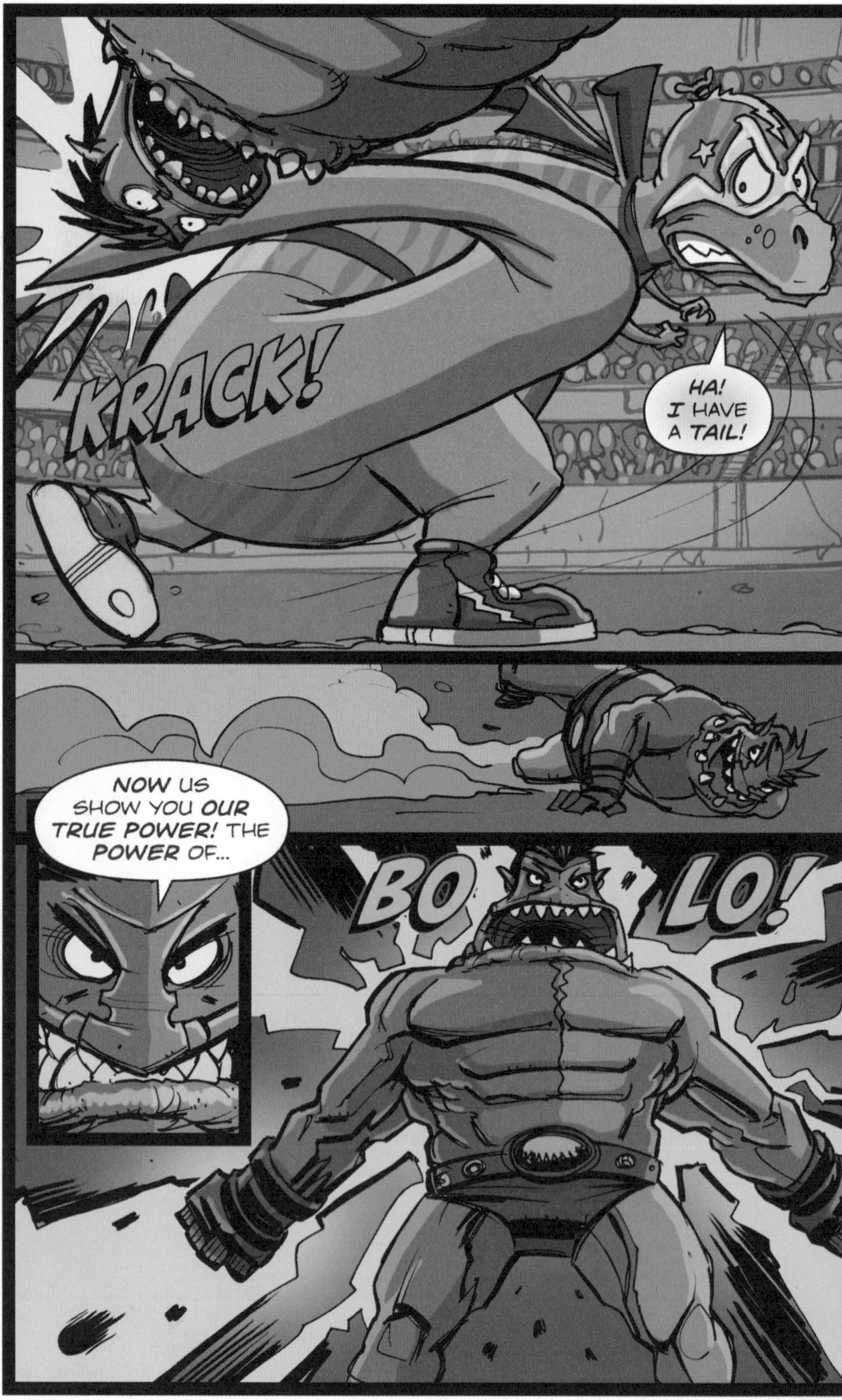
KRACK!
HA! I HAVE A TAIL!
NOW US SHOW YOU OUR TRUE POWER! THE POWER OF...
BO LO!

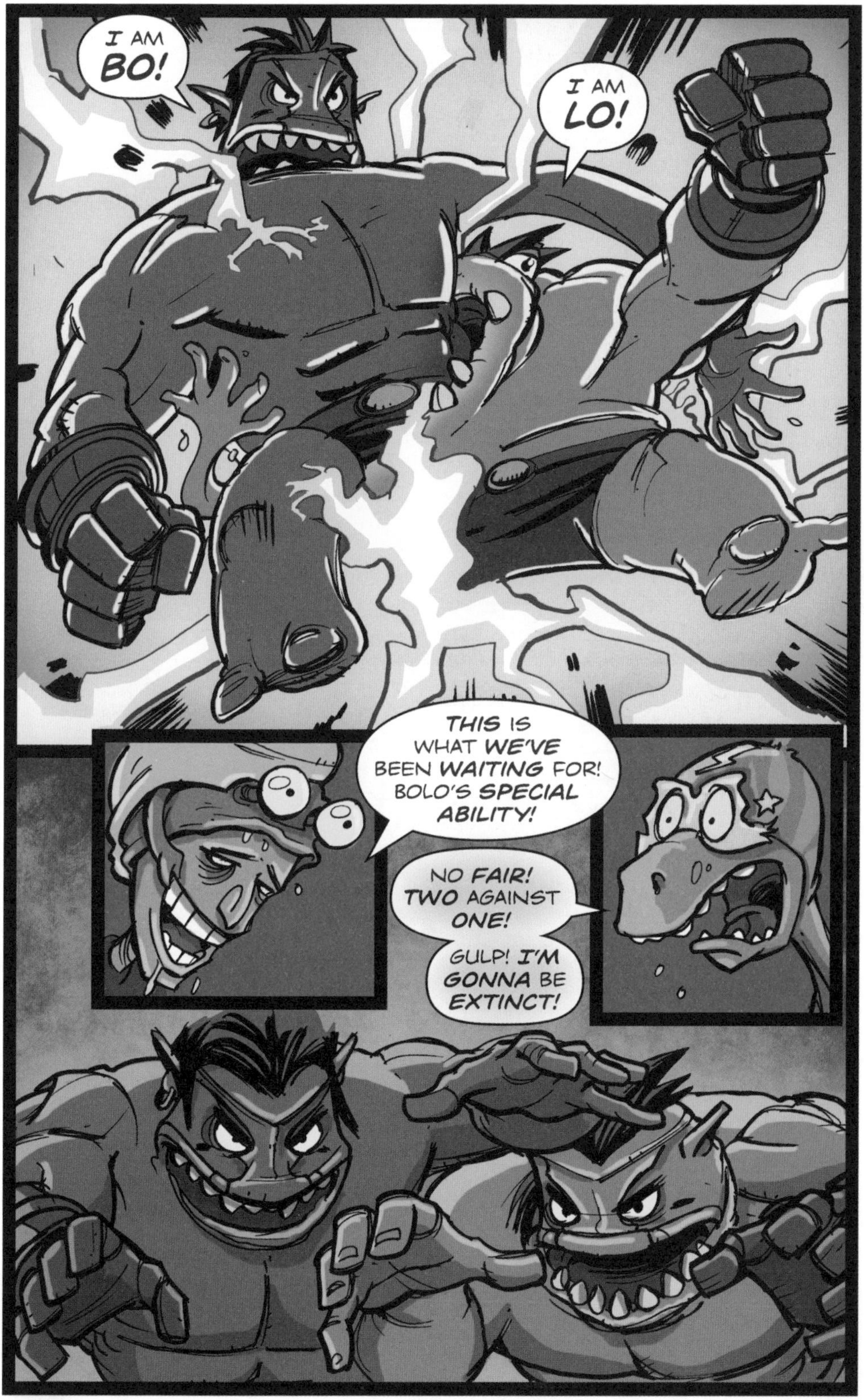
I AM BO!
I AM LO!
THIS IS WHAT WE'VE BEEN WAITING FOR! BOLO'S SPECIAL ABILITY!
NO FAIR! TWO AGAINST ONE!
GULP! I'M GONNA BE EXTINCT!

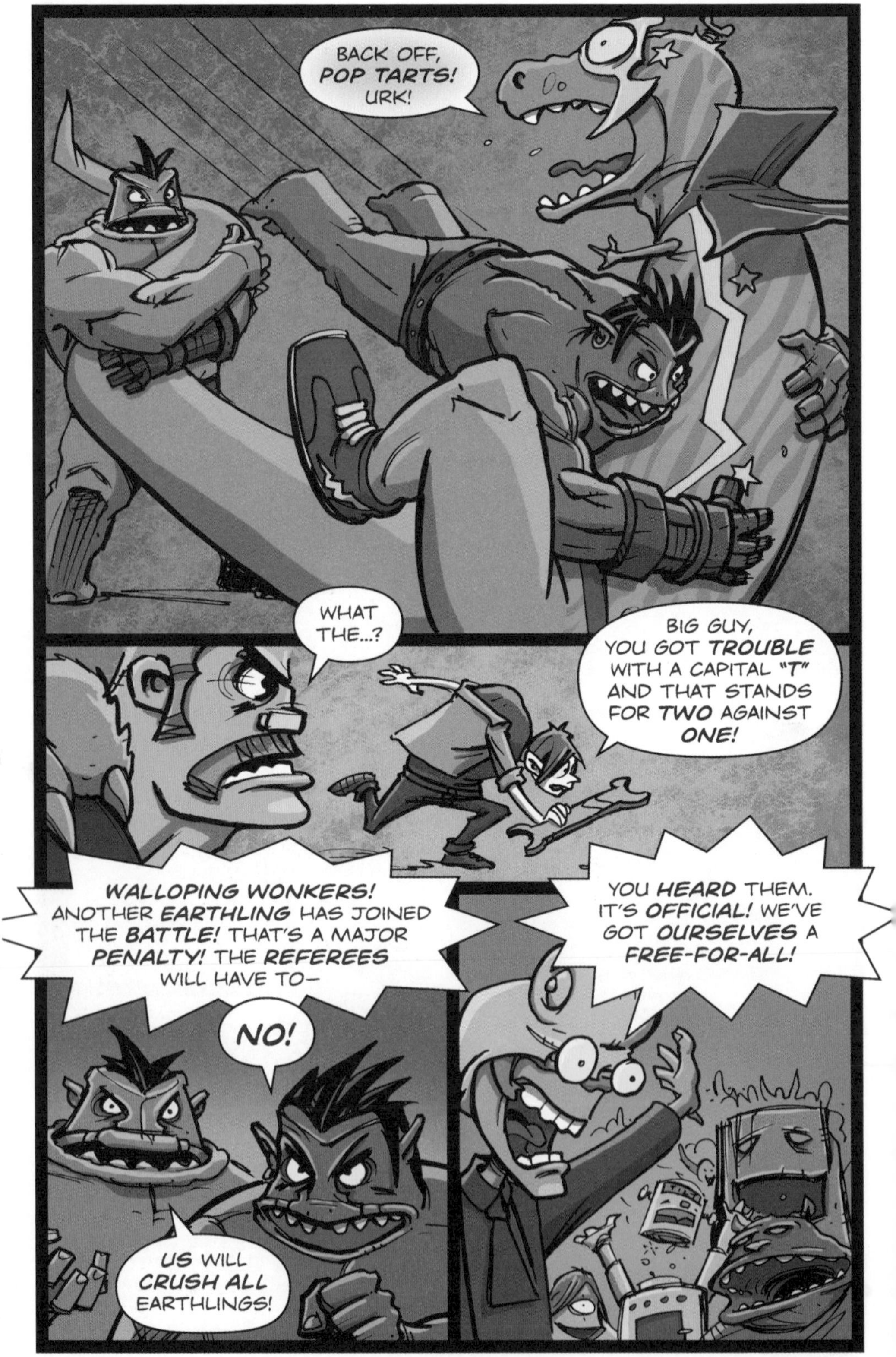
BACK OFF, POP TARTS! URK!
WHAT THE...?
BIG GUY, YOU GOT TROUBLE WITH A CAPITAL "T" AND THAT STANDS FOR TWO AGAINST ONE!
WALLOPING WONKERS! ANOTHER EARTHLING HAS JOINED THE BATTLE! THAT'S A MAJOR PENALTY! THE REFEREES WILL HAVE TO—
NO!
US WILL CRUSH ALL EARTHLINGS!
YOU HEARD THEM. IT'S OFFICIAL! WE'VE GOT OURSELVES A FREE-FOR-ALL!

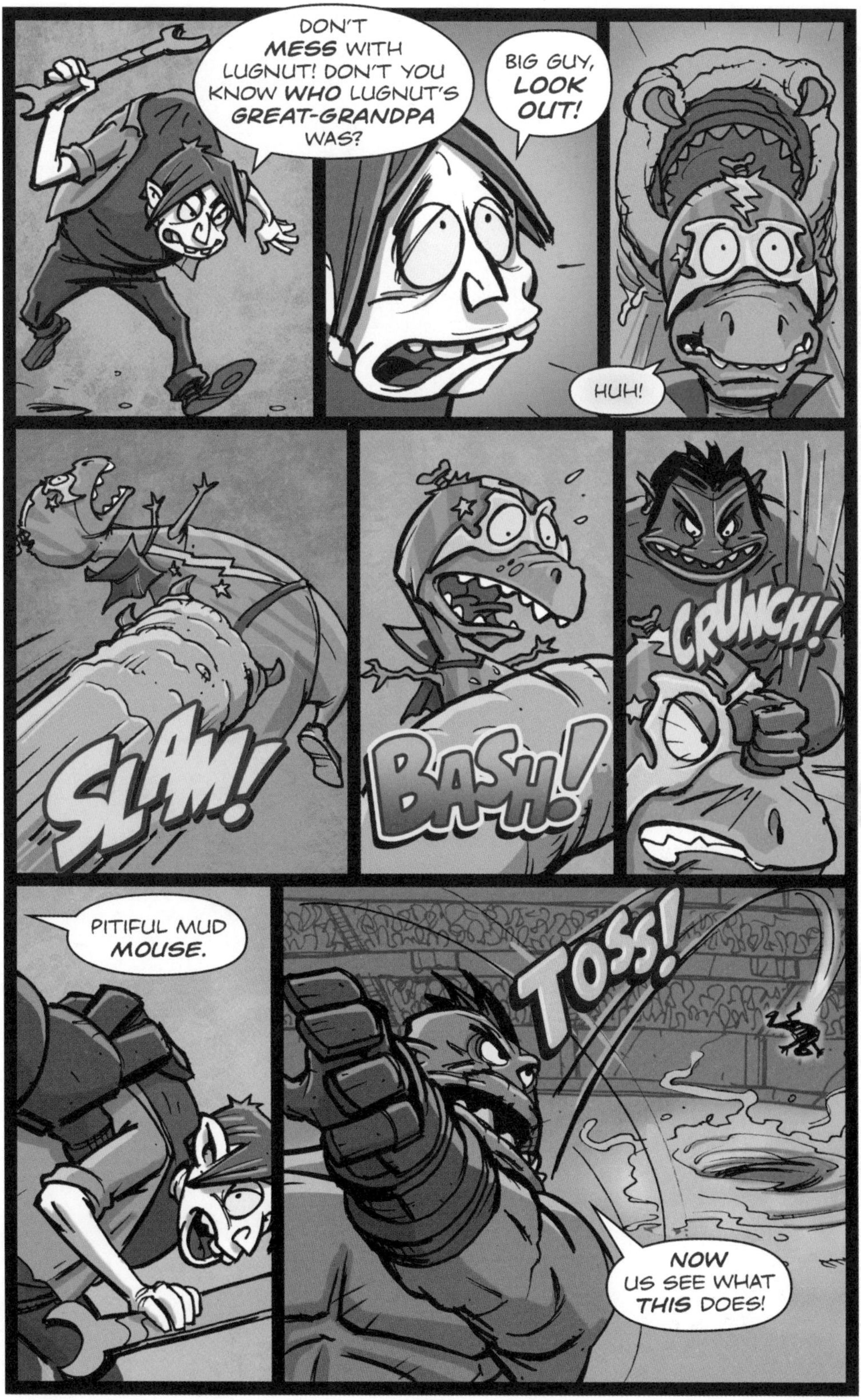
DON'T MESS WITH LUGNUT! DON'T YOU KNOW WHO LUGNUT'S GREAT-GRANDPA WAS?
BIG GUY, LOOK OUT!
HUH!
SLAM!
BASH!
CRUNCH!
PITIFUL MUD MOUSE.
TOSS!
NOW US SEE WHAT THIS DOES!

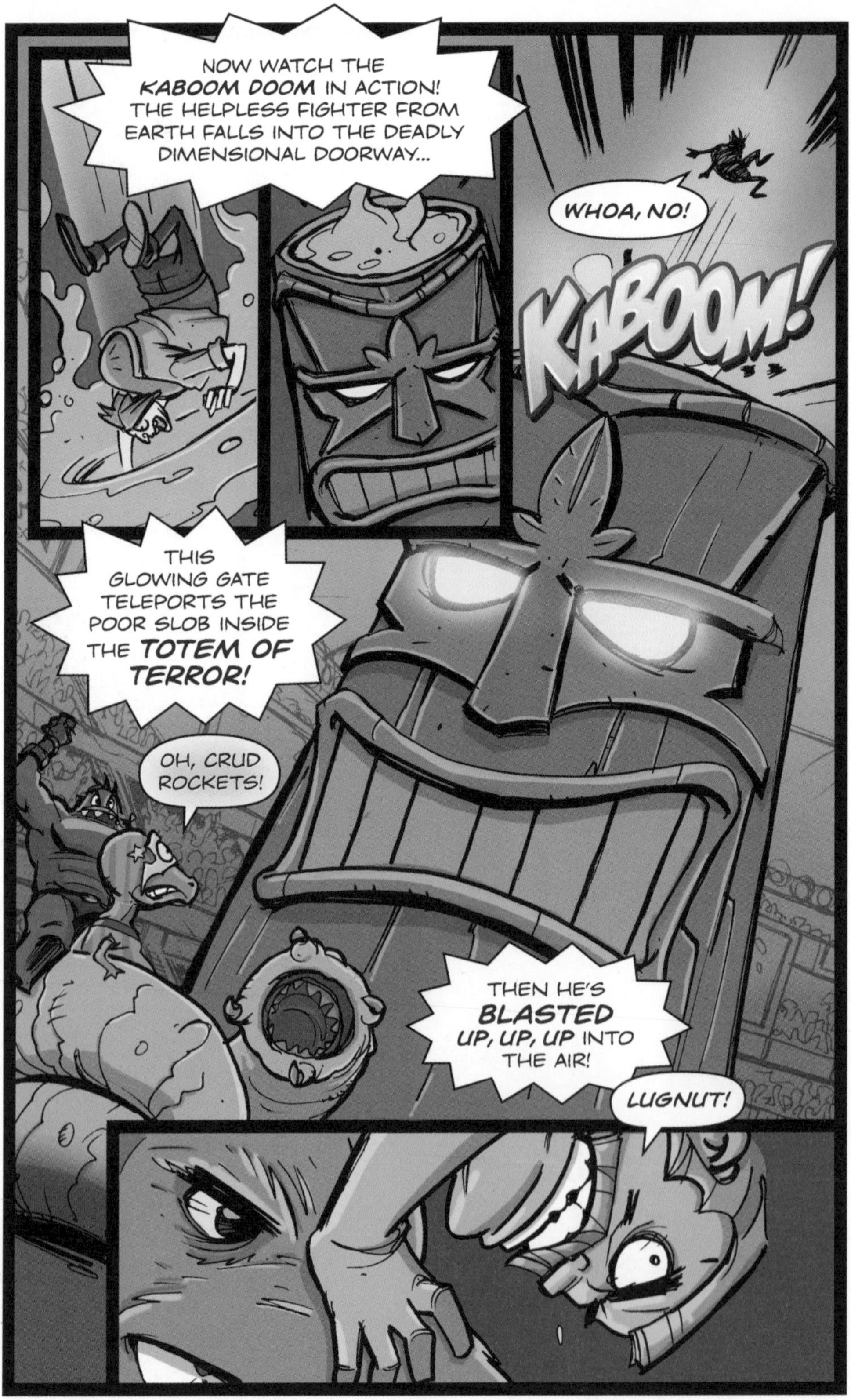
NOW WATCH THE KABOOM DOOM IN ACTION! THE HELPLESS FIGHTER FROM EARTH FALLS INTO THE DEADLY DIMENSIONAL DOORWAY...
WHOA, NO!
KABOOM!
THIS GLOWING GATE TELEPORTS THE POOR SLOB INSIDE THE TOTEM OF TERROR!
OH, CRUD ROCKETS!
THEN HE'S BLASTED UP, UP, UP INTO THE AIR!
LUGNUT!

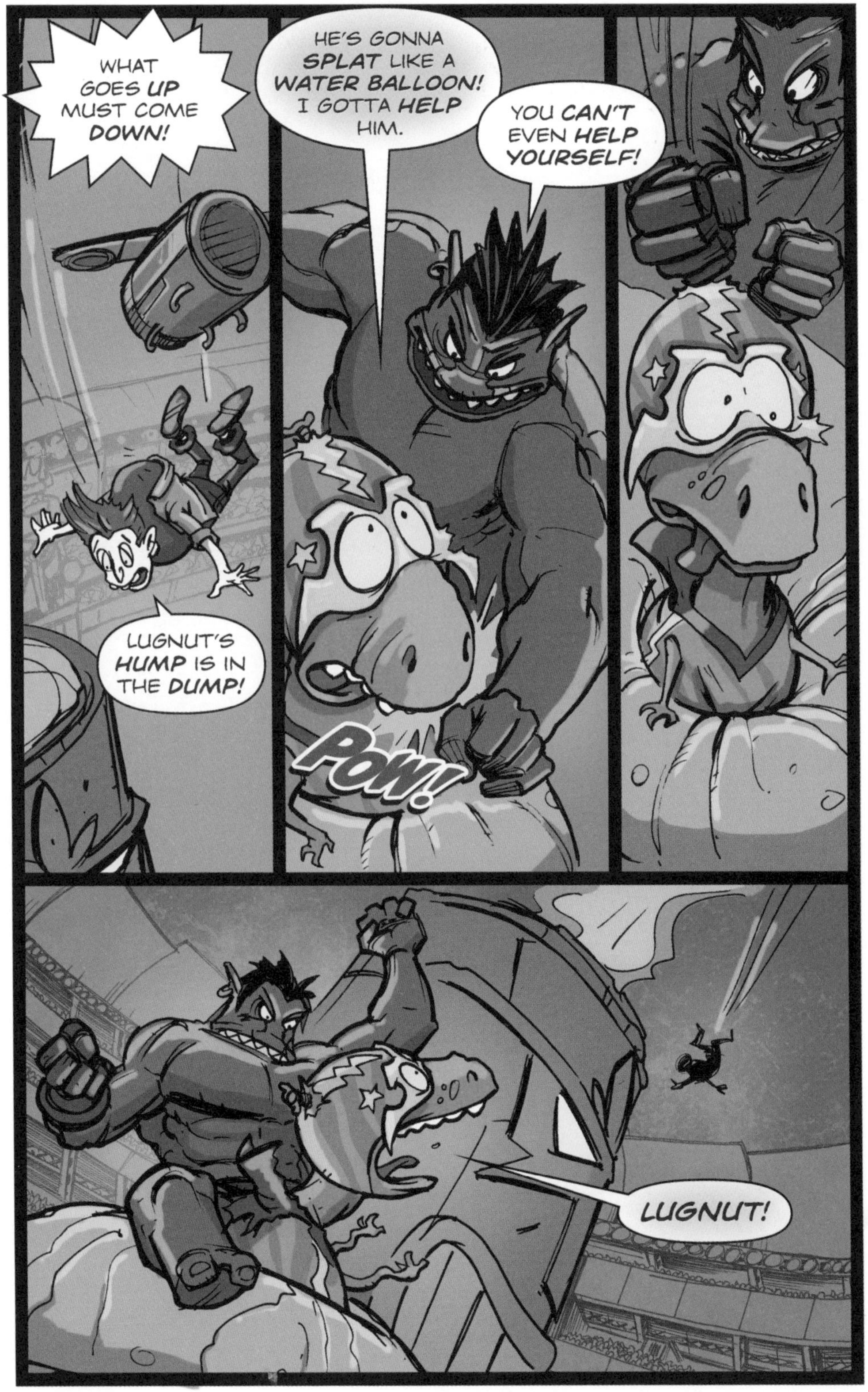
WHAT GOES UP MUST COME DOWN!
HE'S GONNA SPLAT LIKE A WATER BALLOON! I GOTTA HELP HIM.
YOU CAN'T EVEN HELP YOURSELF!
LUGNUT'S HUMP IS IN THE DUMP!
POW!
LUGNUT!

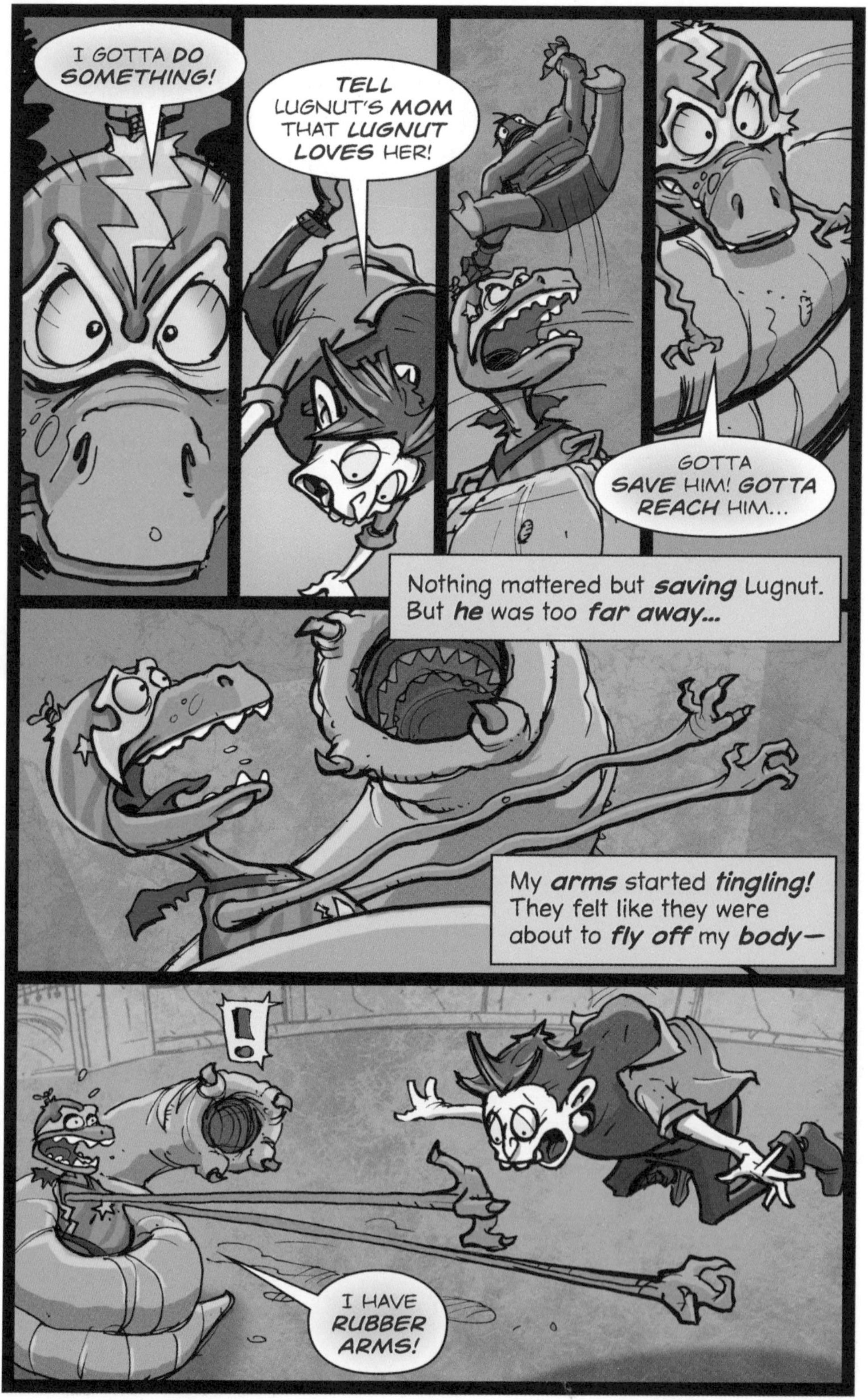
I GOTTA DO SOMETHING!
TELL LUGNUT'S MOM THAT LUGNUT LOVES HER!
GOTTA SAVE HIM! GOTTA REACH HIM...
Nothing mattered but saving Lugnut. But he was too far away...
My arms started tingling! They felt like they were about to fly off my body—
!
I HAVE RUBBER ARMS!

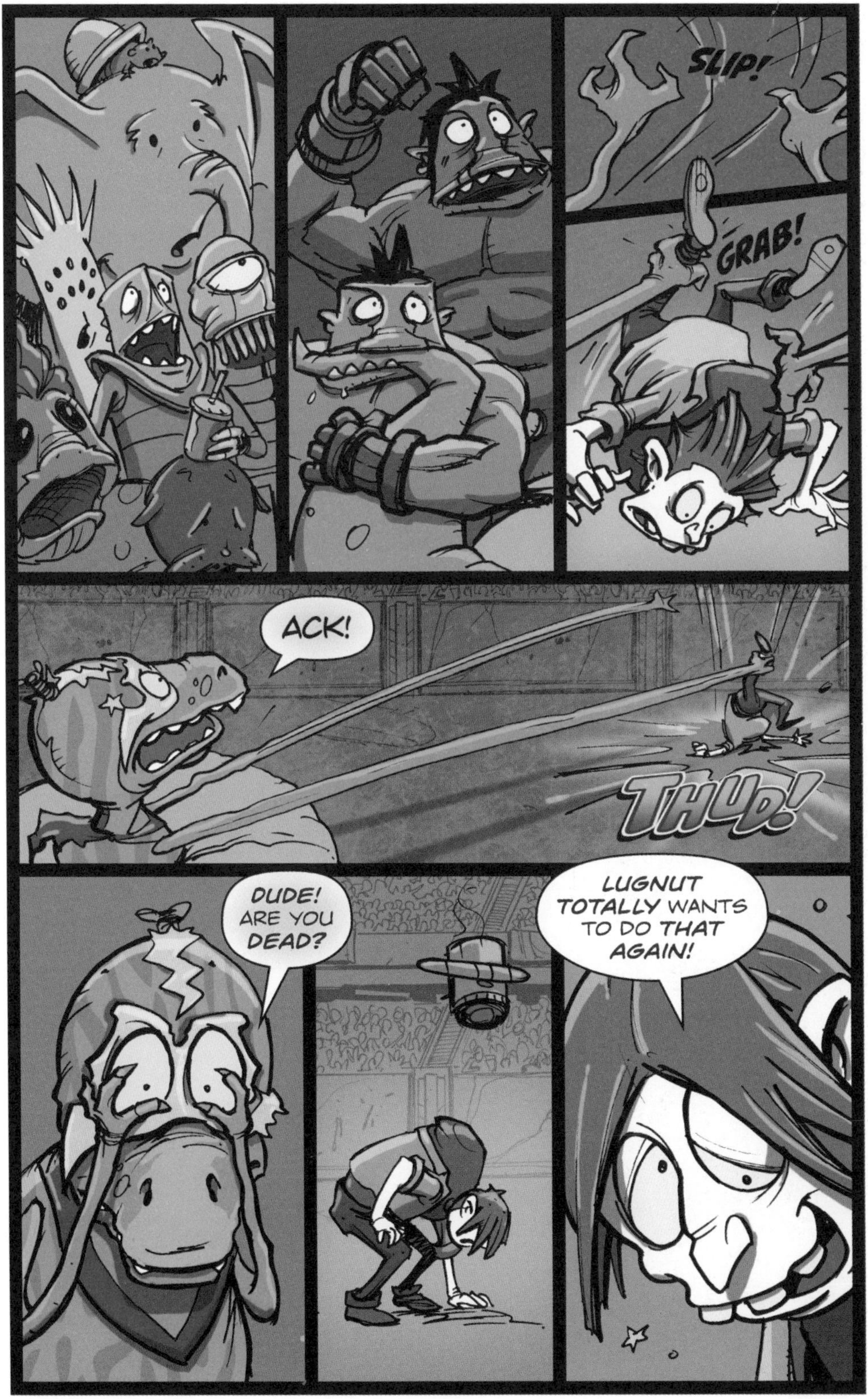
SLIP!
GRAB!
ACK!
THUD!
DUDE! ARE YOU DEAD?
LUGNUT TOTALLY WANTS TO DO THAT AGAIN!

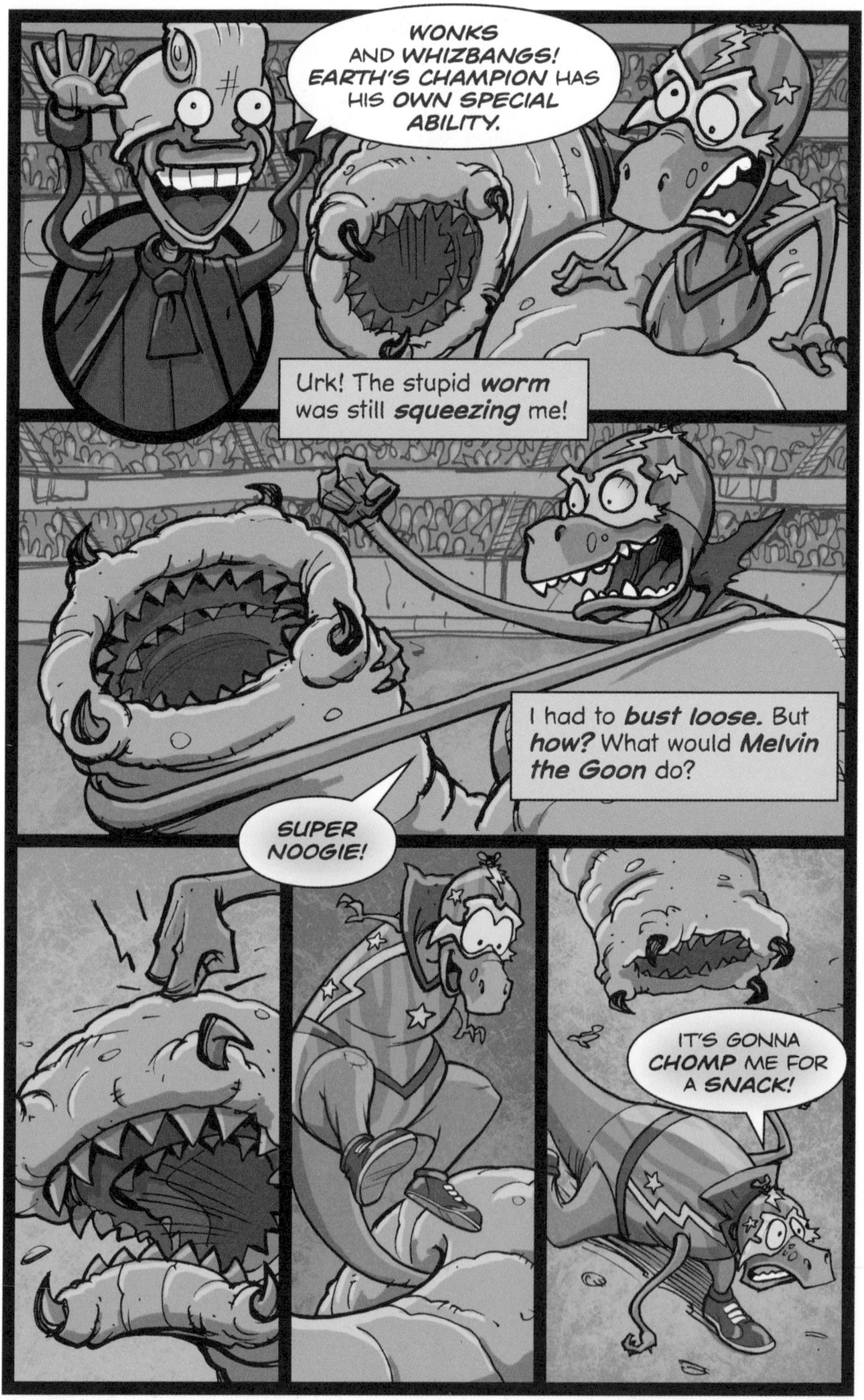
WONKS AND WHIZBANGS! EARTH'S CHAMPION HAS HIS OWN SPECIAL ABILITY.
Urk! The stupid worm was still squeezing me!
I had to bust loose. But how? What would Melvin the Goon do?
SUPER NOOGIE!
IT'S GONNA CHOMP ME FOR A SNACK!

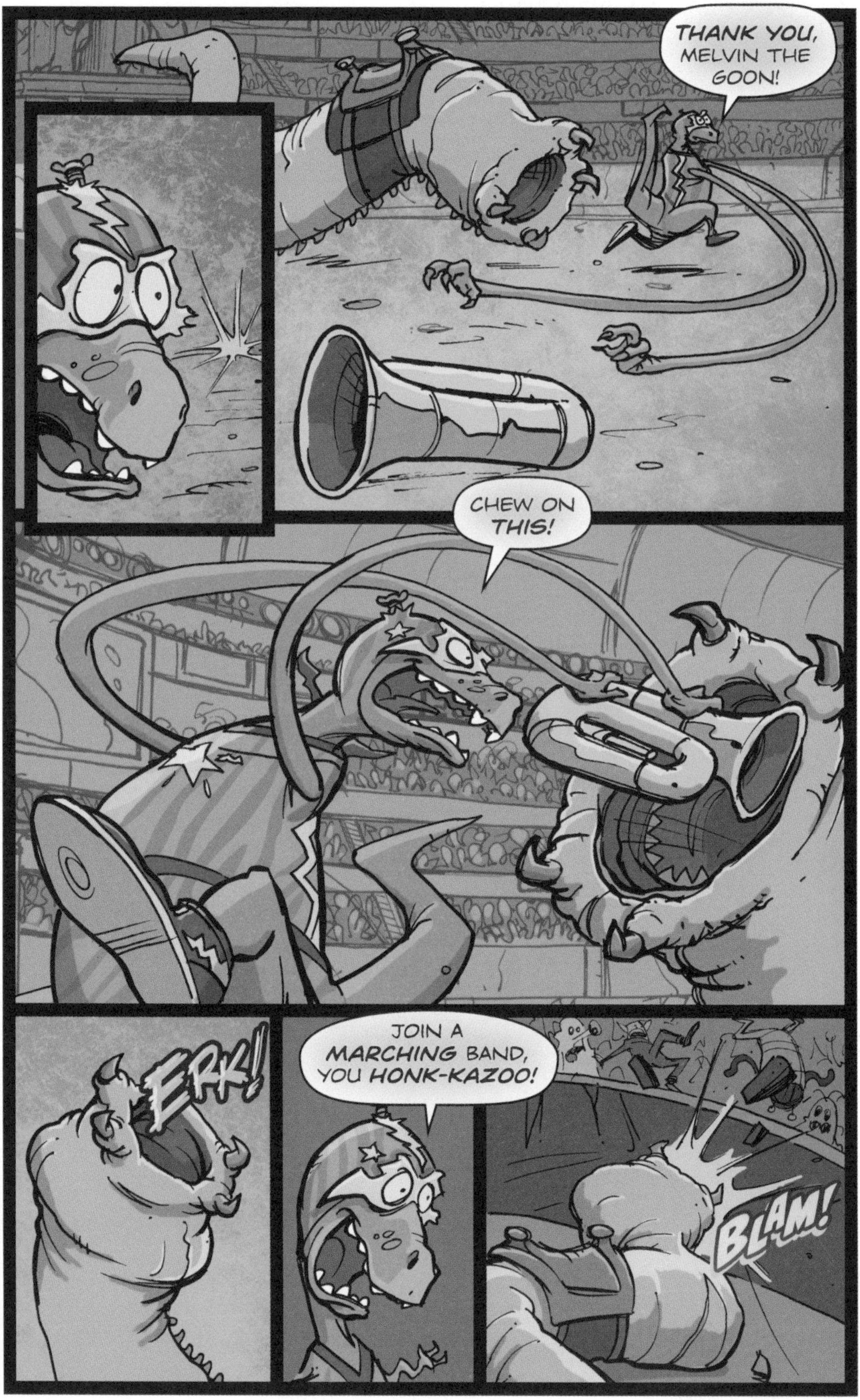
THANK YOU, MELVIN THE GOON!
CHEW ON THIS!
ERK!
JOIN A MARCHING BAND, YOU HONK-KAZOO!
BLAM!

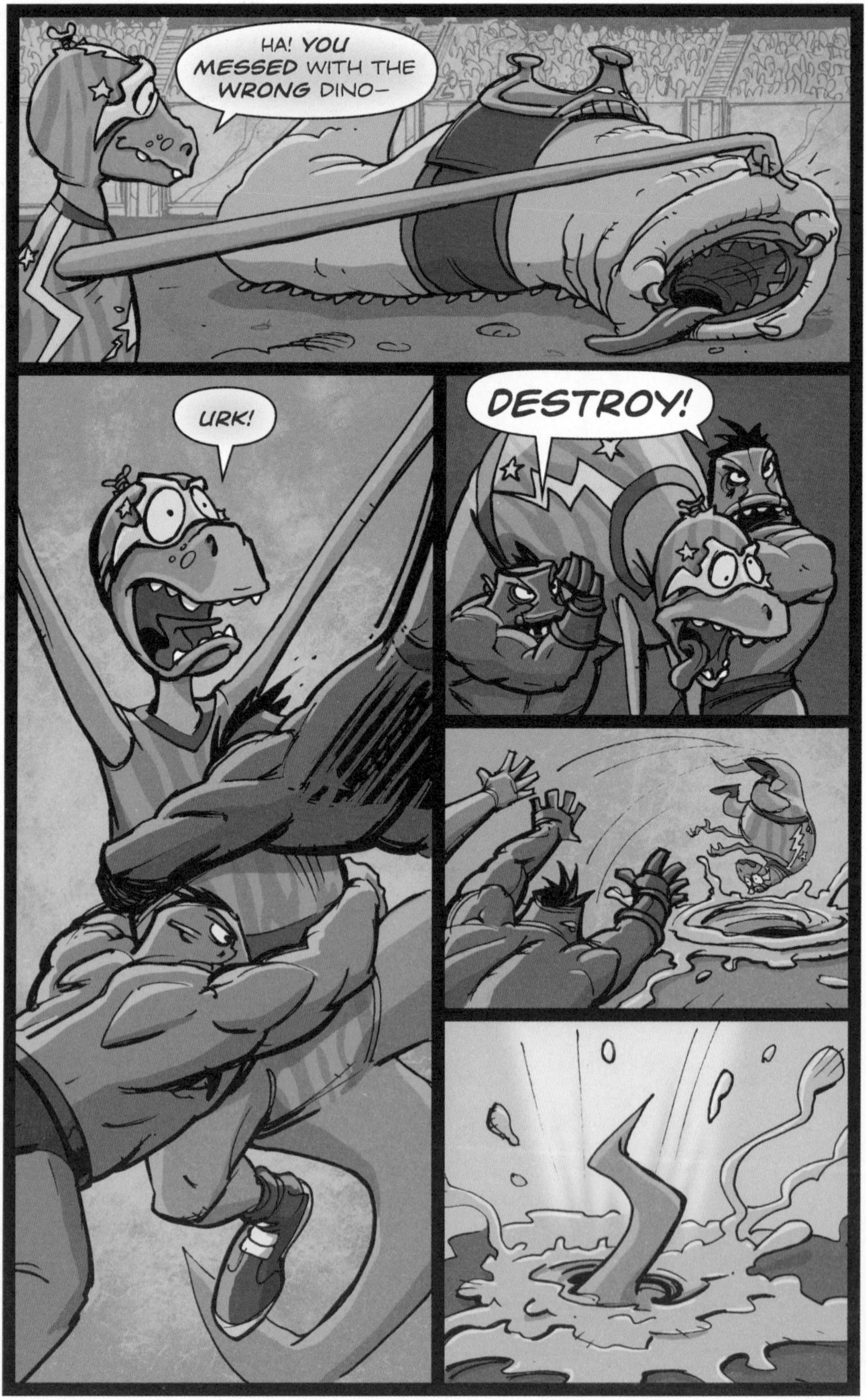
HA! YOU MESSED WITH THE WRONG DINO–
URK!
DESTROY!

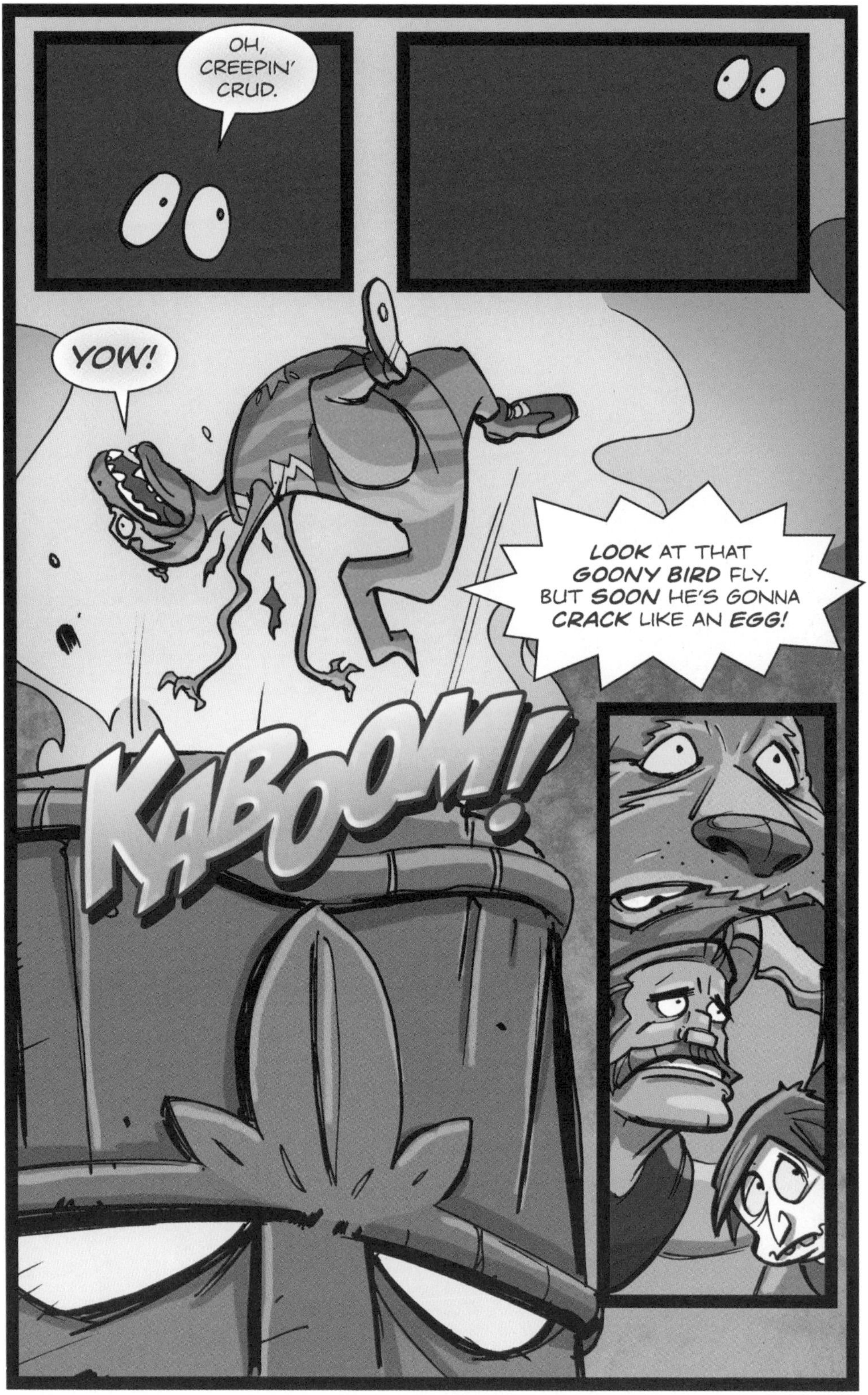
OH, CREEPIN' CRUD.
YOW!
LOOK AT THAT GOONY BIRD FLY. BUT SOON HE'S GONNA CRACK LIKE AN EGG!
KABOOM!

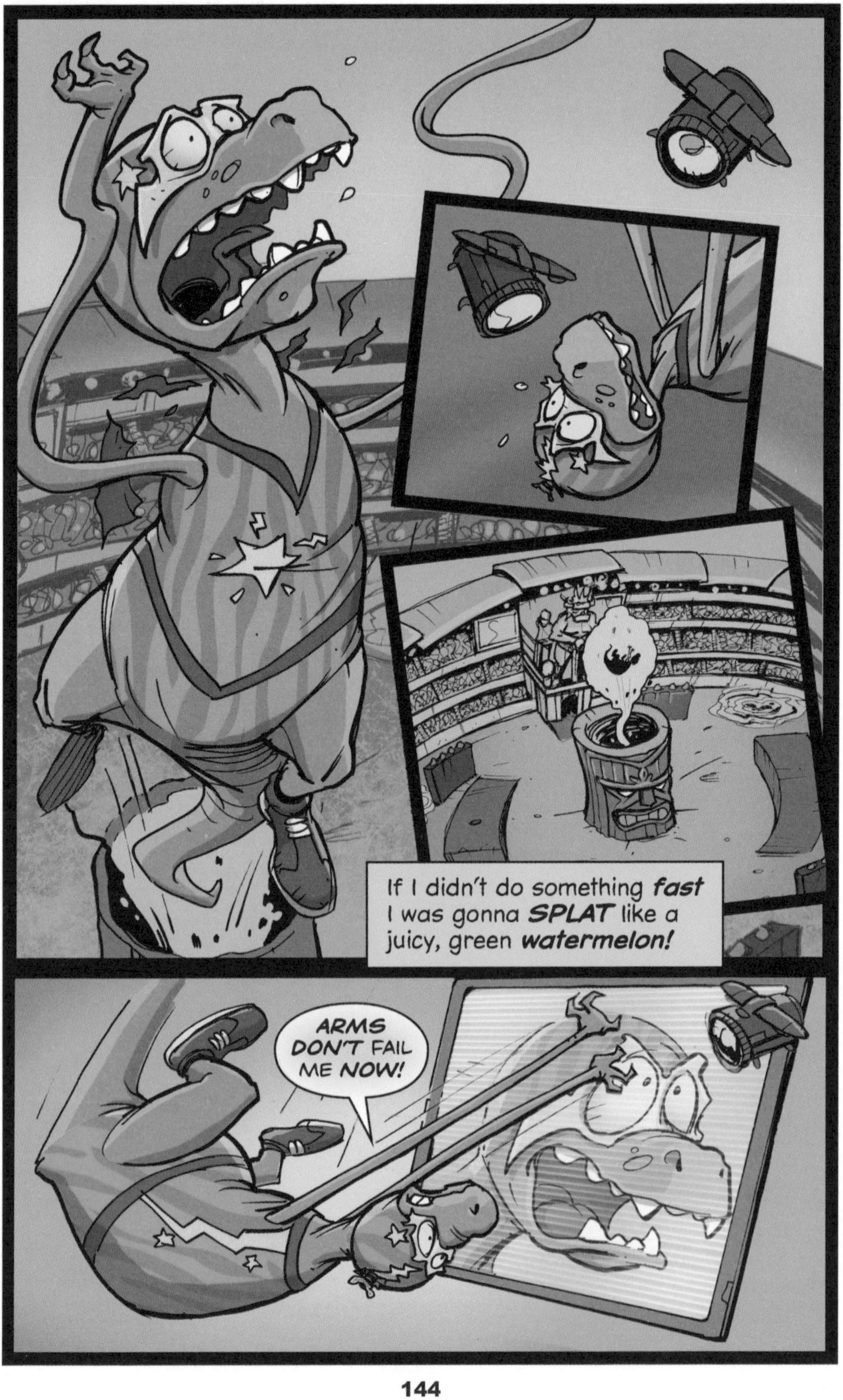
If I didn't do something *fast* I was gonna *SPLAT* like a juicy, green *watermelon!*
ARMS DON'T FAIL ME NOW!

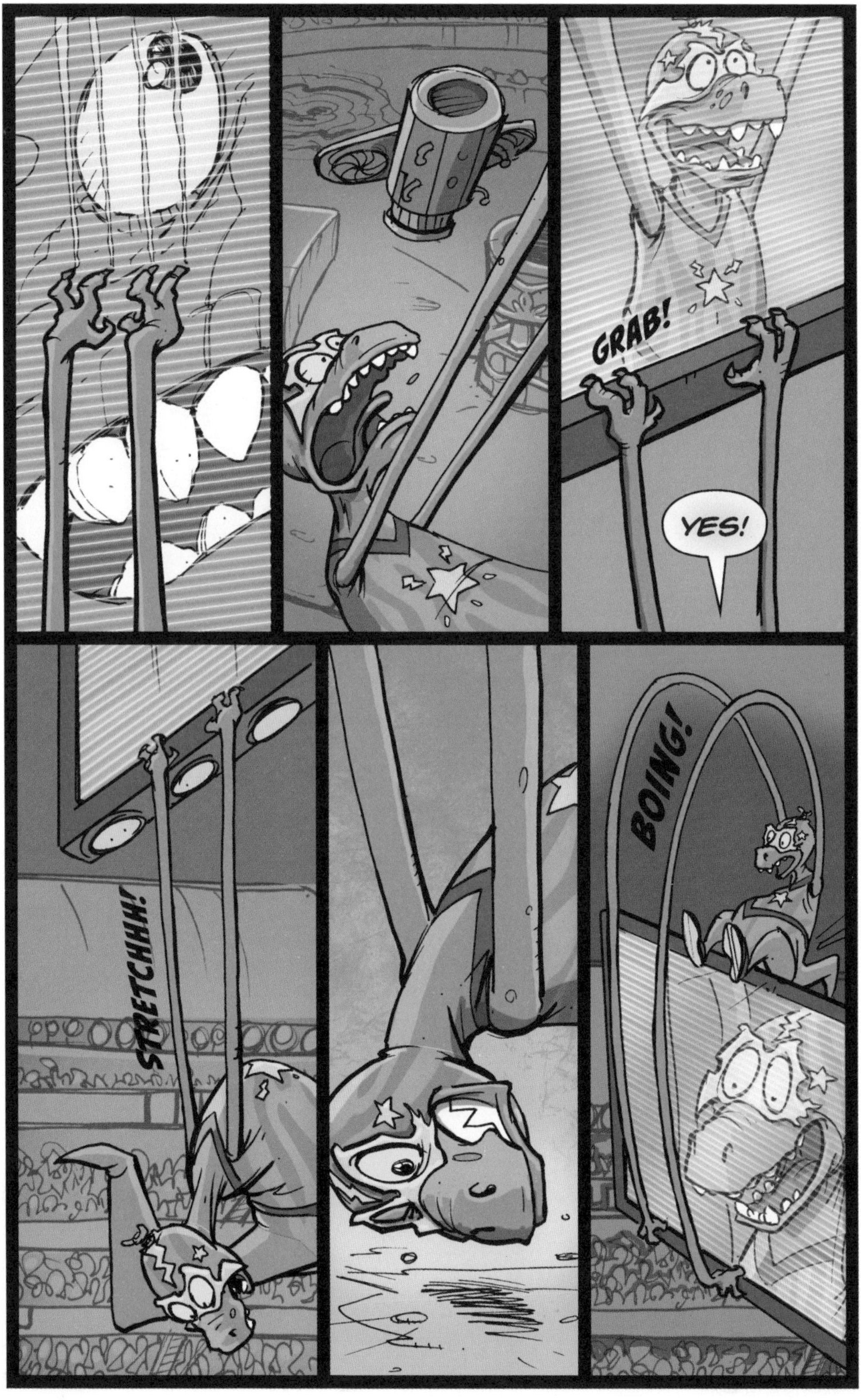
GRAB!
YES!
STRETCHHH!
BOING!

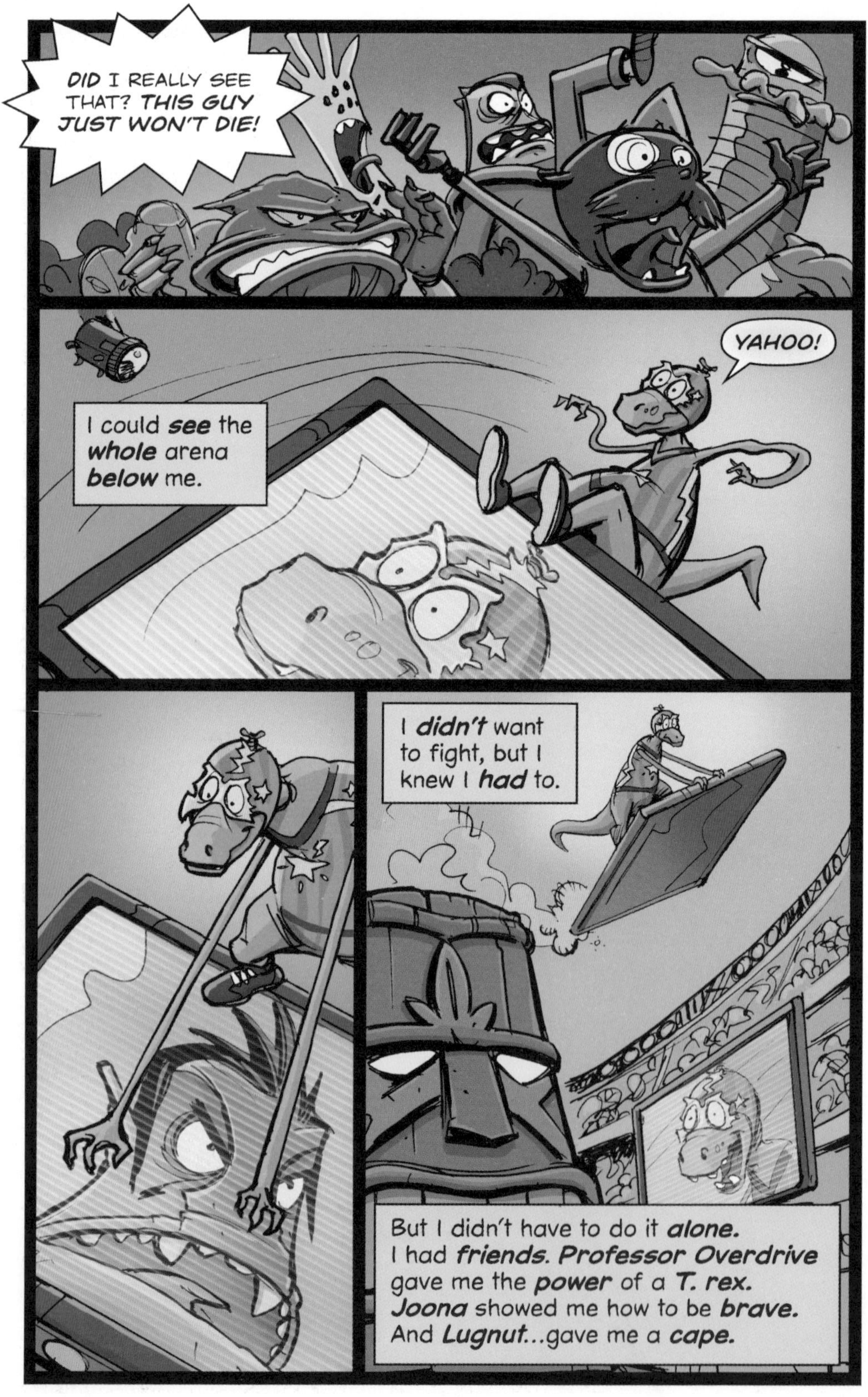
DID I REALLY SEE THAT? THIS GUY JUST WON'T DIE!
YAHOO!
I could see the whole arena below me.
I didn't want to fight, but I knew I had to.
But I didn't have to do it alone. I had friends. Professor Overdrive gave me the power of a T. rex. Joona showed me how to be brave. And Lugnut...gave me a cape.

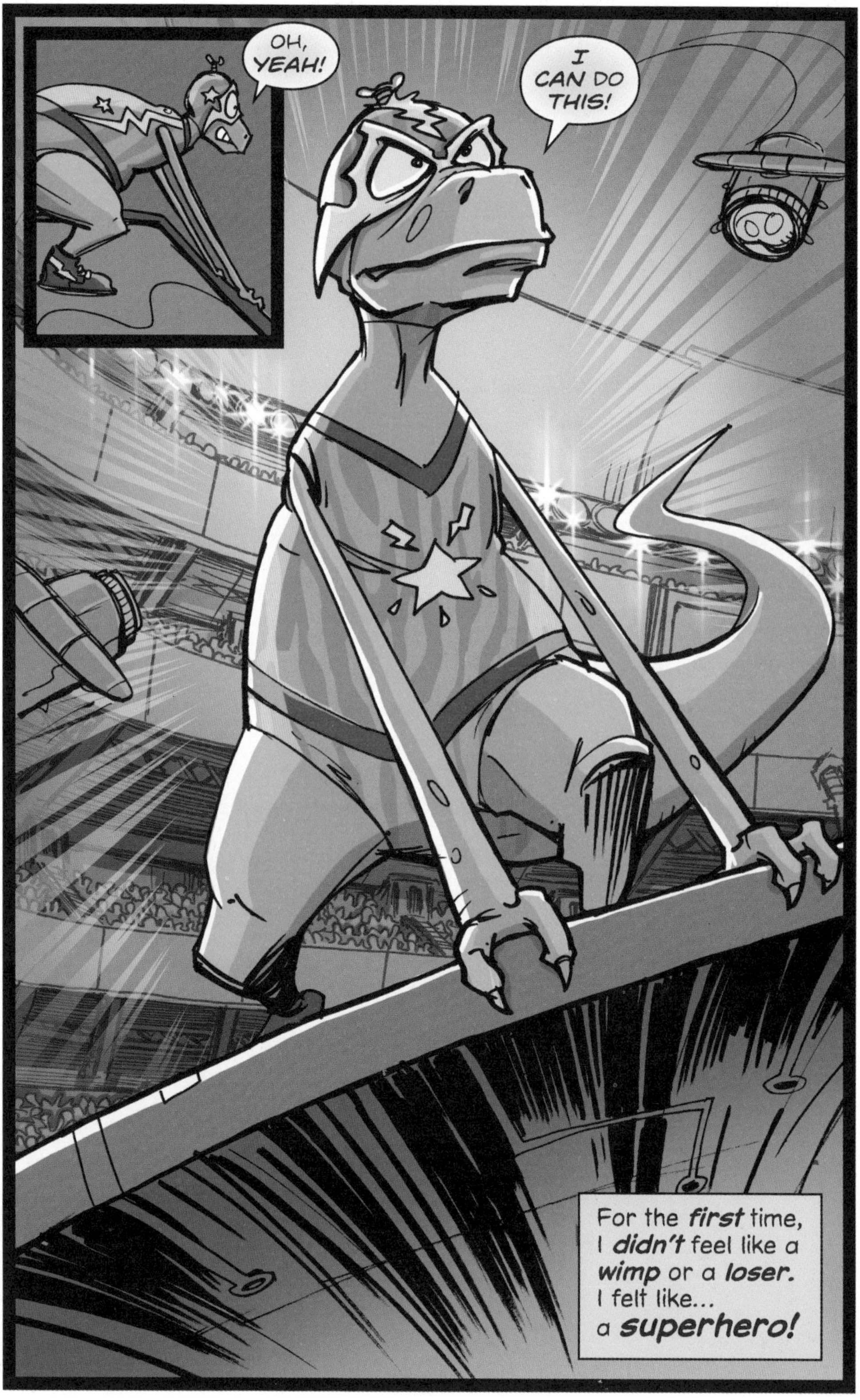
OH, YEAH!
I CAN DO THIS!
For the first time, I didn't feel like a wimp or a loser. I felt like... a superhero!

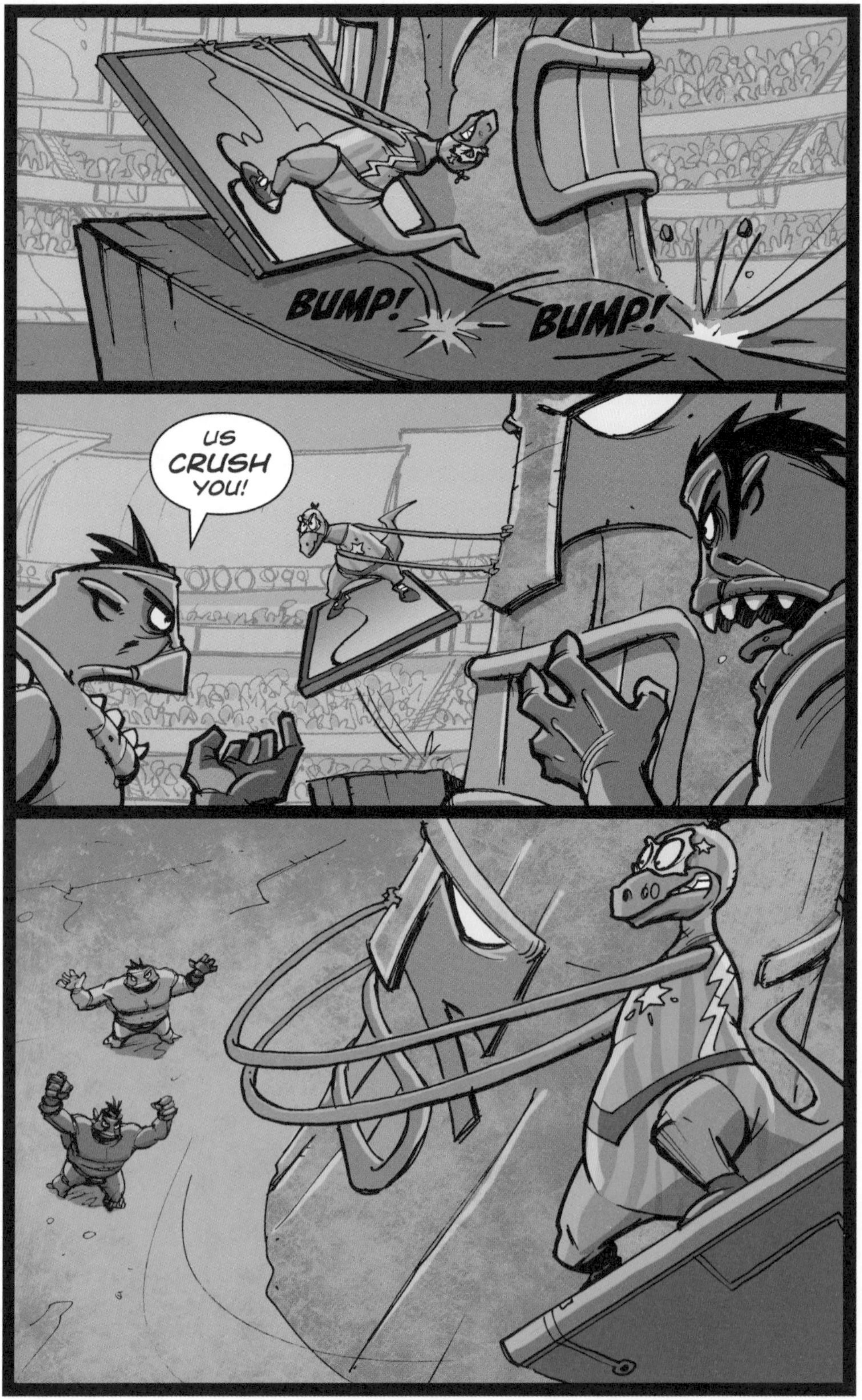
BUMP!
BUMP!
US CRUSH YOU!

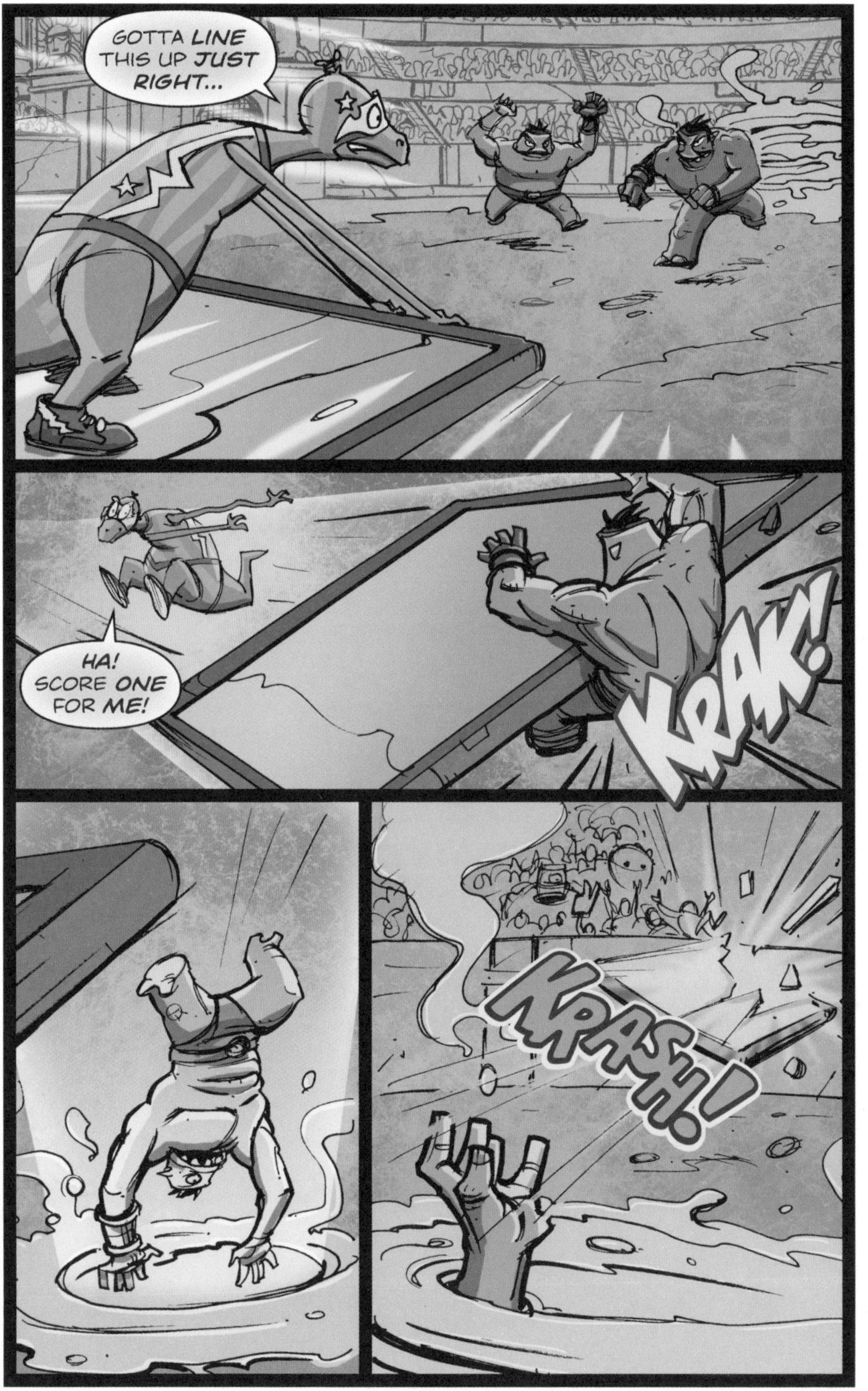
GOTTA LINE THIS UP JUST RIGHT...
HA! SCORE ONE FOR ME!
KRAK!
KRASH!

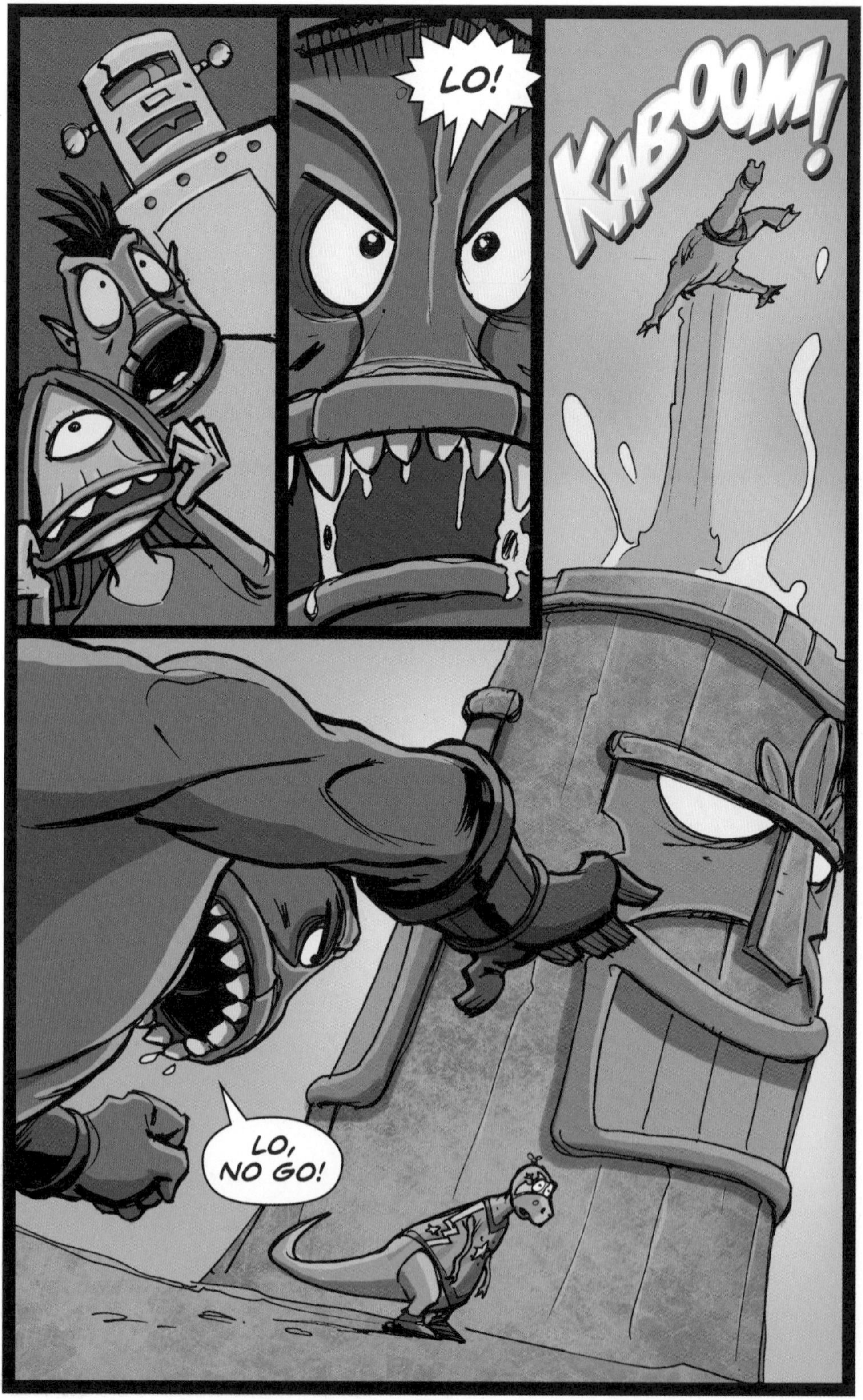
LO!
KABOOM!
LO, NO GO!

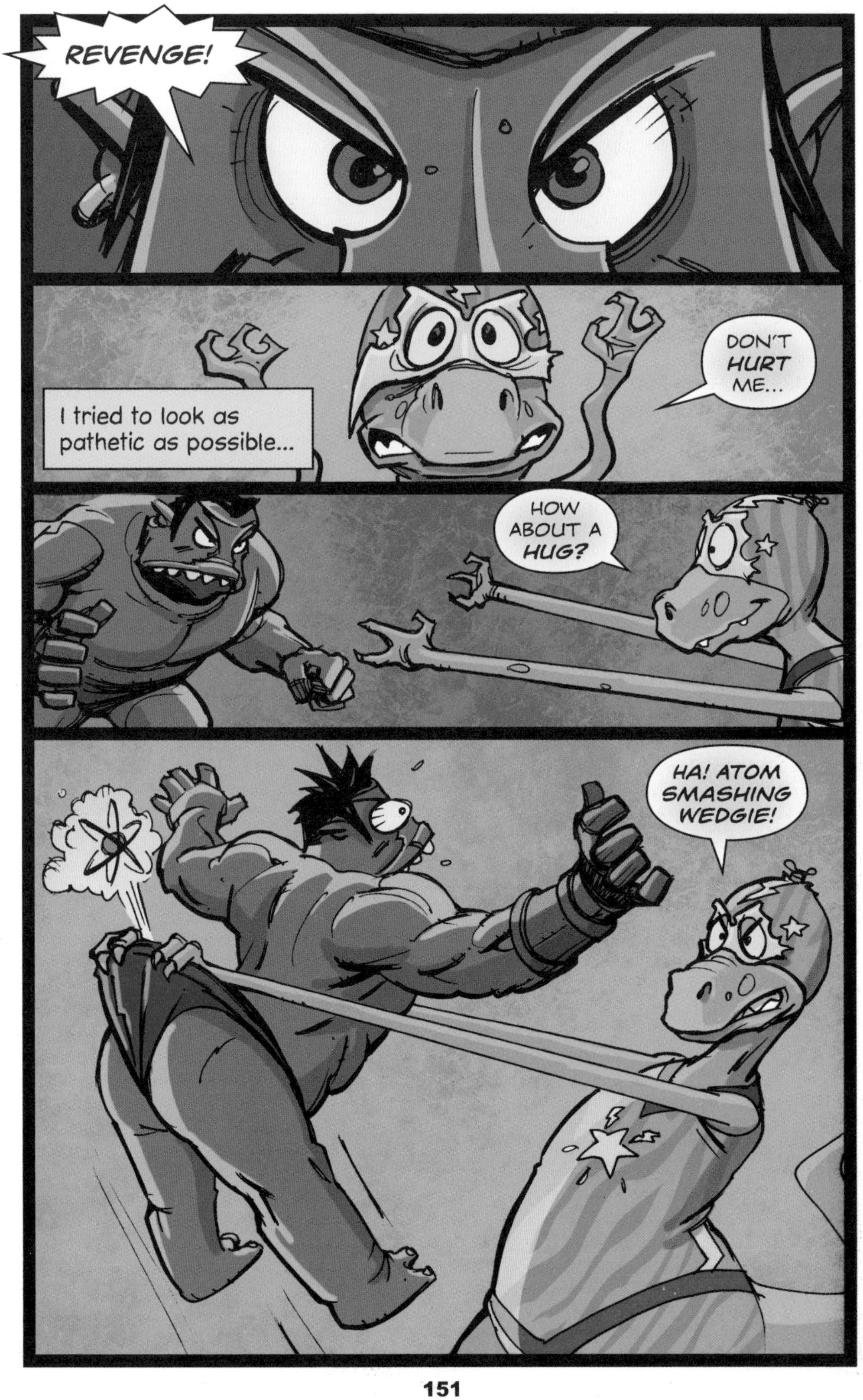
REVENGE!
DON'T HURT ME...
I tried to look as pathetic as possible...
HOW ABOUT A HUG?
HA! ATOM SMASHING WEDGIE!

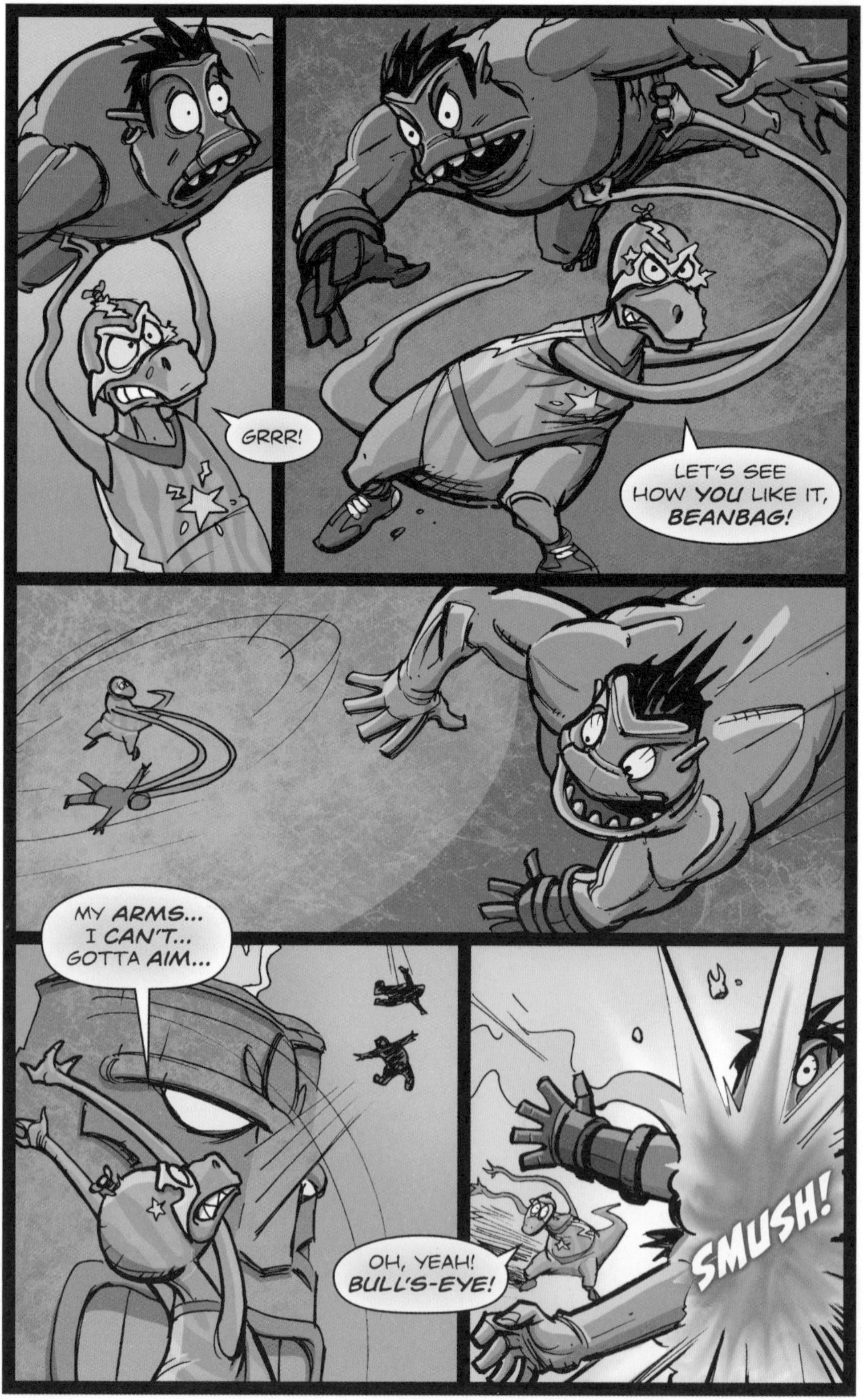
GRRR!
LET'S SEE HOW YOU LIKE IT, BEANBAG!
MY ARMS... I CAN'T... GOTTA AIM...
SMUSH!
OH, YEAH! BULL'S-EYE!

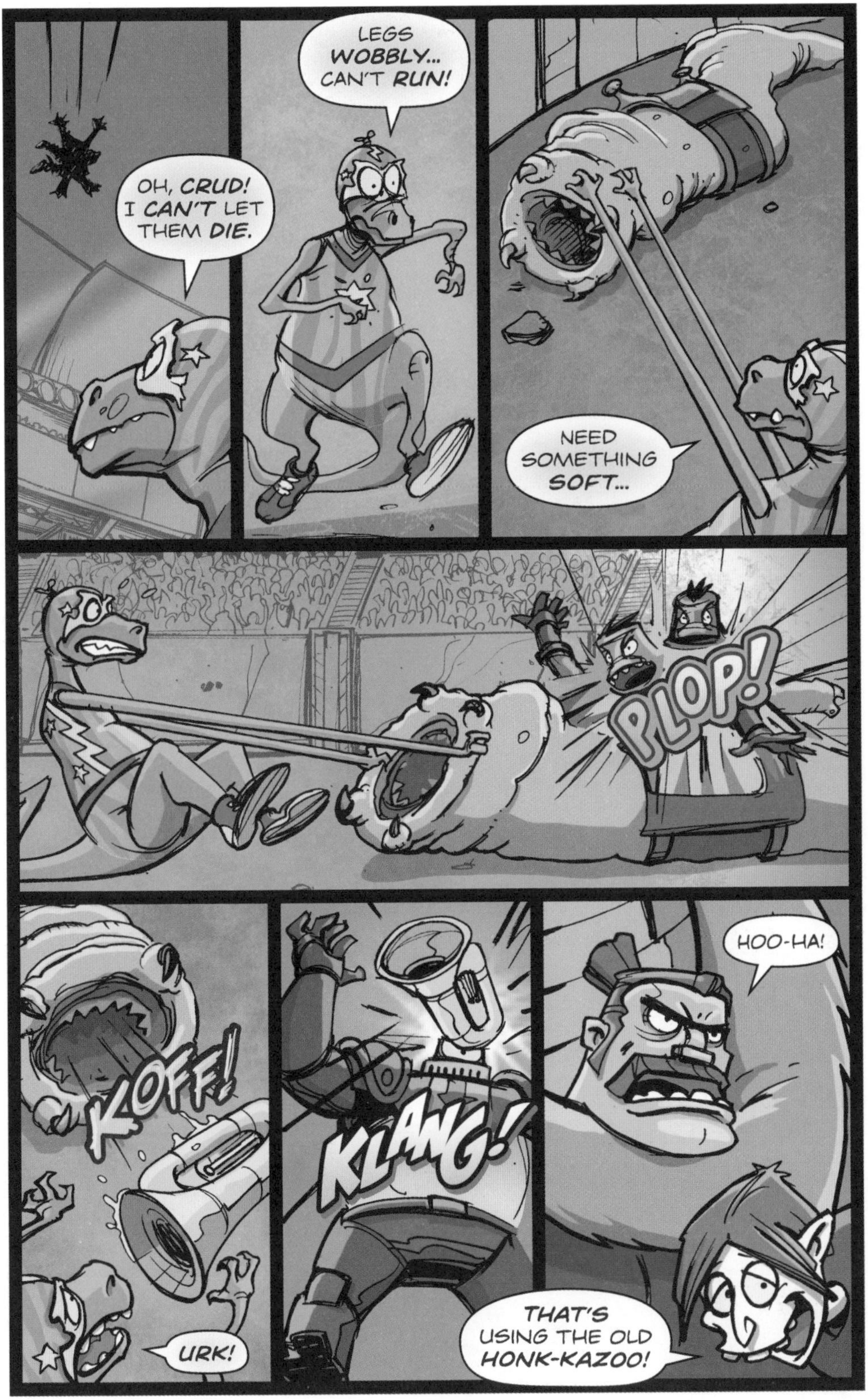
OH, CRUD!
I CAN'T LET
THEM DIE.
LEGS
WOBBLY...
CAN'T RUN!
NEED
SOMETHING
SOFT...
PLOP!
KOFF!
URK!
KLANG!
HOO-HA!
THAT'S
USING THE OLD
HONK-KAZOO!

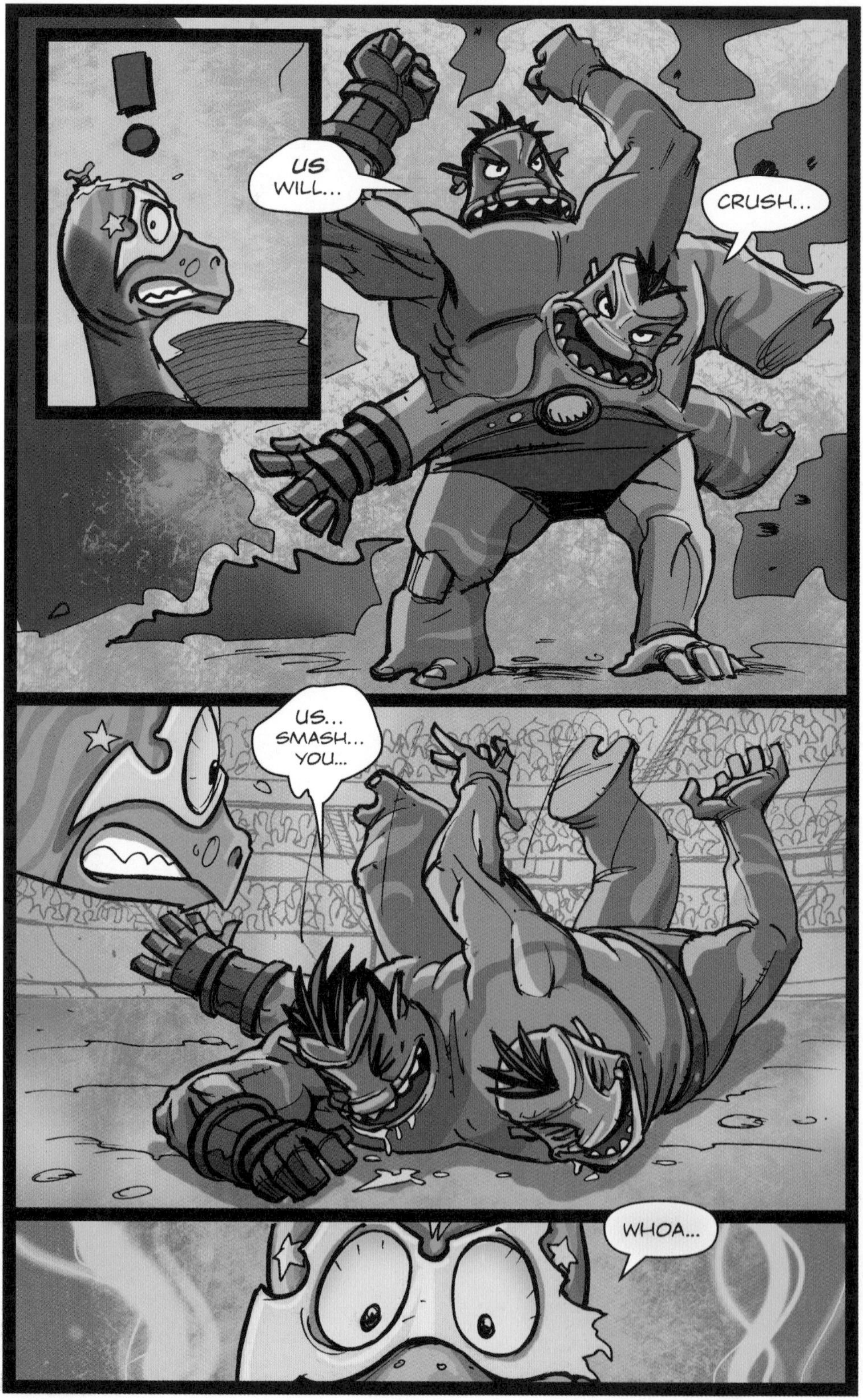
!
US WILL...
CRUSH...
US... SMASH... YOU...
WHOA...

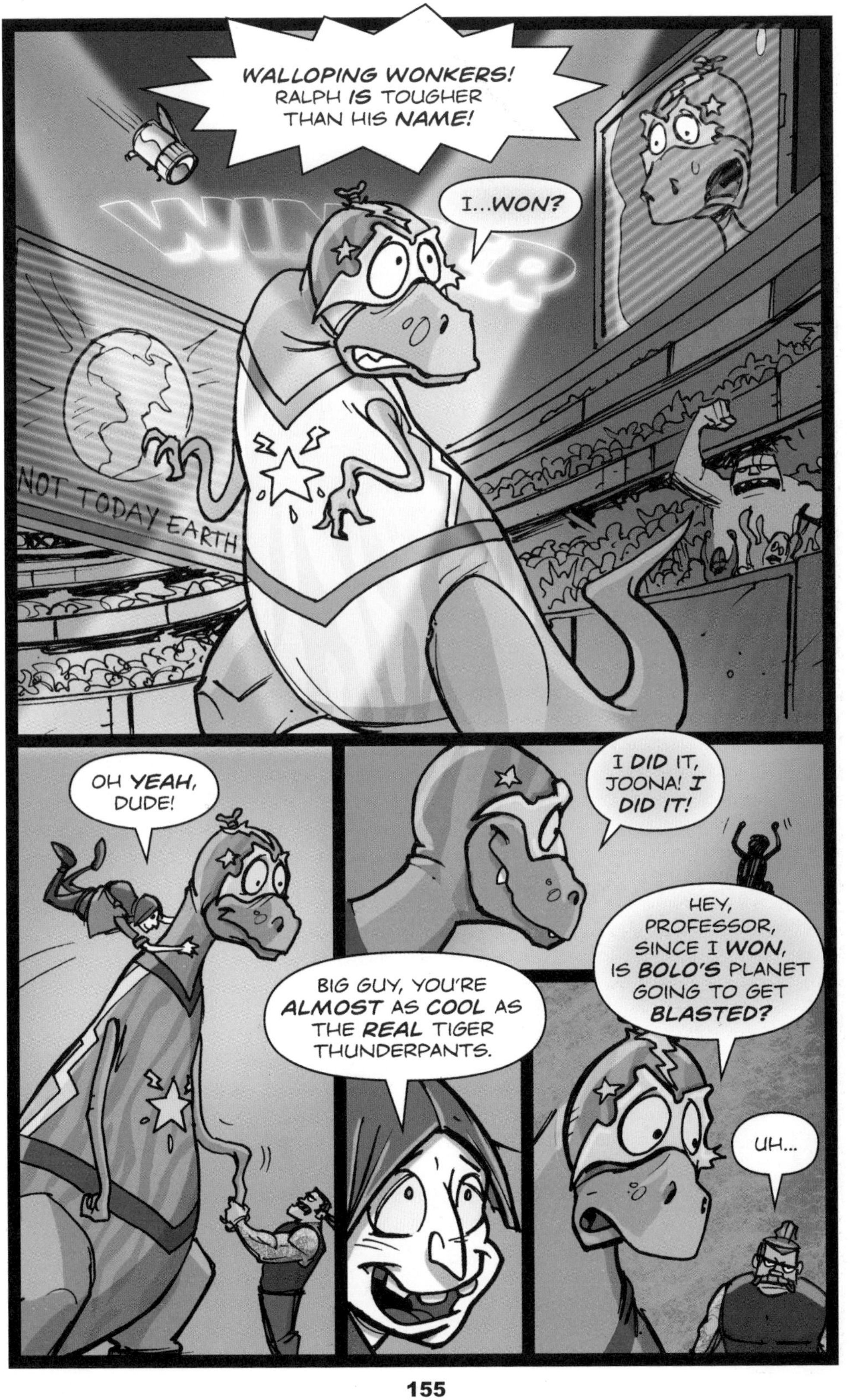
WALLOPING WONKERS! RALPH IS TOUGHER THAN HIS NAME!
I...WON?
NOT TODAY EARTH
OH YEAH, DUDE!
I DID IT, JOONA! I DID IT!
BIG GUY, YOU'RE ALMOST AS COOL AS THE REAL TIGER THUNDERPANTS.
HEY, PROFESSOR, SINCE I WON, IS BOLO'S PLANET GOING TO GET BLASTED?
UH...

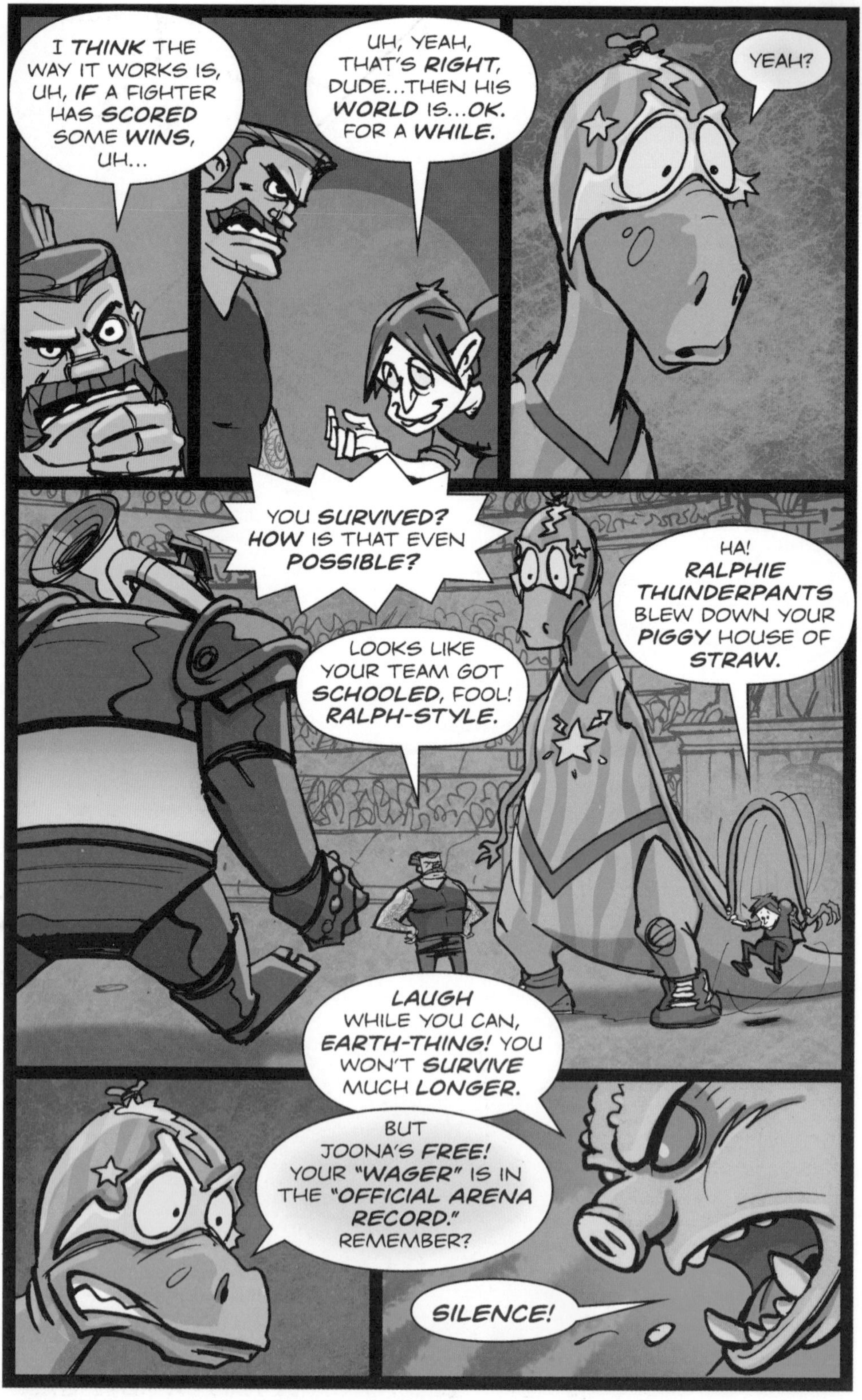
I THINK THE WAY IT WORKS IS, UH, IF A FIGHTER HAS SCORED SOME WINS, UH...
UH, YEAH, THAT'S RIGHT, DUDE...THEN HIS WORLD IS...OK. FOR A WHILE.
YEAH?
YOU SURVIVED? HOW IS THAT EVEN POSSIBLE?
HA! RALPHIE THUNDERPANTS BLEW DOWN YOUR PIGGY HOUSE OF STRAW.
LOOKS LIKE YOUR TEAM GOT SCHOOLED, FOOL! RALPH-STYLE.
LAUGH WHILE YOU CAN, EARTH-THING! YOU WON'T SURVIVE MUCH LONGER.
BUT JOONA'S FREE! YOUR "WAGER" IS IN THE "OFFICIAL ARENA RECORD." REMEMBER?
SILENCE!

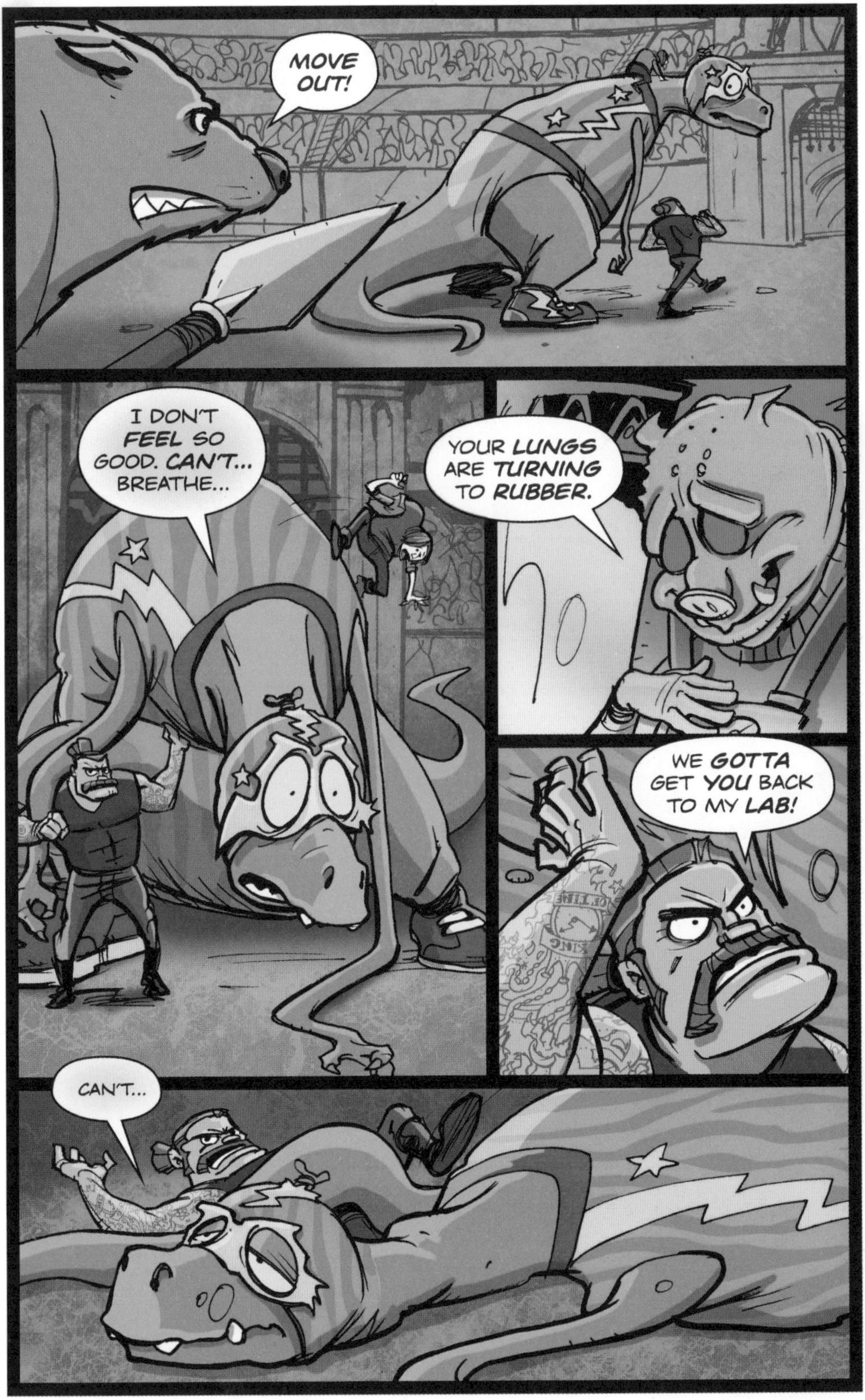
MOVE OUT!
I DON'T FEEL SO GOOD. CAN'T... BREATHE...
YOUR LUNGS ARE TURNING TO RUBBER.
WE GOTTA GET YOU BACK TO MY LAB!
CAN'T...

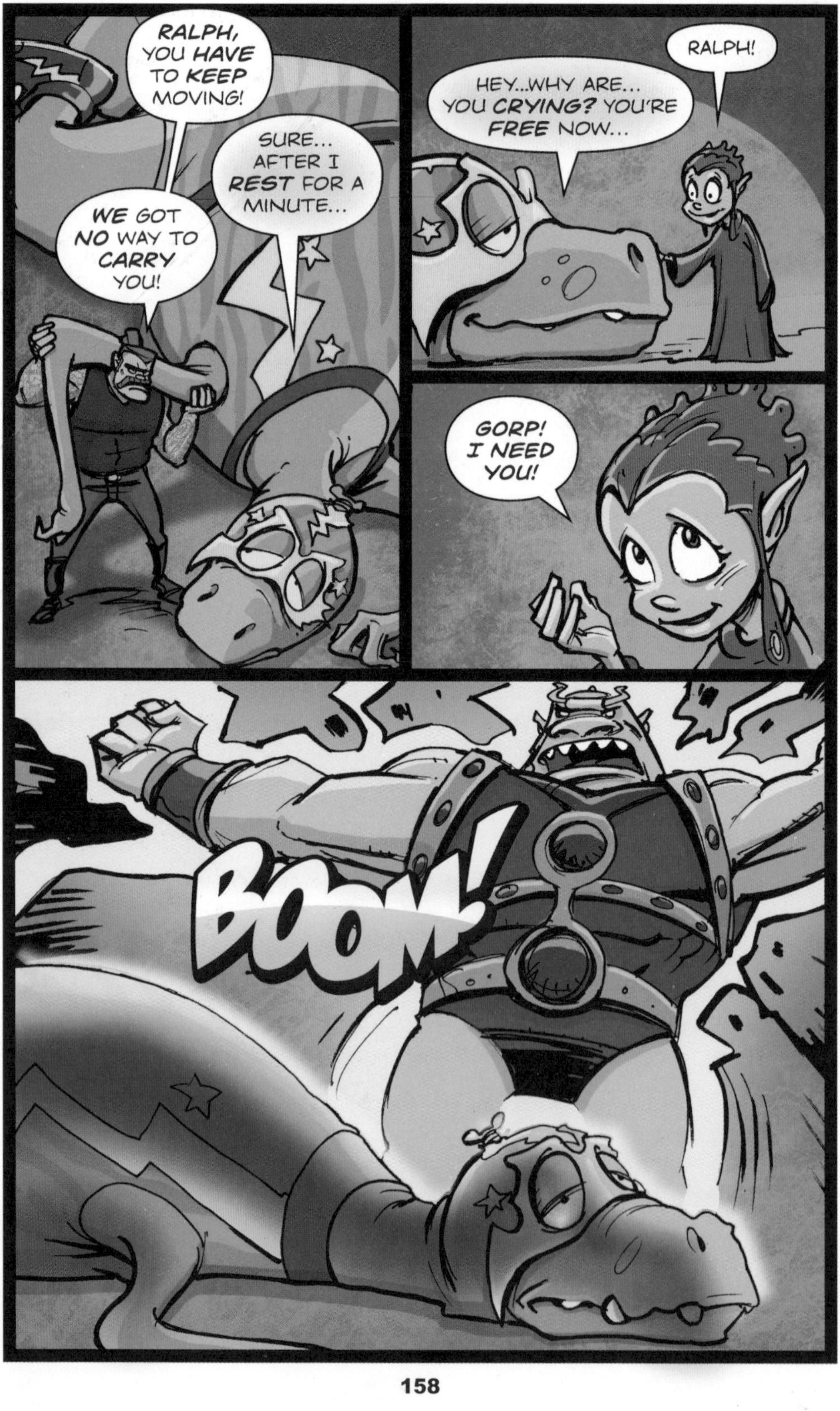
RALPH, YOU HAVE TO KEEP MOVING!
SURE... AFTER I REST FOR A MINUTE...
WE GOT NO WAY TO CARRY YOU!
RALPH!
HEY...WHY ARE... YOU CRYING? YOU'RE FREE NOW...
GORP! I NEED YOU!
BOOM!

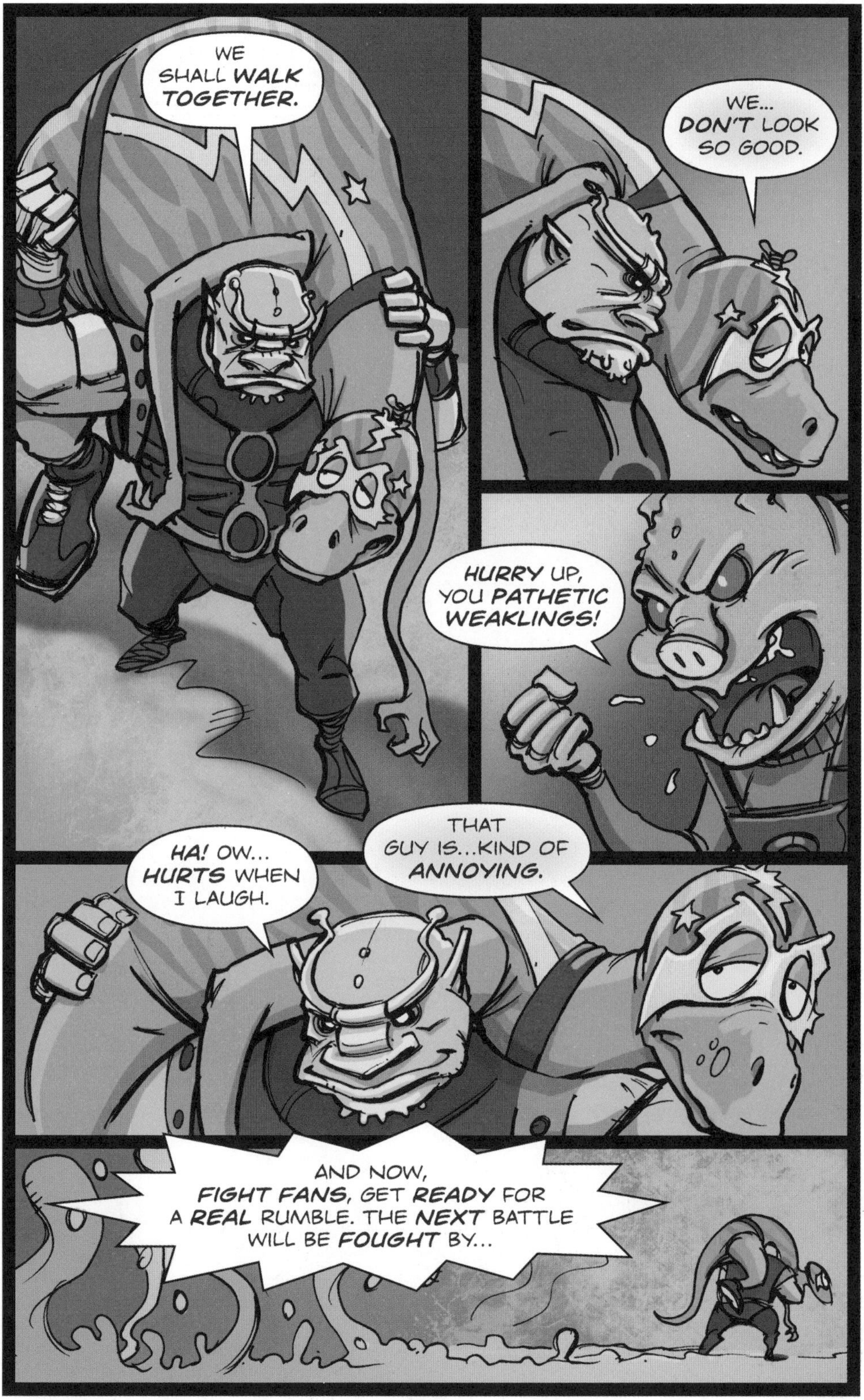
WE SHALL WALK TOGETHER.
WE... DON'T LOOK SO GOOD.
HURRY UP, YOU PATHETIC WEAKLINGS!
HA! OW... HURTS WHEN I LAUGH.
THAT GUY IS...KIND OF ANNOYING.
AND NOW, FIGHT FANS, GET READY FOR A REAL RUMBLE. THE NEXT BATTLE WILL BE FOUGHT BY...

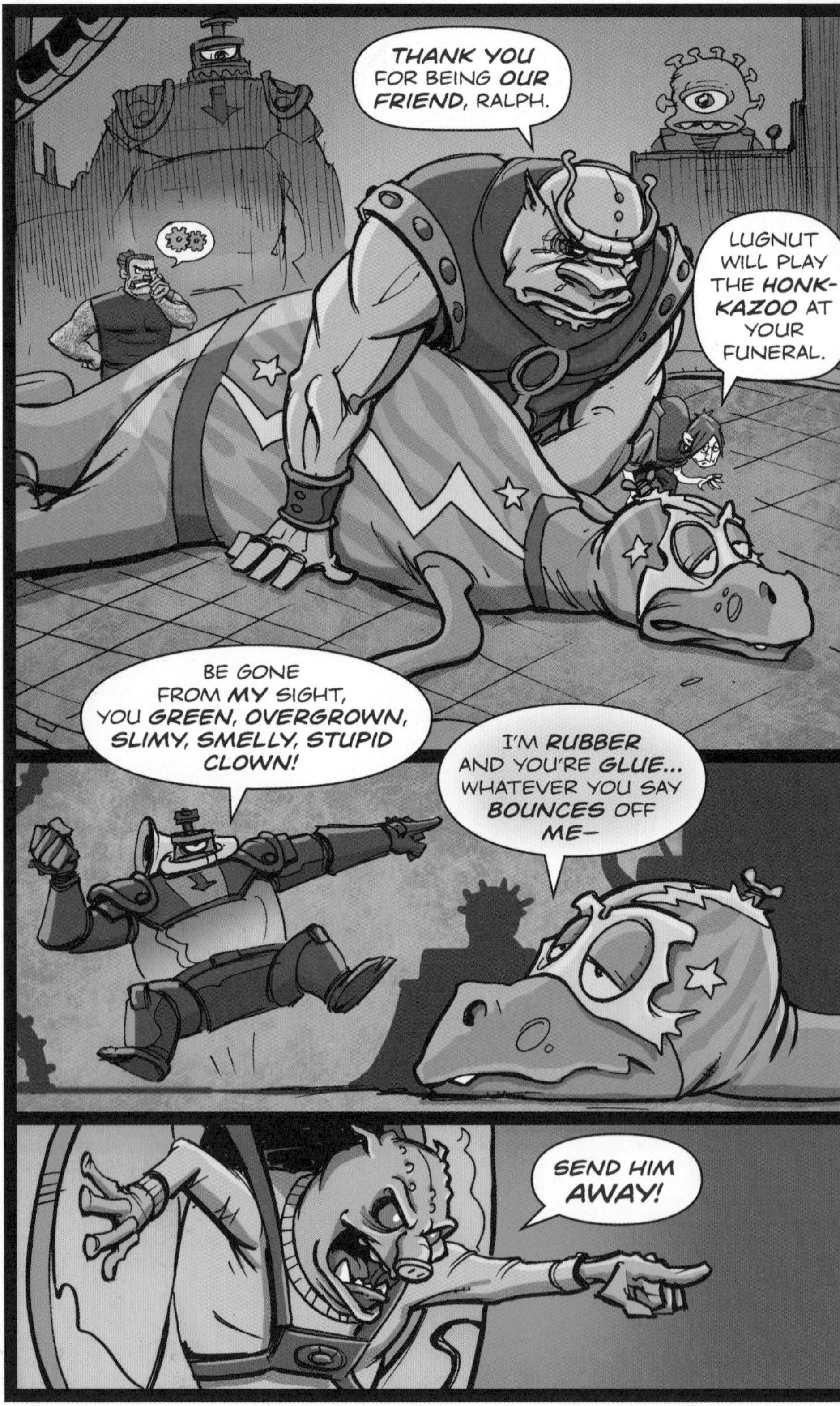
THANK YOU FOR BEING OUR FRIEND, RALPH.
LUGNUT WILL PLAY THE HONK-KAZOO AT YOUR FUNERAL.
BE GONE FROM MY SIGHT, YOU GREEN, OVERGROWN, SLIMY, SMELLY, STUPID CLOWN!
I'M RUBBER AND YOU'RE GLUE... WHATEVER YOU SAY BOUNCES OFF ME—
SEND HIM AWAY!

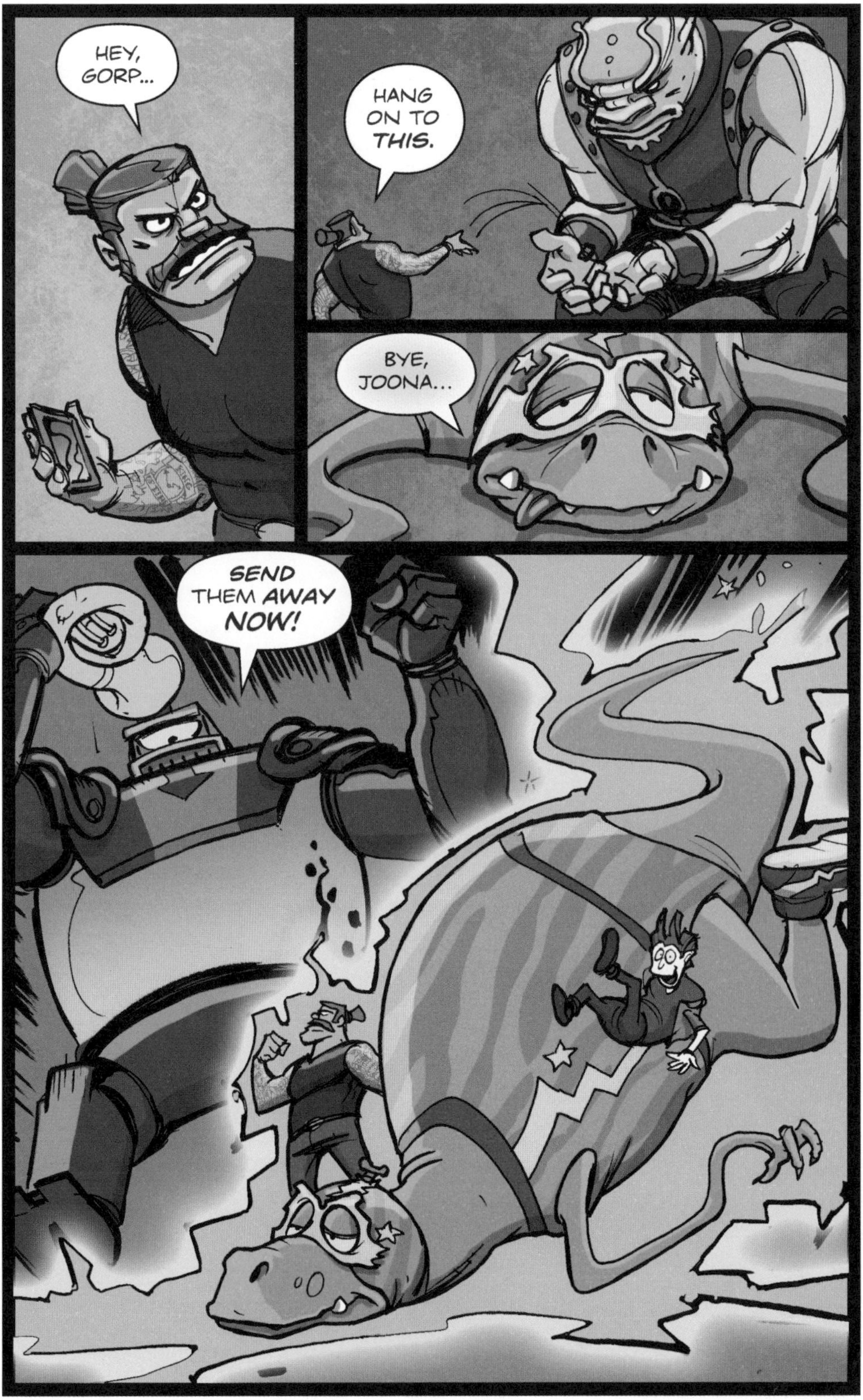
HEY, GORP...
HANG ON TO THIS.
BYE, JOONA...
SEND THEM AWAY NOW!

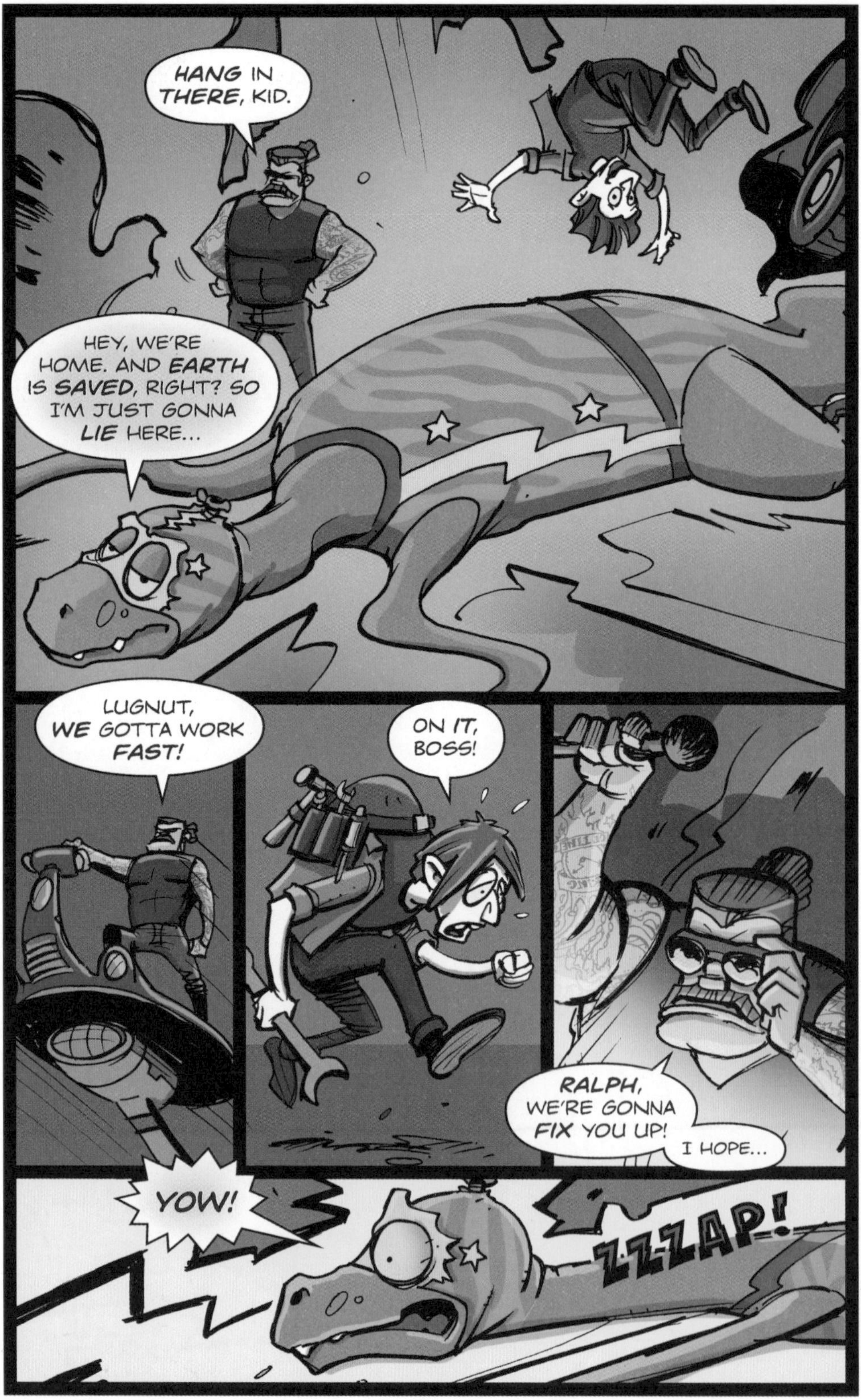
HANG IN THERE, KID.
HEY, WE'RE HOME. AND EARTH IS SAVED, RIGHT? SO I'M JUST GONNA LIE HERE...
LUGNUT, WE GOTTA WORK FAST!
ON IT, BOSS!
RALPH, WE'RE GONNA FIX YOU UP!
I HOPE...
YOW!
ZZZAP!

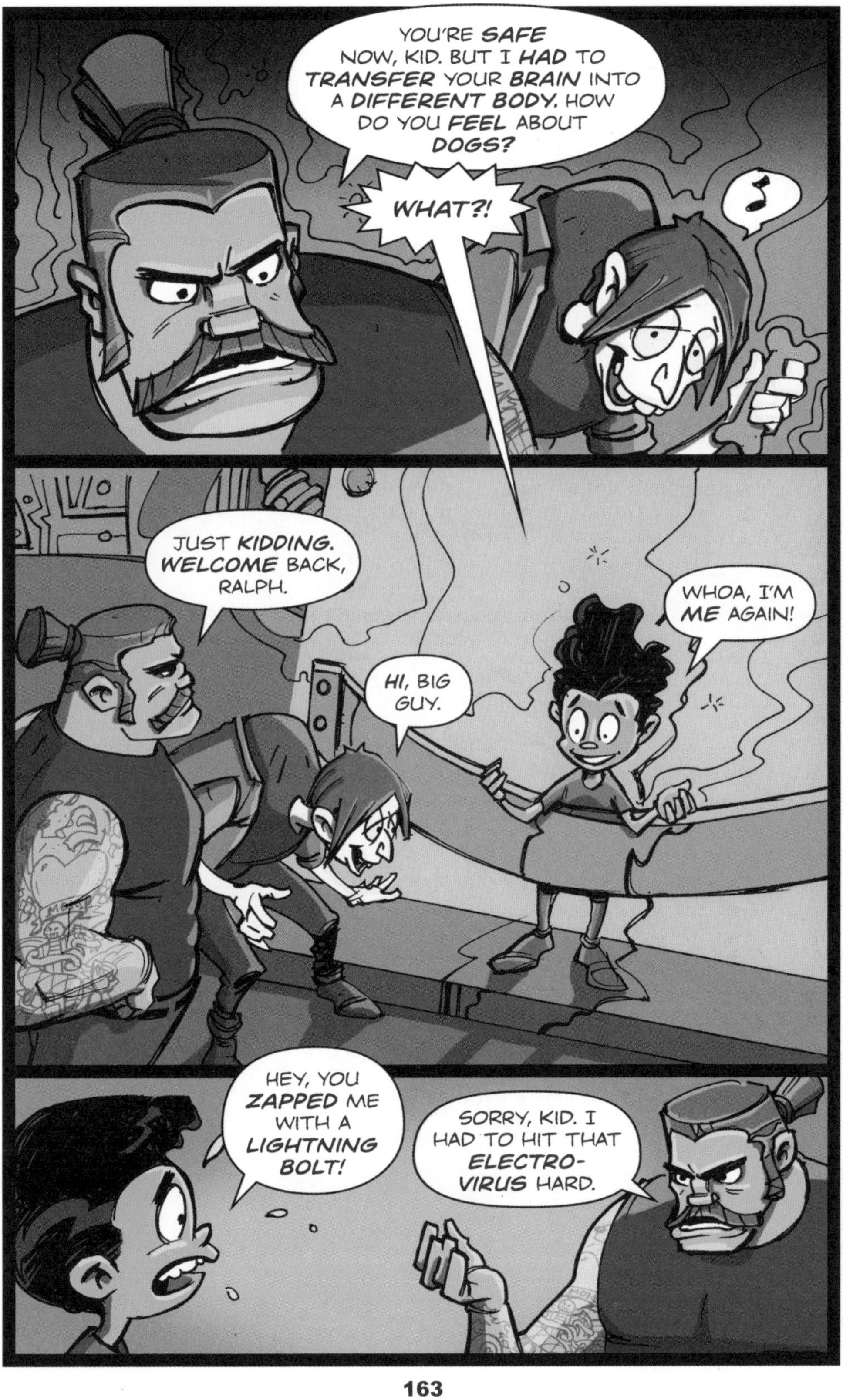
YOU'RE SAFE NOW, KID. BUT I HAD TO TRANSFER YOUR BRAIN INTO A DIFFERENT BODY. HOW DO YOU FEEL ABOUT DOGS?
WHAT?!
JUST KIDDING. WELCOME BACK, RALPH.
HI, BIG GUY.
WHOA, I'M ME AGAIN!
HEY, YOU ZAPPED ME WITH A LIGHTNING BOLT!
SORRY, KID. I HAD TO HIT THAT ELECTRO-VIRUS HARD.

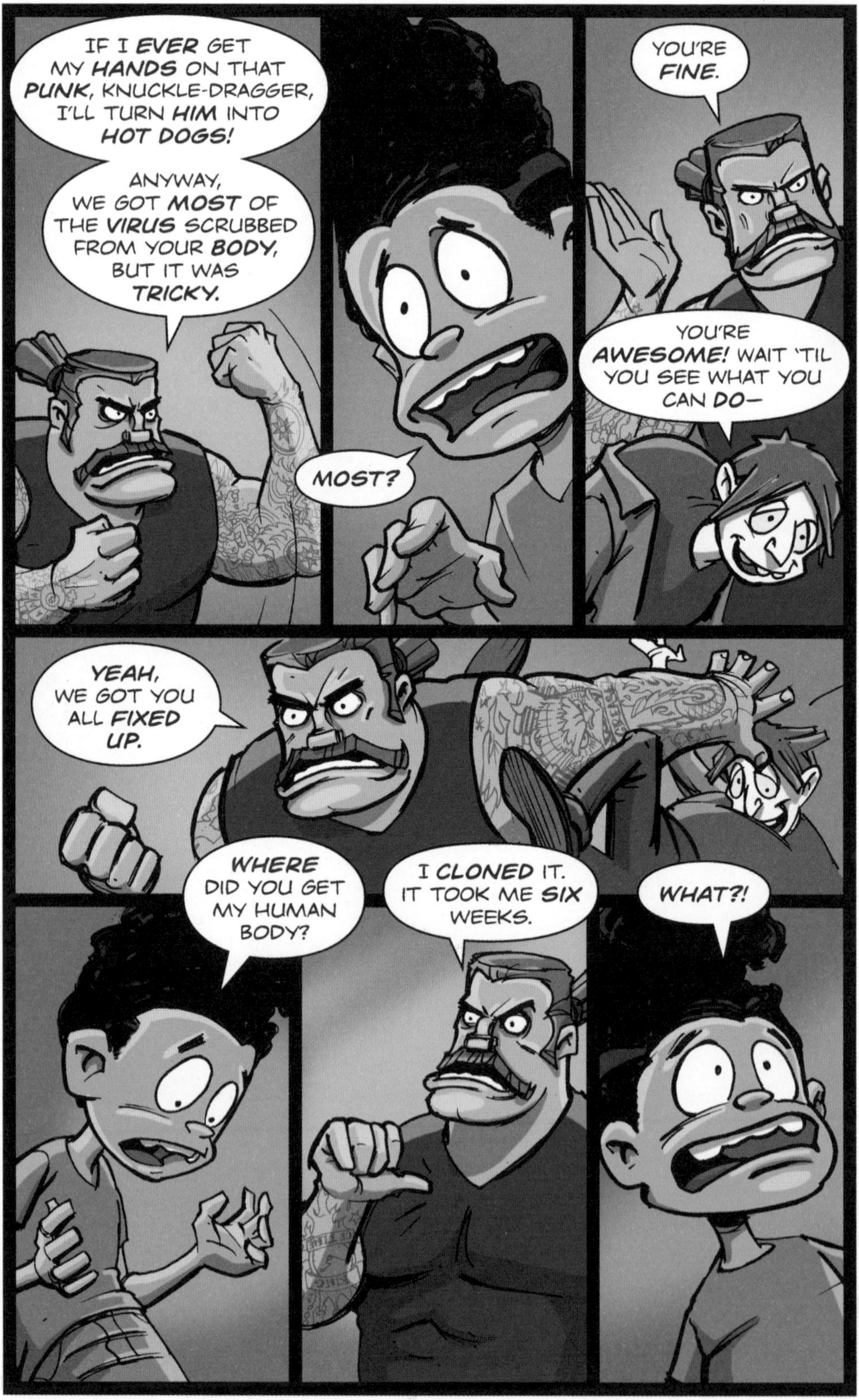
IF I EVER GET MY HANDS ON THAT PUNK, KNUCKLE-DRAGGER, I'LL TURN HIM INTO HOT DOGS!
ANYWAY, WE GOT MOST OF THE VIRUS SCRUBBED FROM YOUR BODY, BUT IT WAS TRICKY.
MOST?
YOU'RE FINE.
YOU'RE AWESOME! WAIT 'TIL YOU SEE WHAT YOU CAN DO—
YEAH, WE GOT YOU ALL FIXED UP.
WHERE DID YOU GET MY HUMAN BODY?
I CLONED IT. IT TOOK ME SIX WEEKS.
WHAT?!

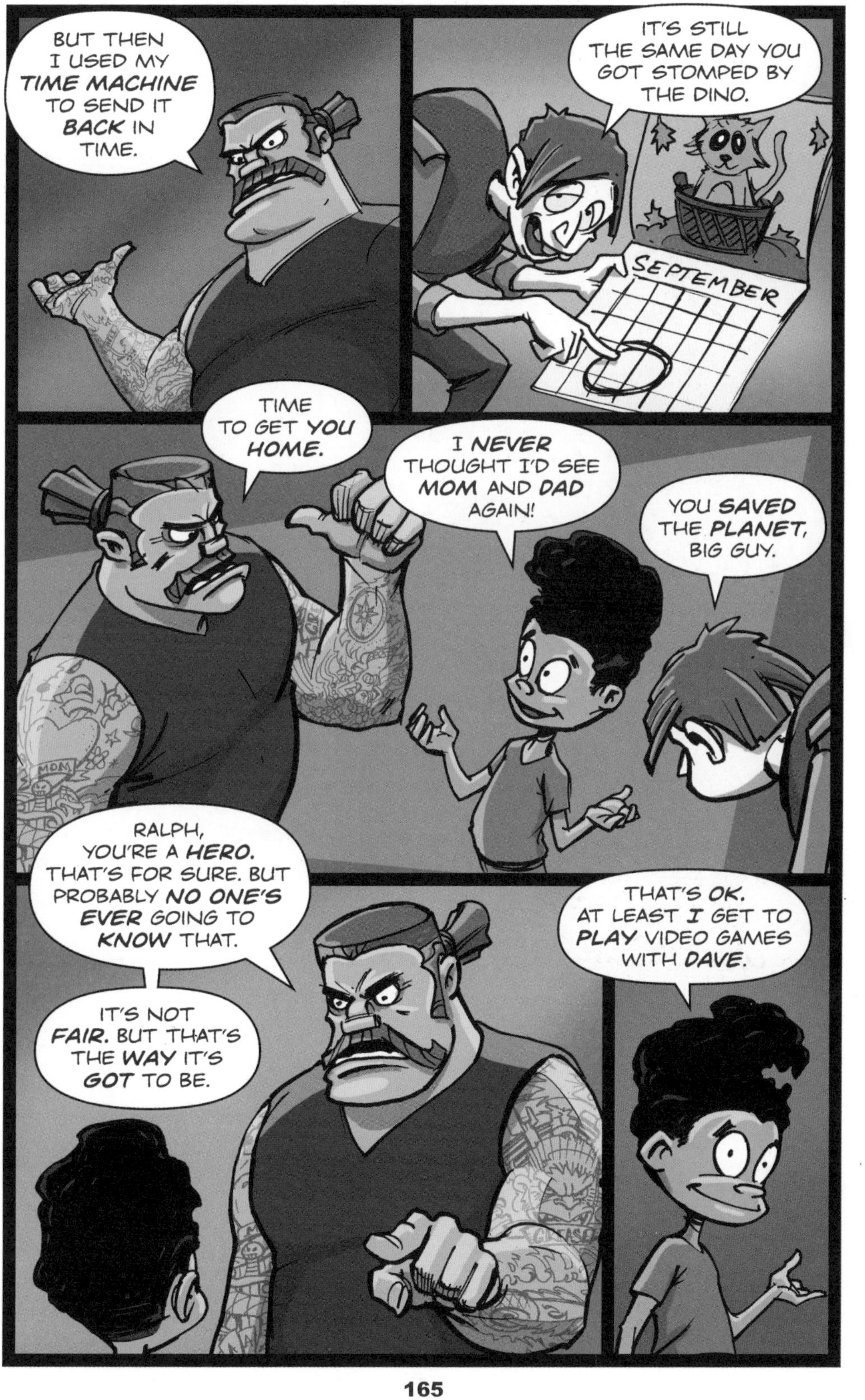
BUT THEN I USED MY TIME MACHINE TO SEND IT BACK IN TIME.
IT'S STILL THE SAME DAY YOU GOT STOMPED BY THE DINO.
SEPTEMBER
TIME TO GET YOU HOME.
I NEVER THOUGHT I'D SEE MOM AND DAD AGAIN!
YOU SAVED THE PLANET, BIG GUY.
RALPH, YOU'RE A HERO. THAT'S FOR SURE. BUT PROBABLY NO ONE'S EVER GOING TO KNOW THAT.
IT'S NOT FAIR. BUT THAT'S THE WAY IT'S GOT TO BE.
THAT'S OK. AT LEAST I GET TO PLAY VIDEO GAMES WITH DAVE.

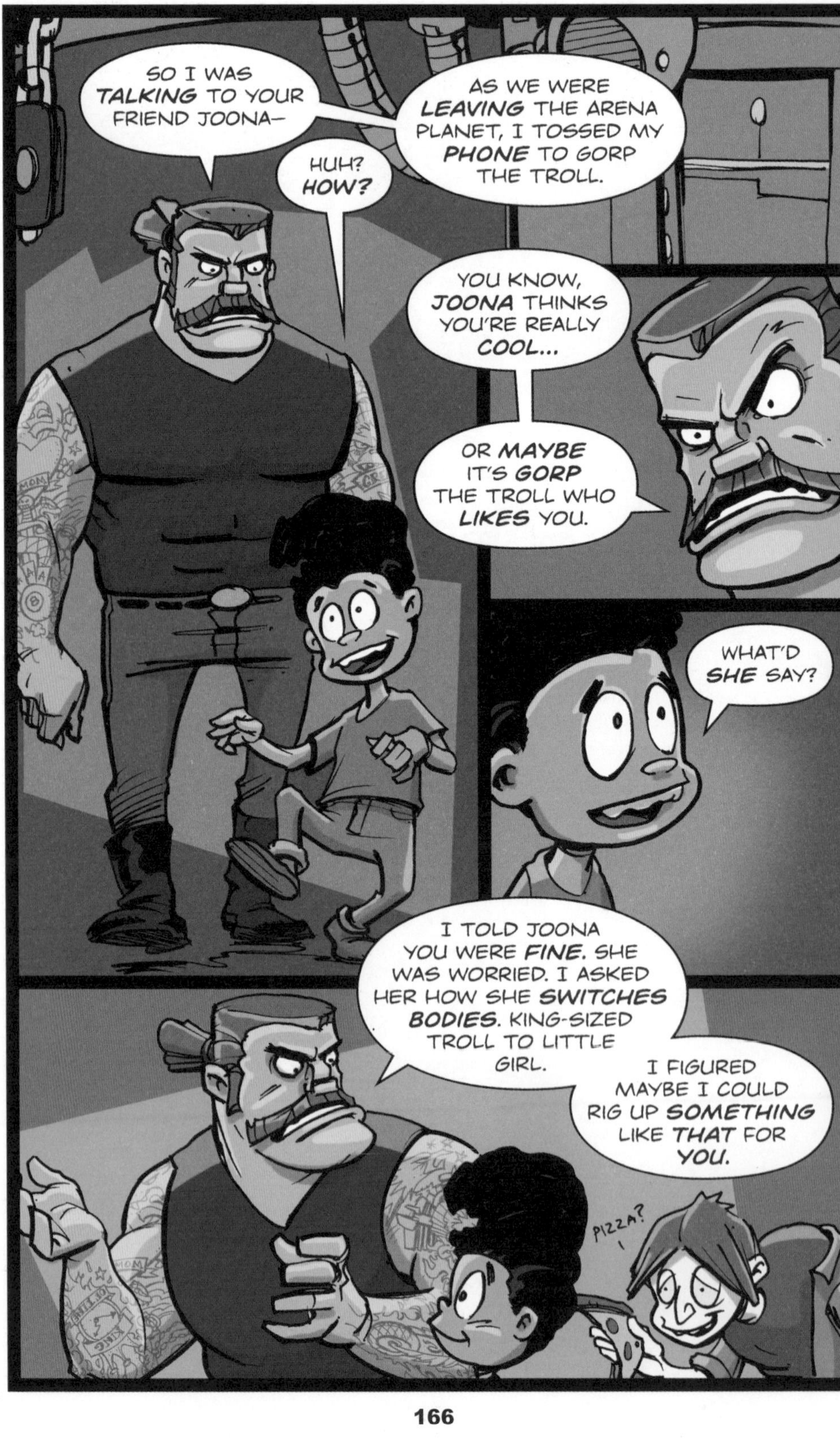
SO I WAS TALKING TO YOUR FRIEND JOONA–
HUH? HOW?
AS WE WERE LEAVING THE ARENA PLANET, I TOSSED MY PHONE TO GORP THE TROLL.
YOU KNOW, JOONA THINKS YOU'RE REALLY COOL...
OR MAYBE IT'S GORP THE TROLL WHO LIKES YOU.
WHAT'D SHE SAY?
I TOLD JOONA YOU WERE FINE. SHE WAS WORRIED. I ASKED HER HOW SHE SWITCHES BODIES. KING-SIZED TROLL TO LITTLE GIRL.
I FIGURED MAYBE I COULD RIG UP SOMETHING LIKE THAT FOR YOU.
PIZZA?

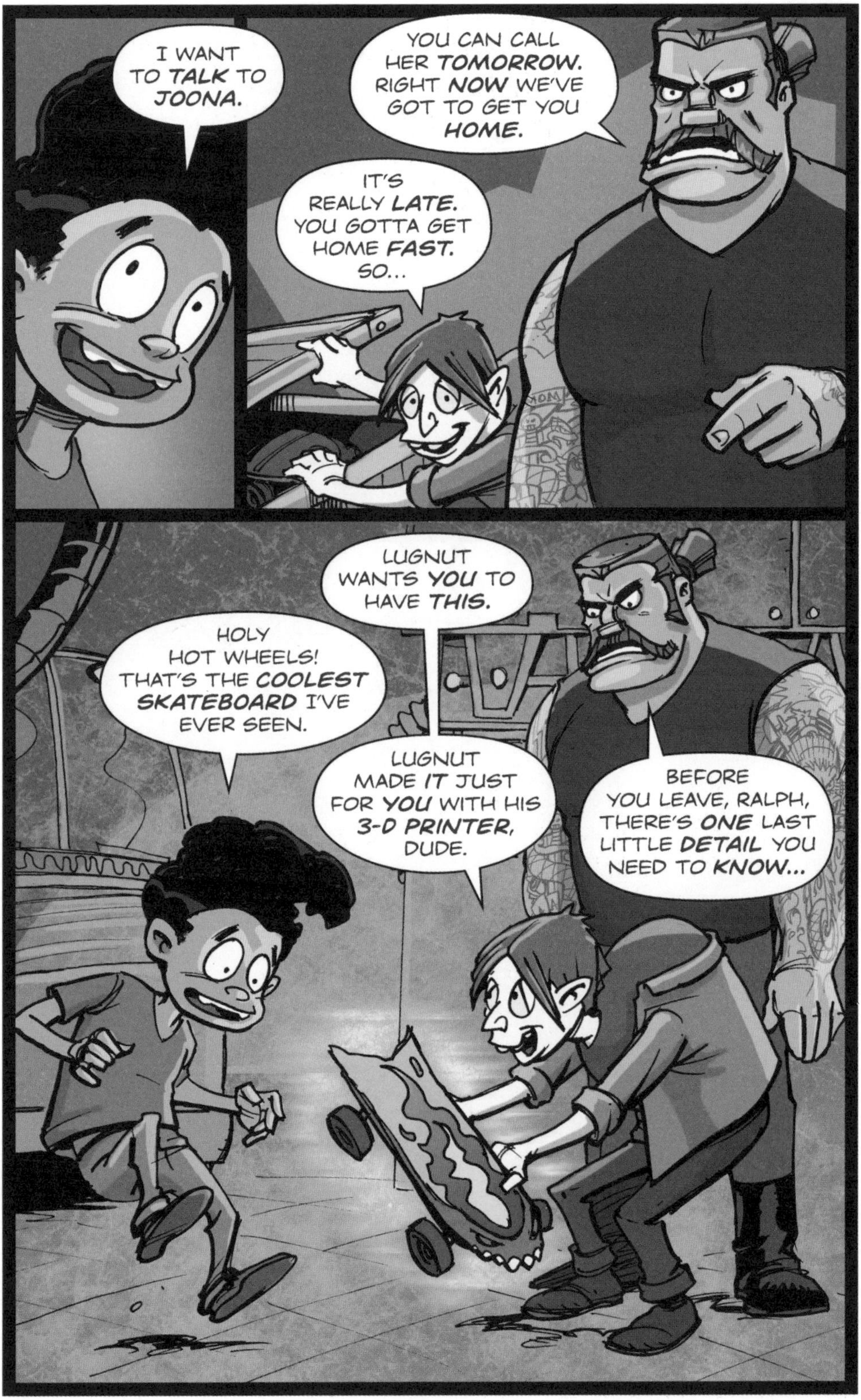
I WANT TO TALK TO JOONA.
YOU CAN CALL HER TOMORROW. RIGHT NOW WE'VE GOT TO GET YOU HOME.
IT'S REALLY LATE. YOU GOTTA GET HOME FAST. SO...
LUGNUT WANTS YOU TO HAVE THIS.
HOLY HOT WHEELS! THAT'S THE COOLEST SKATEBOARD I'VE EVER SEEN.
LUGNUT MADE IT JUST FOR YOU WITH HIS 3-D PRINTER, DUDE.
BEFORE YOU LEAVE, RALPH, THERE'S ONE LAST LITTLE DETAIL YOU NEED TO KNOW...

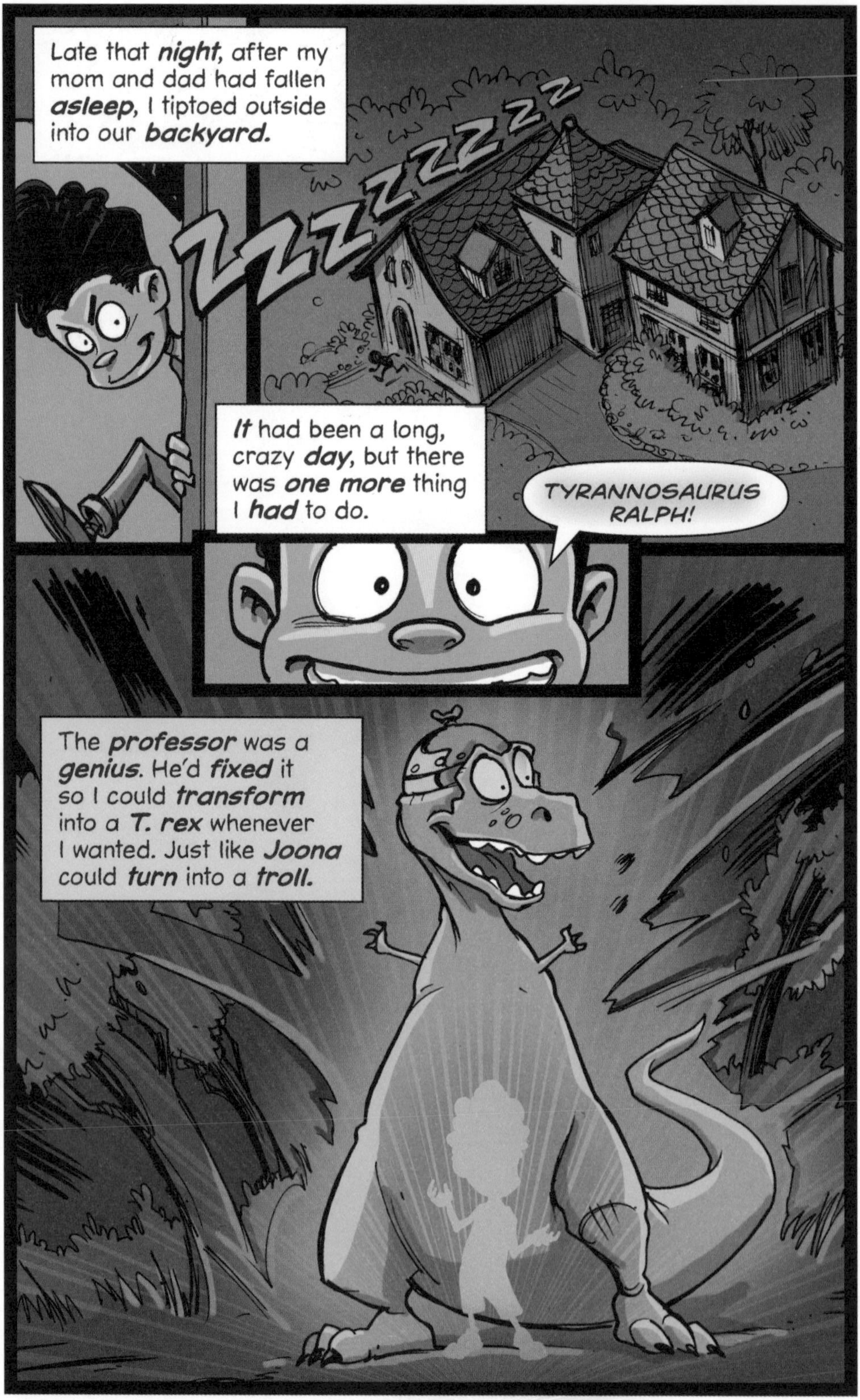

Late that *night*, after my mom and dad had fallen *asleep*, I tiptoed outside into our *backyard*.
ZZZZZZZZZZZ
It had been a long, crazy *day*, but there was *one more* thing I *had* to do.
TYRANNOSAURUS RALPH!
The *professor* was a *genius*. He'd *fixed* it so I could *transform* into a *T. rex* whenever I wanted. Just like *Joona* could *turn* into a *troll.*

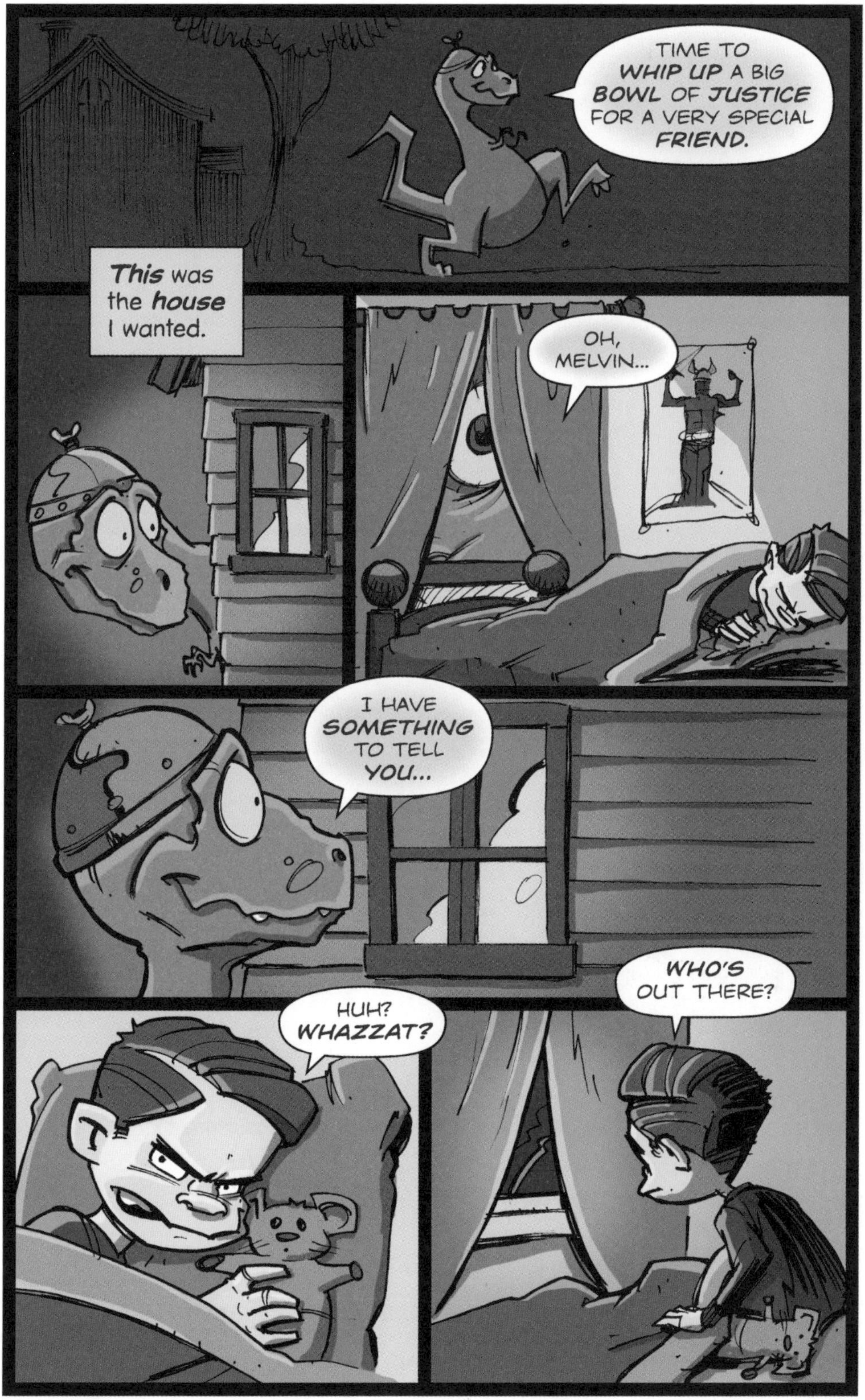
TIME TO WHIP UP A BIG BOWL OF JUSTICE FOR A VERY SPECIAL FRIEND.
This was the house I wanted.
OH, MELVIN...
I HAVE SOMETHING TO TELL YOU...
HUH? WHAZZAT?
WHO'S OUT THERE?

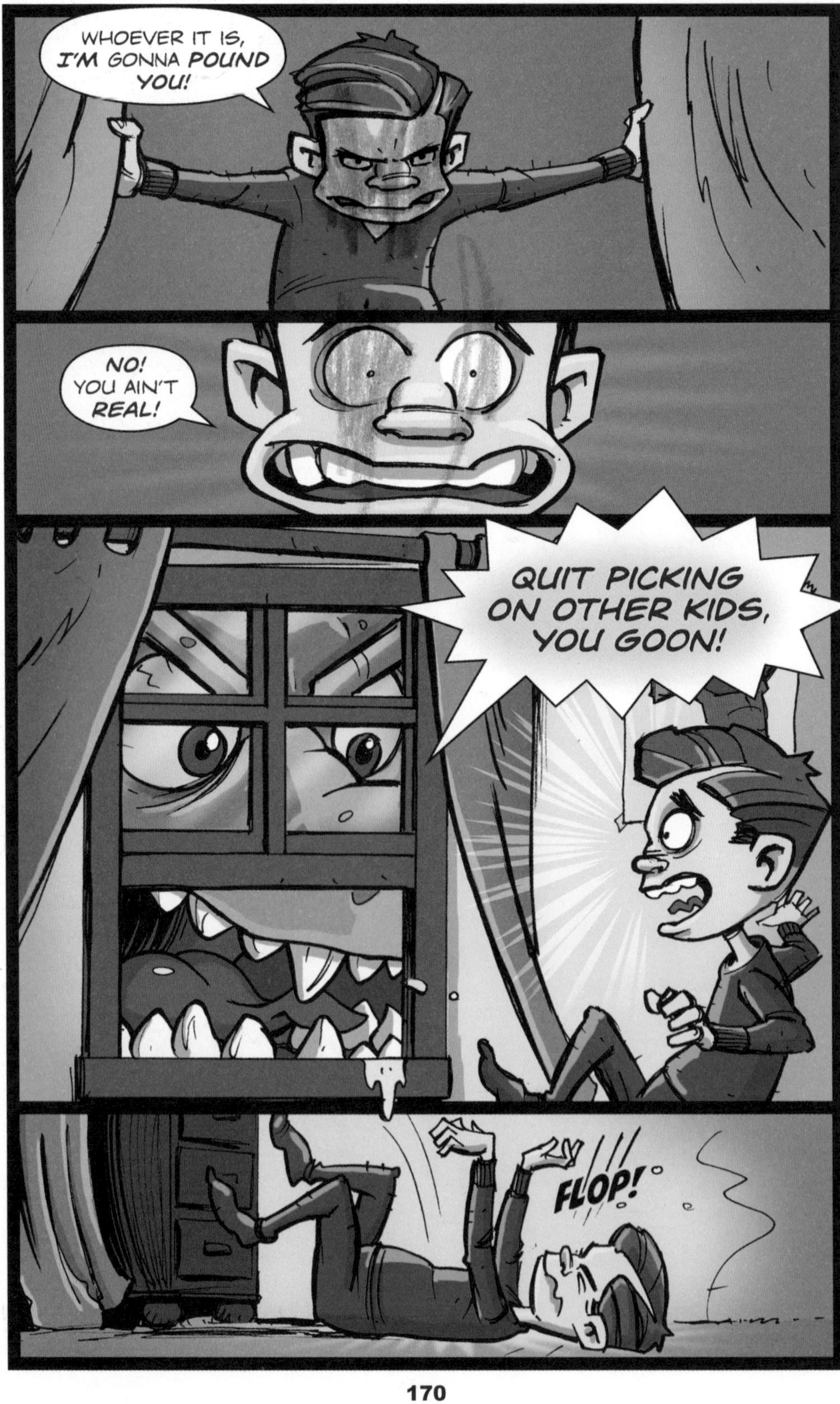
WHOEVER IT IS, I'M GONNA POUND YOU!
NO! YOU AIN'T REAL!
QUIT PICKING ON OTHER KIDS, YOU GOON!
FLOP!

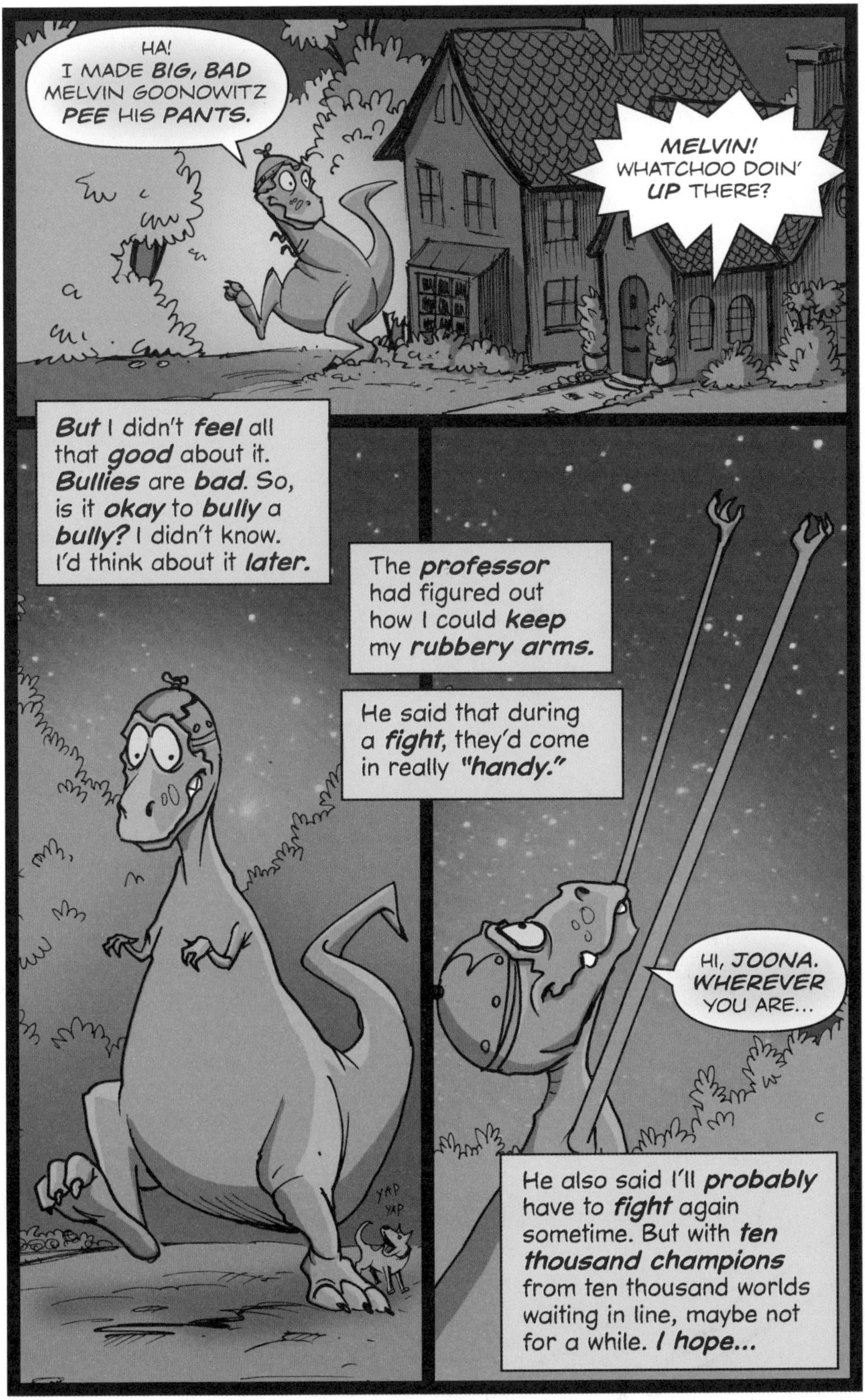
HA!
I MADE BIG, BAD MELVIN GOONOWITZ PEE HIS PANTS.
MELVIN! WHATCHOO DOIN' UP THERE?
But I didn't feel all that good about it. Bullies are bad. So, is it okay to bully a bully? I didn't know. I'd think about it later.
YAP YAP
The professor had figured out how I could keep my rubbery arms.
He said that during a fight, they'd come in really "handy."
HI, JOONA. WHEREVER YOU ARE...
He also said I'll probably have to fight again sometime. But with ten thousand champions from ten thousand worlds waiting in line, maybe not for a while. I hope...

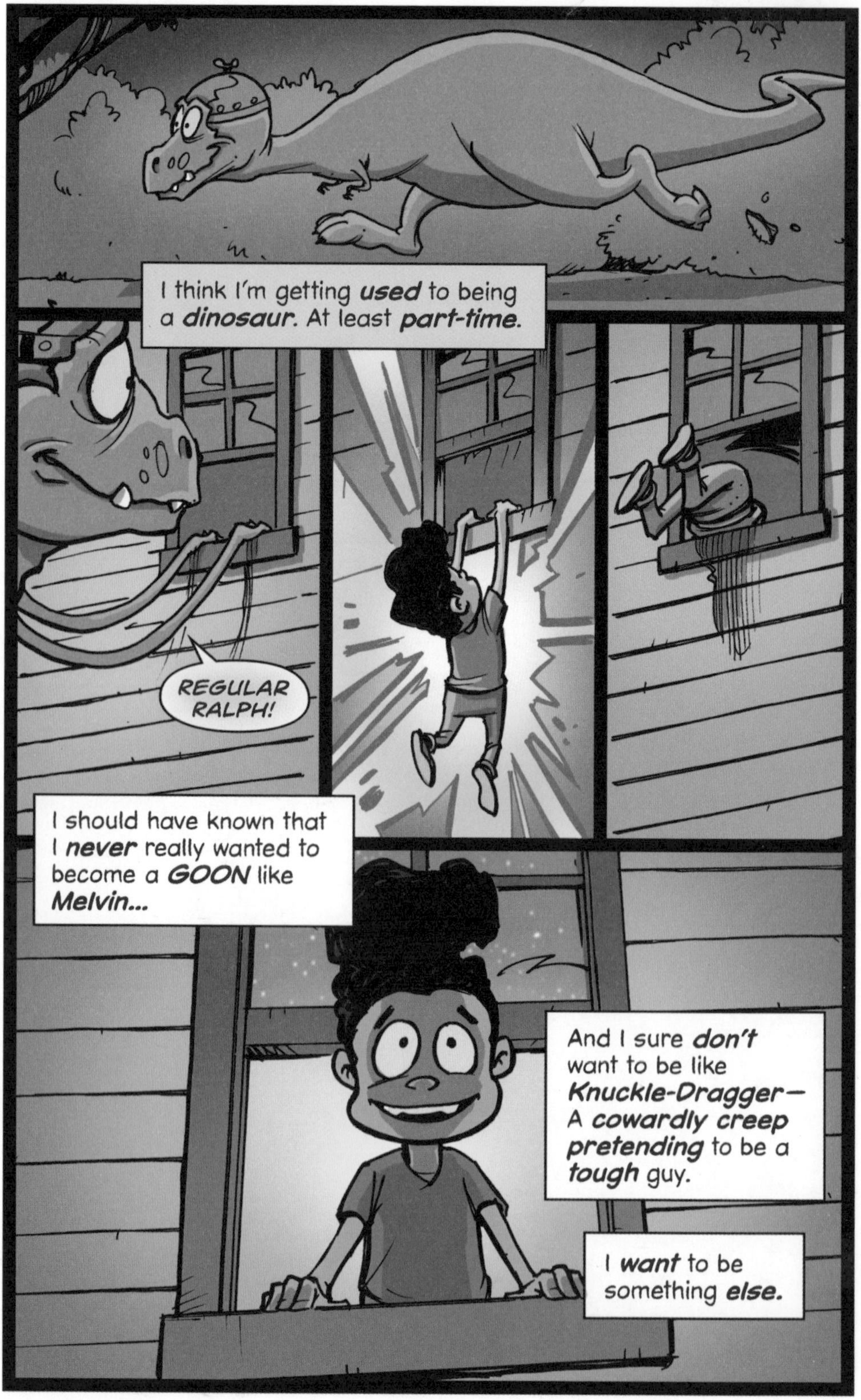
I think I'm getting *used* to being a *dinosaur*. At least *part-time*.
REGULAR RALPH!
I should have known that I *never* really wanted to become a *GOON* like *Melvin...*
And I sure *don't* want to be like *Knuckle-Dragger*— A *cowardly creep pretending* to be a *tough* guy.
I *want* to be something *else*.

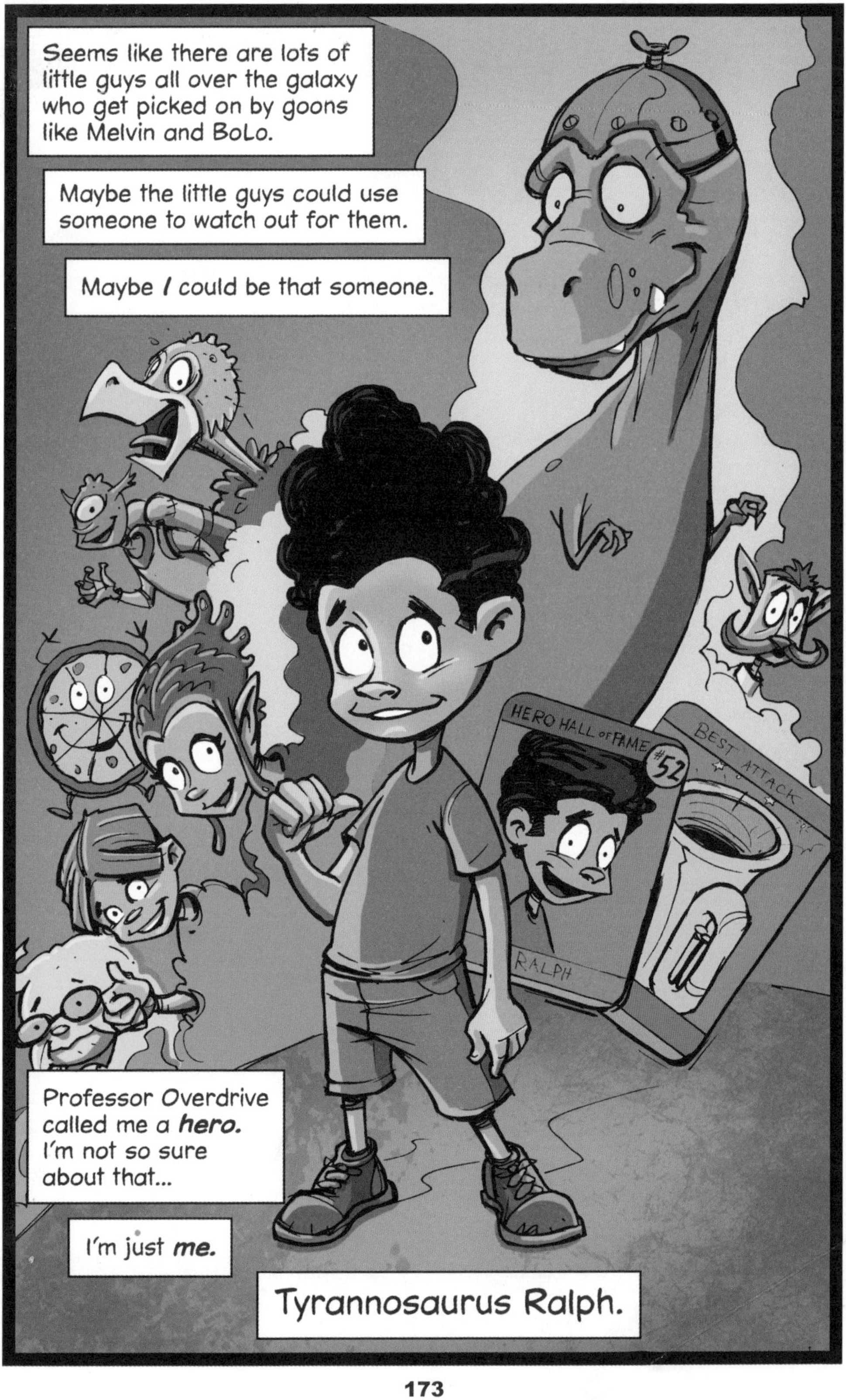
Seems like there are lots of little guys all over the galaxy who get picked on by goons like Melvin and BoLo.
Maybe the little guys could use someone to watch out for them.
Maybe *I* could be that someone.
HERO HALL OF FAME
#52
RALPH
BEST ATTACK
Professor Overdrive called me a ***hero.*** I'm not so sure about that...
I'm just ***me.***
Tyrannosaurus Ralph.

MORE TO EXPLORE
ROMAN GLADIATORS

ARTWORK BY GRACEE ASHLEY

When the sixth graders at my school put up a big display about Roman gladiators, you better believe I was paying attention (and I took pictures). I mean, if I have to fight in King Crunch's awful arena again, I figured maybe I could learn a few tricks from the experts—guys whose whole lives were spent training and fighting in combat arenas.

The first thing I learned is that the gladiators in ancient Rome weren't always guys. Women battled, too. Why not? Joona is an amazing warrior. If Joona had fought two thousand years ago in the Roman Colosseum, she would have been called a *gladiatrix*, not a *gladiator*.

Most gladiators were slaves captured during wars, but sometimes Roman citizens thought being a gladiator might earn them fame and money, so they entered the arena contests. There were even a few emperors who fought. Of course, these royal goons rigged the battles. The opponents were drugged or had to fight with wooden swords while the emperors used metal weapons and armor.

Artwork by Leann Patros

Artwork by Kaylee Holden

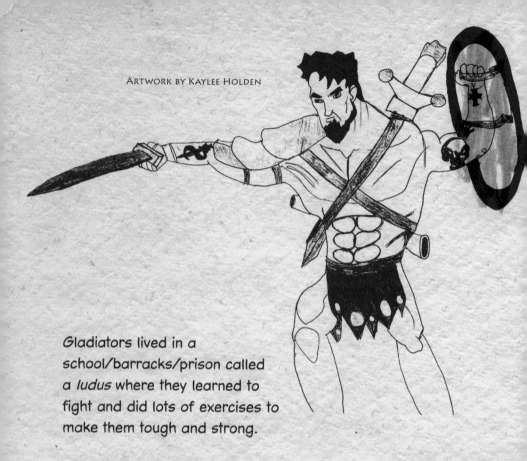

Gladiators lived in a school/barracks/prison called a *ludus* where they learned to fight and did lots of exercises to make them tough and strong.

The best gladiators in Rome were totally famous, just like sports superstars of today. These fighters didn't have their own line of sneakers, but there was lots of gladiator merchandise for sale. The Roman fans idolized these guys. Of course, most of the gladiators didn't make it past the age of thirty, and it's kind of hard to spend gold coins when you're dead.

Gladiators were divided into lots of different classes, and each class fought with different weapons. For example, gladiators in the Samnite class wore heavy armor and a visored helmet, carried a large rectangular shield, and sliced opponents with a sword called a *gladius* (this sword is how the *gladiators* got their name); the Thracian class fought using a small shield and a short sword; and the retiarius used a net to snare his opponent and a trident to skewer him like a fish.

Oh, and you know that whole *thumbs up, thumbs down* thing, from the fight fans and the emperor, deciding whether a gladiator lived or died? Well, I guess we sort of got that mixed up. *Thumbs down* actually meant, "Let the gladiator live another day," and *thumbs up* meant, "Finish the bum!"

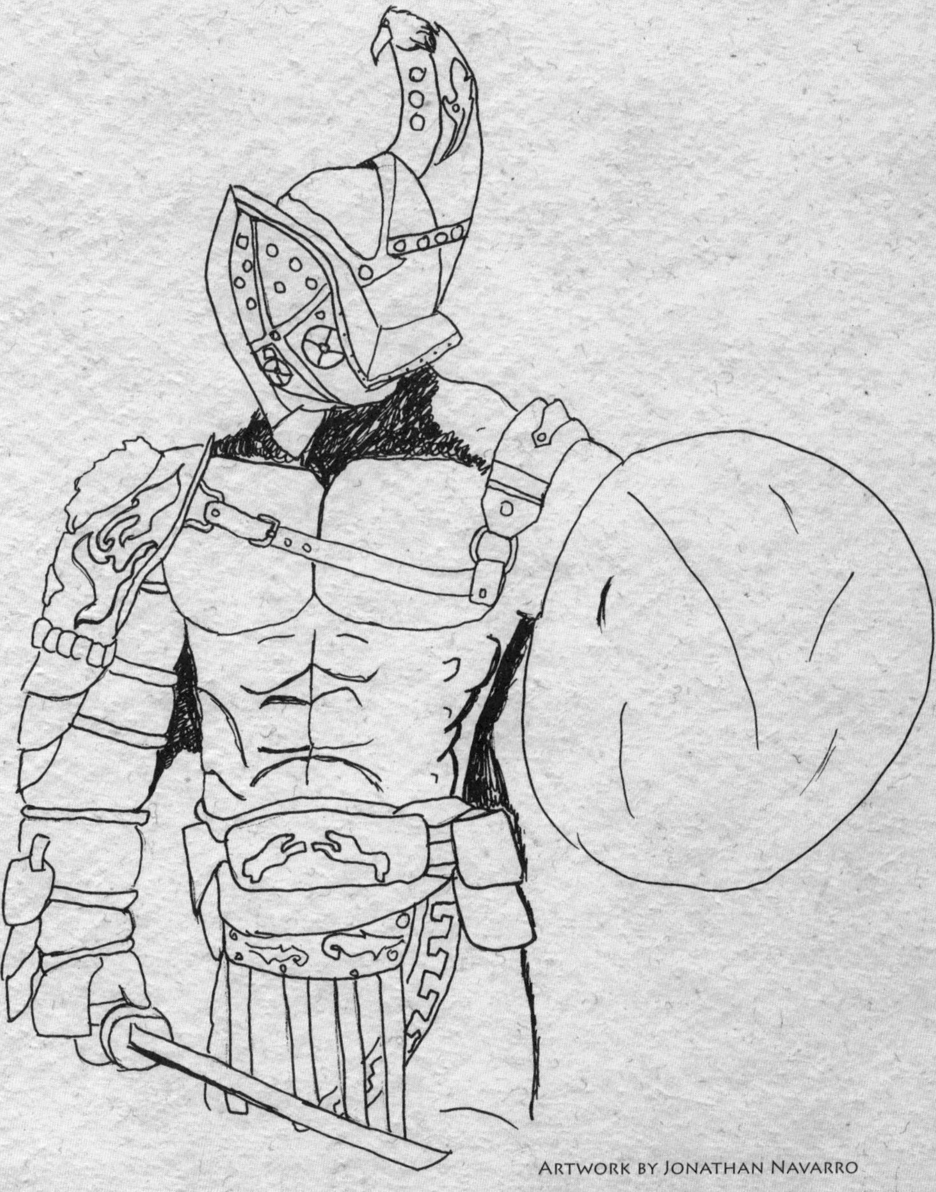

Artwork by Jonathan Navarro

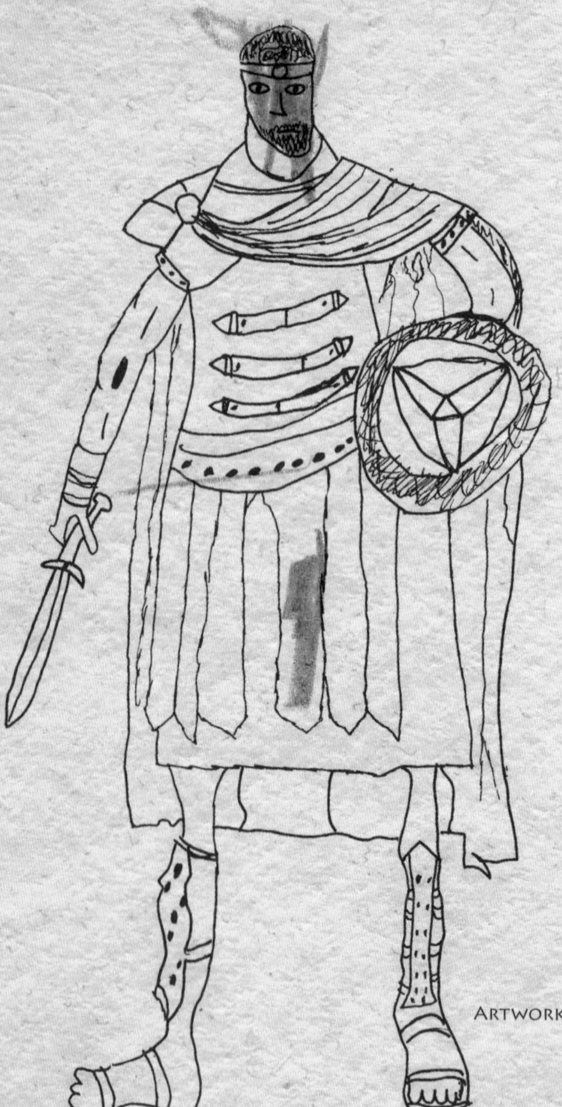

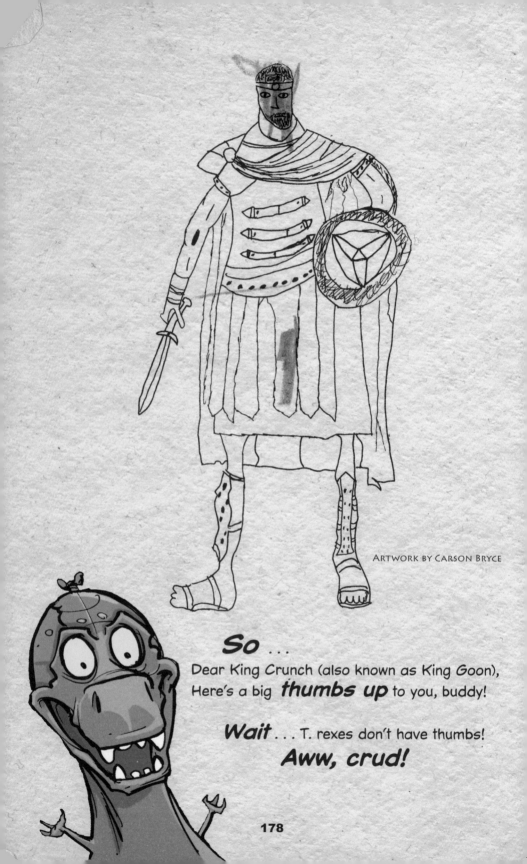

Artwork by Carson Bryce

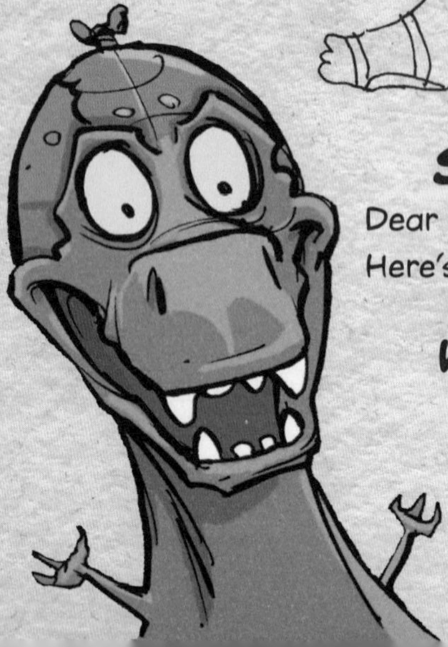

So . . .

Dear King Crunch (also known as King Goon),
Here's a big **thumbs up** to you, buddy!

Wait . . . T. rexes don't have thumbs!
Aww, crud!

Andrews McMeel Publishing
a division of Andrews McMeel Universal
1130 Walnut Street, Kansas City, Missouri 64106

www.andrewsmcmeel.com

17 18 19 20 21 SDB 10 9 8 7 6 5 4 3 2 1

ISBN: 978-1-4494-7208-5

Library of Congress Control Number: 2017943566

Editor: Dorothy O'Brien
Creative Director: Tim Lynch
Production Editor: Maureen Sullivan
Production Manager: Chuck Harper
Inventory Manager: Linda Laming
Colorist: Jason Bays

Made by:
Shenzhen Donnelley Printing Company Ltd.
Address and location of manufacturer:
No. 47, Wuhe Nan Road, Bantian Ind. Zone,
Shenzhen China, 518129
1st Printing – 7/31/17

ATTENTION: SCHOOLS AN

Andrews McMeel books are available at quantity
educational, business, or sales promotional use. F
Andrews McMeel Publishing Special S
specialsales@amuniversal.

amp! COMICS for kids

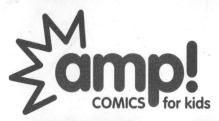

Check out these and other books at ampkids.com

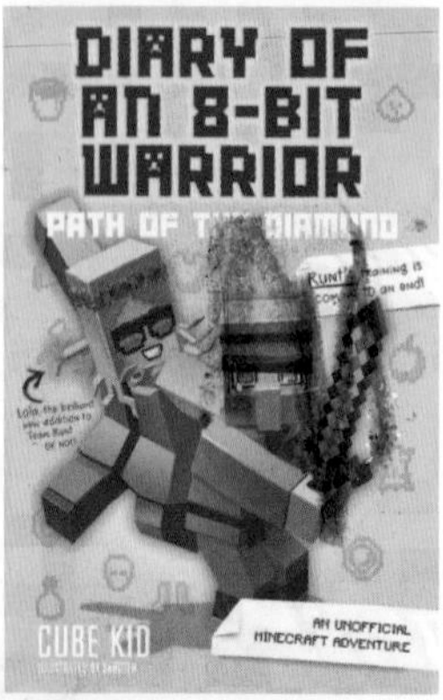
DIARY OF AN 8-BIT WARRIOR
AN UNOFFICIAL MINECRAFT ADVENTURE
CUBE KID

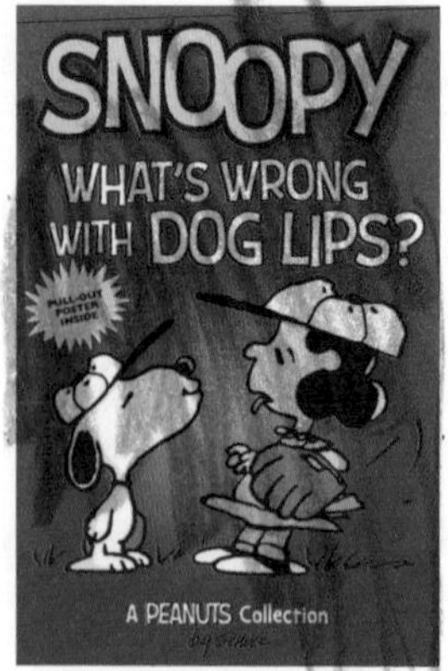
SNOOPY
WHAT'S WRONG WITH DOG LIPS?
PULL-OUT POSTER INSIDE
A PEANUTS Collection

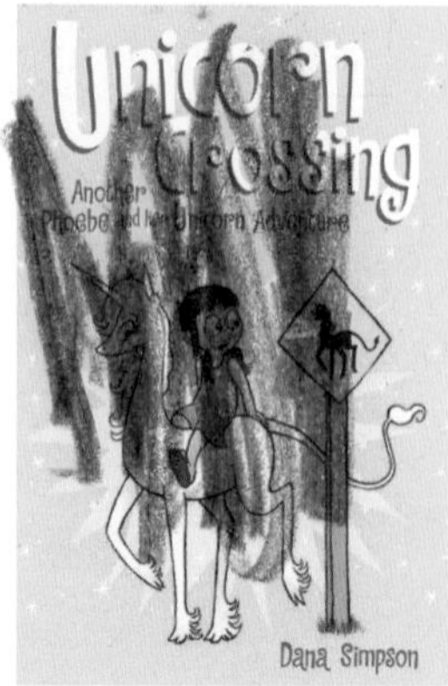
Unicorn Crossing
Dana Simpson

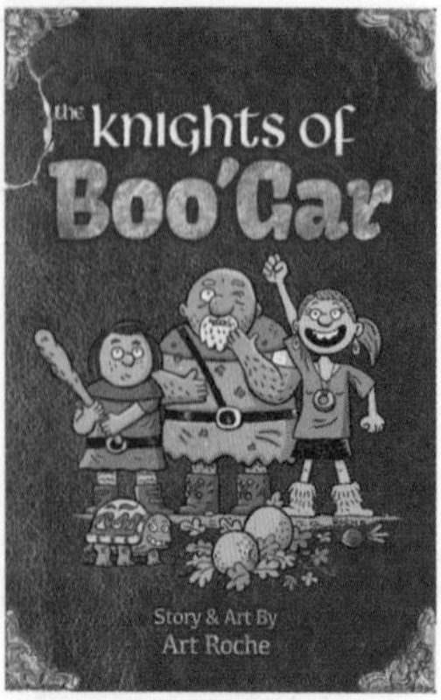
the knights of Boo'Gar
Story & Art By
Art Roche

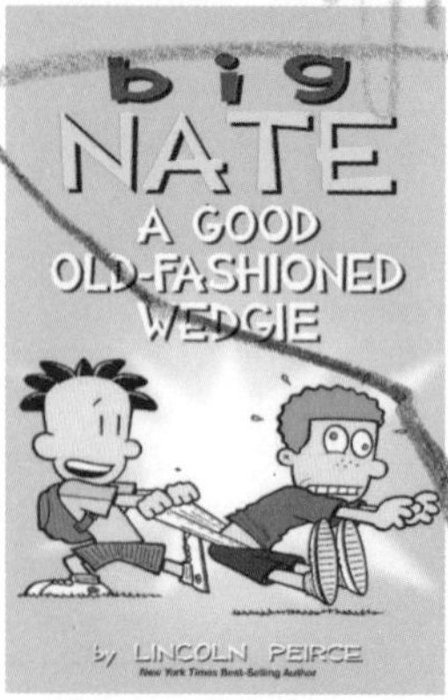
big NATE
A GOOD OLD-FASHIONED WEDGIE
by LINCOLN PEIRCE
New York Times Best-Selling Author

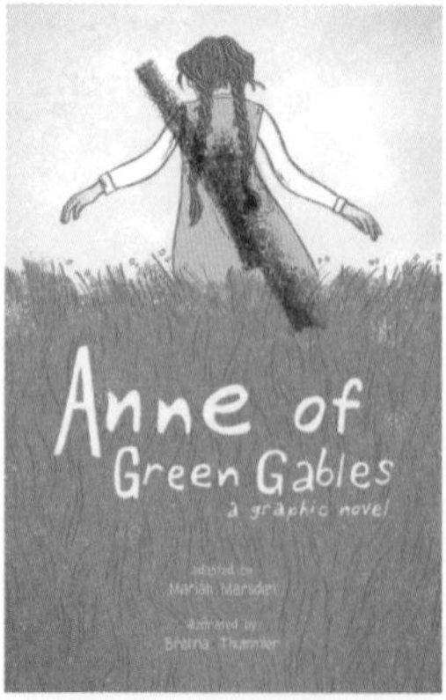
Anne of Green Gables
a graphic novel

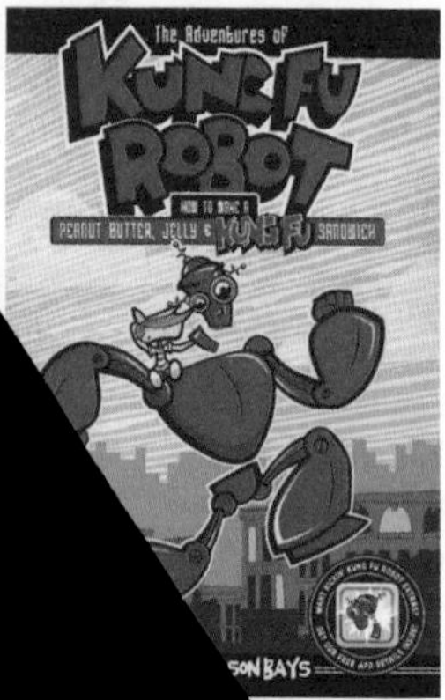
The Adventures of
KUNG FU ROBOT
HOW TO MAKE A PEANUT BUTTER, JELLY & KUNG FU SANDWICH

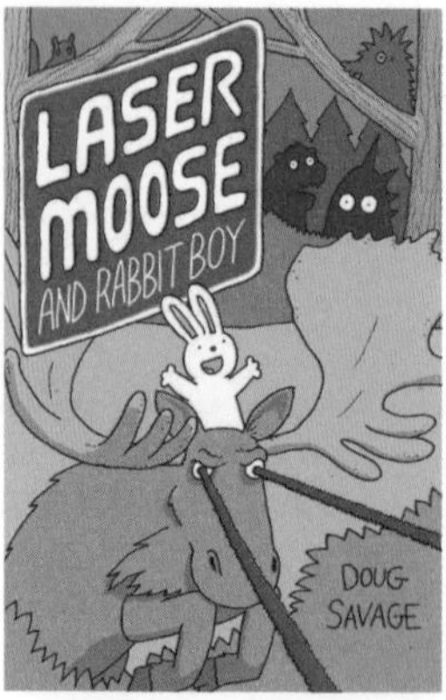
LASER MOOSE AND RABBIT BOY
DOUG SAVAGE

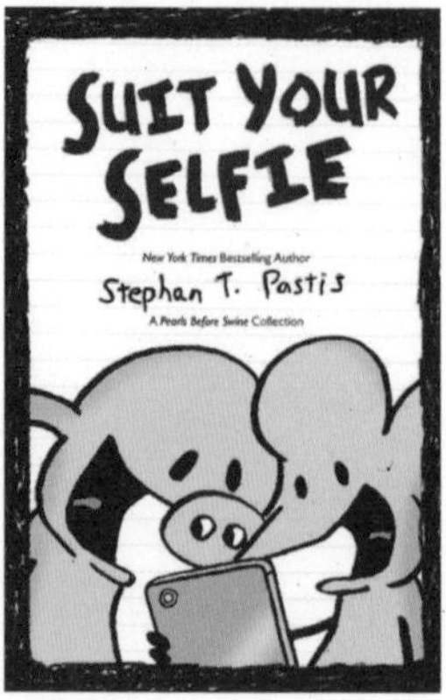
SUIT YOUR SELFIE
New York Times Bestselling Author
Stephan T. Pastis
A Pearls Before Swine Collection

Also available:

Teaching and activity guides for each title.

Comics for Kids books make reading FUN!